D1564672

*"Forgiveness is the only true basis for happiness.
And forgiving life for all its injustices is the
beginning step."*

A LOVE BEYOND TIME

A NOVEL

by

Marsha Newman

Sequel to "The Lightning and the Storm"

WELLSPRING PUBLISHING
Salt Lake City, Utah

Copyright © 1987 by Wellspring Publishing
All rights reserved
Printed in the United States of America
First printing August 1987

ISBN 0-9608658-3-7

Lithographed in the United States of America
PUBLISHERS PRESS
Salt Lake City, Utah

Acknowledgements

This book has been a true work of love and I appreciate the loving help of several people who worked with me on it. Special thanks go to Darla Hanks, Claudette McDougal, Arlene Bascom and Barbara Miller for help in editing. I am especially grateful to my dear friend, Sheela Eames, for background on New York and work in the airlines.

*To all those courageous individuals who
continue to love life with all it's
capriciousness and wonder.*

Chapter 1

A hawk mounted the winds of the canyon. He seemed to soar just for the thrill of it, dipping with the currents, disappearing behind a column of aspen, and then rocketing into view and rolling on the downstream wind. From his height, the narrow road winding between the mountains into Bird's Eye from Spanish Fork, Utah was just a gray ribbon, and Utah Lake was a flamboyant blue gem, undulating in the warmth of the afternoon. On the side of the north mountain, at the mouth of the canyon, was a spot of white in the expanse of spring's new greenery. The spot was moving up and up . . . destination unknown. Curving with the curve of the hillside and drifting earthward, the hawk swooped closer, then precipitously veered off, away from the white thing, wheeled about and headed back toward the narrow canyon. Closer, one could see that the white spot was a human being—not a lamb or a rabbit at all—a girl in a white dress, climbing higher and higher on the mountainside.

It was hot work, even though a spring breeze kept the air slightly cool at that elevation. She stopped as often as she liked and stood quite still, studying the valley spread out below. Catching her breath and wiping her forehead and upper lip, she would press on, not hurrying nor seeking a goal, content in just the climbing and the solitude. A breeze caught the filmy skirt of her dress and billowed it about her legs. At first she had tried to be careful of her dress. It was her graduation dress and it was new. Today was graduation day and she wanted to be alone so she came to the mountain as she had often done over the years. After a while she forgot, and the hem of the lacy skirt picked up dust and a few twigs. The girl climbed, twisting about on the hillside, picking out the easiest path upward, until at last tired, she stopped.

Shielah sat carefully on a large boulder, resting her feet on a smaller one. The valley shimmered below, the sun splintered off her golden head,

1

and in her mind she rambled back in time, vivid pictures capturing her attention and blocking even the breathtaking view before her.

Shielah Sorensen was a tiny, wispy-haired two-year-old, wandering about the huge front yard, gleefully tearing up dandelions, smelling them, then flinging them away in favor of a new flower. Buttercups, geraniums, petunias, her mother's best prize-winning roses—they were all in grave danger. But Ginny caught her up under one arm and carried her back into the house.

Bubbles in a sea of water! The delicate, wisp of a little girl submerged her face in bubbles and came up laughing, blowing bubbles off her fingertips. Ginny knelt beside her on the floor, wet up to her elbows, scrubbing and rinsing small white feet, neck, and arms. The little girl made roads all over the bathtub through the bubbles, while her mother laughed at her antics.

"Dese are my clouds," she told her mother, importantly.

"Are they? What do clouds do, muffin?"

"Dey wain on you!" And she gleefully splattered her mother with droplets of water.

"Hey, it's not my bathtime. It's yours, remember."

"Now dese bubbles are my covers. I go to bed." The little body squirmed under the water until she was covered, all but her face, in the bubble bath.

"You bet you're going to bed! In just about two minutes. Hop out of that tub and let's get you dried off."

Shielah held her arms up obediently, still dripping bubbles, and wrapped them lovingly around her mother's neck. Toweled off and dry, a soft fleece nightie slipped over her head, she reached back into the tub once more and patted Ginny's face with bubbles just as she began to rise.

"Oh! You are a muffin! I thought I was safe from 'dose clouds.' Come back here!" But the flying legs had disappeared around the doorway and hopped into bed in a flash. The covers were all still when Ginny crept into her daughter's bedroom. She pounced on the bed and grasped the giggling, squirming little body in her arms. Dancing blue eyes appeared from beneath the covers, then a button of a nose, and finally, cherry pink lips. "I lub you de mostest, mommy, de mostest in all de world."

Ginny! Oh, Ginny! Her mother was always young in Shielah's memory—young and beautiful as only a mother can be beautiful. I've never looked a thing like my mother, Shielah thought. No wonder Dad loved her so. She was the best, the most beautiful.

Ginny Sorensen had remarkable brown-gold eyes and deep auburn hair. She laughed quickly and brightly, easily capturing Ed Sorensen, the prize of the Clarksville Class of 1949. Broad-shouldered and blonde, he was as perfect a prototype of father as Ginny was mother, in Shielah's mind. And he was as devoted to his little daughter as she was to him. Even when she was just three years old he would take her with him in the old, iron-red pickup, jouncing over the back trails (not to be confused at all with roads) while he explored the hills. She sat on his lap while he drove, stretching her neck to peer over the steering wheel. As she grew older, he allowed her to change gears for him. That was a job of utmost importance, and Shielah knew her Daddy trusted her.

Besides the gears, she was also responsible for their food. The kitchen counter was too high for her to be comfortable, so she prepared all their sandwiches and celery sticks at her doll's table, carefully wrapping and filling a paper bag with lunch for her Daddy. Of course it was her's too, but in her seven-year-old mind it was really for her Dad.

By the time she was eight, they frequently substituted horses for the truck, and could explore the back country properly. Ed taught her to ride. The huge animal that carried her as easily as a dandelion puff obeyed every command, for she learned quickly to use the reins and the pressure of her knees. This was the most responsibility her father had given her, to ride and care for an animal. Shielah remembered her father kneeling in the stable, currying his horse, his blonde head bent, concentrating on his task. The young Shielah, with hair like new corn silk stood opposite him, imitating her dad in every move.

It was one of the few things Ginny scolded him about.

"She's too young, Ed. She can't handle Captain Nemo as well as you think she can."

Ed smiled implacably in the face of his wife's concern. "Just because you don't like to ride, don't think she can't. She handles those horses as well at seven years old as some grown men do at twenty. Just ask Buck, he'll vouch for that."

Unlike her parents, Buck had always seemed old to Shielah. Even when they were young, he was not. Where had he come from, this strange brother of hers? As dark-haired as she was blonde, he was the complete antithesis of Shielah, and his five years seniority seemed a huge gulf. He was handsome even at eight, and devil-may-care in his ways, but he was also terribly intense and moody. Neither Ginny nor Ed understood their son at all. There were dim memories of voices late at night, when the little girl woke to visit the bathroom, voices fretting and concerned. "Buck, Buck"—over and over she heard the name, though she understood nothing of the conversation. And the little girl both loved and hated him.

"Olly, Olly oxen free. I see you, Shielah, you can't hide from me. I saw you right from the start; I was just pretending to look for you."

"You were not. You were not! Why'd you go way over by the barn then? I almost ran in home."

"Naw! You'd never of made it. I had my eye on you the whole time, over behind the yellow rose bush."

"Mom," the little eight year old wailed to her mother, "Why'd you have to go and born him before me? I don't want to be the baby. He's bad to me."

But then, he had pockets full of wonderful things. Shielah smiled at the memory and shook her head. His pockets held a never-ending supply of bubble gum, ten cent rings, paddle balls with the elastic string still attached, tiny packs of cards for playing Old Maid, a few nickels, pretty rocks, and always mouth-sized chunks of candy.

3

He would let her little hand pick out of his pockets just the piece she wanted. Then he'd say, "For a kiss, muffin, for a kiss." Obediently, tiny rosebud lips would pucker up and press his cheek.

They always had to say prayers together at night, and he always made her say them. Always, at least, unless Ginny was there to see that he got a turn. "God bless Buck to go to school and get good grades and do his chores and be nice to me." (With much emphasis on the "be nice"). After a quick hug, snuggling into the covers, Buck would steal one last, teasing kiss on the way back from the bathroom to his bed.

"What are you doing with all those cookies? Mom'll be mad if you eat all those." Buck had opened the door of her room to find six dolls set upright, very carefully, on the bed. They all had on party hats, their best dresses, and in their laps, tiny, colorful plates were adorned with two cookies each. Big blue eyes stared at him in surprise.

"No won't. Mom say tree cookies, and I only take dis many. Dust two." Shielah held up two delicate fingers.

Her nine-year-old lord and master came and sat beside her on the bed. "But, muffin, you've got fourteen cookies here. Fourteen cookies! You can't eat that many cookies. It'll make you sick," he pronounced emphatically in his most adult manner.

"Silly, dese are for my fwiends."

Buck grinned at her. "Come on, now. These dolls can't eat cookies. These are for you. You *stole* these cookies!"

Offended and hurt, her eyes filled with quick tears, pink lips pouted and crocodile tears splashed over. "I not stole dem."

Quickly, the boy leaned over to kiss the soft cheek. "Don't cry, muff, I'll help you." He had popped a cookie into his mouth before the little girl realized it. Then he took three more and slipped them in his shirt pocket. "We'll take some of these back to Mom. Then she won't be mad."

Through the rain, the sunshine came again. Shielah wiped her eyes with a fist and smiled at her brother, adoring him for his wisdom.

Shielah couldn't remember much of the old farm, just vague impressions of a large front yard, dark, narrow hallways, and a warm kitchen. The barn was, of course, immense to her ten-year-old mind, immense and pungent, dusty with the particles of hay ground into the floorboards. She could hear the barn in her memory, the creaking of it under her feet, the eery whistling of it in the wind, and thudding, thumping of horses hooves. Then suddenly the memories stopped. She was ten years old and they all disappeared.

Deliberately, the grown-up girl in the white dress, sitting on the mountainside, forced herself to remember another day she had climbed up a mountain. She was ten and Buck was fifteen. It was late August, the ground was tinder-dry. The grass on the hillside had turned golden, and the dry dust made her nose tickle and itch. They were going on a "before-school-starts" picnic that they had wheedled out of Ginny. She gave them a basket full of sandwiches, cookies, apples and a mason jar full of cold, spring water. She kissed Shielah and put her hair in pigtails, then put her hand on Buck's arm, detaining him a moment.

4

"You be careful with her. Don't take any chances, and don't go off and leave her. I hold you responsible for her."

"I'll be careful," Buck had promised easily.

"I'll make him be good, Mama," Shielah vowed importantly.

He flipped her pigtail as they got out of arms distance from Ginny. Crossing the little ditch that ran beside the long, gravel driveway, and cutting across the corn field that lay south of their home, they looked back, both waving simultaneously to their mother framed in the doorway, who waved obediently back at them. They never saw her again.

They wandered almost three miles from home, exploring and looking for Indian arrowheads. Buck had taken his bow and arrow and shot a few arrows just for the fun of it. A few hours into their picnic they saw smoke in the sky, but paid little mind. After a half hour, the smoke seemed blacker and denser, and Buck grew concerned.

"Better find out what that's about, in case it's a brush fire."

Off they started in the direction of the smoke. After a short way, Buck carried her on his back, so he could go faster. Up one hill and down, then up another, higher hill and around, climbing, picking their way over rocks, around bushes, stopping for a cool drink from the mason jar—until they rounded the side of the last hill and looked down on the monumental incinerator that had been their home. Shielah slid down. They stood stock still. Shielah's hand crept into Buck's larger, harder one, and they stood as though in a dream, mesmerized, unbelieving.

Suddenly, Buck jumped as though shot and screamed with all his might. He tore away from his sister and plummeted straight down the hill. Shielah panicked and started after him, calling him and crying, but he paid her no mind. It was only when she tumbled over a rock and split her knee on the ground, screaming and crying his name, that he paused in his headlong rush and called back to her. "Stay here. Don't come any closer. Stay here, do you understand?"

Usually she would have argued. This was not the time. She was horrendously frightened, and her knee was bleeding profusely. She sat down on the ground and squeezed her skin together to keep the blood from coming, but nothing could stop the tears. The house, the barn, even the corral were all ablaze. Smoke was billowing upward and the air currents were carrying it toward her. Her eyes stung with the smoke as well as tears. It was hot, murderously hot, and ashes were falling like snow from the sky.

The little girl hugged her knees, forming a ball. With horrible fascination she watched the conflagration below. Small whimperings came from deep in her throat as she rocked back and forth, terrified and helpless. She had been sitting just so for nearly half an hour, falling deeper and deeper into a kind of stupor of agony and fear when she heard a soft voice in her ear. Wrenching her gaze from the fire, she raised her tear-streaked face and saw a woman bending beside her. The woman wore a long dress and old-fashioned, dark leather shoes. Her hair was a deep copper and gleamed in the sunlight. But it wasn't her hair that Shielah remembered most. It was her eyes. They were gray-green, direct and sympathetic, and seemed to command the terror in Shielah's heart to be gone.

5

Amazement replaced fear for a moment. "You look like my mother," Shielah stated.

The woman smiled and sat down on the ground beside her. "I know. I've often thought so too. You love your mother very dearly, don't you?

Shielah turned back to the fiery scene below and nodded her head miserably.

"And you're afraid for her right now."

Whimpering sounds began to come again as the little girl resumed her rocking.

"Shielah, your mother is all right. But she is worried about you. She is concerned that you are so afraid. She wants you to be brave and to understand that sometimes things happen that seem very, very bad at the moment. But we have to believe that good things will happen too.

Shielah looked at the pretty woman from the corner of her eye. "What good things?" she mumbled.

The woman lifted her hand as if to pat Shielah's hair, then she tucked her hand into her pocket. "More good things than you can imagine now. Loving someone decent and good, babies and happy days filled with rainbows and sunshine, and most of all, knowing your Heavenly Father loves and watches over you. Do you believe that?"

"Yes," Shielah answered. "But I don't like the fire. It scares me. I want my mother and my daddy. Where are they?"

Love seemed to flow from the woman as she looked unflinchingly into Shielah's eyes. "They are not far away, though it may be a little while before you see them again. But they love you too, so very much. That's why they sent me here to sit with you for a while. Let me tell you about your mother when she was a little girl just your age."

And for the next hour, until Uncle Will came up the hillside to find Shielah, the red-haired woman sat beside her telling stories about the young Ginny. She kept the little girl's interest away from the awful fire below and filled her with beautiful visions of her mother. Years later Shielah would comment to her Grandmother Grace about something Ginny had done or said as a child and Grace would wonder at her knowledge. As Will drew near, he called out to Shielah from a few yards down the hill.

Before she answered him, Shielah asked the woman, "What is your name? I want to tell Mommy I made a new friend."

The woman smiled lovingly at her and answered, "Charlotte. And I'll always be your friend."

Then Will called again and Shielah turned to answer. When she turned back, the woman was gone, and with her the feeling of comfort and serenity that had kept the girl from succumbing to the fear and terror of the moment.

Trucks and cars from neighboring farms had pulled into the driveway of the farm, then stopped. Men jumped out of them and made their way toward the fierce blaze. But no one, not even Buck, who had run until he thought his lungs would burst, trying to get home to Dad and his mother, could get close enough to even start putting water on that inferno. A fire

6

truck came out from Clarksville. The Moritzes from the farm four miles up the road had called them. Buck searched the crowd of neighbors for his Dad's blonde head above the rest. He was not there and Ginny was obviously not, for there were no women in the crowd.

"Where are they, where are they?" Buck was frantic, shoving men out of his way, making his way to and fro in the crowd of cars, trucks, and men. Firemen were bravely inching toward the roaring, blazing animal that had been his home. "Where are they? Dad! Dad! Have you seen my dad or mother? *Mother!*"

Now he was beside the firemen. They were dressed in their uniforms, gloved and masked. Buck was in cutoff jeans and a tee shirt.

"Get back, son, get back there."

"Where's my mom and dad? We've gotta get that fire out."

A fireman shoved him back, "Get back there, I said. This smoke'll get 'cha."

Buck stumbled backward into the arms of his Uncle Will.

"Where's Shielah?" was the first thing Will Skinner asked.

"Where's Mom and Dad?" Buck countered frantically.

"Don't know. Where's Shielah?"

Buck couldn't concentrate on anything but the hypnotic monster roaring. "Mom! Dad! Where's my Mom and Dad?"

Will shook him to get his attention. "Tell me where your sister is. Where's Shielah?" Will already suspected the worst. Ed and Ginny were nowhere to be found. But where was the little girl?

"She's over there," Buck pointed to the far hill, across the acre of corn.

Skinner could barely make out a tiny figure crouched on the side of the hill. "Keep the boy out of trouble," he said in the ear of Harry Moritz, "I'm going after his sister on that hill. Don't think she's in any danger. The fire ain't spreading much, but she's bound to be scared to death."

Fear had taken Buck over by now and he felt frozen in the most awful nightmare of his fifteen years. No one answered his occasional pleas of "Don't you know where my Mom and Dad are?" No one dared.

When it was over, the fire sunken in wet, filthy ashes, both charred bodies were found in the barn, Ginny's pinned beneath a crossbeam, and Ed's just at the threshold of what had been an animal stall. Buck and Shielah had been taken to Will and Maddie's place in Bird's Eye long before the bodies were found. Buck wouldn't believe the reports at first, then demanded to see the bodies to make sure for himself. Of course, they wouldn't let him. Shielah fell into a dream world, punctuated by sobs and screams, and heart-wrenching, pitiful pleas in the night for her Mama and Daddy. Buck disappeared.

Shielah had no memory at nineteen of the funeral held when she was ten. She had no memory of the year she spent with Will and Maddie and their big, bustling family. She was easily absorbed into that family of seven cousins, and she was loved and petted and favored by everyone, from the oldest to the youngest cousin. But she wandered through that year in a daze. Fire destroyed her body hundreds of times in her dreams. Ginny came walking out of the flames with her arms open, but her little girl could never reach her and feel her hug. Ed smiled at her from the window of his old truck night after night. These were the memories, the dreams she would never forget. The days she never did remember.

Will's farm was large and rambling, leisurely stretching over twenty acres. There were three barns, including a training ring and thirty horse stalls, several more outbuildings for hay, tractors, farming equipment, and acres of cultivated land, all neatly sectioned off into rows of vegetables, with orchards of fruit trees bordering the garden. The farmhouse loomed at the end of the long lane, solid and sturdy, roomy and homey. Will worked longer hours than the sun in keeping his property in good repair and all the fences and outbuildings painted. There were no fences falling down or doors hanging askew on their henges. This quiet, shy man was a giant in responsibility and loved the beauty of his property as much as his wife did.

Aunt Maddie was her mother's sister, though the two girls had never looked alike. Where Ginny had been auburn-haired and fair-skinned, Maddie had light brown hair, now fading into a nondescript color. She was a seamstress and made all of her own children's clothes and most of Ginny's. She didn't have the gift of easy laughter that her sister had, but she was gentle and slow and her smile could soothe a hurting heart. Shielah had always loved Aunt Maddie, mostly for the pretty dresses that often came from her house to theirs and for the wealth of cousins she had given Shielah. Now she should have been able to turn to her for comfort. Maddie tried. So did Will, in his way. But the girl could not be comforted. She was alone. Her mother and father were gone, taken away by a terrible, diabolical event, never, never to hold her and love her again. Added to that, Buck was also gone. He deserted her just when she needed him most, not taken away as her parents had been, but leaving of his own choice. And the little girl was deeply alone in her heart. No prayers could help her. God made no sense to her young mind. She should have died with them, or so she thought.

Even now, nine years later, all grown up, in her lovely white graduation dress that Buck had bought her, tears came swiftly at those memories. It's too painful, she thought, watching the cars inch along the ribbon of highway coming into the canyon. I should think about happier things today. I should think of Stephen and the dance the other night. But memories are not always obedient. She was ending an old life, and the future stretched mysteriously ahead. She could attend to the future better if she mastered the past. Slowly, reluctantly, she gave in to the commando memories again.

A smile came at last. Grandma had been their salvation, quite literally.

One day, a year later, Buck had appeared at the Skinner's farmhouse door. Maddie looked up from the trousers she was mending and stifled a little scream, seeing his face so unexpectedly at the screen door. She jumped up, tipping over the chair, then threw open the door, "Buck, oh Buck, I'm so glad you're back."

"Thanks, Aunt Maddie. I didn't know if you would be."

8

"Of course I am. Shielah will be, too. She's missed you so terribly. You'll be surprised to see how big she's grown. She's out with the kids on the horses. They're over by the east pasture." Maddie was rambling on, trying to ease the awkwardness they both felt.

"Here, I'll bet you're hungry. Have some pound cake. I just made it last night. Will'll be so glad to see you."

"Aunt Maddie, is Shielah ok?"

"Why yes, she's fine . . . well . . . she is awfully quiet. Off in her own world, you know. She doesn't talk much lately, but she goes to school with the rest of the kids. I guess it takes time. I think she'll be all right."

Buck was nervous, pacing up and down. He had come to see Shielah. He needed to be with her again. She was only ten, nope, eleven now, but she was his only family left. He felt incomplete. Somehow she could make him whole again—he hoped.

He was sitting on the step of the porch, watching for the horses to come in. At last they came, some trotting, some galloping, one trailing behind. On it was a long-legged young girl with golden hair hanging in tangles down her back. The cousins saw him first and spurred their horses on.

"It's Buck," Drew shouted.

"It is! It's Buck," Allen and Joanie and Katie shouted in glee.

"Hey, Shielah," hollered little Wayne, "It's your brother. It's Buck."

She rode up slowly, reined in the horse just a few feet away, then slid off his back. It seemed such a long way to the ground. Everyone was silent, looking on. From Drew, the oldest at seventeen, down to Wayne, the little six-year-old, they sensed a drama before them. Shielah made no expression. That had become her way now. She stood still and looked at her brother, who stood up and was also watching her. He was so beautiful! He hadn't changed. No, that's not right, she thought. He's taller and his face is older. But he's still Buck. Anger and hate flooded over her. A whole year he had left her to be alone and to hurt alone! Then love came washing over the anger. She blinked and he put out his arms. In a burst, she flung herself into them and he wrapped her up. They both cried and cried, and kissed each other. He swung her around and told her what long legs she had, what pretty hair. How he loved her, how sorry he was he had left her. The words came tumbling out, running all over each other and Aunt Maddie quietly herded the cousins inside to do chores before dinner.

Buck stayed with them that night. The next day he sat at the table with Uncle Will and Aunt Maddie, and told them he had come to take care of his sister now. They were a family, the only family they had left, and he intended to take care of her.

"Where ya been, Buck?" Will wanted to avoid the subject for a while. The boy was only sixteen, too young to be responsible for a little girl.

"Went all the way to Mexico." Buck answered.

"No kidding! Well, that's a piece. What did you wanta go down there for?"

"I dunno. Just had to get away, I guess. I couldn't stand it here. I couldn't drive by the old place. Thought I'd go nuts. I'd just be in the way, anyhow." Will started to speak. "No, it's true. I know you'd have taken me just like Shielah, but I'd just be one more mouth to feed and another bed to buy. I had to get my head clear. Had to be alone. So I thumbed to the Mexican border, and rode a truck on down to Guadalajara."

Will and Maddie glanced at each other in wonder. After a moment he continued, "Got a job working for a wealthy Mexican, owned about three haciendas. I'm a good fix-it man! I kept his cars running, and his plumbing, too. Last February he took me to Mexico City with him. He had a friend who had an airplane of his own and we flew down there. I ran away from him when he started talking about some illegal stuff. Took me a while, but I found something better. Found some scientists—American . . . French . . . some South American archeologists. They were headed out to a dig. I got all their gear and food and transportation rounded up for them, and they took me with them."

By now Will and Maddie were dumb. They sat staring at him in amazement. Buck was tempted to laugh but it would have been impolite. He had run away from the memory of his childhood happiness, the nightmare of the fire, from his guilt. He had never been a good kid, always naughty, making his mother worry and sometimes cry. That guilt was all mixed up with their deaths in his mind. So he had run. He didn't deserve to be taken care of, to be taken in like a poor, hurt puppy. And he didn't intend to go back to school. He could make it on the street. It was a more exciting classroom. He was smart, quick, capable, and nobody's fool. He could lie when he had to, steal if it were necessary, and talk an angel out of his halo. His greatest talent was getting things put together right, especially mechanically. He had kept his dad's truck running for three years, as well as the tractor and his mother's few appliances.

The Spanish language came quickly to him, and he had a knack of making people laugh with his funny, Americanized Spanish. He loved Mexico. It was bright and garish, noisy and seething with opportunities for anyone ambitious and precocious enough to grab them. He had not intended to go home for a long time. But archeology had caught him. He was fascinated with the dig. It was tedious work, precise work, all mapped and catalogued, but it unfolded—like a string of paper dolls—a whole different world. His vivid imagination could picture the living, laughing people who had inhabited an ancient city. It took only three months for him to become thoroughly converted to the science.

The professors who had taken him under their wings were street wise themselves. They stumbled on this American kid, long haired, suntanned skin, looking almost Spanish and obviously without ties. He was probably in the country illegally, but he was bright and tremendously helpful. They knew he must be under age, although he told them he was eighteen. When they saw him falling in love with the project and the work, they went to work . . . persuading him he had to go back to school and get a degree if he wanted to do archeology with them.

Tenacious or stubborn, Buck was alternately called both, depending on who was describing him. Now he hung on like a bull dog. Will and Mattie argued that Shielah was better off in a big family with cousins to

10

play with and a mother and father—a normal family. It would help ease the pain. The country life was good for her; she loved the horses and the wide open spaces. How could he go to school and care for her, too? They couldn't live alone and Grandma was too old to have the worry of two young kids.

Buck answered every objection. He would work after school. Besides, hadn't there been some insurance on the old farm and his dad? Well, yes, there had been, Will admitted. They wouldn't be any trouble to Grandma, Buck assured them. They would look after her. They needed each other, he and Shielah; it was the only comfort either had. Finally, they all looked at the girl. She had been sitting quietly in the chair, eyes big at Buck's adventures, wonder and adoration written in her blue eyes. She had not contributed a word during the whole conversation, but there was no doubt in her mind. She would go with Buck. If he went back to Mexico, she would go too. If he lived in a tree house on the side of a hill, she would too. If Grandma would take them, that was fine. But most of all, she would have a family of her own again. If they were together, Mother and Dad would always be alive between them.

"I will live with my brother," she said softly, "wherever he lives." She could still remember the pride in his eyes and the impish grin on his lips.

So Grandma put the final, adult seal of approval on the plan, and they moved into Clarksville to her tiny brick home with two bedrooms. The children were too old to sleep together, so Shielah slept with her grandmother for the first two years she was there. Later, Buck put up a pre-fab, small storage shed at the back of the house, and he slept there so Shielah could have a bedroom of her own. Grace Thompson's home was one among many in block after block of brick houses. Invariably, they were set thirty feet back from the sidewalk and each one sported a small front porch, at least two trees to shade the front yard, and a narrow, detached garage. Like older ladies in a sewing circle they were neat, tidy, a bit old-fashioned, but emitting a warm, familiar hominess that soothed the heart. In the summer, Grace's home was cool because of the brick and the trees. Irrigation water traveled down each side of the street in narrow ditches, singing its bubbly, siren song to little feet. Shielah spent days in the hot sunlight wiggling her feet in the cool clear water or following it blocks and blocks, lost in her nightmares and dreams. Grace often received a phone call from a neighbor a mile or more away who had taken the little girl in before she could follow the wandering ditch to the outskirts of town.

Grandma became her new mother. After all, she was Ginny's mother, and Shielah asked a million questions about her mom as a young girl. Sometimes, as she sat at the table eating biscuits with honey butter, she imagined that she was Ginny and would grow up to be beautiful, with an easy laugh and everybody would be her friend.

She and Buck had only been in their grandmother's home a week when Grace asked Buck to help her in the attic to get a picture down. It was twenty-six by thirty-six inches of canvas, encased in a heavy, oak frame. And it was the only picture existing of her grandmother, Charlotte Boughtman. The two of them wrestled the portrait through the tiny crawl

11

space up to the attic and eventually hung it in Grace's bedroom. She had been meaning to bring it down for years, but had never wanted to bother her sons-in-law to help her. Shielah saw it for the first time that afternoon when she came in the house for lunch. Entranced, she stood looking at the picture, then inched forward and reached reverently to touch the oil on canvas. Tears started in her eyes and breathlessly she whispered, "That's Charlotte."

Grace was taken by surprise. "Yes, it is. I didn't think you knew about her. I wanted to tell you all about her and how brave she was. You know she lost her mother and father too. Their farm was burned and they were driven out of Nauvoo. Her father died on the plains and she never saw her mother or her sister again. She was a very strong woman, my mother told me—strong and loving and very determined. You know, honey, she looks a lot like you."

Shielah shook her head. "Oh no. She's very beautiful. She looks like my mother. They have the same color hair."

"True," Grace replied, her arm around her granddaughter's thin shoulders. "They both had deep red hair, but your face is like hers. Why, look at you—wide cheekbones, delicate nose, same mouth. I declare! Put gold hair on that portrait and it could be you when you're all grown up."

But when Shielah looked in the mirror, it was with despair. She saw only a very awkward girl there—blue eyes too big for her face, ears too large so she hid them with hair, a tiny heart-shaped face, and a mouth too generous. Everything was wrong. Her legs were too long, her feet too big, her hair was a strange mix of colors—gold, white, even red strands—as if it couldn't make up its mind. She blushed and shook her head vehemently when home teachers said, "You're getting to be a pretty young lady." She knew it was a lie.

Conversation didn't come easily, and she had few friends at school. She did her fifth grade over. It had been lost somewhere in her mind. Consequently, she was a year older than her classmates, and the boys teased her unmercifully. They couldn't get her to talk any other way. The shy, winsome three-year-old had become an introverted young girl. She dutifully answered questions in school, but preferred to play alone at recess, except for a few gentle playmates she trusted. She wouldn't speak to the boys. The only way they could get a response from her was to pick on one of the little kids walking home from school. Then the wall of silence would break, her eyes would flash, and she might say anything. What grand fun! At least once a week she would burst into the house, holding back the tears until she could be alone.

"I hate boys, Grandma. I hate them! They are cruel and awful. They like to pick on little kids, anyone weaker than they are. Why? Why? Why are boys so mean?"

"Who was it this time," Grandma Thompson asked, laying aside her reading glasses?

"Who else? Curtis and Mark! They followed us for two blocks, clear out of their way, just to torment us. Someday I'm going to tell Sister Andell that her boys are real stinkers. Wouldn't she be surprised. She thinks

12

they're so perfect. If those boys pass the Sacrament this Sunday, I'll puke. Honest, I will. Doesn't the Bishop know those boys aren't worthy to pass the sacrament?"

Grandma patted her hand. "I suppose they are pretty mischievous. Boys usually are. Just wait, honey, they'll grow up and you'll, like as not, marry one of them."

Shielah jumped up angrily. "I will not! I never would. I'll be an old maid before I'd marry one of those creeps."

Meeting with no argument or resistance, she sat back down. "Grandma, did boys tease mother?"

Old eyes twinkled. "I should say they did. Boys loved to be around Ginny, so they teased her for all they were worth. She just laughed. Even your father, believe it or not, when he was . . . oh, about eleven and twelve . . . used to steal her papers and pencils. She had a grand time chasing those boys to get her things back and them chasing her to pull her pigtails, or untie her sash."

Shielah listened solemnly, but could not relate to that.

Now, her school days finally over, sitting on the hillside, throwing rocks far down the mountain aimlessly, she smiled almost grimly. Grandma had been partially right. At the beginning of her junior year, before school had even properly started, Curtis Andell had asked her to go to a movie. She was flabbergasted, so amazed she could hardly speak. He was six feet three inches now, and she barely came up to his chin. He was nervous, standing on one foot then the other, looking down at her expectantly. Hurt ran deep in Shielah and forgiveness did not.

"I've already been to that movie . . . with a friend," she said and walked away.

No one else tried, that year. Buck took her to her Junior Prom, against her wishes. She had been sure it would be excruciating to spend a social evening amongst her peers that teased her and scorned her. But they had a good time. He insisted on dancing a few dances with other girls, which meant that their dates had to dance with Shielah. Obnoxious deacons, now grown up a foot, smiled shyly at her and complimented her dress, her hair, her looks. In the ladies room, when no one else was around, she studied herself in the mirror. Were they serious or still teasing? She looked all right. The hairdresser had put half of her hair up in curls on her head, and the rest hung in smooth waves past her shoulders. Buck and Grandma had scrimped and saved enough money to buy her a new gown. It was not fancy. Simple, like me, she thought, but shiny and soft and delicately peach. She ran her hand down the silky fabric and her heart swelled with love as she thought of their sacrifice for her.

After the dance, a group of friends dragged State Street until the cops closed it down to teenagers. Buck and Shielah were in his '59 Chevy. Buck was infallibly the leader, the winner, the instigator. Older than the others and well known for his adventures, the boys tried to emulate him, challenged him regularly and laughed at getting beaten. You couldn't beat Buck. He always found a way to win. It was his nature. They ate hamburgers and milkshakes so thick they had to use a spoon. Finally, they parked fifteen cars in a circle in the church parking lot, turned up the radios and danced and talked until four o'clock in the morning. But best of all, she spent the whole night between her brother—whom she still loved and hated—and his best friend, just home from a mission—tall, blonde Stephen Gailbraith, whom she just loved.

Chapter 2

Stephen Michael Gailbraith was the descendant of mountain men. His great, great grandfather, Michael, had immigrated to America from Scotland, a man who disappeared for months at a time into the wilderness where the deer, the beaver, the otter, and the bear understood the same language. It was a universal language of solitude and survival. He had passed on his love of the wilderness to his son, Josiah. They worked together trapping as they moved west with the Mormon wagon trains, and the boy learned mercy even in a wild setting from his father. Josiah, in turn, passed on his hardiness, endurance, patience, and survival skills to his son, Sean.

Stephen remembered his Grandfather Gailbraith. Sean was also a mountain man, though he did no trapping for fur. He was a forest ranger in the Yosemite Mountains. He loved the forests and mountains as a father loves his only son. Sean's son was Cameron Michael Gailbraith. Cam grew up as rough and hardy as any of his early ancestors. His friends were the animals and the sky, but also withinhim was a certain idealism and dreaminess. Many times Sean would find Cam lying on a big slab of rock, dreaming and wondering and asking the sky all his why's and "whence-cometh-I's."

Sean had reluctantly parted with his son when Cam became college age. He sent him to Utah State College in Logan, Utah for a degree in Forestry. In his sophomore year, Cam met a young, brown-haired, blue-eyed girl he could talk with about his why's and wherefore's. Mary Margaret Stalling was getting a degree in sociology and was determined to help the underprivileged of the world. She would give food, clothing, jobs to those poor souls who needed her help. In their many discussions of life, as they walked the college campus, Cam found his longed-for answers. He came to believe in himself as a literal child of God and intended to prove himself worthy of that honor. Six months before graduation, Cam and Mary married in the Logan Temple.

Stephen was their first child. After him came Mike and finally, the little girl, Tami, that Mary had her heart set on. Through all the years of raising the children, Mary continued her social work, though it meant leaving them with babysitters much of the time. She had a deep need to contribute to society, to feel that she made a difference in the world. Cam tried to dissuade her from it in the first few years. He even took her back to Yosemite, and they lived with his father for two years. She hated it. It was too lonely for her, and she finally persuaded Cam to take her back to Utah. They moved to Springville. It was a compromise for Cam. He disliked working in Salt Lake City at a desk job with the government, but small town life was a liveable compromise if he couldn't be in the forest.

When Stephen was eleven years old, Cam insisted on taking him back into the Uintas on a backpacking trip, just the two of them. Mary had become more rigid over the years and would not give her permission. She feared the dangers of the wilds. She wouldn't even help them get the food ready for the trip. When they parted, she kissed her son goodbye, but let her husband go with never a farewell. Her fears were almost prophetic.

Thursday morning, after three wonderful days of hiking, talking, sharing dreams with his dad, Stephen was separated from Cam, when his father went to catch fish for their lunch. After fifteen minutes, the boy began to be aware of a fine, white ash falling from the sky. It seemed almost like snow. He pulled out his transistor radio and switched stations until he found the news. It was a forest fire, and he and his dad were right in its path. Cameron was nowhere to be seen. Stephen began to panic. Fear knotted his throat. He tried shouting for his father, but only little sounds came out.

At last, he imitated what he had heard his father say so often. Aloud he said, "Now wait a minute here. What is the smart thing to do?" The sound of his own voice calmed him a bit, and he started back to camp, realizing that his father would probably be there looking for him by now. But the trail looked entirely different going back, and he never came to the camp they had made. After twenty minutes of walking and calling and not finding anything familiar, he suddenly stopped in a small clearing and dropped to his knees. If Joseph Smith could ask help of God, so could he. He never doubted that his Heavenly Father would hear him.

He didn't ask for a lot, he just wanted his Dad. He said it over and over, "Please help me find Dad." It was hard to force himself to get up, but Stephen was a survivor, and the survival instinct pushed him to his feet. When he was almost hopeless, he saw through the slender saplings a man dressed in white clothes. The man called him, "Stephen, come this way." Obediently, he followed the white-clothed figure ahead of him, who frequently beckoned and often smiled reassuringly at him. An orange halo seemed to have drenched the sky in its glow. At long last, he came to a road. He stopped. The man was not in sight. He debated with himself which way to go and started west. Again, the man in white stepped out from the trees ahead and spoke, "Not that way. Just a little further the other way." So he turned and had walked no more than a quarter of a mile, when around a bend came a ranger jeep with his father urging the driver on.

Mary never forgave Cameron that trip. Stephen never forgot it. He knew he had received heavenly protection and it became a lifelong touchstone for his faith. But Mary didn't see it that way. She used it against Cam. She was resentful of his need to be a part of the wilderness, and he could not understand her preoccupation with other people and their children. He often told her she had a needy family right at home. Their marriage fell into bitter silence. Eventually, when Stephen was fourteen, his parents separated and finally divorced. Cam applied for a job at the ranger station in Kamas, Utah, and Mary threw herself deeper into social work.

So Stephen became the man of the household—also sometimes the mother, fixing food for his younger brother and sister and helping them with homework. The most fun he had in life was with Buck Sorensen. They were an unlikely pair. He was as fair as Buck was dark. Stephen stood six feet two inches with strong features—a broad forehead, straight, prominent nose and high cheek bones. His shoulders were broad and the expanse from shoulder to hip was lean and well muscled. Blonde hair was the only really unruly thing about him. It was fine and soft, and constantly crept over his eyebrow. Even before Buck lost his parents, he would range from Clarksville into Spanish Fork, thumbing rides or walking if he had to. He was the free spirit Stephen envied but couldn't quite emulate. Adventures with Buck were a dime a dozen, climbing up the water tower and getting shouted at by police, skinnydipping in the river when the spring runoff water was freezing cold. When Buck came back from his year in Mexico and told all his strange stories, Stephen begged Mary to let Buck come live with them. He had almost persuaded her when Buck told him that he was going to live with his grandmother and take care of his little sister. Stephen was disappointed for himself, but he was glad to hear Buck's plans to go back to school and even to college to get a degree in archeology. Even then he sensed that Buck needed to find a purpose in life.

June seventh of 1972 was a turning point in Stephen's life. He went to the graduation services at Clarksville High School with Buck and Grandma Thompson. Shielah had been almost as much a part of his life as his sister, Tami. Yet there was something more tender in his feelings for her. He had watched her turn from a gangly, withdrawn child, groping in a nightmare world of loss and grief, into a beautiful young lady, graduating today in her cap and gown. She was even smiling through most of it. Many of the girls in the bleachers were wiping away tears during their graduation ceremony. Not Shielah. She seemed happy and relieved to be leaving high school behind. She was the oldest in her graduating class and not unmindful of that fact. He glanced over the class. She was also the prettiest by far. Not that she would believe that, he smiled.

"Take me with you," the eight-year-old girl had begged whenever Buck and Stephen would set out on a hike into Bird's Eye.

"No! Go back," Buck would shout.

"Please, please, Buck! I'll keep up, and I won't cry, I promise."

Buck looked at Stephen as if to say, "I'm sorry."

Stephen shrugged. Secretly, he enjoyed Buck's sister. Something in her delicate face and determined courage touched him. He was frequently the one to carry her on his back if she got tired, or if rocks started to hurt her bare feet. She would wrap her thin arms around his neck and lay her head on his back. She was not heavy, and the closeness was something he rarely experienced in his own family. Sometimes he would look back and she would push her head around his shoulder and beam at him in her joy. He was too young at eleven to know what he was feeling at moments like that.

He and Buck showed off for her, leaping across the river on stones or climbing the tallest trees and swinging from their knees from the upper branches. She sat below and clapped her hands, laughing and begging them to help her do it. Of course, they wouldn't. She might fall. They both felt proudly responsible for her.

As they grew older, and Shielah disappeared into her own constricted world after the fire, Stephen missed those happier days. But he didn't know how to reach her. Always delicate, she seemed almost too frail to touch. He watched her grow up. He was the only outsider at her sixteenth birthday. Grandma Thompson had wanted to plan a party for her but Shielah withdrew into a shell at the very mention of it. On that birthday night in mid-April, Buck and Stephen had taken her and Grandma to a play in Salt Lake City. Shielah sat between the two boys and Stephen tried to watch the play instead of her, but he didn't always succeed. Her face was alive with excitement and unrestrained pleasure that he had not seen in years. A few weeks later he left on his mission and carried the memory of her face with him. It was the startling contrast of deep blue eyes against porcelain skin that gave her a haunting quality, and even when her eyes refused tears there was often a wounded look about them. It pained Stephen. It pained him because he still felt protective but could no longer carry her to make things easy, as he once had.

At the end of last year, the night of the Junior Prom, Buck had stopped by his house at midnight and tooted the horn. Stephen joined the impromptu party and spent the rest of the night, until early morning, riding with Buck and Shielah in the front seat of Buck's '59 Chevy, then talking and dancing in the church parking lot. He smiled to himself as he remembered that night. Shielah had grown up all in one day. He had been home from his mission only two weeks and had not been aclimatized back into American society. Buck grabbed him by the shirt collar and hauled him into the middle of things that night. When he helped Shielah out of the car and looked at her in the moonlight in a dress all filmy and clinging, all his missionary reservations melted away. He had been two years in Scotland, completely submerged in serving the Lord as a missionary. He had not thought of girls, except for Shielah, and he couldn't admit that she was anything more than just Buck's little sister who seemed too fragile to touch.

During the summer, he found every reason in the world to visit Buck. Shielah was shy with him, but not bitter as she was with so many of the boys her own age. She was devoted to her brother, though Buck teased her unmercifully. She never truly minded his teasing, even when she complained to Grandma. And Stephen seemed to fall into the same preferred category. One day he asked Buck about her withdrawn attitude.

"I don't think she has ever gotten over the fire and losing Mom and Dad. I also think she is still mad at me for deserting her. Oh, she'd never say that. Maybe she doesn't even realize it, but I feel it. Who knows, could be just my guilty conscience."

"She seems so quiet, almost fragile."

"Yeah, I know. I worry about her. Maybe she'll never get over it—the fire I mean. It was pretty awful. I still dream about it. She probably does too."

"Does she date?" Stephen asked casually.

Buck glanced at his friend, then grinned. "Nope!" Got any ideas?"

Stephen colored slightly. "Just surprised. She's so pretty, you'd think she'd be popular.

"Won't let herself. She has a very long memory and has never forgiven the guys her own age for being bratty twelve-year-olds. Her feelings are pretty easily hurt, and the hurt lasts a long time with her. I heard that Andell asked her out last year and she turned him down. I can see her self-made wall go up when she is with kids her same age. With me, she's an angel."

That summer Stephen and Shielah frequently found themselves alone together, and slowly she began to open up to him, to confide her feelings of rejection by her peers and the debilitating sense of loneliness she had lived with since her mother and father died in the fire. He could see the emotional scars left by the fire and felt frustrated in wanting to help her. But at least she talked to him. They often rode Will's horses across the hills between Clarksville and Birds Eye. More than once they climbed the mountain to her favorite spot, about half-way up, and stayed for hours talking.

The week before her Senior Dance he found out from Buck that Shielah was not going. "I'd take her but she won't go with me," Buck said. "I took her last year to the Junior Prom. Guess she's embarrassed over her rascal brother."

"She should be!" Stephen poked his friend. "No, I'm sure it's not that. It's just too condescending in her mind."

"But, you know something," Buck said thoughtfully. "She's been asked. I heard both Le Roy and Mark have asked her. She just won't go."

Stephen ate dinner that night at Grace's table. Buck went out on the porch after dinner while Stephen stayed behind to help with dishes. He insisted. He said he owed at least that much for a delicious meal.

"I guess I shouldn't spend so much time here."

Shielah looked at him quickly. "Why not? You've always spent a lot of time with Buck. You're good for him."

"Well, my own family is beginning to wonder what I look like." She didn't reply. A fall of silky hair hid her face from him. "I'm just so comfortable here with your family. You're lucky, Shielah. You all have such closeness and so much love."

She handed him a dish. He could see surprise and thoughtfulness on her face. "In the mission field we taught about love. The scriptures say it's the most important commandment and most people don't understand it at all."

"Is it strange to come back from your mission and rejoin the rest of the world?"

"A little. Well, more than a little. A lot!"

She concentrated on the dishwater and the silverware. "You seem to adjust quickly," she said.

"I try, and Buck has been determined to help. He set up my dates for the first two months after I got home. Do you date much?"

She shook her head.

"I hear Mark Jones asked you to the Senior Dance. Don't you like to dance?"

"Sometimes. But I dance alone . . . when no one else can see me."

"I'm not a very good dancer, but I like to try." He put the silverware away. "Maybe you'd go with me, a poor ex-missionary terrified of girls."

With that he got her to laugh. "You're about as terrified as a duck in water. You and Buck are just alike in that."

"I'm wounded! Do you think I'm a Casanova? You're wrong. I'm actually very conservative. Despite my intense charm I'm tongue-tied around blutiful dirls . . . glutiful burls . . . uh, uh, beautiful girls. See? See, what'd I tell you? Would you be embarrassed to take an ex-missionary to your Senior Dance?"

Shielah couldn't help laughing at him. "I wouldn't be embarrassed with you. Everybody likes you. You always fit in."

"Then will you go with me?" The water disappeared down the drain. He took her hands, drying them on the dish towel, and she didn't pull away. "If I step on your feet, I could always just carry you . . . remember?"

She couldn't resist the memories. She finally looked fully into his face and his grin infected her. Smiling with pleasure at the childhood memories she capitulated. "Promise?" she asked.

"Promise," was the answer.

The night of the dance clarified in Stephen's mind his feelings for his best friend's sister. When he took her in his arms for the first dance, and her eyes raised to his, Stephen was flooded with joy. Even as children, there had been a special feeling between them when he had touched her in any way. Now he held her against him and honey warmth swept his body. He couldn't look into her face without wanting to kiss her. So he laughed and joked to hide his feelings, and Shielah enjoyed that night more than she ever thought she would.

The Senior dance was held in an art gallery in Springville. It was elegant, with marble statues and tall, carved columns, and long hallways softly lit. Shielah felt like she was enveloped in a dream. If only it would never end. Years later she would remember that night, wandering down the halls of the gallery, hand in hand with Stephen, too intensely happy to worry about what anyone else thought of her. In her memory, the dim light surrounded the young pair in a quaint, antique glow, and Stephen's face was forever young.

Later, after the dance, they sat in Buck's car with only the yellow glimmer from her grandmother's porch illuminating the front seat. The laughter and jokes all over with, she became suddenly shy.

They talked for a minute, then fell into silence. She sat looking down at the tiny purse in her lap. He looked at the steering wheel and glanced frequently at her. Long, shiny hair shadowed her face, and the longing to touch that softness was excruciating. But, as always, he held back, uncertain whether she would accept him.

Finally, she spoke, still not looking at him. "I didn't think I'd like it. I didn't want to go. But I'm glad I did. You make everything fun. It's a talent of yours, Stephen."

"I like people. I want them to have fun. Sometimes I make myself look like a fool just so people can laugh. Sometimes it's a cover-up."

"I didn't think you ever covered up anything. You seem so natural, so free."

"Well, that's right. I usually don't . . . just sometimes."

"Were you covering up something tonight?" Now she turned to look at him. The stream of gold light from the porch lamp touched her face and hair. Stephen stared at her through the dark. She was exquisitely beautiful with her face half in shadows, half in filtered light.

He didn't answer. They just looked at one another, each suffering an exquisite awareness of the other. He didn't know how to answer. He couldn't tell her that holding her, feeling her body against his had left him shaken and tingling. She wouldn't understand. He was as much a big brother to her as Buck was. He couldn't tell her he wanted to hold her and kiss her until she couldn't breathe, he would frighten her. So he tore his eyes away from her face, opened the car door and walked around to her's. He helped her from the car and stood holding her hand, wanting to say something clever, anything that would prolong the last few moments together. But his easy conversation had deserted him. There was only one thing he wanted to say—and he couldn't say that. They stood painfully close for several minutes. Once she looked into his eyes, searching for something, but quickly dropped her eyes.

"Goodnight," she whispered.

"Shielah, I . . . I. . . . Thanks for taking me to the dance." He cursed himself for being so tongue-tied.

"I am the one to say thank you. I had such a good time. It was wonderful, and you . . . you . . . well . . . I like the way you danced," she finished lamely.

"Goodnight," he said, still holding her hand. And then they were both tongue-tied, and finally, she moved to go. Impulsively he held on and pulled her back. Quickly he took her silky head between his hands and kissed her on the forehead. Her eyes grew wide and blinked in surprise. Her fingers went up to her lips and her breath caught as their eyes locked. Then she backed away and in a moment was crossing the porch. At the door she turned, then tentatively lifted her hand to wave. He saw that salute all night long in his dreams, and he held her and smelled her perfume until he woke the next morning. Stephen sat up in bed and smiled, knowing he would hold her again.

Shielah disappeared after the diplomas and the final march. She had come to them and hugged Grandma, kissed Buck and even, shyly gave him a hug. Then, as they stood and talked with others in the crowd, she whispered something to Buck. He drew his hand from his pocket and put it in hers; then she disappeared. Stephen drove Buck and Grandma home and started home himself.

Rounding the last curve in the mountain road before starting into the valley, he saw Buck's car parked way off on the shoulder. He slowed down and looked up. He couldn't see anything. She was too high. But he knew where she was. Once before, she had shown him her favorite spot on the mountain.

Stephen drove straight home after the graduation, changed his clothes, pulling on jeans and a tee shirt. While he was tying his shoelaces, his eyes wandered to the top of his dresser. A letter. Reaching over, he read "Department of Armed Services." He tore it open and scanned it. His heart fell down to his tennis shoes. "Report to your local draft center immediately." One word seared his mind, "Vietnam." He had been lucky so far. Back from his mission a whole year, he had been working as a carpenter to get enough money to enter college. So far he hadn't been tapped. This was it! Vietnam!

He left the letter on his dresser and jumped in the car again. He knew exactly where he would go. He pulled his car off the highway behind Buck's, locked it up, and started up the mountainside. She had gone higher today than the other time she brought him here. He passed the rock where they had sat and talked last fall. Off to the left, he could hear rocks hitting the ground occasionally, and he veered toward the rocks, looking up. He could see her several hundred yards higher. He jogged back the other way and kept climbing. When he judged he was almost on her level, he walked around the hillside and came up on her from behind. She was deep in thought and was startled at his voice at her shoulder.

"I wondered if you were aiming for the top this time."

"What . . . no . . . I just needed to do some thinking. Some remembering actually. What are you doing here?"

He grinned at her. "Chasing a deer up the mountainside." He sat down beside her. "You did it, you graduated. How does it feel?"

"I don't know. Kind of free, but kind of uncertain, you know?"

"Yeah. There are a lot of those moments in life, I think. I felt that way when I graduated, then when I went on my mission and when I came back. Now I feel that way again."

"You do?" They were sitting side by side, shoulders almost touching.

"Umm hmm. But I don't want to talk about me, I came to see how you were."

She turned her face away, and looked off into the distance. He could make out telltale streaks down her face.

"You OK? I thought this would be a happy day."

"It is," she said quickly. "It is, really. I've just been thinking back over my life. I was almost to the part about what's ahead when I was so stealthily interrupted." She picked up another rock and tossed it.

"You know you almost hit me with one of those."

"Really?" She looked back at him quickly. "I'm sorry. I didn't know."

"It's all right. No great loss, one head more or less. I'd never miss it."

She had to smile back at him, his grin demanded it. Stephen's heart twisted inside him and he knew exactly what he was feeling. Easy, take it easy, he thought.

He ran one finger down her bare arm, sunburned from her hours on the hillside.

"It's been a good year, Shielah," he said, watching her profile.

"Yes," she agreed quietly. Then after a moment of silence when neither knew how to make the next move, she said, "I especially remember the Senior Dance. I had so much fun. Probably the most in my life. Thank you for taking me, even if Buck bribed you."

His finger stopped, and he looked at her in surprise. "You think Buck got me to ask you! That's crazy. I asked you because I wanted to. I . . . I wanted to be with you on your special night."

He could see disbelief in her eyes. He raised his eyebrows and nodded. "Really," he affirmed.

Slowly she smiled. He took her hand in his, very gently brushing his hand over the satin smoothness of her arm. "Are you touchable, Shielah Sorensen? Or will you break if I try?"

"I don't break very easily," she whispered.

Her hair was like warm silk, and the world was all hushed on the mountainside. In the perfect quiet, with just a slight breeze fanning them, Stephen kissed her for the first time. Leaning toward her he touched her lips gently, still afraid she would jump and run away. But she didn't move. Her breath quickened and she began to tremble with repressed emotion. He brushed her lips with his once, twice, ever so careful not to frighten her. Then he began to shake all over and he pulled back. Oh, he knew what it was, all right, the unbelievable pounding of his heart and the delicious fire washing through him. "I love you," he murmured softly against her lips.

She tensed and pulled away, fear showing in her eyes. "Don't say that to me. Not unless you really mean it. It's cruel—too cruel—to play with those words."

He wound his hand in her hair and drew her back. "I'm not playing. I love you, Shielah. I always have, I think. At least since last year in the church parking lot when you danced with me."

"I don't believe it," she whispered in amazement.

"Believe it," he commanded, nuzzling her cheek, her lips. A deep breath escaped her. The tension went out of her body and she relaxed against him. He felt her arms creep uncertainly around his neck. Her lips parted ever so slightly and gave back his kiss with a tenderness that took his breath away.

When at last they parted, they looked at each other, amazed at what had happened. Then she grew painfully shy and wouldn't look at him. He held her lightly in his arms, stroking her hair, her cheek, her arm. "Is it OK?" he asked. She nodded, still looking down, not knowing how to act or what to say.

"Do you believe me?"

She nodded again.

"I don't hear anything."

"Yes," she whispered, looking up into eyes as blue as the summer sky. "I believe you."

"Why are you so surprised?"

In a moment she said in a shaky voice. "Because . . . because I've loved you for so long. When I was little I loved you almost as much as Buck. I blessed you in my prayers, just like I did him. And then, and then . . . I loved you . . . " and she hesitated a moment, "more. And I was afraid and confused and embarrassed. You were my brother's best friend. I thought I was just a nuisance to you."

He grinned a lopsided little smile and shook his head. Then came her more difficult confession. "No one has ever loved me before. Maybe Buck and Grandma. But boys have always snubbed me. I've never had a boyfriend. I'm just not the type they like, especially not the type to win you."

"Why not me."

Her voice was so soft he had to listen very hard to hear it. "Because I always wanted so much for you to like me."

He didn't say anything. He couldn't. He was remembering the little girl who had clung to his back as he carried her across a stream. He remembered the warmth and the comfort of her little body against his, and he remembered how that comfort had turned to fire when he took her in his arms at the Senior Dance.

When he didn't speak, she looked up at him, "You've always been my 'knight in shining armour'. I dream about you sometimes, and once, right in the middle of the day, I saw you in a vision kind of thing. I saw you and me like we are now, only it was just me sitting on a rock. You were standing with one foot on the rock and bending over me. We were both dressed in white, and there wasn't any earthly thing around us. I was

24

afraid—afraid of going to earth, I think— and you were reassuring me. It was like we were getting ready to part and you were telling me it would be all right. I saw us like that when I was fifteen, just before you left on your mission. I've always wondered if it was just my wishful thinking."

Now he tightened his arms around her. She put her head on his shoulder and they sat for several minutes, looking down to the valley, savoring the closeness of each other. Stephen gave in to the rush of love within him and ran his hand over her back, her hair, allowing himself, for the first time, the delicious pleasure of caressing her.

"Life is funny, Shielah. We see everything all wrong. We are so paralyzed by our own fears and self-concept that we don't have any idea what the truth really is. The truth is you're so . . . so beautiful and at the same time, so delicate, that the guys are all afraid of you. Everybody's afraid you'll break if they say the wrong thing. Those guys all know how rotten they were as kids, and you haven't let them forget it. You could have had all the boyfriends you wanted if you'd only known it. But you were too wrapped up in yourself. Even I was afraid of you. Afraid to hurt you. Afraid of what was in your mind . . . afraid maybe you'd push me away."

She listened intently. Could it be true? She was amazed. "Is that how I seem, delicate and wrapped up in myself?"

"Umm hmm."

"If you only knew how tough I've had to be, you wouldn't think I was delicate. I've always felt unaccepted, mocked, made fun of by the other kids, as though they enjoyed my pain—they who have mothers and fathers, a real family life. It doesn't seem fair, and sometimes I'm terribly resentful. Life for me has been separated into two parts—before the fire and after. Only, the after hasn't seemed like living at all. Until today. Until now, with you. I came up here because I knew I had to come to grips with who I am and what I'm going to be. Sometimes I even resent Buck because he seems so unaffected by Mom's and Dad's death. He can still laugh and have fun and never seems to hurt. I feel like I've been living in a cocoon and somehow I have to break out. But I don't know how." Tears started to slip down her cheeks.

Stephen brushed them away for her. "It's all right. You can cry. I think I understand. But I think it's also OK to laugh and have fun. You won't betray your parents by allowing yourself to enjoy life."

Shielah's head jerked away from his shoulder. She stared at him, dumbfounded as the words sank in. "That's right. You're right! I've been hanging on to it, afraid to let myself be happy. Afraid because . . . because the pain is all I have left of them."

"But that's not true. You have your love for them."

She stared intently into his eyes, searching for understanding. Finally, understanding dawned, and with it, hope. Her face brightened. "That's right! Oh Stephen, I think that's right! Maybe I can just remember the good things. Maybe it's time for that now. Do you think they'll understand that I have to let myself forget, at least a little?"

"I'm sure they would want that. It's time. I think it's past time. You need to have fun, to laugh, to love." He pressed her to him fiercely. "To love me." And this time he wasn't afraid she would break.

Only later, on the way down the hillside, did he tell her about his letter.

Grace Thompson was nobody's fool, though her grandchildren obviously thought she was senile at eighty-one. Far from it. She had known for a long time that Shielah's best chance was that Gailbraith boy. "Maddie," she frequently told her daughter, "If that Gailbraith boy would only open his eyes, Shielah might make it yet." But it took him altogether too long, by her reckoning. He was preparing to go on his mission when Shielah was fifteen, and Grace had noticed a subtle change in her granddaughter whenever he was around. After he left, Shielah was even quieter than usual and seemed deflated for months. Now he had been back from his mission a whole year, and Grace watched with interest the frequency of his visits. It wasn't Buck he was visiting, she knew. Of course, that was who he always asked for, but he ended up sitting by Shielah or standing and talking to her long after she should have been doing homework. On Christmas day of her senior year, he brought a large basket of fruits, cheeses and sweet cakes "for a family gift" he said. But he gave it to Shielah.

Grace shook her head. And the girl didn't see what was happening. She would hardly look at him. Grace smiled. Of course when she did, her face beamed like a lamp turned on. She had seen the same thing happen to Ginny and Ed. They had moved a little faster though, and Ginny hadn't been a bit stingy with her feelings. Grace recalled how often Ginny had grabbed her by the arms and said, "Mama, if Ed doesn't ask me to marry him soon, I'll die, I just know it!" No, all her daughter's emotions were worn on the surface, which was just the way it should be with a young girl. None of this hiding your feelings in dark corners for fear people will laugh. Shielah had never learned to trust, at least anyone who wasn't family. Thank goodness for Maddie and Will's family. Will had that farm with ten horses, and Shielah went to ride and to help with chores at least once a week. She seemed to be a natural horsewoman. Must be my grandmother's child, Grace thought. Mother said that Grandma Charlotte was a true expert with the animals.

Grace owned the only portrait of Charlotte O'Neill Boughtman that existed. Her mother, Annie, entered college when she was sixty years old to learn to paint, so she could leave a portrait of her mother. She was afraid that the memory of Charlotte would be lost. She repeated the story often of her mother's life, her qualities of strength and resilience. She repeated often, and even stitched on a sampler, her mother's favorite saying, "We may not know until the last heartbeat of the universe what effect one single choice has upon our lives, but it is true that the sum of all our choices

26

determines our exaltation or damnation." She had said it was straight from the mouth of the prophet, Joseph Smith, with whom she danced one day in Nauvoo, Illinois.

Grace cherished those mementos and kept them. The sampler was wrapped and tucked into her cedar chest. The portrait done in oils she had hung over her bed just after Shielah and Buck came to live with her. Beside it was a picture of her own mother, Annie, then one of herself with Annie and Ginny and Maddie, and finally, one of Ginny with Shielah just before the fatal fire. Even then, if you looked carefully, you were struck by the resemblance between the ten- year-old, Shielah and her great, great grandmother. In the portrait, Charlotte was dressed in a blue gown as if for a fancy dress ball and gazed out with large, gray eyes, shaped so much like Shielah's it was startling. Charlotte also possessed a quality of strength and courage that Shielah had tried to imitate all her life. It seemed to breathe from the portrait, manifested most in the determined tilt of the head. I wonder if Grandmother Charlotte could have done more for Shielah's hurt than I have? Grace thought.

Grace was lying down, resting from all the excitement of the graduation when two cars pulled up in front of the house. She heard Shielah's voice, filled with laughter, as the door opened. Grace roused herself, smoothed her hair, and went to see who was making Shielah laugh. In the kitchen she found her granddaughter pouring a glass of juice for Stephen Gailbraith, and he had one hand on her arm. Grace looked at their faces and knew instantly their secret.

"So, it's cake time. I 'spected as much. Here, let me cut you some lemon cake."

"Thanks, Sister Thompson. I guess I can't refuse after a long hike up the mountain."

"Hmm, my granddaughter's a mountain goat, I do believe. Always climbing something, or riding Will's horses. She got you doing it too?"

"A bad influence, no doubt." Stephen spoke to Grace, but looked at Shielah all the while and grinned.

It was as plain as the nose on your face, as Grace so often said. Something had happened today. Shielah was sunburned, her dress dirty, and she was smiling and watching him. Ought to scold her about that pretty new dress. Here Buck goes and spends a fortune on that dress and she goes hill climbing in it.

But Grace didn't have the heart. She was too pleased to see Shielah happy.

"Buck'll be home in a few minutes. He said to tell you he's got a surprise for you. Another graduation present. Doesn't he beat all? He's a fool with his money for sure."

The fool came bursting in, not five minutes later.

"Hah, hah! Found you. Eating all the cake from your darling brother. And giving the last piece to him." He pointed an accusing finger at Stephen. "See if I trust my best friend behind my back again."

"Oh, quit this foolishness. There's more cake." Grace interjected impatiently.

"Guess you don't want your last graduation present."

"You know I do," Shielah answered, wondering what on earth he was grinning about.

"For a kiss, muffin, for a kiss. Just because you think you're all grown up, you can't get away without a kiss. One kiss, right on the old smacker-oo will get you one graduation present, which any girl in her right mind would cut off her arm to obtain. And you get it for just one measly kiss."

Buck stuck his face right down by hers expectantly. She was embarrassed and blushed, but she kissed him on the cheek and said, "That'll have to do."

He looked over at Stephen in amazement, then something dawned, and he looked back at Shielah. Grandma caught his eye and nodded slightly. He swallowed his protests and pulled an envelope out of his shirt pocket. Without a word, he handed it to his sister.

"I don't believe it! You can't afford these. What are you doing? This is crazy. It's a joke. Oh, Buck, how'd you get tickets to Hawaii?" She had jumped up and grabbed Buck by the arms.

"Simple. They are available in any travel agency." Now he looked like the cat who had licked the cream, satisfied and a little sneaky.

"A trip to Hawaii for graduation, I can't believe it. Everybody talks about it but I don't know anyone who really got one."

"You do now. Of course, I'm a little selfish. You get to go only on the condition that you take me, your angel brother . . . say it, 'my angel brother' . . . with you. I wouldn't turn your gorgeous body loose in Hawaii without constant supervision." Now he grabbed her and squeezed her until she begged for help. Stephen was watching, smiling, but saying not a word.

"I figured I might as well take my graduation trip early. You may not be around next spring when I get my degree, and it wouldn't be as much fun without you. Besides, I got a great deal on them from a very charming young saleslady. What d'ya think? You got time off next week?"

Shielah looked quickly at Stephen. He was smiling. She remembered his letter and the smile disappeared from her eyes. Buck saw it.

"Is it OK?" Anything wrong with that plan?"

"No, nothing's wrong. At least for us. Stephen's got something to show, too."

He handed the Armed Services letter to Buck. Buck read it and the smile left his face. "So they got you."

"Yep."

"So don't go."

"What do you mean, 'don't go?' When Uncle Sam calls, you go."

"Hell no, I don't! I got out of it. You can, too. I got a letter like that once and sent it down to Armand Marceaux in Mexico City. He's been keeping tabs on me. For three summers, I've been his assistant down at the dig and he wants me full time as soon as I graduate. He fixed it with the government. I never heard from them again."

"Well, I don't have Armand Marceaux in my pocket. Physical is Monday." Things had turned sober now. Shielah sat back, eyes only on Stephen. "Besides, someone has to fight the communists, I guess. I went when the church called me to Scotland. I'll go if my government calls me to Vietnam."

Buck snorted. "That's bright! And get your brains shot out! Hey, Steve— buddy! A war is not a mission. The two don't correlate. Serving the Lord doesn't compare with serving a bazooka."

Quietly Stephen asked, "How would you know? You haven't done either."

Buck stopped short. He took a breath for control. "R . . . r . . . right. I haven't. And I don't intend to. The Lord and me, we have a mutual agreement. He doesn't bother me, I don't bother Him. The last time I asked Him for anything I got turned down. They died anyway. So, great, go to Vietnam. Ought to be kicks." Grace clucked disapprovingly over her grandson's blasphemy and shook her head. No one could tell him a thing about religion.

"I'm sorry, Buck, I know it's a sore subject with you." Stephen could feel the anger in his friend. "Listen, if I thought there was any way out, any honorable way, I'd probably do it. But I'm no conscientious objector. It's not me. I'm a 'do-my-duty' guy. You know all that stuff, for God and country? Well, I buy it."

Buck stared at him, shaking his head. "I do, Buck," Stephen continued. "I believe in all that 'America is freedom' stuff. I've seen a little bit of the rest of the world and I believe it. America is the best as far as I'm concerned. And I also don't like communists taking over other people who can't help themselves. Maybe you think I'm nuts. But what if you knew those people? What if they were Mexicans? You love Mexico. What if it were Mexico and you knew all those people would literally be slaves?"

"What about it?" Buck was trying to ignore the question.

"Would you go and help them?"

Reluctantly, Buck admitted, "Yeah, I guess, maybe I would. I don't know. I like to fight, a fair fight, you know, with both guys in gloves. I don't believe in Napalm and grenades. And I don't really know whose war it is. I just don't think it's the little guy's."

"No," Stephen shook his head. "I don't either. I think it's mostly the big boys playing with people's lives. But I'm not going to fight for the big guys. If I have to go, I'll go for the little people."

And that's what he did. Shielah and Buck left for Hawaii the next week and Stephen left for boot camp in California.

29

Chapter 3

*I*t was an evening just like any other evening . . . almost. A girl stepped down from the last, high step of the Honolulu City bus and joined the surging wave of humanity that swept through Kalakawa Blvd. Quickly she struggled through and, reaching the little side street that led to the Imperial Islands Hotel, she soon ducked into the door and made her way toward the dining room. This grand old hotel was the princess of the islands, a landmark of Hawaii since the second World War. Large and bulky, surrounded by tiki lamps and gardenias, and furnished sumptuously with overstuffed chairs and plush wine-red carpets, the hotel catered to nostalgia and the rich tastes of its patrons.

Shielah stood out from the other tourists. Her blonde-gold hair insured that. Tucked behind one ear and secured with a plumeria flowers, her hair fell straight and shining, far down her back. It was, so she thought, her only asset. She had never realized how startling her eyes were. Even as a toddler, her eyes had been the most arresting feature of her face, like blue-cracked glass, they reflected light in little stars around the pupil. They betrayed, despite herself, naivety and inexperience, and unexpectedly . . . pain. They had the child-like quality of innocence and tragedy remembered.

Tonight she wore a long blue dress. Shiny and light, it fit her snugly about the bodice and fell in full, graceful folds to the floor. And she carried herself with the straight, proud carriage of her great, great-grandmother, Charlotte O'Neill Boughtman. She headed for the balcony, where she was to meet Buck and their new-found friend, Bridget. Bridget and her family had been friends of their parents before the fire, but years had separated the two families until Grandma Thompson wrote, asking Thelma and Don Crandall to meet their plane and show them around. In Bridget, Shielah found a lifelong friend, and Buck met one of the few girls not smitten with his charm. He was intrigued, and immediately set about to win the citadel.

She was a polite tour guide who steadily refused to be affected by his leading remarks. They were all to meet on the balcony at nine o'clock and go on to a late show at eleven.

She wove her way between the tables in the dining room and headed for the open doorway. The tiki lamps were already burning on the patio. Piped-in music sounded like birds calling through Paradise. She stepped out into the warm, sultry night air and paused, looking around for Buck's familiar wave. She didn't see him. Twilight had crept upon Waikiki slowly, the sky deepening into inky blue, and strips of pink and gold highlighting the bank of clouds far out on the horizon. Up and down the famous Waikiki beach, lights were winking and blinking like bright jewels rolled out on the sand.

Shielah gazed out across the bay, deep in reflection and caught up in the evening's magic. She'd forgotten Buck and Bridget for a moment. She stood quite still, just beneath the red glow of an overhead lamp, her chin lifted, staring out into the indigo night. In the shadows, a man stood, leaning on a rail, looking over. As he turned slowly to face the doorway, he saw her standing under the lamp, lost in dreams, and something like an electric shock hit him. He stood up very straight and stared. His face went pale, the skin around his mouth and eyes tightened. Everything seemed to stop, the noise, the breeze, the music. Everything disappeared and he remembered another night, some ten years before, when he had seen a girl in a deja vu experience, dressed in a blue gown, standing in a pool of golden light. She had been straight and proud, yet delicate and yearning for love—for him. She had reached out to him and he to her, only to have the vision disappear. He had called her his "golden girl" and had spent the next years looking for her, sure he would find her at any time, sure also that she was meant to be his.

Shielah was drawn to his gaze. She turned her head, looking to find the current that had disturbed her dreams. Then she saw him. He was so much in shadows, she could only see his face and shoulders. Actually, all she really saw were his eyes, holding her like a vise. What was it that ran through her like a memory? She had never seen him before, yet still, she knew him. Strange, unbidden emotions engulfed her, and left her weak and shaken. He held her gaze; she couldn't break away. It was his eyes, dark and direct, deep and full as the ocean—the eyes of a poet, or a saint.

Shielah was immediately, physically drawn to him. He was dressed in a simple aqua blue shirt, his shoulders solid beneath the silk. Slim and graceful, he exuded a sensual fashionability. Warm, tingling sensations flooded her body as their eyes met and locked. She was confused. What was happening? Who was he? Certainly he was a stranger, and she was embarrassed and surprised by her own innate response to him, she who was on guard even with old friends. She wanted to deny the feelings, to escape, but it almost seemed that a spell had been cast over both of them. The force was so intense she couldn't look away, and he would not. A smile came slowly to his lips, his eyes, as he luxuriated in a vision he thought he might never see again. The red light in the ceiling above bathed her face, her hair and turned it into a reddish-gold.

31

Finally mobility returned. Shielah disciplined herself to turn away from his gaze. In a moment he moved quickly and was by her side. He touched her arm, forcing her to turn back. She looked at him, inescapably held by his touch. He was Italian, dark haired, but fair-skinned, with straight nose and features, definitely older than she, and so handsome she was embarrassed to look into his eyes. He was not as tall as Stephen, only a few inches taller than she was, but there was a sense of quiet power about him, and his face was awash with transient emotions. She could see hope and fear, wonder and joy, all in the same moment. He stumbled over his speech.

"I . . . I . . . don't mean to be fresh. I know you don't . . . you don't know me. But, believe me, I know you. At least I saw you once before. I know that sounds crazy. Look . . . can I talk to you?"

A strange thrill of sudden happiness and recognition jumped through her like an electric current, as though somewhere, some other time he had been dear to her. To his surprise and hers, she replied, "Of course."

His voice was deep and urgent. "I know you must think I'm fresh or crazy or something. I . . . I'm not usually so forward, but I know I have seen you before, and just now when I saw you again, I could hardly believe my eyes. Please, can we go somewhere . . . somewhere quiet so I can introduce myself. I'm a very nice person, actually," he smiled slightly, "and not at all crazy."

The sensation of meeting a kindred spirit in a stranger was very disconcerting to Shielah. She had to collect her thoughts. She felt a little dizzy with the experience. Most disrupting of all was the way his hand burned her flesh and sparked the little streamlets of fire that were consuming her. She looked down to his hand on her arm and traveled up the tanned arm. Her eyes caught at his chest and shoulders and self-conscious embarrassment held them there. In all her life in Clarksville, Utah she had never responded like this to anyone. She felt totally inadequate to the moment. Moving slightly, she bumped into a table of four diners and didn't apologize. She knew she should turn away from him and dash back into the lobby, but she couldn't take her eyes away from his. And, surprisingly, she wasn't afraid or suspicious at all.

There was an urgency in his voice, "I've handled this all wrong. I can see I've scared you to death."

She shook her head "No." She spoke so softly that only he could hear her. "No, you haven't. I was just . . . a little surprised at first. Have we met before? It seems as though I remember something . . . but no, I guess not."

Still they stood half in shadows, half in the golden light, a quiet world all their own, separate from the crashing sea and dining room noises. His face was only inches away from hers, and, as she spoke to reassure him, the anxiousness turned to delight. Dark eyes searched her face and played over her hair, her figure and returned to meet her own.

"Please believe me, I am harmless, utterly. I'm not going to steal you away, I just want to talk for a few minutes." When she still stared at him wordlessly, he tried again to reassure her. "Look, I know . . . I know you'd never be a . . . a 'pick-up'. I'm not trying to. . . . What am I doing? This is all wrong. Let's go talk in the lobby, it's quieter there. I assure you, you'll be perfectly safe. I am very trustworthy. I've even been known to help old ladies across the street and rescue kittens from drowning."

There was tension between them, but it came from the uncommon chemistry. Shielah knew she should be reserved, should turn away from a stranger, too disturbing for comfort. But she couldn't turn away. Her whole spirit responded as though she had always known him and merely lost contact for a moment. In the warm Hawaiian night, she shivered with the electricity between them and couldn't have told him her name if he had asked her. But he didn't. He simply bowed from the waist, old-world-fashion, as naturally as if he always did. "I am Paulo Jiuseppi D'Agosta. And you are as beautiful as I remember."

Paulo Jiuseppi D'Agosta, the third son of an Italian mother and a Portuguese father, had a family background of visions. In fact, as a kid growing up on the West Side of New York this would have kept him out of the highly selective gangs except for the fact that his skill with his feet and fists won him no little admiration. When he was five years old his mother told him about a dream she had the month she conceived him. In that dream, she saw him in adult form, dressed in the robes of a priest, ministering to the sick. She told him she had known from the very beginning that he was a special spirit, in a family of highly successful people. As a child, all that meant to him was he got fewer cuffs than the others and collected some coins in the form of bribery when his brother or sisters wanted something from Mama. He could get anything.

Enrico D'Agosta had come to America from Lisbon, Portugal at seventeen years of age with his family, who had been famous for years for the cut of their suits and the fine finishing touches that marked every garment that left their shop. He met, on Ellis Island, a passionate, dark flame of a woman whose hips were made for bearing children. Carmella Gilletti was his senior by two years. She fell impulsively in love with Enrico of the beautiful eyes. They were married on the Island before they could be naturalized, and there she bore his first son. Eventually she gave him six children, the delight of his heart. Two of them died in infancy. Another son died in the Korean War and his body was never recovered. That left Roberto, two years older than Paulo, and Maria, an invalid sister, five years his junior. Carmella Maria D'Agosta was the constant, throbbing pulse of the family. When their tailor shop burned to the ground in 1943, Enrico found a sign advising the "dirty wops" to go home. He brandished it around the neighborhood, inflaming other immigrant Americans who had been spit on and otherwise harrassed. None of them had suffered any real damage, however, except the D'Agostas. Carmella found him, and in the bedroom of Emile Fiorentina's flat, she convinced him to put his vengeance aside.

33

"Our money was not there," she told him, "only our pride. The same men who burned us down last night will be coming to us for their suits a year from now." It actually took seven years for her prediction to come true.

After the war, the D'Agosta name became a byword for fine suits and coats. When Enrico was persuaded to retire by his family for the sake of his heart, his oldest son took over. Roberto Dante D'Agosta, a slender, steel knife of a man, turned the family business into a multi-million dollar concern by the shrewd, sometimes unscrupulous business practices he indulged in. He branched out into women's apparel, accessories and cosmetics, occasionally using bribery and false rumors in places where his money and charm failed to get him what he wanted. They had a board of directors which Roberto always deplored. But it continued to function under the strong influence of Carmella. She saw the hunger for power in her son and found ways to soften the pangs of his appetite. Maintaining her controlling interest in the business, she was the final decision on important matters. Roberto would argue with Mama. She stood firm. After all the arguments had been given on both sides, Roberto would continue to talk, but Mama would press her lips together, remaining silent until her son talked himself out. In the end, he did her will whether he liked it or not.

Paulo never manifested the least interest in the tailoring business except to benefit his wardrobe from it. In fact, as other serious interests defaulted, he decided to follow his mother's dream and become a priest. Before entering the ministry, he wanted one year at a regular college, and he chose the University of Denver. "Why Colorado?" his mother fretted. "Isa so far away." Exactly. He had never been west of Chicago, and he was ready to explore the world. That, however, was only incidental to the need he had to get away from his adored and adoring Mama. He didn't tell her that. He went, at last, amid pleas from Carmella not to forget to write. They both cried a little, and it was when he finally caught his first glimpse of the Colorado Mountains that he knew he really was glad he had come.

He found his first true love in Denver—photography. He never tired of photographing the leaves, the snow on the branches of the pines, the light cutting through the canyons of the mountains like shafts. By the end of his first year, he had a scholarship in art, a steady girl, and he wrote for permission to stay another year. Carmella flew out. She detested flying. She ignored the girl, and she couldn't understand why he wasn't ready to go into the priesthood. How could he communicate to her that he loved his church, his God, the whole religious experience, but didn't want to devote his whole life to it? He took his mother driving through the mountains with him, against her pouting protests. In that setting, he did his best to explain his love of this world. He pointed out the valleys, the crevices, the canyons. He invited her to see the sunlight as he did, splintered through the needles of the pine trees.

"Mama," he told her passionately, "the spiritual world has its joys, I'm sure, but I have given my heart to worshipping God through this." He gestured from the blue, cloud-washed sky to the valley stretching out around them. "This, His world, is my world, too, and I want to share the beauty of it with everyone. I want to capture the glory of it in pictures, make it come to life in the hearts and souls of people hungry for beauty and the peace of the mountains and streams." At last she understood, watching his face glow, and she never again tried to make her dream come true for him.

Paulo didn't doubt that she had had a dream. He had experienced some of his own. He often knew of important events before they happened. He knew of Jean's death before the telegram arrived. He saw his brother walk into a mine explosion one day while he, Paulo, was vaulting up the steps to their flat. The experience seemed to fling him against the door, leaving him so weak he slid to the floor. Mama had opened the door, exclaiming, "Paulo, Paulo, what isa wrong with you, Paulo?" He looked up at her, white around his eyes and mouth, and cried out, "Jean is dead. I saw him blown up." The next day the telegram came.

At Christmas of his first year at college, he was nineteen, and he was making plans to marry Karen. He thought he loved her, and she loved him with all the adoration he had witnessed between his father and mother. Life was good. He took her home one night, carrying an engagement ring in the pocket of his overcoat. He touched it several times, but somehow never pulled it out. He would wait for Christmas Eve. It had snowed that night and the sky still flecked his head from time to time, white on black, as he walked the six blocks from her apartment to his.. He wished for his camera to catch the sudden glints flashing from the quivering bushes. Then, for a few moments, everything around him disappeared. It seemed not to be night at all. He thought he saw a girl at the other end of a room. A slight breeze was blowing her hair—long and red, with a golden sheen glancing off the curls. Twined throughout the curls were flowers. She seemed to stand in a circle of golden light. Her dress was blue, long and full at the bottom, with tiny cap sleeves. She turned and looked at him. When their eyes met he saw recognition and love wash over her face. Tears began in her eyes and spilled onto her cheeks. She reached out as if to take his hand, and he actually took a step toward her. Then the blackness of the winter night swallowed her up, and he was alone again, his hand outstretched, snow collecting on his collar.

He saw her only once, but it was enough to wipe aside all thoughts of anyone else. He could never give the ring to Karen. He knew he would wait until he found her—his golden girl, as he came to call her. Indeed, he knew he must wait, for it seemed to him God had sent him that vision and promised him in a quiet whispering voice, "She is yours, and you will find her, but not soon."

It was ten years later in a Hawaiian Hotel that Paulo turned beside a railing on a balcony and saw her again.

The spell was broken by Buck. He and Bridget strolled into the lobby and he saw Shielah standing with some Latino. We'll break that up, he thought. He wanted his sister to have fun, but he had her earmarked for Stephen, and this stranger seemed very intent on her.

"Howsit? You ready for dinner, Shielah?" He didn't look at the dark-haired man.

She answered Buck, but still looked at Paulo. "Yes, I guess I am. You're late."

"Just a little sightseeing. Besides, I don't think either of us is too hungry. We had a late lunch. Sorry you had to wait." He turned his back on the man, not even acknowledging his presence, and started to head toward the dining room assuming that Shielah was with them.

But she didn't move. Paulo was still smiling at her, holding her with his eyes. Paulo was not offended by Buck. He refused to be snubbed.

"When can I see you, so we can talk?" He went on naturally as though they had never been interrupted.

"I don't know. I'm not sure I should." But her every nerve strained toward him. "This is too strange . . . when do you want? . . . whenever you say."

"Tonight, later."

"No. Not tonight. I . . . I can't."

"Tomorrow? Let me take you for brunch?"

She stared at him, still struggling with the uncommon magnetism between them. "I'm not sure. I really don't know you. . . . "

" Yes you do," he guessed correctly. "I'll meet you here in the lobby. We'll go to the International Marketplace." He seemed amused by her confusion. "You'll certainly be safe there."

Buck paused and called her, "Shielah?"

She glanced at him, then back to Paulo. She knew she shouldn't go out with a stranger. But, on the other hand, something told her he wasn't a stranger. "Time?" she whispered. "What time?"

Now his eyes were shining. "I can live until ten. Ten o'clock tomorrow morning, right here."

The rest of the evening was a blank. Shielah sat on the balcony with her brother and Bridget, trying to enjoy the Hawaiian buffet. She kept looking into the shadows by the railing where she had first seen him. She didn't know Paulo was sitting in the corner of the dining room with a friend, watching her all evening.

Bridget came from a patriarchal family. Don Crandall was a quiet man, tall and rangy, with dark brown hair turned salt and pepper gray. He had bushy eyebrows, almost white now, and his voice was deep and full of resonance. He was the stake patriarch for the Honolulu Stake and had always seemed to his children like an old-world prophet. Bridget adored her father and judged all men by him. Buck definitely did not measure up.

36

She didn't know why she had agreed to show him around the islands—most of the time she didn't like him. Still there was something intriguing about him. Past the flippant talk and the extreme self-confidence, there was something deep, even occasionally tender. It surfaced when he talked about his sister, or his true love, archeology.

He was pushy. "Why don't you come to a real college. The University of Utah is a great experience. Or, if that is too strong a medicine for you," he said, as she shook her head resolutely, "BYU would at least be a new experience for you. Will Papa let you out of his sight."

Her brown eyes flashed a warning at him. "Dad wants for me what I want. We are on the same wavelength and he puts no strings on me. If you think I am such a baby, why are you bothering with me. See, look around you, there are beautiful girls here. I'm sure they would all be more smitten with your curious charm than I am."

He grabbed her hand just as she stepped away from him. "Ooops, hit a nerve, I guess. Sorry. I take it back. Whatever I said. You got a great Dad, you're lucky. And I'm sorry. Maybe I'm jealous."

She looked at him, puzzled. "Of what?"

He glanced around nonchalantly, "Of you, of him." Then he looked at her again. "Of your relationship."

Bridget didn't know what to do with Buck. She never knew where the deep water was, and she suspected him of being far more perceptive and intelligent than his smart talk indicated. With him she seemed to say everything wrong.

Buck just liked to watch her. He deliberately said things that caught her off guard so he could see her true, unplanned responses. He had dated other girls just as pretty. But she was everything he wasn't, sure of her faith, straightforward, nothing hidden, and she was graceful as a deer. He loved to walk with her along the water's edge and watch her dodge the waves as they threatened her long muu muu. Her long, dark hair smelled of plumerias, and he knew from Shielah's remarks that she danced with the natives at the Polynesian Cultural Center. He shuddered with pleasure; would he love to see her in a grass skirt!

He got his wish. On Friday night, she arranged tickets for him, Shielah, and her parents for the evening show at the Center. They had dinner before at the Hawaiian buffet. He kept wondering if she would join them. But, no. As they ate he talked with Don about archeology, his experiences at the dig, and then later the history of the Hawaiian Islands. For such a straightlaced man, Don took great interest in all the fascinating heathen worships of the old islanders. It was curious to Buck that Mr. Crandall could so vehemently oppose the bikini bathing suits that women wore throughout the island, and yet be unconcerned to have his daughter dressed in a grass skirt. He shouldn't have wondered.

They sat in front row seats, and when Bridget came out for her first dance, she was just a few feet away from him, across a narrow strip of water. He shook his head. She was too pretty . . . and too modest. Of course, he shouldn't have expected anything different. He settled back and enjoyed watching the dances and watching Bridget move. She danced in the Tahitian group, and he had to force himself not to sit bolt upright, as she came out in a white, artificial grass skirt along with ten other girls, and the grass began shimmying in a fascinating undulation. Too much for a young man to take!

The Crandalls took Buck and Shielah back to the hotel, and he had a moment alone with Bridget while the others went to look at a huge aquarium in the hotel lobby.

"I liked it!"

"Did you?"

"Umm hmm. You're good, very good. Wouldn't have known you weren't a native."

She was flattered. "Well, thanks, that's a real compliment."

"Nope. I forgot to say how beautiful you are. *That's* a *real* compliment."

She blushed then and turned quickly in the direction of the lobby. "I wonder when they are coming back."

"Never." He took her arm and walked down the sidewalk to the cross street. "I guess I haven't made a very good impression on you. You act like I have leprosy."

"That's not true. I've tried to be very nice to you."

"Ooh, that hurts. 'Tried to be very nice to you.' Is it that hard?"

"No, I didn't mean that. You always twist my words. I . . . I think we've had fun together. At least I have."

They stopped and he tipped her chin up. "Have you?" he asked softly.

She held his gaze for a moment, then moved away. "Yes. I have. Now it's definitely time to be getting back. Mom and Dad are waiting by the car."

He didn't speak until they were approaching the car. "Want to go to Hanama Bay tomorrow?"

She answered too quickly, "No. I . . . I can't. I have dance lessons."

Just before she opened the door, she paused and said, "I'm not finished until three o'clock. That's too late for skin diving."

"No, it's not."

"Well, you rent the gear for all day. You'd only get half your money's worth."

His eyebrows went up. "You think so? I don't think so. I always get my money's worth. Meet me at 3:30 at the refreshment stand at the Bay?"

She did.

About four in the morning, all the music stilled, Honolulu quieted down as if in weary repose. Now Paulo looked on in inexpressible admiration as the morning paraded before him. His best friend, the sun, rolled out a carpet of gold and rose tapestry across the sky. The sky was transluscent white, and the sun was resplendent in gold and salmon spears of light fingering the clouds. The sun and its light was a continual amazement to Paulo. It could turn simple leaves and ponds into flaming objects of beauty. From simple old boards and sooty corners, it made a magic land of cobwebs and dust. When the light traveled on, one saw that, in reality, beauty was mostly potential. What was humble and unattractive today, might be glorious tomorrow when it was light infused.

So he wondered if he would find his "golden girl" still imbued with light, or was that his memory only, a fluke of last night's romantic spell. After so many years he had stopped looking for her. Indeed, in the last few years he hardly knew if he believed she existed or if he had made her up, and kept her alive in his determination. But last night he had seen her again. He had hardly slept that night. Suppose she didn't come. Suppose everything he said was wrong and she didn't believe him. It was a fantastic story, but he had to tell it. She must come. She must! When dawn had spent her beauty on the grateful hills and heavens, Paulo lay down to sleep for a few restless hours.

The International Marketplace was a confusion of little shops and a cacophony of voices. The little paths wove their crooked labyrinths so expertly one could almost get lost there, in an area half a block square. Beneath the great banyon tree that sentineled the entrance, farmers, businessmen, schoolteachers, policemen, accountants, movie stars, and thousands of servicemen entered and succumbed to the lure of grass skirts for sale, and luscious frozen chocolate bananas. It truly was the safest place to be in all of Honolulu. No one was free of curious eyes. Yet it was also private in the very self-centeredness of its vagrant inhabitants. Couples walked aimlessly, arms wrapped about each other, or shyly, hands just touching, or briskly, trying to see everything on the tour. From the seventeen-year-olds to the seventy-year-olds, they were all so involved in their own ecstasy that they were hardly aware of Shielah and Paulo.

Those two were, however, exquisitely aware of each other.

Morning did not diminish the power Paulo held over her with his eyes and his quiet, persuasive manner. Every thought seemed to vanish from her head when she walked beside him, and he did not prompt her to talk. They found a small, white, round table in the Colonial House. It was ridiculously incongruent with the rest of the native atmosphere. Shielah liked it. It was so prim and proper one expected to see women dressed in long, elegant lawn dresses with oversized picture hats. Instead there were muu muu's, lei's, and sunburns hastily acquired and peeling off. He ordered coffee, then ignored it while he told her about himself and his family. He told her about the many flashes of premonitions.

"My mother wanted me to be a priest. I almost was. I mean, I loved all the symbolism and the security of the faith, but something happened that threw it all out."

She waited. He seemed to be sorting out his words, and he spoke carefully choosing just the right ones. "Ten years ago, when I was nineteen, I was in Colorado, going to school. I was about to become engaged to a girl I knew there, when one night, walking home from her apartment, I experienced a very vivid premonition."

He paused, watching her closely, then continued. "I was walking in the snow. It was freezing, and there was snow all over my hair and coat, but I saw . . . or seemed to see . . . up here I guess," he tapped his forehead. "I saw a beautiful young girl in a blue dress standing in a golden light. She reached out her hand to me. And I reached out to her. I seemed to already know her, and to know that I loved her deeply, wonderfully, completely. I reached out, and in just that moment, she was gone. Just that fast. Too fast. I shook my head and wondered if I had gone to sleep on my feet. But no, there was no real doubt in my mind. It was another of my premonitions, and I had seen the woman that was to be mine someday."

Her breath caught and held. She didn't dare look at him. An awful pain in her heart made it difficult to talk. He spoke softly. "That girl I saw was you."

"Are you sure?" she asked when she could speak. "Really sure?"

"I've never been more sure of anything. A baby could have knocked me off my feet last night when I turned around and saw you standing under that lamp. It was the same golden light that surrounded the girl in my vision, the same blue dress, and the same, lovely face." He paused and looked thoughtfully at her hair. "The only thing different at all was your hair. Do you mind my asking if it has always been blonde? Has it ever been . . . red, or strawberry blonde?"

She blushed and looked around. "No. My mother had deep red, auburn hair. But I look more like my father, blonde . . . naturally."

"I've made made you very uncomfortable, haven't I?" he asked.

"Yes, and no," she admitted. "You seem so certain about your experience. And you seem too familiar to be a stranger, but I know I've never met you." They sat together for several minutes, not talking, just sipping their drinks, before she decided to tell him her own experience.

" Yes, the whole thing . . . I mean meeting you last night and feeling as though I already knew you . . . that all made me . . . nervous. I've never really had anything like that happen before. I'm not usually . . . good with strangers. I like people, but I just don't make friends too fast. But I believe you," she said to him. Paulo looked up expectantly. "At least I believe that you saw someone you believe to be me. I have heard of that happening before." It was an eternal naivete that made her believe in the honesty of others. She sometimes found out afterward that she had been a fool, and knew that they must have laughed at her. Many years later she would look upon her young self and wonder that so many people had dealt so gently with her innocence.

She paused. This was difficult for her. He was so obviously sincere, and something inside her didn't want to let go of the special, romantic spell that he seemed to cast over her. Then too, she wasn't used to talking so intimately, so soon, with anyone. But he had a right to know.

She struggled with the words, "In fact, something similar happened to me. I was only fifteen and afraid of my own shadow. My brother had a best friend . . . Stephen. He was . . . well, he is . . . just everything perfect, I guess. He never noticed me at all. I was too young, and not very pretty anyway. I tried not to think of him, you know. I didn't ever even dream of being in love. I was too busy just trying to make it through school, through life. But one day . . . right in the middle of the day . . . everything seemed to change around me. The porch swing on Grandma's porch faded out, and the steps and the chair I was sitting in—they all went

40

away and I could see myself sitting on a rock, and I could see Stephen standing beside me, leaning down to talk to me. I was frightened about something, and he seemed to be reassuring me. I looked up to his face and I could see love there. There was nothing else around, just him and me, and we were both dressed in white clothes, and I just knew that we were meant to be together."

There, it had been said. She didn't want to look at him, to see the anguish in his eyes. But she couldn't take her eyes away from his. Doggedly she went on, "That's all, except that I never told him about it until just a week ago, when he finally told me he loved me. I couldn't have said anything until then . . . until I was sure he felt the same way. Now he's gone . . . to Vietnam."

Paulo didn't hear the last words. He was a grown-up man. He was twenty- nine years old. He had lived in a fast world all his life and had mastered it. New York City was his backyard and the other cities of the world, playgrounds out of school. But she took him back to eight years old again, with a present in his hand for the prettiest girl in class and the agonizing hope that she would respond. But this time the answer was "No." The pain of disappointment was intolerable. He couldn't even look at her now. He got up carefully, pushed the chair in and said, "Wait for me, please. I'll be back."

Then he was gone, walking quickly through the crowd, anywhere just to get away from the words, from the pain, from the innocence of her eyes, and from the memory of last night. He was gone a long time it seemed to Shielah. Just when she was about to give up and leave, she saw him threading his way through the crowd. She watched him. His every movement was controlled and smooth, nothing brisk or off-handed. He paid careful attention to each detail or person that surrounded him. If he jostled a person's shopping bag, he would pause slightly to apologize. She had never met anyone like him.

When he reached the table he was smiling. "Sorry. Hope you weren't worried."

"I'm sorry too," she said. "I knew it would hurt you to tell you about Stephen, and I didn't want to tell you. But I had to. It was only fair."

He inclined his head, "Right."

"You are the only other one to know that except Stephen."

He nodded his understanding. "Shall we go walking?"

Reluctantly she said, "I think I'd better go back to the hotel, and let you go your way too."

She arose, sure the episode was over. But he put his arm around her shoulders to guide her through the crowds. Electricity flashed through her, and she looked again into his deep, brown eyes just inches from hers. "Not on your life," he said. "I don't go my way without you. I'm not a quitter. And I am a very sore loser. Does it matter which way we walk?"

"No," she answered, in spite of herself. Surrender was easy. His touch was enchantment enough.

"All passengers with reservations on Northwest Orient Flight 515 for San Francisco please board the plane."

All the way to the airport Paulo had argued with Jim Polanski, and finally gave up the argument, simply saying, "I'm not going. I'm due for a vacation and I'm taking it now."

Jim reminded him of the special project he had just completed. "You don't think Zimmerman is going to let you get away with it? He sent you on a pet project of his and he's going to want you there to spell it all out for him. He'll have your butt if you don't show up Thursday in New York for briefing."

"He won't have my butt. It'll be parked on the beach at Waikiki. Look, Jim, don't sweat it. It's all spelled out in the ten folders I gave you. He doesn't need me to tell him a thing. He's just too lazy to read. So, this time he can earn his salary."

When Paulo did a special project for Izzie Zimmerman, the Senior Vice President of Vista Color, Inc., he spoon-fed the results to him. He knew that was why he had aced out the Jews Zimmerman had working under him, to become the Vice President of Public Relations. He was really the Vice President of Trouble Shooters. When there was diplomacy involved, Paulo was sent. And he did what he was supposed to, flattered egos, soothed feelings, covered up flaws, and turned out pictures and layouts of superb sensitivity and class. That was the case on his last assignment. He had been sent to Eastern Europe to do a travel brochure on the border Iron Curtain countries—Romania, Bulgaria, Poland. Hoping to warm relations between the Soviets and the Americans, the State Department thought it would be nice to have a classy, tasteful travel brochure to show the Soviet Ambassador. So, Paulo and Jim had just spent two months traveling behind the Iron Curtain.

He put together the layout for the brochure, wrote the accompanying copy, and had it ready to lay on Zimmerman's desk. Normally he would have put it there himself, and then sat for several hours repeating to Izzie everything that was so clearly spelled out in the folder. Izzie would finally pick it up, glance through it, nod in appreciation a few times, and stick it into his briefcase to pull out and pore over later with the Secretary of State. This time, if Zimmerman wanted to know what Paulo had found and what he thought, he could do a little work himself.

"Tell Izzie I'll call him in a few days. Any questions, he can ask then."

Jim shook his head, and Paulo gently pointed him in the direction of the plane. "Look," Paulo said. "What's to worry? He can't fire me. I own too much of the business. You can tell him, the next time he sends us on an assignment, he'd better give us new equipment. Half our shots were missed because this lighting equipment is out of date. Kodak has us beat all the way with lighting technique."

Polanski said, "Shut up, Paulo, and say something that means something. You gonna bring this girl home?"

Paulo didn't answer, thinking about Mama's reaction.

Jim went on, "You better prepare Mama first. Write her. Want me to go over and break her into it gentle?" Jim Polanski was undoubtedly the best friend Paulo had. He had a knack for getting the most out of equipment, cameras, lights, developing, and he had a knack for getting the most out of Paulo. They worked projects where Paulo fumed over irritations and blocks, and Jim kept him shooting until they had the pictures they needed. Jim had come to work for Vista Color five years ago with a degree in photography, and after Paulo worked once with him he never asked for anyone else. Jim made it fun.

He made everything fun, which was why he had such success with girls. He didn't think he would ever be contented with being fenced in. Not that he was particularly good-looking. He had what you might call a crooked face—a nose a little crooked from those teen years of Polak remarks, mouth a little crooked mostly from his cockeyed sense of humor. He always had a half smile on his face. Carmella D'Agosta adored him almost as much as she did her Paulo. Jim let her bully him and baby him. He would bring his girls, the ones that lasted more than a month, to meet her. If his date wore a corsage, he brought one also to Carmella. It was to her a constant sadness and bewilderment that he never married any of those nice, pretty girls.

"No, not this time," Paulo answered Jim's offer to break the news to Carmella. "I'll write her if something develops. Who knows, she may never meet this girl anyway."

"I'd never lay odds on that. It'd break your record to come up with a miss. She looks like the roses and white cottage type. Get her into the sack once and she'll be all yours—if that's what you want."

"See ya, Jim. Take care of New York for me, OK?"

Bridget was more than a conscientious tour guide, she seemed to know every nook and cranny of the islands—best places and worst places to eat, best buys and worst buys for tourists, and most of all, when to let Shielah bow gracefully out of the tour excursions. Buck tried to be interested in all the places his sister went and how she spent her time, but he was clearly busy seeing that Bridget spent her time with him. That was fine with Shielah. She didn't want him looking over her shoulder, and there was someone else she would rather spend her time with than Buck and Bridget.

The day after Shielah's talk with Paulo, Bridget took them through the Ala Moana shopping center and up to the Pali, regaling them with old Hawaiian myths about the goddess Pele. It was a comfortable threesome. Along the beach road they stopped and bought fresh pineapple so sweet there was no acidic taste, and a coconut they split open to find white milky meat, tender and delicious. About dusk, they wandered through the crowds on Kalakaua Boulevard and stopped for a light dinner at the Jolly Roger.

"I think I'll go back to the hotel," Shielah said as they were finishing.

"What for? You're on vacation," Buck asked.

Sheilah looked at Bridget briefly, then at her brother with his arm draped casually along the back of Bridget's chair. "Exactly. And on vacation you get to do whatever you want. Tonight I just want to read my book, and take a long, long bath."

"What, no dancing with your loving brother?"

"Bridget will fill in for me, I'm sure."

She left them at the restaurant, finishing their drinks. She really did intend to spend the evening with a book. She took her long, luxurious bath, soaking until her skin was pink and soft, washed her hair and did her nails. She had just slipped into her nightgown about ten o'clock when a knock came at her door. Thinking it was Buck, she wound her hair a little more securely in the towel, threw on a dressing gown, and opened the door.

"You were going to bed," Paulo observed. "I'm sorry." But he was smiling at her, not at all like he was sorry, and she could see his amusement at her embarrassment.

"No, you're not. You're smiling! You look like the cat that stole the cream. I *was* going to bed."

"Is it too late for a walk along the beach?"

She hardly dared admit to herself that it was just what she wanted, what she had been hoping for all day. "I think it's probably never too late in Hawaii. Wait for me in the lobby. I'll be right down."

She took a few minutes to dry her hair, then quickly changed into shorts and blouse and ran, barefooted, down the hall to the elevator. She didn't see him when the doors first opened. He saw her though, and watched her for a moment, interested in her reactions. She glanced quickly around, searching for him, then disappointment registered. After a moment, he stepped out between the sliding glass doors that led to the darkened lanai and was delighted with the look of relief he saw on her face.

"I'm not so sure I didn't prefer you the other way." He made a circle around his head to indicate the towel turban.

"That was a fluke. I never let anyone see me like that, except family. I thought you were Buck. I should have known it was too early for him to be in."

"You must have left the party early." He touched her arm to start their walk toward the open lanai that led to the Waikiki beach.

"I thought they would want some time alone."

"Umm hmm, and did you too?"

"Yes. I guess I'm quite a private person."

"Am I intruding? Maybe I shouldn't have . . . interrupted you?"

He was trying to bring their relationship out into the open. But Shielah was cautious. Even to herself she wouldn't yet admit what she felt about him. Determinedly, she looked down at the sand beneath her toes. "No . . . no, I . . . I enjoy talking to you. You're an interesting person."

"Is that all?"

"Yes, that's all. That's all there can be!" Then, when he didn't reply, she confessed, "Well, . . . that's not . . . quite true. You . . . you . . . this is very hard for me. Sometimes I feel as though I've known you . . . have always known you . . . and I'm not the kind of person who usually allows that."

" 'Allows'?" He sounded surprised. "Do you 'allow' your relationships? You must have a lot of control over your feelings."

"I never thought of that. Maybe I do. Maybe I do, too much." The water was warm as it lapped their toes. There were a few couples still walking the beach as they were, and the tiki lights were burning in many of the hotel lanais they passed. They came to a concrete wall that broke the onrushing water at high tide. Paulo jumped it lightly, and held out his hands to help her. She gave both hands to him and stepped up on the little wall. Then she was over, jumping down in front of him, he still holding her hands. She was afraid to look at him, afraid of what would happen, and what was already happening inside her at being just a breath away from him.

He rested his hand on her head and let it slide down the length of her hair, then brushed the strands away from her cheek. "Sometimes relationships just happen and we don't have much control over them. Feelings aren't always predictable. More like bad boys out of school, they become rebellious and run away with us. Are you always going to be such a strict schoolteacher? You'll miss a lot in life if you are."

"Lately I haven't been strict enough," she said, wanting his arms around her, and shocked that she should want it. She never imagined she would want anyone but Stephen. In the shadows he couldn't see her face or he would have taken her in his arms then. But he had no idea what she was feeling, and he didn't want to push her too hard. So he simply held her hand and turned to walk on down the beach.

"Tell me about New York," Shielah invited.

"Some people say 'It's a nice place to visit, but I wouldn't want to live there.' But that's not how I feel. I live in the city, and I love it. New York is a microcosm of the world. You can see all colors, all heights, all races of people, usually in one square block radius. I'm a 'people' person. I love people. I love watching and knowing, and sometimes photographing them. So New York is a perfect place for me. Listen to me. I sound homesick, don't I?"

Now she smiled at him. He did sound like a boy away from home and missing it. "You're a good public relations man. New York ought to hire you. I feel that way about my mountains in Utah. The most excitement there comes on the Fourth of July when the school shoots off fireworks and Buck usually finds a way to get the police on his neck."

They laughed together. "But the mountains," she went on. "They are like my other soul. They are a part of me. I see them, at night, in my mind while I am trying to go to sleep, and they comfort me, like a mother's presence comforts her child."

"Tell me about your family," Paulo probed.

She paused a moment before answering. "There's not much to tell. I live with my grandmother and Buck." He sensed her pulling away from him now. There was a discomfort that hadn't been there a moment ago. Where had it come from?

"What are those lights out on the water?" she asked.

"I think it's a dinner ship that leaves from the wharf at sunset every evening." He let go of her hand as she pulled away, giving her all the space she wanted. "They have dinner and dancing on board. Looks like it's coming in now. Would you like to go out on it?"

"Oh, yes!" Pleasure and moonlight lit up her face.

He chuckled at her enthusiasm. "Done! Thy wish, O Princess, is my command. I'll see if I can get tickets for tomorrow night."

"Do you treat every girl like a . . . like a . . . 'princess'?"

"I try to. My mother schooled me in old world manners. It's her fault."

"I think I'd like your mother."

"I'm sure of it. And she would be ecstatic over you. She despairs of me. She thinks I'll never marry. I began to think so too."

Shielah turned away from him and started back toward the stretch of hotels. He caught her by the arm. "I don't want to push you, and I don't want to frighten you. I know I have already rather upset your carefully laid plans, but I have a feeling about us, and so do you. That's why you keep distance between us. You feel more than you show, don't you?"

Now her heart was beating wildly. The night was too warm and too dark, and the pull of his body too strong. "Shielah," he urged, "can't you admit what's there? You recognized me almost as uniquely as I recognized you. I saw it. Why are you so determined not to let it be?"

She was fighting to hang on to her practicality. Now he was holding both her shoulders, and she could smell the fresh cool scent of him even while the warmth of his hands muddled her thoughts. "I don't know that it *can* be. I don't think it can be any more than a few pleasant days with an interesting stranger. I wouldn't fit into your life any more than you would fit into mine. We come from different universes."

"No, we don't. We're both from the planet earth, and we're both two adaptable human beings. Anything can work, *anything*."

She could see he wanted her to believe that. And, almost, she did. But even as his persuasion beckoned her, reality pulled her away. She could not always walk hand in hand with him in the moonlight on some warm beach. There would be next week, returning to Clarksville, while he returned to his world, and it was best to leave it so.

But each day her resistance grew weaker. They spent the next day lying side by side on the beach, dozing intermittently, talking and eating chocolate covered bananas. Buck had gone skin diving early with Bridget, so Shielah hadn't mentioned to him her date with Paulo for that night, nor her midnight walk the night before. She was enjoying her time with Paulo too much to risk spoiling it with Buck's interference.

They boarded the old, restored trading ship-turned-restaurant about eight o'clock. She was not disappointed. They stood at the rail as it slowly made its tour of the bay. The sky sank into deep inky blue and the white clouds blushed a vivid peachy-rose. By nine o'clock lights were beginning to wink from the shore. Dinner was an elegant affair, native style, with Hawaiian waiters dressed in traditional costume. Paulo D'Agosta was as comfortable here as he was in a hamburger stand. Obviously, special treatment was second nature to him. He expected no less, but was, nevertheless, gracious to those providing service.

During the main course, Shielah observed, "You're used to expensive restaurants aren't you?"

He cocked his head. "Expensive? I guess so. I'm also used to very inexpensive restaurants. Try a polish dog stand on the street corner in the city."

"A polish dog? I've never had one."

"Umm. That's bad. Next to Italian food, polish dogs are the best. It's a polish hot dog, reminds you of sauarkraut. They put sauteed onions and pickle relish all over it. It's twice the size of a hot dog and a million times better."

"You seem so . . . so . . . at ease, anywhere you are."

"I am. Comes from going a lot of places."

"I'm jealous. This is the farthest I have been, and next to this, St. George, Utah, with the girls' basketball team. I'd love to travel, to see a world full of exciting places."

His gaze was direct and open in its invitation. "I'd love to show them to you."

She could not look into his eyes for more than a moment when he looked at her like that. They were hypnotizing. She looked away and changed the subject. She had told herself a hundred times in the last three days that she couldn't keep seeing him. Obviously it only complicated things. In her heart she knew the vacation would end and she would never see him again. Vacations were made for romance and this was her turn on the merry-go-round. Selfishly, she relished the mercurial emotions that touched her when she was with him. But it could not be any more than here, than now. She only wished he weren't so intent on persuading her that she was his "golden girl." She very much wanted to dismiss it all as his imagination.

"Did you get sunburned today?" he asked.

"No, not much. Looks like I'm a little pink."

"Does it hurt?"

"No, not at all. I had a pretty good base."

He pushed back his chair, and held out his hand. "Good. Let's dance then."

He led her to the tiny dance floor. There were two other couples there. Paulo drew her into his arms, brushed aside her hair to put his hand on her bare back above the top of her sundress. The next moment he was holding her close, his body warm and solid against hers. The faint scent of his skin, and the soft brushing of his breath on her cheek sent waves of honey coursing through her. They danced without speaking. Neither of them wanted to interrupt the privacy of their thoughts with talk. By the end of the first dance they were moving together as one, smoothly, in perfect co-ordination. Shielah eventually relaxed against him, closed her eyes and drifted through the dances, oblivious to anything else.

Once Paulo drew back slightly, looking into her face. Neither of them spoke. Then he tightened his arm around, drew her closer yet, and they were locked in gentle rhythm, swaying to the love songs of Kui Lee. At length he murmured against her cheek, "You're a wonderful dancer."

"I could say the same about you."

"But I said it first. You'll have to think of something else."

She smiled at his gentle teasing. "Are you really twenty-nine?"

His eyebrow lifted as he smiled back. "Is that ancient to you?"

"No, not ancient."

"But very, very old? Right?"

"Methuselah," she teased him back. "No, no, not even that. You're just . . . extremely sure of yourself. It must come with experience. I never feel as confident as you seem."

"Looks can be deceiving."

"Are you trying to tell me something?"

"I'm not so extremely sure of myself where you're concerned." The music stopped and he took her hand, threading their way between tables, until once more they stood beside the railing of the ship. The slight breeze of the trade winds was warm as it stirred her skirt and his hair. He resumed as though nothing had interrupted him. "In fact, I'm as scared as a twelve-year-old boy on a first date. Scared of doing or saying the wrong thing, and losing you when I have looked for you for ten years. I don't know where you are inside there," and he touched her temples, then brushed her cheek with the back of his hand. "Where are you, Shielah? What are you thinking? What are you feeling?"

She didn't answer. When uncomfortable she turned back to her old shelter- silence. She turned away from him, gripping the top rail, wanting the breeze to clear her thoughts. She summoned up Stephen's face in her memory. He was there, smiling, teasing, laughing as always. But Paulo persisted.

"Why won't you look at me? Why won't you just say what you feel?"

"I can't," she answered softly, looking across the water to the far away lights on the shore.

"Yes, you can. It doesn't hurt. You just put your thoughts into words and trust them to me. You can, you know. I promise I'm trustworthy. Look at me. Come on, Shielah, turn around. Look at me."

Turning her shoulders, he drew her around and held her there, just inches away from him. "Now, then. Stop avoiding my eyes. No, don't look down. You can look at me. I won't bite." Nervously, she had been looking everywhere but into his face. He was too close. She was on edge. It was simply too painful to look at him and tell him she was not his dream. She had already decided to love someone else and there was no room for him in her life.

"Here, right here, just look here into my eyes and say what you feel right this moment."

Involuntarily, her eyes obeyed, found his and were held there by the intensity of his will. She stumbled over the words. "I'm . . . I'm not . . . sure . . . what I'm feeling."

"Don't hedge with me. If there is nothing here for you, tell me so."

She couldn't lie while she looked at him. "There is something . . . I don't know what. I feel . . . safe . . . safe with you. You are like a memory that I can't quite remember, . . . like a friend . . . that I never had . . . like . . . like a special love that I never knew. I don't know who you are, but you're . . . you're very hard not to love." There, she had said it, and a smile of delight started in his eyes.

"It wasn't so hard was it?"

"It was . . . awful." And she didn't smile.

His smile widened for a moment, then disappeared completely. He bent slightly and softly covered her lips with his own. She couldn't think of anything then, not Stephen, nor their two separate worlds, not his religion or hers or all the very sensible reasons why she shouldn't get involved with him. It was impossible not to be involved with him. His kiss, his touch, his magnetism stirred sensations throughout her that she had never known. The waves rocked them gently, like two babes, and Paulo carefully slipped his arms around her, holding her securely within his love. This was what he had waited for, prayed for, and never dreamed would be as sweet as he had wished for.

Five days! It had only been five days since they arrived at the Honolulu Airport amidst flower leis and excited reintroductions to the Crandals. Bridget and Shielah made an instant connection, which was unusual for Shielah. She rarely trusted anyone. She was too easily hurt and so she protected herself. Don't trust, don't love, don't share. If they betray you, you'll die. But she protected herself right out of satisfying friendships, all except for Bridget who was a kindred soul. Shielah sensed that Bridget was not damaged as she had been. Bridget was frank, and seemed very strong, but also very compassionate. She knew exactly who she was and responded to the world openly, happily. Shielah admired her immediately.

Buck was late, and the two girls were sitting by the breakwater on the small concrete wall.

During her life Shielah only felt truly comfortable and at peace when she sent her spirit out searching to join the soul of the universe. It was as though she were a tiny white cloud, separated from the mass of looming whiteness, and seeking always to rejoin that mother cloud—a homing pigeon flying ever homeward and never reaching a resting place. It was that unanswerable yearning of hers that the mountains satisfied, and now the ocean as well. Shielah was a deep spring, unplumbed and hardly realizing herself what depths and what heights she was capable of. Her naivety and inexperience masked those depths. It took someone as perceptive as Paulo to see past the little girl that often peered through her eyes and to see the woman she would become. Even Buck had not glimpsed the woman within, and Stephen simply loved the little girl, with just a vague sense of her potential.

"Bridget, I've been seeing the most curious man." Shielah told Bridget about the meeting Monday night and about her lunch with Paulo on Tuesday. She described the vision Paulo had when he was nineteen.

"I may be a fool, but I believe him. At least, he surely saw someone, and he seems so certain it was me. But it doesn't make sense does it? How could that be? I almost wish it were true. It means so much to him and he was absolutely crushed when I told him about Stephen."

"What's he like?" Bridget asked, tracing her toes through the damp sand.

"Paulo? Well, he's very dark, not at all like Stephen. Very intense, and serious. He's Italian," she smiled a little, "and very romantic."

"Uh uh," Bridget shook her head in warning. "Not nice. Not nice at all for a girl who is supposed to be in love with another young man."

"I know. I know. That's the worst thing of all. I like him, Bridget." She was staring off across the ocean, seeing Paulo's face in her mind. "I really like him. It would be hard not to. He touches me somehow."

"Sounds dangerous. You're too vulnerable, Shielah. How long is he going to be here?"

"I don't know. All I know is that he is a photographer from New York. He is Italian and Catholic. His name is Paulo Jiuseppi D'Agosta, and he loves me. It's such an odd feeling when a perfect stranger comes up to you and says, 'I saw you in a vision and I love you.' I wouldn't believe anyone else who told me that, but I believe him. What is so strange is that I feel like I've known him forever. And yet . . . yet I love Stephen. Oh, I'm getting confused!"

Darkness crept around them like a warm, dark comforter. Both girls were lost in thought, picturing the strange men who had entered their lives. Shielah tried to remember that sunlit afternoon on the mountainside with Stephen, but it seemed so long ago. All she could see in her mind were dark eyes and a touch like fire. Bridget was right. It was dangerous. All at once, she hoped fervently Paulo D'Agosta would go away.

Buck was hoping the same thing. He spent three precious, Hawaiian hours asking questions and placing phone calls to find out about this Latin fellow that Shielah was seeing. He was a New Yorker, almost thirty, and much out of Shielah's league. He must be playing "rob the cradle." Buck didn't like him. Even if it weren't for Stephen, he wouldn't like him. He didn't trust him and he was amazed that Shielah would, she who never opened up to anyone.

He found the girls at the breakwater.

"I know, don't tell me. I'm late. I apologize. I was chasing girls on the beach and sprained my leg."

Bridget feigned disgust. "It's OK. We weren't waiting for anyone in particular so you fit right in."

"Ouch. You got me." He put his hand atop Shielah's head. "Is she leading you astray? Fess up. How many dates does she have lined up for you?"

"Thirty-five today, and twenty-three more tomorrow." Shielah smiled up at her brother. How could anyone resist him?

50

He wondered the same thing . . . but they did. Particularly Bridget. She had been steadily resisting, and now it was almost time to go home.

He sat down beside Bridget and conveniently put his hand on her knee. "Ladies, I must break the sad news that we leave this Hawaiian paradise in just two more days. I know . . . I know it will break some hearts, not to name names, you understand. But Hawaii won't be the same when we go . . . will it Bridget?"

She looked away. Out in the bay, a light from a boat was bobbing around. "No," she admitted. "It won't."

"Good! I'm glad to hear you admit it because I go on record as advising you to follow us as quickly as possible to enroll at BYU. The place needs some Tahitian dancers there."

This time she didn't laugh. Shielah turned in surprise. "Really? Are you really thinking about going to Utah? I can't believe it. That'd be wonderful, fantastic. Please think about it, Bridget. I've been dreading our flight home. But it wouldn't be half so bad if I knew you were coming later."

"I haven't said so. I just told Buck I'd think about it. And I have. I don't know. I'd miss my family too much, I'm afraid. I've never been to the mainland for more than a couple of weeks."

"You're a big girl. You can make it," Buck reminded her. "And you, little sister, over there, has it been all you hoped? This trip to Hawaii was supposed to be your big celebration. How's the party been?"

"Perfect," she answered.

"Perfect? I can't believe that. If Stephen were here, then it would be perfect." He was probing now.

"Well, then, almost perfect. I've had a good time, and," she touched Bridget's hand, "made some new friends."

"Ummm hmm. So I see. Bridget. And some others?"

Shielah knew where he was taking her. Subtlety had never been one of Buck's strong features. "Paulo is a very fine man, Buck. He has been a perfect gentleman."

"I'm sure. He'd better be. But I can't figure out why you spend so much time with him. He's ten years older than you are. He can't be interested in someone as young and naive as you."

Her head jerked around and she looked at him quickly. Her eyes turned hard and he knew he'd gone too far. "People are people, Mr. Sorensen, no matter how old they are. And some people are natural gentlemen, and some people aren't. Not to name names, you understand."

They didn't lock horns often. It was a good thing, for they both had a hard streak in them. Shielah's was well hidden in her quietness and softness. But it was there all the same, and Buck had no idea what she would do if she were ever truly angry.

"I didn't mean anything by it. I just think it's a little unusual for an older man to take such an intense and, at the same time, *platonic* interest in a young innocent girl."

51

Bridget interrupted. "Oh, come on, Buck. We're not dense. We get the message. You're a big brother worrying about his little sister's purity. I think you can stop worrying."

Under her breath, Shielah said, "I should be so worried about yours."

Bridget stood up, letting warm waves swirl about her calves. She didn't hear Shielah's remark, but Buck did. Brother and sister stared unflinchingly at each other for a moment. Then he caved. He put his arm around her and said, "Sorry. I'll stop meddling."

"Promise?" she demanded.

"Promise," he agreed, but his fingers were twisted behind his back in the Kings X of his childhood.

There was an enchantment about those four days since Paulo had met his "golden girl." When Jim had left, all ties to the normal life were broken, and all that remained was the heavy, perfumed, sultry days for which Hawaii was famous . . . and Shielah. He was a reasonable man. He told himself to go slowly, she was very young. He knew instinctively that her brother must consider him a lecherous older man. At that thought, he smiled wryly. An older man, at twenty-nine! Then he thought of his brother, Roberto, and how he would see Shielah. A child—pretty, but inexperienced and naive. That's exactly what Roberto would say. Again a flickering smile crossed Paulo's face. Roberto was determined that he would marry Elaina Maretti. It would be a smart liaison. Elaina was the daughter of Vincent Maretti, the king of furs in New York City. She had teethed on New York society, and had social and personal contacts all over the world. Elaina! Paulo had wished from time to time that he could love her. She certainly was not shy about letting him know how she felt. They had fun together, she could make him laugh, and she was a daredevil who frequently appalled the more conservative members in their circles. But she got away with it because she was Vincent's daughter, and because, if called to account for her outrageous behavior, she turned cool and competent immediately, assuming haughty command of the situation. In short, she was a shark. She had never turned her teeth on him, but Paulo knew very well that she could. So he never let the struggling romance get very far.

No, Roberto would not approve of Shielah. That concerned Paulo not the slightest. Whenever he even thought of her name, a sweet warmth enveloped him. He was not blind. He saw the naivety and inexperience that Roberto would criticize . . . and found it charming. There was a quality of vulnerability about her that haunted him. The professional in him wanted to capture that essence in pictures. He had tried, without success, to get her to permit him to photograph her. But she was steadfast. No, she said, she didn't photograph well. He would only be disappointed.

It was their last day together. She would be leaving tomorrow and Paulo yet had no plan as to how he would continue their relationship or how long it would take to win her. Certainly, when she went back home,

52

he would lose whatever ground he had gained. In small town Utah life, this incident in Hawaii would seem more and more like a dream. He was determined not to let that happen.

The elevator opened and she came out, smiling. The last four days had melted away all her attempts at being sensible and he knew she was completely comfortable with him now.

"Were you waiting long?" she asked.

"No. Besides I never mind waiting. I love to watch people. I always think that each one is a picture in himself."

In that week of sun, Shielah had tanned to a deep, honey gold, and her hair was bleached out into shiny strands of silver and gold. She wore her beach jacket belted at the waist, trimmed in pink to match her bathing suit. With her long, slender legs and silky hair she was a tempting model for a vacation poster.

"Well, what will it be, more sunbathing, or sightseeing. Is there anything we haven't seen yet?" he asked as they walked outside.

"I heard there is a waterfall back toward Laie. Then too, there is a temple not far from the Polynesian Cultural Center . . . if you're interested."

"What kind of a temple? A native temple? I've never heard of that!"

A smile lit up her eyes, "No, not a native temple. A Mormon temple!"

"What, no fertility rites! I don't know if I'm interested," he teased.

"Well, it's pretty. You're the photographer, I thought you like to photograph pretty things."

"I do. And the prettiest one of all won't let me point a camera in her direction."

She blushed, "I told you, I take terrible pictures."

"But I don't. All you have to do is stand there. I guarantee a beautiful picture."

"Oh, you don't know. All the pictures of me—my smile is too big or my eyes are crossed or something." She made a face at him and he snapped an imaginary camera at her.

He opened the car door. "So, which is it, the temple first or the waterfall?"

"I don't know. Let's just go and see."

A perfect expanse of blue sky hung over them. The wind came rushing through the windows and tangled her hair. They stopped at the blow hole so he could get pictures, and they stopped once more at a section of the beach Bridget had told her about, where banyan trees grew roots downward from their branches, making a weird, tangled forest. At last he got a picture. She had walked ahead of him slightly and turned to look for him between the twisted branches and verticle roots of the trees. Through the leaves and shadows, a shaft of light hit her face and hair, and Paulo cherished the picture for many years. A look of expectation and delight, anxious for him to come—that was what the camera caught. And her eyes were not crossed.

Afterwards, they drove straight to the temple. The wide boulevard that led from the beach road to the temple afforded an impressive view of the structure. Paulo had seen cathedrals in Europe more spectacular. But it reminded him of the exquisitely made Taj Mahal in its simplicity. They parked and obediently followed a guide around the grounds, listening to the narration about the purpose of the temple. He wanted to see the inside. No, he wasn't permitted. It was reserved only for members. Could Shielah go in? No, she had to be recommended by her local religious authorities. His eyebrows raised. Very peculiar.

"I'm sorry," she apologized. "I know it must seem strange to you."

"A little. Our cathedrals are open for the enjoyment of everyone, believers and unbelievers alike."

"I know. This isn't really a go-and-sit-and-enjoy place though. It is a place where we do baptism work for the dead, and where people are continually being instructed in eternal principles."

"Sounds like a busy place."

"It is . . . I guess. At least, that's what Grandma tells me. I've never been. When I get married I will get a 'temple recommend' from my bishop which will certify that I am worthy to go to the temple. You have to live by certain rules to be worthy to go there."

He was curious. "Really? What rules?"

"Mostly rules of purity. No alcohol, smoking, drugs, coffee—those things that are bad for your body. And of course, no immorality. You have to be morally pure as well."

He watched her profile. She was sitting on a bench beside him, looking out past the pools of water leading down to the temple entrance, out to the ocean beyond. Love and pride welled up inside him. Purity was so obvious in her that it radiated a kind of light he had never known. In fact he had never even considered the quality before; it simply wasn't a part of his environment. Only on the faces of children had he glimpsed it, and then, not all children possessed it. Many of the street urchins were worldly wise from the time they could toddle.

She turned to look straight into his eyes. "This is the place where I will be married. If not this temple, then another. That's the only way for me."

He knew what she was telling him. Her gaze did not waver, and she didn't drop her eyes as she so often did when their eyes met. He had no answer for her. He simply bent his head and touched her lips with his.

He felt her shudder. And he felt his heart jump up to his throat. His eyelids stung and his breath stopped. He had walked beside her, lain beside her on the sand, and watched her face for four days. But he was cautious. And he was smart. He knew he could scare her off so easily, like a wild bird, if he didn't move very slowly. But, oh, the longing had become unbearable. And the sweetness was just as unbearable.

He pulled away first. She sat completely still, staring straight into his eyes. He couldn't read her thoughts this time. There was no pulling back, yet there was no surrendering. She was studying him openly, trying to understand what there was between them. Then, suddenly she raised her hand to his cheek, and pressed her lips to his. Her hair was silky and soft when he touched it, and she leaned against his shoulder. Love came flooding over him, engulfing all his senses until he was almost sick with longing for her.

Again he pulled away. Then he tucked her blonde head against his shoulder and sat stroking her hair and cheek until he could compose himself again.

Later, in the car, he held her hand while he drove, and she was content to let him. Sometimes she looked away, out across the ocean, for several minutes, but mostly she watched his face. He could sense her puzzlement still, but also a relaxing of the defense that had kept him at arms distance.

They found the waterfall after several attempts and retreats up narrow roads. It fell straight down, about one hundred feet from between green, mossy rocks and overgrown banks above. Where it splashed to the ground there was a natural pool, big enough for a dozen people to swim in and enjoy. The water was warm and they stood with it spilling on their heads, laughing and holding hands. They stepped behind the sheet of falling water and he pulled her into his arms and held her for several minutes. She came willingly and lingered there with her face against his shoulder. Then the children who had been watching them like hawks began to dash in and out of the waterfall, giggling as they stole a look at the couple.

Paulo laughed. "They think we're lovers."

"I guess they do." She smiled back at him.

His eyes lost their smile, "Are we?"

She held his gaze for a moment then turned away. "I don't know." And she disappeared through the sheet of water and plunged into the pool on the other side.

In the late afternoon sun, lying on the beach in the scorching sun, she suddenly sat up, drew up her knees and hugged them, staring far out into the horizon. "I don't know what we are. I suppose because I don't know who I am. I have been alone all my life it seems. No one has gotten inside because no one wanted to. Even Stephen doesn't know me, though I have known him since he was eleven years old. Even Buck . . . and I love him more than anyone else in the world . . . even Buck doesn't know me. He seems so sure of himself, I have never been able to let him know how terribly unsure I was. And now here you are, making me more and more unsure of life, of what I had pieced together of myself."

Paulo was listening intently. It was the first time she had shared her real thoughts with him, though he had told her all about his family, his life, his hopes and dreams.

"If I am the girl you saw in your vision, then what of Stephen and the vision I saw. Where do I go from here? What do you want of me? What shall I be to you? I don't know your world, but I have a feeling that I will not fit in. I know only my mountains, the small town I grew up in, my horses on Uncle Will's ranch. The biggest city I have ever seen is Salt Lake City."

She looked at him to see his reaction. He made none. He had felt the same questions pestering him, but he would not entertain them. As he watched her he tried to picture again the woman he saw that cold winter's night in Denver. She was much the same, very much, yet different than

55

what he had thought she would be. He touched her hair as it blew softly in the wind. Blonde, shining and gold. Didn't he remember red hair only touched by gold? But, even more than that, Paulo had sensed an intense, powerful personality about the woman of his vision. Shielah's aura was much more vulnerable, much more fragile, with none of the strength he had expected.

Shielah was still lost in reminiscing. "On my graduation day, I sat on the mountainside and vowed to myself that I would not stay in my little cocoon. I never liked it there. I want to spread my wings. I want to prove myself to myself. Does that make sense? I have a sneaking suspicion that I am just as capable and bright as anyone but I feel like I have chains on. Shackles that bind me all up. I don't want that anymore. Before I left home, I sent in an application to be an airline stewardess. What do you think of that?"

Now she waited for his response. "You'll do very well at whatever you decide to do. There's no doubt about that. Is that what you want?"

"Yes. No . . . I don't know. I just know I need to get away from home. I have to make it on my own, without Buck and Grandma and Aunt Maddie looking over my shoulder. I'm scared, Paulo. I haven't told Buck yet. He'll try to talk me out of it. Maybe the airlines won't take me anyway. I haven't had any college yet." She became fierce in her determination. "But I know I can do it, just as well as anyone else. I'm a hard worker, I don't panic easily, and I'll give it all I've got. I told Grandma to forward any letters I got while I am gone."

He was watching her, learning. Here was the determination that he had only partially sensed, and the explanation of her reservedness. Where had it come from?

"Tell me about your family?"

"There isn't much to tell. There is just Buck and Grandma and me. I lost my mother and father in a fire when I was just ten. Then Buck took over. He was fifteen, and he and I went to live with Grandma Thompson, my mother's mother. Of course, there's Uncle Will and Aunt Maddie, mother's sister. They kept me for a year while Buck was bumming around in Mexico. Aunt Maddie's family is the closest thing I can remember to a normal family life. I almost get lost in that family. They have seven kids, and all of them busy all the time. Uncle Will has a farm, well a ranch. I . . . I don't know what it is. He grows things— corn, wheat, vegetables, fruit. But he also has ten horses and breeds his stallion and gives riding lessons. He has a golden palomino that is my favorite. She is a mare, the most gentle horse, and the most beautiful. Do you ride?"

He shook his head no, not wanting to interrupt her at all.

"The fire was the most important event of my life. Everything else is put into place before it or after it. Of course, I don't remember much before it. I was too young. But I do remember my mother. She was beautiful! I always wanted to be like her. Her hair was deep reddish brown, and she made everything fun. She always made us laugh. I'm more like my father, in looks and personality. Dad was more quiet, as I remember. He was a Sorensen, a Swede. I got my blonde hair from him. I don't know where

Buck came from. He isn't like either of them. Everybody has always called Buck wild. He wouldn't go to church, even as a little boy. He'd sneak out the window, until it was over, then meet Mom inside the door and pretend he'd been there all along. When he got to be thirteen he refused to go at all. He thought people there were hypocrites. He said, at least he knew the other *boys* were. You see, the boys in our church are given the priesthood when they are twelve, and certain small duties to carry out, like passing the sacrament, preparing it, blessing it. Buck knew all their pranks, all their mischief . . . he usually led it . . . and he said they were sanctimonious hypocrites. Sometimes I've felt that way too, but I still have my faith in the church. I believe it is true, but Buck has lost all his faith. I can't imagine what I'd be without my belief in my church. It has given me what little bit of self-confidence I have. Paulo, do you believe you are a true child of God?"

She had jumped around rapidly, and his mind was filled with a thousand questions. Now she was talking theology. "I haven't considered it," he answered.

She was amazed. "Really? That seems so elementary to me."

"I was taught that God is the supreme creator. To consider myself his 'child' seems a bit presumptuous."

"Then you don't believe He is your Father?"

"No, He's my creator, my God. Fathers are fallible. My father was a terrific man. I adored him and still do, though he died before I went to college. But he was certainly very fallible. We all used to laugh about his mistakes and tease him about them. No. God is supreme, infallible, all knowing, unknowable. He is as much beyond us as the next galaxy is."

She looked at him quietly for a minute, then said simply, "I believe He is my Father."

He made no reply and after a few minutes she went on, "Life seems so big to me, like this ocean stretching far away beyond sight. For a long time after the fire, life seemed unbearable and too long. I wanted so much to lie down and sleep forever, and not have to face life without my mother. It was too much time to have to be alone. Sometimes I still feel that way. But love helps fill up that time and make it not so empty."

A smile touched her mouth and he guessed she was thinking about the young man, Stephen. He put his hand on her shoulder to call her back.

"Shielah, love is all around you. There are a million sources, not just one or two. That is the real secret of being happy, understanding and seeking those sources of love."

Her face was a mercurial wash of emotions. "I think I'm beginning to believe that . . . at least I want to. Stephen showed me a little of that and you have made me believe it even more. And everywhere I look there is beauty and so many people in love. For a very long time I never believed that anyone would ever love me."

He sat up and took her face between his two hands, demanding that she meet his gaze. "I can't believe that. You are the most lovable person I have ever met. You're like a . . . like a tropical bird, beautiful, bright, singing a haunting song all your own. Love is all around you," he repeated. "Just look, just look."

He wouldn't let her turn away. He held her securely. His voice lowered to a whisper, "Just look . . . at me."

There was no doubt possible in Shielah's mind. It was clear as the Hawaiian sky. He loved her. It flowed from him into her with the touch of his hands, the penetrating look in his eyes. It was warm and reassuring. It made a place for her to rest from her struggles, and she crept inside his love and lay down. She put her hand over his, and brought it to her lips. Then she rested her cheek in the palm of his hand.

"You are good for me, Paulo. I feel so at peace with you. You seem so much at peace with yourself. I envy that."

"It'll come. Life hasn't treated you so very well, but I have a feeling it will all change. That is, if you will let it. You can be happy if you want to. Or you can go on being unhappy if you want to. It is only your decision."

Twilight crept up on them unawares. They had walked the beach together, her arm around his waist, his arm around her shoulders. They had rented boards and ridden the waves, laughing and splashing around in the foam. They had watched a native boy climb a coconut tree, and bought fresh pineapple at a roadside stand. They had dinner at a charming, little restaurant where they ate deep- fried bananas at a tiny table under the trees. And he had bought her a flower lei and a grass skirt as souvenirs. Time was passing in slow motion for them, and Shielah felt almost intoxicated by newly found freedom. Freedom to be herself. Freedom from fear and loneliness.

She forgot all about the time. The moon escaped the clouds and tangled in the treetops as they were finishing dinner. Night stretched interminably before them. The sky was a mottled, moving quilt of clouds and moonlight. Paulo persuaded her to let him get a picture of her. He walked around her in every direction clicking to his heart's content, and she paid him no mind. She faced the sea and seemed lost in a dreamworld of her own. When he finished, he stepped behind her and clasped his hands in front of her. She leaned her head back on his shoulder, and they stood for a long time just watching the ocean roll in, swaying in the mounting wind. All Shielah's reservation was gone. He had broken the shell that surrounded her, and she was open and trusting as never before.

As they headed back to Honolulu, he pulled the car over at the "enchanted forest," which is what they called the tangle of banyon trees with its twisted roots growing downward. Earlier, they had found a pathway through the trees leading to a secluded beach, a picturesque spot. Paulo couldn't bear the thought of taking her back to the hotel just yet. He carried a blanket and they made their way to the small beach. A squall had been building out over the ocean was sending the clouds scurrying across the moon. Now you see it, now you don't. There were nightbirds calling back and forth, and the wind was mounting, whistling, and crashing through the trees. The deep-throated roar of the ocean was constant and tempestuous as the sea flung itself repeatedly on the shore. It was a wild, strange night, a night of unreality after a surrealistic day in Paradise. The beach was somewhat protected by the banyon trees. They lay on the blanket together, and he began brushing her hair, stroking it free of the tangles of the day.

When he put the brush down, Paulo said, "I can't leave you yet. I don't want you to go. I don't know how I can go back to New York and simply forget this. I can't. I'll never forget this day as long as I live."

She lay back in the warmth of his arms, allowing herself the great relief of enjoying his touch. The uncommon chemistry between them since she first met his dark eyes had tormented her natural reserve. But the days together, and his very apparent love for her had melted away the barriers she used to keep from being hurt. With Paulo, her instincts told her there would be no hurt. When he looked at her she saw a more beautiful Shielah in his eyes. It was delicious water to her soul.

"Neither will I. It has been too sweet." Her arms went around his neck. "Kiss me, Paulo. Please . . . kiss me." The wind wrapped her hair around them. His hands on her arms, shoulders, back stirred feelings deep within, feelings sweet and turbulent like the storm around them. A new desire rose up in Shielah, a fierce desire to open her soul to the world, to fly free, to lose herself in the wild, tumultuous night.

Paulo sensed the barriers were down. He wanted to lock her in his arms, so she would never leave him, but she would not be captive. In a moment, she pulled away, swaying and humming, obeying an unfamiliar primitive instinct. She moved like flowing liquid, and her face was transformed as though dreaming. She had long been a captive of her loneliness and pain. Tonight she was free and the most elemental force, the thunder of the tempest, picked her up and joined her soul to nature.

She touched his lips with her fingertips, silencing any words he might have intruded into this moment. "Paulo, can you hear the music? The wind, the sea, the music of the night. I hear it! Oh, it's beautiful! It's so unbearably beautiful. It's the song of my heart and I've never heard it before. I can't stand it. I feel like I'm going to burst!"

He couldn't reach into her world at all. She left him behind and now obeyed only the song of her soul. She opened her beach bag. Inside it was the grass skirt he had bought as a souvenir. Its strands were artificial, but pure white. She shook it out and flung off her beach jacket. She clasped the skirt about her waist and turned to face him, radiant in childlike joy. For just a second she stood still, then something seemed to erupt within her and she began to move. Swaying and turning, leaping and reaching, her arms enveloped the joy of a world she had rejected for so long. Often he could not see her face for the golden film of hair that flew about in the breeze. It was her moment of emerging. The cocoon was cast away. She danced until she was breathless, dancing in and out of the waves that lapped the shore. Coming close enough to touch his face, then leaping away and whirling to her own private music that filled her mind.

59

Shielah hummed lightly, a song only she could sing—her soul's music. She became lost in her world, one with the sound of the sea crashing violently on the sand. The wind whirling through the trees seemed to play separate, distinct melodies, soft, then faster and wilder. The tone changed moment by moment as though a thousand voices called eerily to her. All reality disappeared and she moved in space, lost in time, suspended in eternity. There was no yesterday, no tomorrow. She had left this world for a more ethereal place, an island alone, beyond time. Paulo watched her face, dreamlike, entranced. He never heard the music she hummed to herself, but he saw her move, glide, whirl and sway with it. She danced around him while he lay back on the blanket. The artist in him cried for a camera, but the moment was too precious to share, even in pictures. She had taken on a timeless quality, and Paulo felt as though the modern world with its inhibitions existed in a different plane and sphere. This moment, out of time, out of place, she came to him open, trusting, innocent, passionate with desire for life and love long denied.

Slender, smooth legs flashed in and out of the silvery skirt. Her body swayed, arched, arms up to the night sky. She shook her head and her hair fell in shimmering waves about her shoulders, then far down her back as she offered herself to the stars. Moonlight seared her face and hair. She was inutterably beautiful to Paulo.

To Buck, she was completely mad.

When Shielah failed to meet Buck and Bridget in the Ilikai for dinner, they ate hastily and went back to the hotel to look for her. She had not been there. They went to the Imperial Islands and Buck asked for the extension for Mr. Paul D'Agosta's room. The phone rang and rang. It was perfectly plain to both Buck and Bridget that he must be with Shielah. Buck checked his watch. It was midnight.

"Don't worry about her. She'll be all right."

"It's midnight. It's too late for her to be out with that guy. He's a smoothie. He knows just what he is doing, believe me. I don't trust him a minute. Gees, I wish I had some idea where they might be."

"She said something to me about going down to Laie today and showing him the temple. Maybe they stayed for the show at the center."

"I doubt it. She saw that with me when you were dancing." A definite fear had gripped Buck. He should never have let her get involved with an older man.

"Come on, I can't stand around here."

"Where are we going?"

"I don't know. To Laie I guess."

The beach highway was picturesque in the tropical night but they drove without speaking. Bridget had not seen Buck unnerved by anything. Buck was struggling with a sick feeling in the pit of his stomach, a fear he wouldn't put words to. They almost drove past the enchanted forest , when Bridget said, "That's the place I pointed out to her one day. It used to be my fairytale forest when I was a little girl."

"Why do you say that?" Buck's interest was caught. He slowed down.

"I don't know. I just thought it was kind of neat and I pointed it out to her as we drove past. She seemed intrigued."

There was one car parked in the small auto clearing. Buck pulled in beside it. He had no idea if it was Paulo's car, but instinct was guiding him now.

"Stay here."

"I don't want to stay here alone."

"Do it anyway. If it's not them I'll be right back. If it is them . . . I'll be right back. Where does that trail lead?"

"To the beach. Be careful."

"I will."

Buck made his way through the leaves and trees. It wasn't difficult, really. The moon was bright when it broke through the clouds, and the trail was well used. A storm blowing in beat at Buck, whipping branches and leaves around him. At the last turn of the path he stared straight out onto the protected little beach and saw his sister in her private moment of freedom. She was dancing in the moonlight to some kind of music of her own. He watched her for a moment, incredulous. That she had any such passion in her soul was a revelation to him. Shielah, of the quiet reserve. Shielah, with whom he had sat in the dead of night, holding her in the aftermath of a nightmare. So prim, so properly Mormon, so reserved that no one would date her. He couldn't believe his eyes. What had he given her, wine, Kalua? That stinking. . . .

She was leaning over Paulo, enveloping him in her hair, and he was reaching up to pull her down into his arms. Out of the shadow Buck plunged, jerked Shielah backward, and in the same movement jerked Paulo up. She screamed in terror, her dream world shattered, and by whom she yet had no idea. Paulo guessed at once who it was. Buck's fist shot out and glanced off his cheek. Then in rapid succession Paulo took a foot in the chest and another blow off his eyebrow.

He could have responded faster, at least to protect himself, but Shielah's screams unnerved him. Still, it took only a moment for Paulo to get his street stance, and then Buck couldn't reach him. Paulo had learned from the best fight arena in the world, the streets of New York, and it was something he had never forgotten. He crouched like a cat about to strike, his foot and his arm coming up simultaneously. "Get away!" he warned Buck between clenched teeth.

"Go to hell." Buck spit out.

By then Shielah realized who the attacker was and flew into a rage. She screamed at him to leave them alone.

"Who do you think you are? Don't you touch him again! Buck, don't touch him!"

Buck was still intent on Paulo.

"He's a dirty wop. He only wants one thing from you. I know his game." He challenged Paulo, "Did you get it yet or are you still working on it?"

Paulo hit him before Buck could see it coming. He took it in the solar plexis and it knocked him to his knees. Shielah was crying by then, and shrieked at Paulo, "Don't. Leave him alone!"

Paulo stood back, and Buck struggled to his feet, and croaked out, "You're going back with me, Shielah. Now!"

"I'm not."

"You sure as hell are." He grabbed her arm, twisting it, and shoved her toward the path. "Now! Move!"

"Leave her alone," Paulo warned.

"So you can have her? Wrong! You don't come near her again. You hear me good? And you don't call, and you don't send your precious flowers. This is it, buddy! Vacation's over. Go make your conquests somewhere else. She's not yours, do you hear. She's not yours! Shielah, have you lost your mind. Are you drunk? Doesn't Stephen mean anything to you?"

No, she didn't remember Stephen. He was in another world on the other side of the universe. She looked from one man to the other. Tears were streaming down her face. The rage left her and she shook her head. "We weren't doing anything wrong."

Buck pushed her before him. Paulo followed after. They reached the clearing. Paulo spoke to her, "You don't have to go with him."

Her face was blank. "I do."

Buck opened the door. Paulo said, "I want to see you before you go tomorrow."

She started to speak, but Buck interrupted, "Forget it. It's over. It never was. Get of out the way. I'm responsible for her and I'm taking her home."

No one spoke all the way to Bridget's house. Buck walked her up to the door.

"Will I see you at the airport?" he asked.

"If you want to."

"I do."

"Don't be too hard on her. She's just too . . . too . . . trusting."

"Yeah. I know. I'll be nice." Buck put an arm around her shoulders and pulled her to him. It wasn't the way he had wanted it. "I'll miss you," he said and kissed her.

"I'll be there in the morning. United?"

"Right, that's it. Departure 8:30 a.m." He started to walk away. Then turning back, he came and kissed her again, more softly this time, and held her for a moment. "I wanted it to be different than this. This last night was supposed to be special, romantic, the way girls like it."

She smiled wryly at him, "You've experience in that?"

"Not enough. I wanted to have some experience in it with you." Now he held her for another long moment. "Now I'm gonna say something I've never said to any other girl, so listen carefully. I love you."

She pulled back so she could look at his face in the moonlight. It was set, and his mouth was a hard line, but when she looked into his eyes she saw it was true and how hard it was for him to say it.

Bridget touched his mouth with her fingertips and his lips relaxed. "A man of many words," she said smiling quietly.

"Not so many. Just three. *I love you*. That's enough."

"Yes, it is," she agreed, and kissed him long and sweetly. "I'll remember those three."

"Good, now we can get on with the other stuff, like when you are coming to Utah."

"I'll have to talk to my parents about it. They might not like it."

"Make 'em like it."

She shook her head and laughed. He was so sure of everything, so determined to have his own way. He probably would too.

"We'll talk about it at the airport."

He opened the door to the car and paused for one last look at her, then waved and he was gone.

Shielah stayed in the back, her head resting against the back of the seat. Buck drove silently, still overwhelmingly angry at Paulo, and dismayed by what he had seen of Shielah. He didn't know who to blame, himself or her. He should have been more assertive with her and made her lose that guy in the first place. She'd better grow up fast. This guy from New York won't be the only shark looking for bait. Fragile things get broken.

All the way up the elevator they didn't speak. Walking down the hallway, they were still silent. He opened the door to her room and followed her in.

He closed the door and started to speak.

"Don't start in now, Buck. We'll both say the wrong thing."

Buck ignored her warning. "What's he got over you, Shielah? It's weird, you know. He's too old for you. Not nearly as sharp as the guy you've got in the bag, and, boy, you almost blew it."

"What do you know?" she asked quietly. She was tired and didn't want to talk about it then.

"Plenty. A lot more than you do. You've never been outside your little world. You have no idea what's on the mind of a guy like that."

"And you do?"

"Yeah, I think I do!"

"Is it the same thing that's on your mind? Is going to bed with Bridget all you think of? Is that how you know?"

63

He almost slapped her then. They stood glaring at each other, neither giving an inch. Buck walked over to the window, trying to regain his composure. Patience was not a virtue of Buck's.

"Does it make you feel dirty? That's how you make me feel," she said icily. "You had no right to humiliate me in front of him and Bridget. You're not God, you know."

"I don't mean to make you feel dirty." He was staring at the boulevard far below him. "It's just that I'm responsible for you, and he's a guy who has obviously been around."

"Well, don't be responsible for me. I'm not ten years old anymore, and even when I was, you felt so responsible for me you cut out and left me to handle it alone. Responsibility is when you love all the time. Not just when it's easy!"

He was incredulous. "You think it's easy for a sixteen-year-old boy to go to school and go to work to take care of a kid sister?"

"Did I ask you to? Did anyone ask you to? I was living with Aunt Maddie. She's the one who held my hand, and rocked me to sleep that year after Mama and Daddy died. You didn't care what was happening to me. Don't come off so righteous. You only cared about one thing—yourself! Don't you know I needed you then! I lost everybody, *everybody*. Mama and Daddy couldn't help it, they died in the fire. But you could help it and you left. You just plain left of your own free will and choice. Now, don't you try to make me feel guilty. And don't try to keep me in that prison I've lived in. I am a grown- up woman now. I can do whatever I choose. And I don't choose you!"

She was alive now, moved by overwhelming anger, anger that had been boiling for years. Thoughts she had never dared express before came tumbling out. She had experienced with Paulo the first peace and freedom of her life and she would not go back to the old world.

"Fine. Choose the wop."

She screamed at him, "Don't call him that!"

"I have some other names if you'd like to hear them." Rage filled him now also, rage at her ingratitude, throwing up his mistakes and not allowing for his own pain.

"You're sick, Buck. You're filthy. Paulo is twice the man you are, and you're too blind to see anything but sick prejudice."

"You're too blind to see anything but daydreams. You want the world—the big, wide, wonderful world. Good, go for it! It'll pull your pretty wings off, little butterfly. You don't want to be fragile, do you. You want to be tough! It's easy. Go spend a year on the streets. One year. You'll be tough. The world isn't daydreams, Shielah. Everybody's shielded you from it long enough. Don't hurt Shielah anymore. Be nice to Shielah, she's been hurt enough. Don't shout at Shielah, she'll break. Let's see if she will?" By now he was shouting in her face, "Will the china doll break?"

They were standing face to face now, he taller and more intimidating because of the vicious streak that could cut even a loved one to ribbons. But rage had turned Shielah's fear into ice, and she was beyond his power to hurt her. She had admitted few people into the special places of her heart. Self-protection was almost the strongest instinct in her. Once her trust was outraged, fear, anger, even hurt ceased to function and only the need to protect her vulnerability existed. Buck had violated the sensitive line of their love. Now no amount of intimidation or ridicule would break the steel of her resolve.

She stepped back, away from him, her face ashen, set in granite. Tears were a revelation of weakness and her eyes were clear and dry now, though streaks crisscrossed her cheeks. When she spoke it was with deathly coldness. "No, she won't break. Don't worry, Buck, you'll never need to be careful of me again. My hurt does not concern you anymore. You have 'given up' nine precious years trying to make up for the fire. Who knows, maybe Mama cursed you that last day when she made you promise to take care of me. But you are free of that now. I give you your freedom! And I take my own! So far you've been in charge of my life. Well, no more. Now it's my turn! And you are free of me for good." She opened the door and slipped away before he could grasp the full meaning of her words.

Buck stood alone in the room for a few minutes, his shoulders heaving, his breath ragged. Then he opened the door, looked up and down the hallway and, much more subdued, went down to the lobby. She was nowhere to be seen. He checked around the coffee shop in the hotel. No luck. Similarly, she was not out beside the pool. He finally had to give up. Obviously she had left the hotel. It was 3 a.m. She shouldn't be out alone. Only drunks were on the streets now. "You're free of me for good." He heard those words over and over and grew increasingly afraid that she meant exactly what she said. Buck's anger cooled as quickly as it flared. He had not dealt with his sister's anger since they were children together. She always protested his teasing, but never grew really angry with him. But he had seen her quiet, unrelenting rejection of childhood bullies and play-mates who hurt her, and he knew she did not forget quickly. He also knew he had terribly humiliated her. Regret was sharp. He had always been her hero, her protector, her favorite. Even as late as a year ago, he could take her on his lap and chase away her blues with his teasing. "Damn it," he said under his breath. Then he went to his own room and began throwing his things into a suitcase.

Downstairs, at the front desk, she left him a message. "I'm not going home with you. Ever again."

Shielah walked and walked along the boulevard, ignoring whistles and curious glances from the few nighttimers who were still out at three a.m. She really didn't care where she ended up. Any place was all right. No place was better. She refused to let herself be frightened. Buck was right. She had never taken care of herself. There had always been Grandma and her big brother. They had faced the world for her. Now the time had come for her to face it alone. Childhood was over. She would get a job. She would move away, and she would make it on her own. He would see; the china doll had resources of her own that he didn't dream of.

The street was empty and she stood on the street corner, senselessly waiting for the light to change. A Hawaiian boy, smelling of beer, leered at her and reached out to touch her. Outrage flared and she slapped him as hard as she could. "Don't you touch me." she lashed out at him. He rubbed his face and backed off mumbling, "Sorry, sorry."

The pull toward Paulo and comfort was strong. The agony of self-examination seemed out of place in the romantic surrounding of Waikiki beach and tiki lamps, but the time had thrust itself upon her. Paulo could not help her now. He was a stranger, for all the feeling of kinship. They hadn't had enough time together for him to be able to counsel and console her now. This was a family matter, a personal crisis, and she was an extremely private person. She had to face alone the accusations Buck had thrown at her. It was a hard look she took that night, sitting alone in the sand, coming to grips with the way she dealt with a world that had deprived her of her family, her security, her self-confidence. It didn't occur to her that Life had no axe to grind with her, no grudge match. But it did finally become clear to Shielah that, difficult or not, she had to become independent so no one could scorn her as Buck had, and she had to bear the burdens alone. She thought she had done that from a very young age. Apparently, she had not been tough enough. Buck had seen her weakness and now had used it against her. She wouldn't let it happen again.

It was daylight when she sank down in a cushioned chair in the lobby of the Imperial Islands Hotel. It was not easy for her to apologize, but she felt that Paulo deserved an apology for last night. He had not been at fault— she had, and her brother. She sat for a few minutes in the chair, framing in her mind the words of an apology and goodbye. Within minutes she was asleep. Paulo was six floors above her and was still not asleep. He was waiting for seven o'clock so he could start to the airport and see her before her departure. He didn't blame Buck. He had a sister too, and had seen a glimpse of what the relationship between Shielah and her brother had been. But he was afraid for his time with her to end this way. He could lose her for good. At five after seven he walked out of the elevator and into the lobby. She was asleep in an overstuffed chair, her legs drawn up beneath her, her hair tangled and strewn over her arm and legs. He knelt down beside her and looked at her for a few minutes before he spoke.

"Miss, you can't sleep here. There are rules in the hotel against it."

She opened her eyes to find him kneeling in front of her, his eyebrow bandaged. He was smiling at her, but she had no smile to offer him in return. He got a room for her and took her to it. She apologized for the night before, both for her own bewitched behavior and for Buck's enraged conclusions, and she told him that she was determined not to go back on the flight with her brother. She would not be his little sister ever again. Paulo got no satisfaction from her story. He tried to get her to see it from Buck's perspective, but she merely grew angry.

"You're too tired to discuss anything now. Go to sleep, and we'll talk about it later."

"I won't change my mind," she whispered as her eyes closed.

Paulo let himself out and closed the door.

It was noon when she woke. He was sitting in a chair by the window. "Ah hah, the morning glory blinks."

She tried to smile. It wouldn't come. "What are you doing here? I thought you'd gone."

"I went out for a while. Wanted to talk to you before you 'flew the coop.' "

"I'm not flying anywhere. My tailfeathers got trimmed last night."

He was studying her. She was morose and completely deflated.

After a minute he said. "Don't let yourself be embarrassed by your brother. He didn't understand you last night. And he doesn't know anything of what's between us. I am not embarrassed and I hope you won't be either. That memory will always be precious."

She shook her head. "No. It was just a dream, some kind of drug of the islands. Buck was right—I was drunk. This place is too powerful, too romantic. Things happen that aren't real." She looked up at him. "I'm not real. I'm not your dream come true. I'm just plain, simple Shielah, a backward girl from a small town. You wouldn't give me a second look if it weren't for your vision of some girl ten years ago."

Now he was treading close to the edge, and he knew it.

"I know what you are, and a little of who you are. And what I know, I like. I look at the dream as a catalyst. Without it I would certainly never have been bold enough to walk up to you, introduce myself, and tell you how beautiful you are. Reality is not necessarily dull. It can be as wonderful as you make it."

She sighed. "Well, reality is that Buck is gone. Check out time from our hotel is two p.m., and I've got to get my things out. Then I'll decide what to do after that. Maybe I'll just stay here in the islands and work for a while."

Walking over to the old hotel, Paulo tried to take her arm. She pulled away. When he proposed a day at the open air flea market that Honolulu was famous for, she shook her head silently. The spell was broken. She had retreated from him, and her silence was a barrier he couldn't breach. In her room he sat and watched while she packed her suitcase. Occasionally, he caught a glimpse of concern on her face, but mostly it was an unreadable mask. It had taken him four days to penetrate that mask and in a matter of hours it was back, thicker than before. He had no idea what was in her mind. Did she blame him? Was she afraid? She had never been on her own before. But she wouldn't talk. Try as he would to revert to their easy exchange of the day before, she answered monosyllabically. The door was tightly shut.

"That's it," she said, looking around.

"You can stay in my hotel for a few days. I've paid for the room for the week." He hoped to reassure her.

She glanced at him, determinedly. "You shouldn't have. I can take care of myself."

"I know that. But the hotel only rents rooms for a week at a time," he lied.

"Hopefully I'll have a job and be gone before the week is up," she answered stoically.

The door was open, Paulo held her suitcase while she checked the bathroom and the dresser one last time. "What's this letter for me. I haven't seen that before. Buck must have stuck it in this drawer. I wonder how long it's been here."

She opened it quickly and scanned it. Paulo waited patiently, holding the luggage. She looked up, puzzlement and incredulity lighting her face. "It's from an airline company. New World Airways wants to interview me for a stewardess job. They sent it to my home address, and Grandma forwarded it. I have no idea how long it's been here, but they want to see me in Salt Lake City on the twenty-sixth. What day is it?"

He looked at his watch and pushed a button. "It's the twenty-fourth." He smiled at her bewilderment.

"Day after tomorrow!" Her voice rose, excitement taking over. "Oh, Paulo, hurry. I've got to get my ticket home exchanged for tomorrow morning. I've got a job interview," she exclaimed with a new sense of importance. "Hurry, let's get down to the travel agency."

Chapter 4

*T*he flight home from Hawaii was interminably long. She waved goodbye to Paulo at 6:30 a.m. His flight left before hers, scheduled into Los Angeles International, then direct to New York City. She was routed through San Francisco. The night before she left she called Fort Ord, California—the telephone in Stephen's barracks.

"Hello, could I speak to Stephen Gailbraith?"

"Out on night patrol." The answer was terse.

"Can you tell him I called . . . Shielah called . . . Shielah Sorensen. Can you tell him I am flying in to San Francisco International tomorrow at 3 p.m. If he can meet me, I'll be at the United Airlines ticket counter just after three."

"I'll tell him."

"You won't forget? It's . . . it's important."

"I'll tell him. Fat chance he can get there, but I'll tell him."

Shielah also thought it was an outside chance that Stephen could meet her plane. He probably didn't have many off-base privileges in boot camp. Still, she had to try. The week with Paulo had shaken her faith in herself, in her ability to make an emotional commitment and stick to it. Her love of Stephen had never been in question that week, but Paulo D'Agosta had definitely touched a responsive chord that disturbed her. She needed to see Stephen again to tell him about the airline interview, but mostly to reassure herself about their love.

Walking down the long concourse to the terminal, Shielah passed several knots of flight attendants in their uniforms and a secret, delicious feeling flooded through her. Perhaps she would soon be one of them. Strangers she would never have even looked in the eye, she now smiled at as she approached. It was a huge airport and rather awe inspiring to an inexperienced traveler, but she took a deep breath, paused to read the direction signs carefully, squared her shoulders with determination and

69

refused to be daunted. She took the escalator down to the main terminal floor and headed toward the United counter. Crossing the terminal, dodging people all the way, she smiled. That was what an airline stewardess did!

She saw him leaning back against the counter, his long, khaki-covered legs crossed at the ankles, and smiling slightly as he watched the cross section of humanity parade before him. He saw her before she was aware of him, and grinned as she approached with her head high.

"Here's a young lady, looks like she just came back from Hawaii! Do you have a date, Miss Hawaii?"

She stopped in front of him and beamed up at him. "Not yet. That's why I'm here, looking for a date. You got some time, soldier?"

"Time enough," he said. "Time enough for you, always." Then he unfolded himself and a second later she was wrapped up in his arms, her face pressed against rough material, smelling his hair and neck. He smelled so good, so clean, so familiar. Her mind, indeed her whole soul, relaxed as she leaned against him.

"Oh Stephen, I missed you. How I missed you. How did you get here? Did they give you time off? I didn't dream you could really get here to meet me. It was just a hope, just a chance. I'm so glad you came."

"Me too. I got back to camp at five this morning and Jonesey said some girl named Shielah had called and wanted me to meet an airplane in San Francisco at three. 'Shielah who'? I asked." He laughed at her indignant pulling back and just squeezed her tighter against him. "But who can ignore an invitation like that? So I hit my sergeant up for a day pass. I want you to know I sold myself into servitude for you. His personal slave for a month, that's what I had to promise. Then I thumbed. Must have been meant to be. I got a ride in the first fifteen minutes. Dropped me right at the airport entrance. Now all I have to worry about is getting back by midnight."

"Guess what?" she challenged him, and he immediately sensed a new excitement about her.

"You love me."

"Yes that, of course. But something else too, something new."

"You're joining the army and me down at boot camp."

"No, silly! I'd be a joke at boot camp."

"Well, you're already a byword."

"Can't you guess any better than that? This is something wonderful, something neat, something really exciting and it involves my future."

"Your future belongs to me. Are you proposing to me?"

"Will you stop that and guess. My future, my future . . . work." she hinted to him.

"Oh, that's more like it. I have to have something to go on. Let's see, your future work, beyond having my kids and keeping my house, you mean." She pushed his arm in exasperation. "OK, OK, I'm sorry. Your future work? You're going to be a dance hall girl?"

"Stephen!" she cried in frustration.

"No? Not a dance hall girl? Gee, you'd be cute, and I could start a career as Billy the Kid. Ouch! I'll be good. Let me think. I'm not good at guessing games, even Charades. Your future work is . . . is . . . a scientific expedition to the Antarctic to study the reproduction habits of penguins!"

This time she shoved him away from her and stamped her foot. "Alright for you. I'm not going to tell you now."

"I'm sorry! I told you I was a terrible guesser. Don't make me guess. Just tell me, and I promise I'll be good. I'll be happy and excited for you . . . I hope."

Stormy signs cleared and her face lit with expectation as she told him. "I sent a letter to New World Airlines applying for a stewardess position. I got a letter back from them while I was in Hawaii. Tomorrow, I have my interview at the Airport Inn in Salt Lake. Stephen, I'm going to be an airline stewardess. If they won't take me, I'll keep applying until I find someone who will."

"I'll take you. Where would you like to go? How about Fort Ord, California? *There's* a beautiful vacation spot."

"I've had enough vacation. I'm going to work. It's time I became independent and stopped leaning on . . . on Grandma . . . and . . . and Buck."

There was a new sound in her voice. Was it just a little hard, a little bitter? Stephen wondered. "A woman of determination, huh? Does a working woman also need food occasionally? I'm starved! How about something to eat? You can tell me about Hawaii over lunch. How's Buck? Is he heading to Mexico for the dig?"

Carefully, she answered as they walked to the coffee shop. "I don't know what he has planned, except he mentioned he might have to go to summer school this year to catch up his credits. Hawaii was gorgeous, warm! You can see my tan."

"And approve! You definitely pass inspection." Just at the entrance of the door he pulled her back into a corner off to the side and buried his face in her hair. "Only one thing a hungry man likes better than food." He kissed her, long, and with deep satisfaction. "I miss this more than food. This could be addictive, I can tell. I can't believe all the times I looked at you and wanted to kidnap you and hold you as a love hostage. Maybe this is the time." He nuzzled her neck and cheek.

"I'm shocked, Mr. Gailbraith. I had no idea you had such devious thoughts."

"Dr. Jekyll and Mr. Hyde. Proper Mormon elder on Sunday and," he gave a wicked laugh, " . . . love-starved outlaw the rest of the time." He held her face between his hands and kissed her eyelids, the tip of her nose, her cheeks, her forehead, and her lips, lightly, then more and more demandingly. After a few minutes he eased the tight hold of his arms around her and drew away, sighing. "You don't know how I wish I had taken Buck up on his offer to try and get me out of this. I hate being so far away from you, from home, from everything I care about. And the training is the pits. They have one goal, to turn me into a killer. That's not me. I'll never be a machine that kills because I'm supposed to."

With the top of her head pillowing his cheek, he relaxed, leaning against the wall, savoring the smell of her, the softness of her body against his. He let his hand run down her back. "I love you," he said in her ear. "That's what keeps me going, knowing that I love you and that you love me. You're my dream, my hope, the star I wish on. And to think I used to carry you piggy-back. Now I just carry you in my heart."

Shielah was content. This was what she had wanted, this moment with Stephen. Everything was plain with him, just as it should be. There were no disturbing undercurrents that she couldn't understand, no strangeness. His love for her was as clear and wholesome as her love for him. It was so right between them. Here in his arms, the world seemed fine again and she could meet the future with all the confidence she needed.

"I do love you. You know I do. I have ever since that day when I was eight and you were an older man of eleven. I cut my knee on the way home from school and I was crying, sitting on the curb with my toes in the irrigation ditch. Do you remember? You came and sat down beside me and washed the cut and squeezed the edges of the skin together so it would quit bleeding. You didn't laugh at my tears or tell me to quit crying. You carried me home, and I bled on your jeans and you didn't care. At least, you acted like you didn't. I remember how warm your shoulder was when I put my cheek on it. And that was the first time I knew, really knew, I loved you, and it was different than my love for Buck."

"Gee, I didn't realize I had captured your heart so long ago or I would have climbed that mountain sooner. Will you wait for me there when I come home?"

"I'll be there. No matter when you come home, or where I am, I'll come to the mountain." She hugged him fiercely and returned his kiss with a passion of her own. The cobwebs of last week were gone, the romantic merry-go-round of Paradise had stopped, but the true love, the right love remained.

He saw her onto her flight to Salt Lake an hour later and stood for another twenty minutes watching the plane take off, then Stephen walked out into the cool San Francisco afternoon and stuck his thumb out.

She arrived in Salt Lake about seven p.m., which with the time difference was about the same time Paulo landed in New York. But she wasn't thinking of Paulo D'Agosta or even Stephen much on that flight. Her mind was in turmoil over the upcoming interview. Would they think she was too young? Could she walk in high heels all day long in an airplane that sometimes turned and wavered? Could she smile all day at the people? Would she get air sick? No, she had flown twice now and she hadn't gotten air sick either time. Would she be afraid? No, she wasn't a bit afraid. It was fascinating to go through take off and landing. What questions would they ask her? DeeAnn London's sister had interviewed for the airlines two years ago, and she hadn't been hired.

Just before they landed she counted her money again. She didn't want to go home just yet. Besides, the interview was at eight a.m. the next morning, and she would just have to find a way back up to the city if she went home tonight. Tucked into a usually empty pocket of her wallet were two fifty dollar bills. She knew she hadn't put them there. Either Buck had, sometime when she hadn't been aware of it, or Paulo had. Her mouth pinched more firmly together. She wished neither of them had. She had quite enough money, thank you. She wasn't destitute. Yet.

Actually, without the extra bills, she had just enough money to pay for her hotel, a dry hamburger and french fry dinner, and a bus ticket to Springville the next day. She was fine.

The screener was a woman. Shielah had expected a man and was much relieved to talk to a woman instead.

"Shielah Sorensen?" the woman began.

"Yes."

"You have a terrific tan," the woman looked across the desk at her, smiling her approval.

"Oh, that. Thank you. I . . . I just came back from Hawaii."

Pencil eyebrows shot up. "Hawaii! Lucky you. Wish I were in Honolulu."

She responded to the older woman's easy manner with a smile of her own. "It was great. It was my first time and I loved it."

"How long were you there?"

"Ten days."

"Family vacation?"

"Well, it was a graduation present, really."

"I see. You have generous parents. When I was eighteen I tried to get my parents to consider a trip to Hawaii. No luck. We lived in Des Moines, so they took me to the State Fair instead, and we stayed overnight in a real hotel. Not exactly the same."

Shielah felt more and more at ease. The woman was probably in her late twenties and stylishly, if conservatively, dressed. Her hair was bobbed at shoulder length, very sleek and shiny. She could have been a model. Shielah thought, I wonder if I'll ever look like that?

"Let's see, from your application you are nineteen, a high school graduate, and speak French and Spanish." She looked up. "Three years of two languages?"

"Yes, I love languages and my brother speaks Spanish."

"Good. Are you fluent?"

"Fairly fluent. In my last year I tutored the other students," Shielah answered quickly.

"That's good. The tests will show just how fluent you are. Languages add a lot to tip the balances in your favor. No college credits?"

Shielah knew that was a mark against her. "No. I just graduated. I'm a little older than most of my classmates. I . . . I was held . . . I repeated the fifth grade."

The woman looked at her quizzically. Shielah was self-conscious lest she seem a slow student. "That was a bad year. I lost . . . my . . .

73

parents . . . in a fire at our family home. It threw me off for a while." She continued eagerly, "But my grades in high school will show you I am not a slow learner. I pick things up very quickly, and I'm an exceptionally hard worker. I've had to be."

"I'm sure," the lady said. "Tell me why you want to work for New World Airlines?"

Shielah wasn't expecting that. "I'm not sure . . . well . . . yes, I am. I'll tell you the truth. I have lived in a small town all my life, and I know there is a more exciting world out there. I have read about cathedrals in Europe, and Stratford-on-Avon, and the Versailles Gardens for as long as I can remember. My whole world was books, a farm, and pictures upon pictures of far away places. Is there any chance I'll ever see anything if I get a job waitressing at the Dairy Queen? No, there isn't. And before much more time goes by, I want to go and see and do and be."

The woman was watching her with gentle amusement. Shielah continued, "You must have been like that once if you came from Des Moines. I've been to as many state fairs as I can stand. Now I want to go to Vienna, or even Manhattan. But whether I get on with your airlines or not, I won't stay here."

"You sound a little like the Unsinkable Molly Brown." The lady smiled. Then she turned serious. "Flight attendant work is not just visiting wonderful places with tempting names. It's work, hard work. You'll take a six week course of training, and after that you'll have the exciting privilege of seeing those 'far away place with strange sounding names'. In addition to the cities you work in, you'll be able to get passes on other airlines, so you can literally go anywhere in the world. You'll be a representative of New World Airways, responsible for public relations, and will have the chance to meet celebrities and a chance to serve the public." Watching Shielah's eager attention, her eyes became amused. "I can promise you it will be the most memorable year of your life."

Shielah was sitting on the edge of her chair, listening, watching the woman's face. Excitement radiated from her. "Do I have to take a test or something?"

"Yes. I've sent for your SAT scores. They were fine but we want to test you ourselves for your aptitude for our kind of work."

"When?"

"Testing starts at noon. It's a three-hour test."

"When will I hear, one way or the other?"

The woman stood up and extended her hand. "About the time you think you're going to die of suspense. Good luck, Miss Sorensen. I'll give you a recommendation."

It happened much too fast for Grace. Lately, she felt like her head was in a spin. Why had Buck come home from Hawaii without Shielah? She tried to get him to tell her, but he joked and teased her, and said that

74

Shielah had met her Prince Charming who was building a palace for her on one of the islands of the sea. So exasperating! Then Shielah came home all excited about an interview with some airlines lady. Grace hadn't even known that her granddaughter was having an interview. Now she was leaving. Just three weeks. She'd been home just three weeks, and she was leaving for good. Oh, she might say it wasn't really for good, but Grace knew better. That was the way of it. Children are only yours for a little while, then other people, other interests, other firesides come and steal them away. "I'll come back" they say. But it isn't true. They never come back. They visit. They come and say hello and kiss you on the cheek, but they never, never, truly come back. Grace fished for the handkerchief in her apron pocket and wiped away the moisture from the wrinkles under her eyes.

"Grandma, are you all right?" Shielah asked, looking up from the letter she was writing.

"Sure. Just getting a little tired. Probably ought to go on to bed now. My program's over. TV isn't what it used to be anyway. Who's that you're writing to?"

"Stephen. I promised I'd write every week. Next week I'll have something really exciting to tell him."

"Buck taking you to the airport tomorrow morning?"

"No, Grandma, Drew is. Uncle Will said he could take the truck." She was almost finished with the letter. She looked thoughtfully into the darkness behind the window. "I'll miss Uncle Will and Aunt Maddie. They've been good to me. I'll miss that palomino mare of theirs too. Don't guess I'll get much riding in during training."

"I 'spect not," Grandma agreed, although she hadn't the slightest idea of what training entailed.

Outside the window, darkness was slow in coming. Night seemed to dawdle, leisurely lowering its shadowy blanket. The crickets were chirping so loudly, they set up a perfect chorus of reedy, raspy noise. Shielah absentmindedly signed her name, then stood up.

"Maybe I'll just go sit on the porch for a while before bed, Grandma."

"There, that's a good idea. It'll comfort you sometime when you're far away from home." Grace began wiping her eyes again.

Shielah stopped and looked at her Grandma for the first time in weeks. She was old, Shielah thought. Grandma was eighty-one years old now, but beautiful all the same. Her hair had turned perfectly white and still had a bit of wave to it. She kept it just so, and sinned, or so she thought, in her pride over it. Her eyes were weaker now, Shielah noticed. Grace frequently asked her to read small passages. Impulsively Shielah knelt down beside her grandmother's chair and touched her cheek.

"Grandma, I'll miss you. More than I can tell. Sometimes I hardly know what I am doing, going out into the world without you. I must be crazy. Gone loco, like Uncle Will says."

Her grandmother shook her head wordlessly and continued, unsuccessfully, to stop the moisture that kept collecting.

"If I bomb out will you let me come back? I might not even make it through flight school. They say it's hard."

Her voice raspy, Grace whispered, "You'll make it. But you can come back any time, any time you want to." She grasped Shielah's hand and clutched it tightly. "You be happy way out there in Orlando, Florida, you hear? I want you to be happy. I know you haven't had too much happiness growing up. I didn't do as well by you as your mother could have. I tried, but Ginny, she had a touch. Just knew what to say to make things better. And say your prayers too, honey. That's the only way to be happy. Don't get in with any crowd that drinks and smokes and chases around. God says that 'wickedness never was happiness,' and that's the truth. Only the good are truly happy. Oh, the others, they might have some pleasure. Least they think it's pleasure. But happiness, that's not easy to come by. Just say your prayers and be a good girl, and I'll be saying mine, here, for you."

Shielah put her own wet cheek against her grandmother's softer, wrinkled one. Then she kissed her, and they both spent the next few minutes wiping their eyes and trying to smile in reassurance.

"I love you, Grandma. You were the only thing that saved my life after the fire. I'd have been lost without you. My faith in God was all gone for a while. You're the one who gave it back to me, slowly but surely. The church has got to be true if an angel like you believes it. I love you, and I'll be back. It won't be so long. I'll be back."

But Grace knew it was a lie.

She sat on the porch, smelling the soft, warm earthy smells, listening to the crickets, and letting the darkness soothe away her anxiety. Shirley Whitney and Mark Andell walked by and waved to her. They came up on the porch, arm in arm, to tell her they had heard she was going to be a stewardess. It was the talk of Clarksville. DeeAnn London's older sister hadn't made it. Shielah was lucky. She must have interviewed at the right time, when they were hiring. Yes, Shielah replied, she must have. Oh, had they forgotten to tell her they were getting married next Christmas? The date was already set. Maybe she'd be home for Christmas and could come to the wedding. Maybe, she answered. Married, she thought, and shuddered.

The light had long since gone off in Grace's room. Shielah had rocked enough. Time for bed. Everything was packed, but she'd have to be up and ready for Drew by seven. Still she lingered. It felt so good, so comfortable. Then Buck's car swung around the corner and came slamming to a stop in the driveway. Shielah got up and started to the screen door.

"Can't you say goodbye, at least?" Buck was up the stairs in seconds and grabbed her arm, pulling her back into the shadows.

"Goodbye," she responded matter-of-factly.

"Gees, you're cold when you wanta be, aren't you?"

She brushed him off. "It's late. I have to go to bed."

"Shielah, whatd'ya want me to say? I'm sorry about Hawaii? I'm not. I'd do the same thing again if I saw you dancing a wild dance for some stranger. I am sorry I hurt your pride and embarrassed you. Maybe my methods aren't the most tactful, but I was concerned, and I guess, a little shocked."

"Yeah, that's fine," she replied and turned back toward the door.

"What's fine?" His voice began climbing. "Damn it, talk to me. I just apologized to you. Can't you even accept my apology? What's fine? That you're going away tomorrow, and you haven't said five words to me in three weeks? What's so fine about losing your sister over one lousy fight in Hawaii? It's not fine by me."

He tried to put his arms around her. "Come on now, muffin, let's not part like this. You know I'm a hot-head. I always was. But I've still got bubblegum in my pockets." He thought that would get a smile out of her.

He was wrong. No smile. And no goodbye hug. She slipped under the circle of his arms and opened the door.

"Bubblegum's not enough any more, Buck. Give it to some other kid. I've grown out of it." She was inside the screen door and halfway across the living room before he regained his composure.

"Well, I'll be damned," he said.

"Your choice," she said over her shoulder and closed her bedroom door.

Shielah stepped to the door of the DC-8 and paused on the threshhold to survey her new world. The skies were startling blue, and she could smell the sea in the hot, humid breeze. She took a deep breath and a smile crept over her face. A flight attendant her elbow cheerfully wished her well.

"Good luck," she said. "You'll love it once you get into it."

"Thank you," she replied, noting the perky uniform of bright blue, white, and gray that she would someday be wearing.

Then others followed and there was no more time for pausing. Down the escalator, into limousines, six girls to a car—perfumes clashing then mixing, excited chatter, "what-if's", "I-never-dreamed", "so lucky" repeated over and over. At the flight school complex the limousines were met by doormen and the girls were directed to the hotel dormitory that was to be their home for the next six weeks. It all moved fast for Shielah. They were to find their rooms, get their baggage stowed, freshen up and report to the lobby all in the next hour. Three girls shared a room with Shielah, a room on the third floor that looked out over the white sands of Florida, to the ocean hardly five miles away.

Sixty-seven trainees gathered in the lobby and took a tour of the flight school facilities—dining room with lunch already being laid out, training center where classes were given in everything from mixing drinks to first aid. The training coordinator was a featured attraction for the girls. At six feet tall, in his middle twenties, with an amused smile and fair, all-American good looks, he had no trouble securing and holding the girls' attention. At times, however, the noise rose until even he had to call for more attention and less chatter.

Shielah was stunned with the elegance of the facilities. The complex included a swimming pool and tropical gardens, beauty salon, theater, and convenience store. All their needs had been anticipated. The flight school was fully self-contained. It even had a doctor and two nurses to supervise any medical needs. It all came from between the pages of Life Magazine and Good Housekeeping. The pool was a free-form structure with a small waterfall created at one end, imported rocks bordering the rim, and a refreshment stand created to look like a thatched hut at one end of the pool. The tropical gardens surrounding it, covering almost a city block, were lush and gorgeously groomed. Little footpaths wandered in and out through bushes of flowers so big and colorful Shielah had no name for them, and white wrought iron benches were tucked into the garden in every convenient spot. Small, white lamps lit the paths at night, and floodlights by the pool lit the whole area until midnight. If she hadn't recently spent ten days in Hawaii, Shielah would have been overwhelmed. The amazing thing was that this had all been created just for them, just for potential flight attendants. She had no idea they were to be treated so royally.

The surroundings were royal, but the training was very practical. They were out of bed the next morning by 6:30 a.m., showered, dressed, breakfasted and in classes in the flight training building by eight o'clock. From the very first morning they were weighed every day, and required to maintain a pre-set weight level despite the extravagant smorgasbord that awaited them every meal in the dining room. They all gained five pounds in the first two weeks, and some of the girls had a good deal of trouble even after that. If they exceeded their specific weight limitation three times during training they were dismissed and sent home.

The girls were divided into groups of about twenty for classroom purposes. There were six class periods a day, each class for a different area of study. They learned to load carts with drinks, to serve food, to work in the different models of airplanes, and to recognize each of the models at a glance, even in flight. They were taught the safety features of each plane, and how to handle emergency situations. None of it was hard for Shielah, even the memorization, but the first woman who had screened her was right—it was definitely work.

Each day of training started with personal appearance and grooming. A flight attendant for New World Airways need not be beautiful—though Shielah knew they had that reputation—but they had to be as well-groomed as any model. Six beauty specialists from New York came in to work with the girls. Shielah had always worn her hair long and pulled back into one long stream down her back. The only make-up she had worn was a little eye make-up and blusher, when she remembered it.

She was the first model the trainer used. He was a man about fifty-five years old, with black curly hair, a very business-like manner, and a critical

78

air. She was immediately afraid of him. She knew she was all wrong in her make-up and was exquisitely self-conscious as she sat before the group, pointing out her features.

"If you have a heart-shaped face like this one, you are lucky. Wider at the top, high cheek bones, tapering to a smaller chin. Almost any hairstyle you desire will work with this face. Of course, some are better than others. Let's see if we can find a better one for Miss Sorensen."

He piled her hair on top her head and looked at the effect critically in the mirror. Some of the class commented their approval. Then he pinned it into a long page-boy style. He gave her bangs, he swept it back from her forehead, he teased it all about her head and gave her "the lion look". Finally, he decided upon a shoulder length page-boy cut, that could be set for elegance or simplicity.

"I'm sorry, but I won't cut my hair that short," she spoke softly.

He looked down at her, puzzled. "Pardon me?" he said.

"Perhaps I do need a trim, but not that short . . . please. I'd just never be comfortable."

Vincent Danilov was not used to objections. "My dear, you look like a school girl. You are supposed to look like a competent flight attendant. The two don't mix. As long as you wear your hair in ponytails, pigtails, or hanging free down your back, you will continue to look like a school girl." He was not angry, only perplexed at her stubbornness.

"You're probably right. But can't you find a way so it won't have to be cut that short?" She was looking up at him apologetically. She didn't want to cause problems, nor to question his expertise, but after all it was her hair— her only asset as far as she was concerned.

His face was set, his authority being challenged. Then he saw the uncertainty in her eyes, the pleading. And what eyes! He would use her for make-up demos also. You almost couldn't make a mistake with this face. He softened under the pleading of those blue eyes. His hand went out to her hair, and his voice became gentler.

"How do you want to wear it?"

"I could perm it," she said eagerly.

He nodded. "You could. Only let it be a very soft perm. No curls, just soft waves. One side drawn back with a comb, like this, ear just slightly showing, long bangs, softly waved, pulled over to the other side. You will be beautiful . . . " Then he stiffened up again. "However, it must be trimmed, at least three inches. Only then will it be manageable. See if you can schedule the perm tonight."

He also used her the next day for the first make-up demonstration, stating that it was beneficial for the girls to see a complete make-over. He was a master with color. She emerged. Eyebrows plucked and shaped, blue, translucent eyeshadow and teal blue liner, highlighting already large eyes, blush applied high on her cheekbones, and her mouth touched with a light, luminescent pink lipstick. The perm had been done the night before. She did not get to bed until eleven-thirty, but it was just what the master wanted. He turned her chair around, explaining every step as he went, talking about different colors of shadow and how to use them for individual coloring. He lectured on the shades of foundation, blush and lipstick. Certain combinations for certain faces, and for certain looks—daytime, nighttime, elegance, simplicity. Applause started and spread through the group. The girls were all excited. They all wanted the chair. He was pleased and smiled his compliance. She got up to give her place to another, dark-haired girl. He held her arm for a moment and said, "It is perfect. You are a beautiful model."

One by one the girls were assigned to one of Danilov's staff for individual attention and instruction. Each of them went through a professional make-over session, and each one was finally inspected by Danilov himself. He was a perfectionist and insisted that every detail be exact. No one really liked him, but everyone wanted to please him.

Shielah blushed and went to sit at the back of the group. Several times she stole a look at herself in the mirror. She liked her hair. It had come out softly waved and still well past her shoulders in the back. But the rest of her! Grandma would shake her head. Too much blue eyeshadow. Too much eyeliner, too much blush, and she had never needed lipstick; her lips were naturally pink. Did she look like a clown? She needn't have worried. All day long she got comments from the other girls on her make-up. Some of them were envious comments, but most were honest expressions. She was very self-conscious before the day was over. But she also found that she liked it too. She was slowly gaining confidence that perhaps she was not so backward, after all. She had lived so long feeling unaccepted, even mocked, that she believed in her own inferiority. Now, in the space of a few short weeks, the episode with Paulo starting an upswing in self-confidence, she began to recognize the signs of approval from her peers and teachers. It was like cool water to a parched soul, and she drank it in, blossoming as the days went on.

When the course on grooming was finished, she had learned a great deal about how to dress and how to present herself. She was grateful and amazed at how much there was to learn. Still, she was a little uncomfortable. The other girls seemed to take it all in eagerly. Shielah felt like an imposter. Simplicity was her way. Beauty was either natural or it was fake. Shielah refused to be a fake. Pretense was not easy for her. It was hard to spend the half-hour in front of the mirror with her roommates, poring over her looks and pretending to be something she wasn't. But she told herself over and over that old ways were gone, there was no going back. She was right.

When Friday came, it was over. The course had taken three weeks. The New York people were to leave early the next morning. After dinner, she took a book out to the patio and relaxed with a long, appreciative sigh. Next week she would have experience in the mock-up airplane. That she could do well, she felt sure. The hotel was busy on Friday night. The lobby was a mecca for the young pilots and flight crew trainees as well as the counter help at the local airport. The girls never lacked for male companionship on the weekends. It was all in fun, of course, and very fickle. Sitting alone in a chair on the patio, she had several young men stop to talk and flirt and try to set up a date for the next night. She was determined not to fall into the zoo. She was friendly and smiled a good deal as she was now trained to do, but she would not date. She mentally compared each young man to Stephen . . . and to Paulo. She had tried to forget the incident in Hawaii. She was sure she would never see him again and she told herself she wanted it that way. Paulo D'Agosta could only upset her life. Stephen was her heart's choice and these young, fresh, trainees didn't compare. They were all so brash and glib. They scared her off. If any one of them had been more subtle and patient in his approach, he might have been successful at getting a date. But the fast-talking, "hello-sweetheart" line only left her tongue-tied.

One other trainee came out to sit on the patio. She was also not a part of the zoo. Her name was Brandy, and she was black. She watched Shielah turn down two young men dressed in blue uniforms. When at last she spoke her voice was husky and lazy.

"You engaged or something . . . I mean, why aren't you're not going out? It certainly isn't for lack of offers."

Shielah answered, "I don't like the type."

"Oh, I see. You have a boy friend back home?"

Clarksville flashed through her mind, then Stephen's face. "No, not exactly. I do have a boyfriend, but he's in boot camp in California. We're not engaged or anything. I'm just not much on the fast life. I come from a small town, and I guess I haven't grown out of it yet."

"I come from a small town too," Brandy nodded her understanding. She spoke with a soft drawl, but perfect English, and Shielah found herself listening just for the music in the voice. "This all seems so big, so elegant, doesn't it? Three years ago I'd have laughed if anyone had speculated I'd be lounging around a hotel like a rich person." Her laugh was even musical and Shielah couldn't help but smile. "Who knows, maybe I was meant for the rich life. Heaven knows I told my Mama that a hundred, no a million, times. I've always known I wasn't born for a small town in South Carolina. 'How you gonna get rich?' my Mama asked me. 'Marry a rich man,' I told her. 'Gotta meet those rich men someway, sugar,' she said. And this seems the best way right now for me to do that. College certainly didn't do it. I tried that for two years, going part-time and working part-time. Sure, I was getting an education, but not meeting the kind of men I wanted. You've got to go where the rich men go." She was grinning by now, white teeth gleaming from her dark face. Her eyes sparkled and she leaned forward. "And where do they go? All over the world, if they're rich. And they fly, honey, they fly. So, how do you like this flight training?"

"This part has been fun. I've never done much with make-up. In my home town people would think I was putting on airs," Shielah confided.

Brandy nodded. "Well, you're a natural. That's why Danilov picked you. He is no fool. He picked you because he knew he couldn't make a mistake on you."

Shielah blushed. "I don't think so. He was very helpful, and taught me a lot. I've just been afraid I looked like a clown."

"Honey, you're not a clown . . . you're a doll." Brandy surveyed her, shrewdly.

"Thanks," Shielah said in embarrassment. "You're very nice. I feel like the dumbest one here. I have to work twice as hard, because I haven't had any college like you and the other girls have. I just graduated from high school in June. This is all like a dream to me. I still can't believe I'm here, and I'm afraid all the time I'll flub it and they'll send me home."

"You have trouble with your weight?" Brandy asked.

"Oh no, it's not that. I just feel that everyone catches on faster than I do."

Brandy sat back and shook her head. "Don't worry about that. I noticed you, you do OK. Hey, don't be uptight. If you have to work twice as hard as everyone else, I have to work *three* times as hard."

"Why?" Shielah asked.

Brandy's eyes roved to one side and then the other, and she jerked her head, "You notice any other chocolate colors around here?"

Shielah blushed a bright pink. "Sorry. I wasn't thinking."

"Hey, no problem. So you're color blind. I think that's great. I've been color blind, too, lately. All I see is white, white, white. It's boring." They laughed together.

There were dozens of questions Shielah wanted to ask her but she didn't know where the sensitive line was. "I guess that's why you're not going out tonight."

"That's right. I figure six weeks cold storage for me. Probably do me good. Cool down that hot blood my Pa warned me against. Of course, on the other hand, it might just make that hot blood boil." She laughed and clapped her hands together in delight.

They sat talking until the sun went down, forgetting to read, learning about each other. Brandy came from a little town called Window, South Carolina. It was a window all right, Brandy said wryly. Everyone could look in and see your business, and you could look out on the rest of the world, but looking was all you could do. There were still certain clothing shops where she could not try on a dress she wanted to buy, certain restaurants she wasn't allowed in, even with a white person. It was only five years ago she had been allowed the privilege of using the restroom in Woolworth's and other white establishments. Her family would probably always stay in Window. Her Pa owned a garage just on the edge of black town. Her brothers worked it with him. She had a sister already married at fifteen, three younger sisters and twin brothers just younger than she. They were all content with their town. She was the only one with the wandering itch. Not that she hadn't loved her home as a child. She loved the singing of the pine trees that dominated the South Carolina landscape. She remembered swinging on the old tire swing in the back yard, and the little schoolhouse where she had first read about whales and NASA and a place called Europe. Now they were bussing the black kids and none of them enjoyed school anymore. Her younger sisters hated the big brick building in nearby Jefferson. She was glad she had grown up when they still attended the white schoolhouse on the outskirts of Window. Lunch time had been spent playing tag, singing, and flirting with boys.

Brandy sighed, remembering. After a minute she looked over at Shielah, "Someday I'd like to take you home with me." She whooped in delight at the thought, mischief written on her face. "Boy, wouldn't that make a sensation." She calmed down and continued. "Of course I couldn't really, we'd both be run out of town."

"Really," Shielah was amazed. "Hasn't all that changed by now?"

"You must be in another world, sugar. There hasn't been much actual change. Oh, I can't say that really. A lot of things are better now. At least I can use a public restroom. But some things don't change and that's color. They also don't mix. The blacks would be more polite to you than the whites." She grinned again at Shielah. "Still, I'd love to see the look on my Mama's face when she saw us together—ebony and ivory."

Shielah thought about Grandma. How would she react if Brandy came home with me, she wondered. She might be surprised, but Shielah couldn't imagine her as anything but kind and sweet as always. Unwillingly her thoughts turned to Buck. No doubt he would be ecstatic. His chief complaint with Clarksville was its small town mentality. He enjoyed different cultures, foreigners, different, unique people—as long as it wasn't Paulo D'Agosta—and Brandy was certainly different from the run-of-the-mill Clarksville crowd. He'd probably take her to a movie, so they could be seen by the whole town, and if anyone so much as breathed an insult, he'd clobber them. A wry smile began on her lips but she banished it quickly.

"I think I'll go swimming," Shielah started to get up. "Do you want to come?"

"Thanks. I don't think so. I was in last night. The water has too much chlorine for me. Some day let's go down to the beach, OK?"

"OK. Sounds good to me." Shielah was standing beside Brandy now, smiling at her. "I'm glad we got to talk. I've noticed you in classes, but it's hard for me to talk to strangers. I'm trying to overcome my shyness but it's not easy. You made it very easy tonight. Thank you."

Brandy smiled back. "Hey, it's all right."

"You sure you won't come with me to the pool?"

"Thanks, but there's a movie I've been waiting to see all week."

They parted, both wishing the other one would come with her, but neither being sure enough of the new friendship to change her plans. As Shielah changed into her swimming suit, she was immediately flooded with memories of Hawaii and Paulo. She sat for a minute on the edge of her bed seeing his dark eyes, and remembering his touch. Then, deliberately, she walked over to the desk and took out her latest letter from Stephen, reread it for a few minutes, then put it back and headed for the pool.

The floodlights were brilliant against the dark sky, and the pool had lights in the water that changed from pink to blue to yellow on a pre-set schedule. She recognized some of the trainees with their dates, and the beauty people from New York were also there, holding drinks and chatting on the far side of the pool.

Shielah moved smoothly into the water, backstroking, sidestroking, and swimming laps across the deep end of the pool where there ws no one to get in her way. After her workout she lay back, floating, feet gently fluttering in the water, and looked up at the night sky. Without the floodlights the stars would be dazzling. The water was warm but refreshing, and occasionally a breeze ruffled the water. Where was Stephen tonight? Was he in his barracks, or at a movie? The thought occurred to her, perhaps he had found a date and was with a strange girl. No, she wouldn't think about that. She thought back to the Senior dance last May. She smiled now, thinking how much she had wanted him to kiss her and how she had thrilled when he held her in the airport. Thank goodness he had climbed up the hillside after her on graduation day.

"You are a loner, Miss Sorensen." The remark came close to her ear. She rolled over in the water, treading quickly. Mr. Danilov was floating beside her on a white flotation board, holding his drink balanced on the front of the board.

"Oh, hello. Not really a loner, I was just enjoying the night and the water." Shielah knew that the airlines insisted on the girls being friendly. There was no place for a loner as a flight attendant.

He was not accusing, simply observing with curiosity. "I thought I detected that in you, even in the classroom. It surprises me. I would have thought a lovely girl like yourself would surround herself with friends and admirers."

She was embarrassed and tongue-tied. "You . . . you're very . . . kind."

"Not really. I'm glad to see you here. If I had known you weren't going out, I would have invited you to join us."

"Thank you, that's very thoughtful, but not necessary."

He cocked his head and looked at her sharply. "How old are you?"

She always hated that question, and wished for the time she could say twenty-one.

"I'm twenty years old. Why do you ask?"

His eyebrows went up, and he continued to stare at her appraisingly. "Really! I'm surprised! You seem much older than that. Of course, before I made you up you looked like a sixteen-year-old schoolgirl. But I've been very happy with your appearance these last few days. And you certainly act older— I'd have guessed about twenty-two."

Shielah was flattered, but still at a loss as to how to talk with this smooth, cosmopolitan man. She couldn't even guess at how old he was. He was in excellent shape, slim, and firm. Still she knew he must be old enough to be her father, and she was uncomfortable with his familiarity. She began to move back toward the groups of people at the shallow end.

"Have you ever considered modeling?" He moved smoothly through the water, maneuvering himself directly in front of her.

"No. No, I haven't. I . . . . I'm not tall enough. I understand models all have to be at least five foot eight. I'm only five-six. Besides, I don't like to be photographed. I don't take good pictures."

"You could, with the right help. I have helped hundreds of girls become successful models. I think I could work with you if you were interested."

"You're very nice to say so, but I think I'm going to like being a flight attendant."

He moved out of her way and motioned to her. "Come on down and join us."

Her heart was not in it. She really preferred the quiet and privacy of her own thoughts after all the socializing required during the week. But she knew courtesy required it, and any good attendant would not refuse. The instructors told them often that public relations was their major work.

So she smiled and thanked him again. For a half-hour she mingled with the New Yorkers, sipping Seven-Up and listening to talk of Gucci's, Wall Street and the latest show on Broadway. It was a world apart, but fascinating.

"Have you ever been to New York, Miss Sorensen?" Danilov asked.

"No. I never have, but I do have a friend from there."

"Really? Who?"

"Paulo D'Agosta. He's a photographer and his family is in the clothing industry. Have you heard of them?"

Danilov and the others stared at her, astounded. Shielah realized she must have said something gauche. Then the older man laughed, "Of course! D'Agosta? Who hasn't? D'Agosta suits and Maretti furs—its the latest love affair in the fashion section of the papers. How did you meet the D'Agostas?" Clearly he was incredulous.

"In Hawaii. It was just an accident. I met Paulo. I . . . I'm not sure he works in the family business. He's into photography."

Now the chic New Yorker group looked at her with more interest. Danilov nodded as though he understood. "I see. Of course! And he wanted to use you. I told you you'd make a good model. I'd be happy to work with you, if you want to go into that."

But she laughed away the suggestion. Conversation went on about fashion and Shielah began to grow increasingly uncomfortable with his eyes constantly on her. After a polite time, she excused herself and thanked them all for their instruction of the last few days. Then she offered her excuses and extricated herself from the party.

He watched her as she dried off and put on her beach jacket. Reluctantly, he turned back to his group of friends. Shielah didn't really want to go back to the room. She wished she and Brandy were better friends so they could talk. She walked to the end of the pool, and, glancing back over her shoulder, could see Danilov engaged in conversation. She paused, then turned abruptly and walked into the gardens. She would be alone there.

She wandered around, promising herself to get pictures of the flowers to send home to Grandma. Tiny lights were strung along the foot paths and the base of trees. There were a few couples sitting on the benches, one couple half lying, half sitting on the grass. But the gardens were big enough to accommodate many couples. She was bending over to smell the huge pink blossoms of the azalea bush when a familiar voice spoke close to her shoulder.

"You should see the beautiful gardens of Tivoli. They are enchanting." Danilov had followed her.

Shielah was visibly startled. "Oh, Mr. Danilov, you startled me. What happened to your friends?"

"Nothing. They are still enjoying the water. I noticed you venturing into the gardens and thought I'd enjoy them with you."

"I . . . I was just coming in for a moment. I do love the flowers, but. . . . "

"Do you know you have remarkable eyes. I noticed them the first day. You could do anything with eyes like that." She tried to move past him. He moved in front of her and put his hands on her shoulders.

"You don't believe me, do you?"

"No. And I don't want to talk about it. I have to go."

"Not true. You *want* to go. I make you nervous. I'm sorry. I admire you very much, and would love to know you better. You're rather intriguing for such a young girl. Come, let's sit down and talk."

"No, I really can't." Obviously he had more in mind than she was comfortable with, and she was afraid she wouldn't know how to respond appropriately. He used his authoritative voice like a weapon. Fear was threatening to take over and she was afraid she would do something stupid.

"Come now. Here's a bench right here. I'm a perfect gentleman, I assure you. Besides, you're too young for me and much too naive. I prefer the more sophisticated woman. I just want to get to know you better."

He was pulling her toward a bench, set back amongst the flowering bushes in the shadows, well off the path. His face was uncomfortably close to hers. He was very forceful and she was completely unschooled in handling situations like this. She felt his hand go up under her beach jacket and touch her bare back. Then another hand was on her hip and starting to move. At the same time his lips brushed her cheek, just by her ear. The smell of alcohol about him was sickening, and his touch made her skin crawl.

Instinct told her to slap him and run. That's what she would have done a few short months before, but she forced herself to meet him on his level.

Quietly, but firmly, she spoke, "Take your hands off me. If you were a *perfect* gentleman, you'd behave like a man your age should—like my father."

He stepped back, startled. He'd expected a protest, a token protest as usually happened, then submission to his charm and will. She took him by surprise.

"That's a rude thing to say," he said coldly.

"That's a rude thing to do. You didn't come here to seduce the girls. You came to teach us about make-up. You do that very well, but you should leave the seduction to younger men."

He was furious. She looked him straight in the eye, and watched him grow red with anger over her insult. She jerked her arm loose and turned to walk away.

"Little prude," he said bitterly to her back. She heard him, but didn't reply, she just kept on walking . . . straight to Brandy's room.

The door opened, and a dark face appeared in the crack. "Hey, what's doin?" Brandy opened up wide for her to come in. Shielah came in silently, walked over, and sat down on the bed.

"You OK?" Brandy asked her anxiously.

Shielah stared up at her for a moment, then she began to laugh. Through peals of laughter she said, "I just knocked Mr. Danilov off his Casanova pedestal. I told him he was too old to seduce me." Brandy sat down beside her and listened intently to the story. They laughed together over the thought of Danilov being put down by an inexperienced little stewardess trainee. What a blow to his well-heeled ego.

"I almost slapped him, and ran away, like a teenager, but something told me I had to handle it like an adult. And I did! I did! I put him so far down he'll have to get a ladder to climb up."

A black hand squeezed her white one. "You did OK, sugar. You're growing up!"

The service class was easy for Shielah. Courtesy came naturally to her because she had been taught it all her life. How to stow carry-on's, check seatbelts, how to handle small children, where the blankets were stowed, how to serve the meals—farthest seat first—how to mix drinks, she learned it all quickly. In the class on airplane design they studied more than ten mock-ups of airplanes. She learned to recognize them inside and out. They learned the safety features of the models as well as the peculiarities of serving from the different galleys. At the end of the course they were tested in an actual flight situation. She was surprised at how some of the girls had to be shown several times. She and Brandy always volunteered to work together whenever there was a choice. Role playing was fun and Brandy gave her the hardest time imaginable.

"Sugar, I don't think you put enough vodka in this drink. Why can't I get up to go to the bathroom when that red light is on? I tell you I have *got* to go and I'm gonna embarrass myself and you, if you don't let me go right now."

"I know this is the fifth time I have asked, but could you get my bag for me one more time. It's halfway back on the other side of the aisle."

"You'd think a big airline like this could keep their food hot."

Many times Shielah would remember and smile, thinking that Brandy prepared her well for reality.

First aid training took two weeks and it was thorough. Instructions included medication, and how different medication mixed with alcoholic beverages, how to bandage, how to help a choking victim, treat puncture wounds, concussions, and do CPR. It was an intensive nurses training course. The girls were up late studying for the tests that went with the course. Brandy was the best at CPR. She was very efficient, firm and quick. Shielah was too gentle.

"Get tough," the instructor told her. "If you want to save someone's life, you have to be fast, like Brandy. Don't pussyfoot around, get that head back, both hands, both hands on his chest and push, harder, Shielah. All your weight. That's a girl. That's it. Again, keep pressing."

Her weight went down. She forgot to eat. She studied until the others made her turn off the light. And she bandaged and re-bandaged Brandy until she declared she felt like a mummy. But Shielah and Brandy both passed. Not everyone did. Three girls in the school went home. Every night Shielah looked in the mirror, while washing off her make-up, and marveled at the stranger looking back at her. But it was a happy stranger, more self-confident, more capable, happier than she had ever been—and succeeding!

The last leg of the course finally came—simulated on-the-job training. The girls were taken up in an airplane and they went over and over the location of all the safety features, the cooking facilities, the medical supplies, how to evacuate the plane from the emergency exits. In the DC-8 the pilot had the time of his life tossing them around. He dropped the plane ten thousand feet in seconds, simulating an air pocket. One girl had to use the air sick bag, but Shielah swallowed hard a few times and was all right. She turned to look at Brandy, sitting right behind her. The black girl grinned and stuck her thumb up. Shielah smiled back and followed suit.

The day they showed the film on an airplane crash Shielah almost lost it all. In the film, the plane crashed on landing. Attendants were manning long, rubber slides from the wings, pushing people into them, jerking them off at the bottom and pointing them in the direction of ambulances standing by. Then a fire broke out just above the tail section. The attendant jumped into the rubber slide herself and streaked away from the airplane. Fire spread instantaneously and, as the ambulances and crews were scrambling to move back, the structure burst into huge billowing flames. She covered her ears, her eyes, she wanted to scream. She began hyperventilating, and Brandy shoved her head down between her knees, and started rubbing her back, whispering in her ear.

"It's OK, Shielah, it's all right. Come on, get a hold on yourself." She kept rubbing her back until the lights came on. Then she grabbed her shoulder and dragged her to an upright position. Only a couple of trainees had seen. No one said anything until they were outside.

Shielah was not the only one affected by the movie. All the girls were very sober.

"Ladies," the instructor's voice began. "You must understand that you have to be prepared for any eventuality. You have the lives of hundreds of people in your hands and you'd better be prepared. This afternoon we will do a prepared landing. Tomorrow morning we will do an actual evacuation."

Over lunch, Shielah told Brandy about the fire that killed her parents. The black girl listened silently, imagining what it must have been like for a little ten-year-old to sit on a hillside and watch her home and parents burn up. Her big brown eyes filled with tears and, when Shielah looked at her, her own eyes overflowed and their friendship was cemented.

"Thanks for listening."

"Thanks for telling."

"It wasn't easy."

"I know it wasn't, but I'm glad you let me in."

The prepared landing instruction was carried out quietly and efficiently. The girls were to be prepared for any emergency. The girls were all still very sobered by the movie. There were no smart remarks or funny jokes, just intensive training, and attention to minute detail. Every seat belt checked. Oxygen masks in place. All carry-ons stowed securely. Don't sit down until every passenger is secured. Sit near the exit doors and be ready to slam your weight against them to make sure they open quickly.

It was almost over. Tomorrow was practice in evacuation. They were to learn the jump and slide routine. After that came a day of study, then the final testing. They had already put in requests for the cities in which they preferred to be stationed. Shielah chose Chicago. So did Brandy. They would room together.

The night before finals, Shielah called Stephen. She had talked to him only once during the summer, when he had called her grandmother's place just before she left for flight school. This time she called him.

"Fort Ord, California," she told the operator. She got through to the phone in his barracks.

"Stephen? Oh! Stephen Gailbraith, please." The noise in the background was distracting.

"It's Shielah. Yes, really. I'm almost finished with flight school, then I'm leaving. I don't know where. I've put in for Chicago. I have a friend who will room with me. Stephen . . . I . . . I miss you."

She could tell he had put his hand over the mouthpiece, and she heard his muffled voice say, "Shut up, you guys."

He responded after a moment, "Me too."

"I guess this is a bad time, huh?"

"It's just that I've got these clowns around me. I want to talk to you when I can get away alone." Whistles and catcalls in the background. "Can I reach you Friday night? I think I can get a pass and get out of here."

"I guess so. Finals will be over then."

"Good, I'll call you Friday night. Good luck tomorrow."

"Thanks. I could still flunk out."

"You won't. I'll . . . I'll keep my fingers crossed for you."

"Good, I need all the luck I can get. Goodbye," she said reluctantly.

"I'll call you tomorrow when we can really talk."

"Ok. Tomorrow. Goodnight."

She hung up, very unsatisfied. She had wanted something else. She needed his strong, warm arm around her shoulders. She was very nervous.

She sat at her window, looking out at the moon over the dark body of water in the distance. Six weeks and she had only been to the beach once.

One Saturday she and Brandy had started off walking. They had been picked up by Jeri and her date. Shielah roomed with Jeri. The girl was a redhead and just as saucy as her hair. Shielah hadn't liked her at first, but after several weeks of rooming together, found that Jeri's easy going style coaxed her out of her own reserve. Jeri was never home on the weekends. From the time school was over at 4:40 on Friday afternoon, until Sunday night at 10:30 curfew, she was either out or on her way out.

Shielah and Brandy rode to the beach with the couple—then separated. They didn't want to be a liability to Jeri. It had been a lazy, quiet day. The Florida beach was dazzling white, the grains of sand pure despite the millions of feet that crisscrossed the beach every day. Palm trees were set blocks away from the water, lining the yards of the beachfront bungalows. The beach itself was a brilliant ribbon of white edging the blue, undulating sea. Shielah found herself telling Brandy about Paulo and their encounter in Hawaii.

The other girl whistled. "Whew, sounds like a dream come true to me. You sure this guy is for real?"

"I think so. Sometimes now I wonder. It does all seem like a fairytale doesn't it? Do you believe in visions, Brandy?"

The black girl didn't even roll over. "Nope." That was it, no consideration. Just, "nope." Brandy was too practical to believe in any such illusionary stuff. "If you can't touch it, taste it, feel it, or love it, it isn't real."

"Don't you think there's anything besides this place, this earth? Don't you believe in life after death, or angels or anything?"

"Who knows, Shug? You can believe whatever you want to believe. But I tell you, the only thing that's real is what you can see and touch. You ever touched an angel or a vision?"

"Well, no, you can't touch them. But sometimes I see things."

Brandy opened one eye and shaded it to look at her. "What things?"

"People, mostly. I saw Stephen and me once. Not like we are now, but like we were before we came to earth. And I couldn't hear any words—but I could tell I was worried about coming, and he was reassuring me. Then once I saw my mother, like she is now, an angel, and she was brilliantly white, sort of like a brightly shining star. And there was someone else. I saw another woman when I was on the hillside and the farm was burning. I felt like I knew her, but I didn't. She was there to comfort me, and I've always remembered her. When I moved in with my grandmother I saw that woman again. It was my great, great grandmother, Charlotte. She was in a portrait that Grandma took out of the attic and hung in her bedroom. I swear I had never seen the picture before. But the woman was the same woman I saw the day my father and mother died."

A wave rolled in and soaked their towels, but Brandy wasn't paying attention to the waves. She was sitting up now, staring at Shielah. "Wait a minute, wait a minute. Whoa down. You lost me way back. What do you mean, 'before we came to earth?' There wasn't anything before we came to earth. We just started living. That's all."

Shielah shook her head. "I believe that we lived before this earth, in heaven with God, and that this body is just sort of a temporary house for our spirits. When we die our spirits will leave this body and go back to God. It's a perfect circle."

Brandy stared at her. "I haven't *ever* heard that before. Ever!"

"I grew up with it."

Brandy was examining the new thought. "Well, it does kinda make sense . . . a little. I always wondered how it happened that, just out of nowhere, a spirit would spring up, jump into a body and live happily ever after. I know there's a next life. Mama always tells us we must be good if we want to get into heaven."

"What she didn't tell you was that you had to be good to get into *life*. Into earth life. Only the best of Heavenly Father's children got to come to earth and get a body. The others followed the wrong guy and got kicked out of heaven."

The rest of the afternoon was spent telling Brandy about the war in Heaven led by Lucifer and his rebellious angels, the plan of salvation, and the three degrees of glory.

Brandy was respectful, though skeptical. "That's all new stuff on me, Shielah. Just tell me one thing. You believe we are all children of God?"

"Yep."

"Then why are some of His children white and some black?" The question reflected a lifetime of prejudice and injustice.

Shielah sat up, praying for the right answer. She looked Brandy straight in the eye. After a minute she said. "I don't think it matters to Him what color our skin is, or where we are born, or how smart we are. I think it just matters that we do the best we possibly can with what He has given us. Who knows what problem in our lives will teach us the love and faith we need to go back and live with Him some day." She looked off over the ocean and tears of understanding filled her eyes. "Maybe some learn it through a black skin, maybe some learn it by a fire."

Finals seemed like the longest day of her life. The questions were endless, multiple choice, diagrams, essays, true and false—every conceivable kind of question. They started at seven a.m. and were required to be finished by noon. There were a host of examiners who went right to work checking. By three o'clock the results were in. Ten of the girls failed and were out of the hotel and flying home within an hour. The other girls, including Shielah and Brandy, had two hours to get packed and ready to go. Along with the test results came the station assignments.

Shielah didn't get Chicago. There were too many others applying. Her assignment was New York. Brandy came bursting in the door with a paper in her hand and determination on her face.

"I'm not going to Atlanta. They can't put me in Atlanta. I won't go. I asked for Chicago, and, by damn, I won't fly out of the south."

Shielah went with her to see the department head. Brandy flung the paper down on the desk in front of the cool, efficient woman who ran the flight attendant training school.

"Please take a look at that, and tell me why headquarters assigned me to Atlanta. I specifically requested Chicago."

The woman glanced down at the paper, puzzled. "Atlanta is a beautiful city, and one of the easiest stations. You can fly all over the country from there. It would be a great experience for you. I don't know why you're so upset."

"Miss Borgstein, look at me! In Atlanta I'd have about as much chance as a snowball in . . . " She stopped and tried patiently to explain. "They wouldn't accept a black flight attendant. They have only recently let me eat at the same counter and go to the same bathroom with them. The whites would hate me and the blacks would accuse me of slumming. I tell you I'd be miserable. I've lived in the South all my life and I simply must get out. Please, can't you help me? Send me to Chicago, or better yet, New York with Shielah. Isn't there something you can do?"

"I think you're misjudging the situation. Blacks and whites have been living together for centuries. The black freedom movement has done its thing very well. For more than a decade now, blacks have enjoyed all the privileges of the white society."

Quietly, Brandy looked at her. "You ever been black?"

When the woman didn't answer, but still looked accusingly at her, Brandy asked quietly, "You want to try it for a while?"

Silence reigned and finally Miss Borgstein said, "Girls, will you wait in the outer office for a minute?"

When the two friends left, she put in a call to New World Airways central dispatching in New York, where the assignments were made. A short explanation and suggestion that perhaps her black graduate might have a better experience in New York brought the desired results.

Smiling, she opened the door and spoke to Brandy, "They've assigned you to New York."

A smile of relief broke over Brandy's dark face. She drew herself up erect and saluted the older woman. "Thank you, ma'am. Thank you very much."

They heard her say as they went out the door, "When you're right, you're right."

There was no waiting for telephone calls. By the time Stephen called Shielah's room at ten p.m., Florida time, she was circling New York City.

Chapter 5

*L*ast week's garbage didn't look any better the day after Labor Day than it had the day before. Paulo came up out of the subway, two blocks from his office on Eighty-Fifth Street, and kicked a stray can over to the edge of the sidewalk. Mayor Walker would take it on the chin come time for elections in October if he didn't clear up his garbage strike. The garbage workers were hitting for more money and newer equipment. Who wanted to pay it? On the other hand, who wanted week-old garbage perfuming the air? He covered his nose and mouth with a handkerchief and walked swiftly down the street, dodging other handkerchiefed faces. He thought it was rather comical, like a sci-fi movie with B grade actors walking around in masks to keep out the radiation ions that ate up red corpuscles. He was the only one smiling on the elevator.

"Stow it," Jim Polanski commanded him as he fell in beside him, walking the shiny hallway to Paulo's office at Vista Color, Inc. "You think this is funny? You should have lived in my neighborhood when I was a kid. Lettuce wasn't even edible 'til it had been thrown out once from somebody's kitchen."

"Thump, thump, thump," Paulo put his hand inside his suit coat and patted his heart. "Hear that? My heart is pumping Kool-Aid for you."

"Make it a little white wine and I'll buy it." Jim shut the door behind them.

Paulo's secretary came in. She was a mod dresser, with different color hair every month. Her make-up was right off Broadway, and she walked around with a pencil stuck somewhere in her hair. But she took shorthand in a day when the talent was dying, and she typed at one-twenty words-a-minute. More than that, she organized his life in the office and she never pried into his private life. Jim tried to date her, just to see what base she was on. He was not successful. She was beyond his charm. She only joined the human race for the Broadway set.

93

"Clarisse, have you seen that update on the research and development department? I've got a meeting with Zimmerman and Welsch today at eleven."

"I gave it to you last week. Wednesday. You said you'd look it over then."

"Well, I didn't get a chance. See if you can dig it up again."

"How's Mama?" Jim asked. Paulo knew what he was referring to. Carmella had felt some mild chest pains a week ago. "Just heartburn, just heartburn," she had reassured Roberto, but he had called Paulo just the same. Against her protests he admitted her to the hospital in Albany where tests revealed fibrillation of the heart. Paulo left the office early on Friday and spent the Labor Day weekend at home with Mama and Maria.

"She says she's fine. The doctor says she's not so fine. He has her on digitalis. She hates it. Ruth can hardly get her to take it. She only does it for Maria's sake."

Maria had taken more pills every day since she was a child than Mama would ever see. And she never complained. What was to complain? She had been an invalid since five years old and knew nothing else. Her legs were deformed with polio, her heart was weak, and her pancreas went into spasms without medication and sometimes even with it. "I'm the one the doctors practice on when they've got a new medicine," she joked good-naturedly. Carmella could hardly fuss at taking three digitalis pills a day in the face of Maria's calm acceptance of her fate.

Jim was sitting on the edge of the desk. "I tried to get up this weekend, but I couldn't get away."

Paulo glanced up at him, and shook his head. "What did Teresa do, handcuff you to her?"

Jim grinned and waggled his head, "Better than."

"Great. Mama says you'd better come see her before Thanksgiving, or she won't make your plum pudding special for you on the holidays." He glanced over the report Clarisse stuck on top of his other papers. "Is that it? Thanks, I won't let it get buried again. If Zimmerman tries to call me this morning, I am not in. I can't talk to him and prepare for this meeting too."

He turned back to Polanski. "I also can't talk to you and prepare for the meeting."

"OK, guess you don't have time for this either." Jim tossed a letter down in front of him. Paulo didn't understand at first. It had his name written in strange, wiggly letters, carefully made. The postmark was Clarksville, Utah.

While Paulo was tearing it open, Jim said, "I noticed it on your desk Friday after you'd gone. I thought it best not to leave an important piece of correspondence lying around. Besides, I thought it might get me some mileage."

Paulo didn't answer. He was reading a note!

"I'm sorry to have to return this. My granddaughter no longer lives at this address. She finished airplane school in Florida and is on her way to New York. I'm sure the operator could give you her phone number and address if you just asked." His own letter to Shielah was enclosed and still unopened. During the summer he had written a dozen letters; all of them had been returned. He looked up absentmindedly at Jim.

"What kind of mileage do you want?"

"An introduction to Elaina Maretti."

Paulo sat back, staring at his best friend. "Now, what do you want with that?"

Jim shrugged and fished around in his suit pocket for a cigarette. "You don't want her. I might as well have some fun."

"You ever hooked into a shark?" Paulo asked him.

"No." Jim said matter-of-factly, starting to light up. "You mind?"

"Uh huh. You know I hate the smell of your smoke."

"OK, OK. So I'll quit some day. She hasn't got any teeth I haven't."

"You might be surprised."

"I'm willing to risk it."

Paulo shook his head. "Her pond is too big for you, Jim. You're a hell of a guy, but she plays with the big fish. Really big fish, and they're not always the ones on the right side of the Internal Revenue Service."

"So?"

"So, it's not healthy. I don't wanta see you get mixed up with her."

"Big brother thinks she's all right for you."

"I disagree. If Roberto likes to play toesy with Maretti's friends, that's his business." He stuck a pencil in the air at Jim. "And *I never ask*. I don't want to know who he knows or why. That's why I'd never get involved with Elaina. We were childhood friends. That's all." He shook his head. "Forget her, Jim. New York is full of girls. Go get 'em, fella."

Jim stood up, disappointed. "Hey, do me a favor. Don't protect me from myself."

"Let's talk about it some other time. I've got work."

"Yeah. Later!"

Paulo watched him close the door, then picked up the telephone. "Zimmerman, who do you know in the airlines?"

"Everybody of course," Izzie Zimmerman spoke in a silky voice. He made it his business to know people in every major industry. That was how he got to be Senior Vice President.

"Kroc is the big man with Pan Am. Bellefond with TWA."

"What about New World?"

"New World? They're a takeover. Bought out American West three years ago and merged the two companies. Let's see, Douglas is out as of June. None of the original big boys are there any more." He hated to come up empty. Izzie prided himself on being on the inside. "I have a nephew on the counter though. He puts together all the big charter flights to Europe. What do you need?"

"I'm trying to find somebody. What's your nephew's name?"

Sam Jacobsen, my sister's boy. He'll do right by you. You gonna have that committee report at the meeting?."

"Yep," Paulo answered. "No sweat. Thanks Izzie."

He hung up and put in a call to New World Airways' main desk at Kennedy International.

Sam Jacobsen had a long, narrow face and looked a little like his uncle. He had discarded his spectacles for contacts and was squinting at Paulo across the table in the airport coffee shop.

"Who are you looking for?"

"An old friend of mine." Paulo smiled. "Dates clear back to last summer in Hawaii."

Sam nodded, "Oh. That old. Go back a long way together, huh?"

"Uh huh. How can I find out where she lives and her phone number?"

"I don't know. I guess the company has records, but they are confidential or the girls would have stew bums underfoot like mice."

"You can't get a peek at them?"

"Nope. Against the rules. I'd get a reprimand, maybe taken off the desk."

"You don't have friends in that office?" Paulo kept probing, not about to give up.

"No, none that would risk it for me. None that I'd ask."

Paulo was getting impatient. He pulled out his wallet to pay the lunch check, and folded up a twenty dollar bill, put it in a napkin and shoved the napkin over to Sam. "I don't want you to get in trouble. I don't want to do anything against policy. But I *have* to find her."

Sam put the napkin in his pocket. "Who is she?"

"Shielah Sorensen. She's new, just came in from flight school in Florida. She can't have been here more than a week. Don't you ever notice the new girls? Come on, Sam, you're not too married for that."

Sam Jacobsen blushed. He had been married for six months and only saw one beautiful woman in New York, Sarah Jacobsen, and she worked across the concourse from him in the Pan Am offices.

"There are about twenty new stewardesses that came in just before Labor Day."

"A blonde? Real pretty, with long—I mean long—blonde hair. Looks like a vacation poster?"

Sam nodded thoughtfully. "There was one like that. Big blue eyes, and kind of overawed by it all."

Paulo began to get excited. "That's her. It must be her. How can I find out her flight schedule? If I can't get her address or phone, I'll just come and be here when she arrives for a flight."

Sam shook his head. "She's too new to bid a line of flight and get it. She'll be standby for a while, at least until another new batch comes and some others move on."

"How does standby work? Doesn't she get any kind of a schedule?"

"Nope. She just stands by the phone and waits, literally. She can't go to the corner drugstore. She can't even wash her hair, because the crew desk could call at any second and she'll have to be at the airport in an hour."

After a second, a hunch came to Paulo. "You know anybody on that crew desk?"

Sam thought for a minute and started to smile. "Joe Cohen. Nice guy. Got married about the same time Sarah and I did." He glanced about casually. "There might be a price?"

The napkin between Paulo and Joe Cohen held a fifty dollar bill this time. He pushed it toward the crew desk attendant. Joe was embarrassed to pick it up.

"Joe, I am not a rapist, a bum or a kidnapper. I'm an executive with Sam's uncle's company, Vista Color. I met a girl in Hawaii last summer that I've been looking for all my life, and I fell in love with her. It's that simple. But I lost track of her. Now I know she's here in New York working for New World, and I have got to find her. Can you identify with that?"

Joe nodded. "I can, but I'm not supposed to help you. It's strictly against the rules. I could get canned."

"OK! OK, let's say a "friend" of yours needs to go to Chicago, and you happen to know when a certain flight is leaving. Could you call that friend and tip him off?"

It was carefully worded. Joe understood. "Yeah, I think I could. Of course, I don't know how long it would be before space available came open for Chicago."

"Let me ask you another question. If this same friend is looking for an apartment—a particular apartment—and hasn't had much success in getting a good one, if you knew of a place that would really fill the bill, could you give him the address?"

Joe didn't answer. Finally he said, "Maybe."

Paulo sat back in his chair and pushed his plate away. "Does your wife have birthdays?"

"What?" Joe asked.

"Birthdays, like when you take her out to a nice restaurant?"

"Sure, only we don't go out much."

"Charlemagne's is fine, really fine. She'd like it there, and I can guarantee it wouldn't be expensive. Complimentary, in fact." Paulo smiled.

"Mr. D'Agosta, I feel like an undercover agent." Joe Cohen was blushing furiously.

"Silly, isn't it?" Paulo chuckled. "But, seriously, I am looking for a nice apartment—a very special apartment—in a certain part of town."

"You better be straight with me." Cohen warned.

Paulo held up his right hand. "Straight as a ruler."

Joe put the napkin in his pocket. "I'll see. If I hear of a nice place for you, I'll let you know."

97

And that was the way Paulo picked Shielah out of the masses of New York City and sent her the first yellow roses she had ever received.

Flying into New York City was like taking a trip through Alice's weird looking glass. The city shimmered like pirate's jewels from Shielah's vantage point abvove, but the airplane circled Kennedy International for hours because there was an air traffic controller's slow-down. If they hadn't landed when they did, they would have had to leave the flight pattern and land in D. C. Their fuel was getting low. But they got in. Up close, the city still sparkled like a big, brassy lady, but acid smog hung over them due to the garbage strike. It was well after dark, and the girls were bone tired from the excitement of the day. Was it true they had been in Orlando, Florida just that morning? Shielah wondered if she would ever get used to the magic carpet she was newly licensed to work on.

Limousines waited to take them on their first tour of New York. Windows were all securely up, shutting out the smog and the heavy night air. But there was definitely an odor about the city, a combination of sea air blowing in off the Hudson and the pungent smell of humanity. Humanity in New York was like nothing Shielah had ever seen. The city was a solid maze of lights and people. It was ten thirty on a Friday night and people strolled, they walked, they zoomed the sidewalks on rollerskates, they lounged, they staggered, they hunted for scraps and they hailed cabs by the score.

Shielah's face was pressed against the window, like a little kid at a candy store. Brandy was right beside her. They could hardly take time to grin at each other for "oohing" and "ahhing" at the sights. At the sorth end of Central Park, Brandy said to Shielah, "I think I'm gonna fit right in around here."

Black faces carried the day (or in this case, the night). In every conceivable mode and color of dress they ambled down the sidewalks and gathered on the street corners. Shielah had no idea there were so many black people anywhere. Her only contact had been Brandy. Other than her, she had seen a few, a very few, black faces in downtown Salt Lake City. Brandy was waving ridiculously at nobody and everybody. "Hey, I'm here! I'm really in New York City. This is going to be Brandy's city before I'm through. I have come home, honey! This is it!"

Shielah laughed with her and waved too. What they were waving at, they had no idea. Certainly the New Yorkers on the sidewalks couldn't see their two faces in the limousine through the darkness. They were waving at their future, making friends with it, opening their hearts to all the adventure of whatever lay ahead. Suddenly, Shielah looked at Brandy, then she looked around at the other new flight attendants staring just as excitedly out the other windows. Then she allowed herself to comprehend the immensity of the city they were traversing and realized with satisfaction that she was not scared. In all this strangeness, she was not afraid.

Three months ago, she couldn't have said that. In six short weeks, she had left Clarksville behind and come to know that she was capable and competent. She shook Brandy's shoulder.

"Brandy! Brandy, we're gonna be good, aren't we? I mean, as attendants? We're gonna be great at it, the best."

"You'd better believe it, Shug. I've known it all along. I'm glad it finally hit you."

In the morning Shielah would walk outside and be dumbfounded with the unending stories of buildings mounting up to the sky, but tonight they were a magic land of lights. She fell in love at first sight!

She awoke between silk sheets in the Lady Grace Hotel. Not too soon, she wouldn't jump up too soon. She rolled over, savoring the silky touch on her body. Sitting up, she could look out the window and see Central Park. The driver had pointed it out to them last night. It was the pride of New York— the only natural greenery in a concrete jungle.

"Brandy, wake up! How can you sleep when New York is waking up?"

"Waking up? Are you kidding, New York never sleeps, but I have to sometime."

"Sometime. Not all the time! Wake up and feel these sheets. I've never slept between silk sheets before. Have you?"

"No, but I think I could get used to it."

"And this is my first, my very first, luxury hotel!"

Brandy grinned impishly at her. "I have this feeling that 'you ain't seen nothin' yet'."

"Me too. So let's go see it."

On the sidewalk, Shielah couldn't keep herself from staring upward. Obviously she was a tourist. New Yorkers never looked up. She didn't care that she looked like a tourist. She had to see it all. It was simply phenomenal. Can buildings stand that tall? Mountain cliffs, yes—they were a natural part of the earth. Mountains she knew. But buildings— giants that men had made—giants with paned faces would take her a while to comprehend.

They walked for blocks, stopping to look in shop windows. They didn't take time to go in and browse. That would be another day. This was their first day. It would never come again, and they wanted to use it to see everything they could. Furs and diamonds, imported dresses, beauty make-over salons. The girls giggled like a couple of kids over that. They had been made over once. Would the salon reverse the process? Doormen greeted cars and ushered well- dressed men and women into elegant hotels and apartments. It was Saturday. Businessmen with their briefcases were off the streets. Their wives were out shopping and luncheoning. Traffic whizzed by them, dashing madly for the airport, or the ferry, or the tunnel, or the country beyond the hubbub of the city.

In Central Park, the bag ladies were having a heyday. The uncollected garbage was a windfall for them. Shielah and Brandy watched an old woman go through three big, green bags of garbage she had hauled into the park from behind one of the apartment buildings. She collected bottles of all sizes, labels she cut off of boxes and cans. Once or twice they saw something shiny disappear in the voluminous pockets of the black overcoat she wore, although it was one of the hottest days of the summer. That was one aspect of the city Shielah never remembered with relish—the bag people. Later she would see them still picking through garbage in the snow.

The girls walked on. The park was the gathering place for New Yorkers. At one time or another during the year, everyone came to Central Park. It was huge and like an injection of normalcy serum reminding them that beneath the concrete there was earth—earth that mysteriously grew trees, bushes, flowers, and grass, if given half a chance. Even the smog didn't kill the Park. It survived muggings, killings, gang wars, garbage, and acid rain. And New Yorkers rejoiced in that fact, though not overtly, of course. They seemed to take it very much for granted. But they always came back.

Bordering the park up to 100th Street were expensive, exclusive homes. Above that, Spanish Harlem emerged and gradually blended into black Harlem at the northern end of the park. Lining the park at the southern end were sidewalk cafes, student hangouts, and strange little shops with curiosities from all over the world. They smelled pungently of perfume, incense, tea, coffee, pipe tobacco, leather and new cloth. And oh, the bookshops! There, Brandy had to pull Shielah away. She would have spent their precious time standing and poring over shelf after shelf of remarkable books.

They walked and walked until their feet were sore. At last, they hailed a cab and gratefully rode back to the Lady Grace. Each girl had her turn at soaking in luxury in a perfumed bubble bath, then napping. And at eight o'clock they met the rest of the girls in the hotel lounge, then went as a group to dinner. Shielah was glad that night for Mr. Danilov. Somehow the sophisticated look he had given her in Orlando had seemed too ultra, but in this setting it was perfect. "Bless you, Danilov," she said under her breath as she surveyed herself with approval in the full length mirror of the ladies room.

The girls were given two weeks of luxury life at the Lady Grace and, by then, were expected to have found an apartment of their own. None of them could afford the rent of a nice place by themselves, so they split off into groups of four. Jeri Rhodes, Shielah's redhaired roommate in Orlando, was in the group sent to New York. Brandy, Jeri, and Shielah went looking for a place together and found a two bedroom apartment on Eighty-Third Street, not far from the U. N. Building, in the heart of the fashionable business district. It was more expensive than they could afford, even among the three of them. But it was right on the main line to the airport, close to everything, and young executives of every hue and height swarmed about the place. They loved it. Besides, there was even a doorman for their safety, though they later came to realize he was nearly always drunk. On the last day before they had to sign the contract and put down the money, Jeri came up to Shielah's hotel room with a new roommate. Jeri was very excited about recruiting her. Shielah was relieved. Brandy spent her time staring out the window. The girl was Marci Chestney from Little Rock, Arkansas. Her southern drawl hit Brandy like Mickey Mantle's bat.

Marci looked from Jeri to Shielah, then to Brandy. She was obviously surprised at a black girl being included in the group. She had never even eaten lunch beside a black person in Little Rock. Not that she had any prejudice, mind you, but she thought they preferred to stay within their own group. After a slight hesitation, she extended her hand to Brandy.

"Pleased to meet y'all. I was afraid I'd never find myself an apartment. I was about ready to ask for an extension here at the hotel. Jeri says you have a place on the boulevard. I sure hope we'll all get along fine. Where y'all from?"

Of her own accord, Brandy wouldn't have touched the southern white girl. She caught the look in Marci's eyes, and felt the slap she had experienced dozens of times as a child. But she glanced at Shielah, and she couldn't bear making a scene in front of her. So she solemnly shook hands with the girl and then went to stand by the window. Shielah understood instinctively what was happening in Brandy's mind, but felt that she could make it all right. Prejudices fade, even Brandy's. Besides they wouldn't all be together in the apartment very frequently, or so they had been told. Marci gave them a check for her part, and the foursome was formed.

Brandy went out first. The crew desk called in with a flight to Pennsylvania for her. From there she went on to Detroit, then Deluth, back to Akron, then home. But by the time she staggered in, exhausted and wrinkled, Shielah had been sent on her first flight. She flew into D. C., then Charlotte, down to Jacksonville, Miami and finally home. The puddle jumpers were the worst possible lines of flight. They kept you hopping every moment and the attendants were ragged when they dropped into bed. It was one a.m. when Shielah crawled into her bed. When she awoke in the morning, Brandy and Jeri were both gone. She wanted to tell someone about that first day, but Marci was still a stranger. Consciously, Shielah made the choice to open up communication.

"Have you gone out yet?" she asked Marci.

"Yesterday. It was just a short flight up to Vermont and back. I hardly had a chance to do anything but shake hands and get blankets for little old ladies. I liked it, though. I think it's fun doing all that stuff I've seen real attendants do." She frowned. "Not that we aren't 'real'. "

Shielah laughed. "I know what you mean. I don't feel 'real' yet either. Although if I get many more days like yesterday, I'm gonna feel 'real' in a hurry."

"Where'd you go?" Marci asked.

"The coast—D.C., Charlotte, Jacksonville and Miami. Watch out for the puddle jumpers."

"They run your fanny off?"

"That and a little more. I was afraid I'd be nervous, but there wasn't time. It was just like flight school, only worse. The senior kept me too busy

101

to think about being nervous. Up and down, up and down, fasten seatbelts, unfasten seatbelts, blankets and drinks, and I spilled Seven-Up on a lady's sleeve. I was lucky. Could have been her lap. Then I had to wrestle a carry- on away from a seventy-year-old grandma. It had a dog in it. Would you believe that? She brought her poodle in a big beach bag. About half way between Jacksonville and Miami, it began to bark. Poor thing, he was probably suffocating. The poor woman. I felt so sorry for her. She was almost frantic about her dog. I sat by her most of the way and listened to her life story."

It was only the first of many puddle jumpers, and Shielah often thought back on her first interview when the screener had told her it would be the hard work . . . but the most memorable year of her life.

One morning at the end of September, Shielah opened her eyes after a long exhausted sleep to see yellow roses in a vase beside her bed. She was nonplussed. Where had they come from? There was no note with them. She asked Jeri, who was up doing her nails, waiting for a call to come in.

"Don't know where they came from. Ben, the doorman, sent them up, saying they were delivered for Miss Shielah Sorensen. I think he stole one. There's only eleven."

She knew it would not have been Buck or Grandma. Stephen, by now, must be either out on the Pacific or already in Vietnam. Who else but Paulo? She could picture him as she first saw him, standing by the railing at the hotel in Hawaii. That image had returned to haunt her many times that summer, but she had decided it was best to drop the whole thing. He had an unsettling effect on her. She had never let down her guard so far with anyone before, and she didn't want to again.

Three days later Ben handed her a dozen white roses as she came back to the hotel after shopping. Again there was no note, but they kept the thought of Paulo alive in her mind. She began to grow anxious. If he knew her address, he must know her telephone number. She didn't want to talk to him. She didn't want to see him. She was not his "golden girl", and it was best to let it drop. She gave the word to the girls that she would not talk to any man that called, unless it was the crew desk.

"Aren't you being a little unromantic, Shielah?" Jeri asked.

"That's right," Marci added her bit of wisdom. "After all, if a man's got money for flowers three times a week, he can't be all bad." They giggled at that.

"Marci, you'd just love him. Paulo D'Agosta is rich and handsome, black hair and delicious brown eyes. He's just your type. And he is very romantic. That's the problem, he is too romantic. I'm not ready for that stuff yet. Flying is about as romantic as I care to get."

"You sick?" Jeri asked.

"No, I just love my work. After I get tired of that, maybe then I'll be ready for a man."

"Got anything against double dating? Eddie has a friend he wants to fix you up with."

"When?"

"Whenever you're free?"

"Who's the friend?"

"T. J. Barry. He works baggage claims."

Shielah wasn't very interested.

"Listen, he's cute, really he is. Brown hair and blue eyes, and he's had his eye on you."

"I don't have any time off until next week."

"He'll keep." Jeri eyed her critically. "You know you really should go out. You can't work all the time. You need some comic relief. Don't you know how to have fun?"

Marci answered for her, "I can teach her," she drawled softly.

Shielah had the uncomfortable feeling they both knew far more about the "fun" of dating than she did. If it was really just for fun it was all right. Anything beyond that she wasn't interested in.

"You're right. I probably do need to start dating. I'll go if we are with you." She hastily added, "But not alone. I won't go alone with him. I really hate blind dates. It'd just be a favor to Eddie."

Her first date was a disaster. T. J. Barry was the Don Juan of the baggage room. Every female from age thirteen to sixty came under his scrutiny. They either passed or they didn't. He was merciless in his judgments. A ten was his highest rating. Shielah rated a nine in looks. By the end of the evening, she had dropped to an overall average of three— there are other things to be considered besides looks.

The two couples went to a wonderful little corner restaurant—the Knickerbocker Saloon. It was teeming with people, half of them girls, and T. J. kept busy all night ogling anything in a skirt, while trying to convince Shielah he was actually interested in her. He didn't succeed. After dinner, Eddie suggested dancing. Shielah wanted to go home. Then T. J. began his irresistible approach, an arm around the shoulders, suggestive whispers in the ear, a little nuzzling. He was so transparent Shielah was disgusted. She stood up and accidentally stepped on his foot. He jerked back and lost his balance. The spindly chair went over and he floundered on the floor. Jeri was embarrassed by the scene. Shielah was not.

They left Eddie and Jeri at the restaurant, and T. J. took her home by the subway. The waiting ramps were still teeming with people at eleven o'clock, and they didn't try to speak over the noise of the trains. In silence, he walked her home from the subway exit. Just before they reached the door of the apartment, he stopped her and asked to come up. She couldn't believe it.

"Go check your baggage," she told him coolly. "You've misplaced the one called courtesy. But I'm sure you'll find it on the streets. That's just the place for what you want."

He grabbed her by the wrist and pulled her back, and up against him.

"You owe me one," he said gruffly, determined to get at least a kiss.

"One more, you mean," and this time she slammed her high heel down on his foot on purpose. Before he could recover, she was dashing past Ben and into the elevator. So much for T. J. Barry and blind dates.

The call came through Paulo's office at three-thirty on Thursday afternoon at the end of October. "There is space available to Chicago on New World Flight 326 at 5:20 today, if you can make it."

If he could make it! Good point. Traffic would be murder. Paulo grabbed his coat, forgot his briefcase, and dropped his day's work.

"I may not be in early tomorrow, Clarisse. I've got a quick trip to Chicago."

The doorman signalled a cab and Paulo jumped in.

"Can you get me to Kennedy by 5:00?"

Cabbie O'Brian was whistling. "Be tight," he commented, starting off with a jerk. Then he called back over his shoulder, "but we'll make it." The clock in his cab showed three-forty.

Paulo sat back, trying not think of her, trying not to be nervous. He had been right, the traffic was murder. The cab meter kept ticking. O'Brian was still whistling. Paulo saw her a dozen times in cabs they passed. This is stupid, he told himself. I can't imagine anything. If she had wanted to see me she would have called. She knows where I am. Vista Color is not hard to find. She wouldn't have had to bribe anyone.

He was not really surprised that she didn't want to see him. He knew when they parted in Hawaii that she would put him out of her life if she could. He disturbed her. She had embarrassed herself with him. She didn't know what to make of him and was too inexperienced to try to understand their relationship.

He paid the cabbie at 5:03 and strode up to the New World desk. "Pardon me," he said, discreetly pushing past a couple hesitating before the counter. "I'm going to miss a very important flight. I need a ticket on Flight 326, first class." He got his ticket and ran down the concourse toward the open door at the end.

Shielah was at the main entrance to the airplane, greeting, smiling, and taking tickets. It was her usual assignment. The senior attendants often gave it to her because the passengers responded to her so pleasantly. More than once in the last month she thought, "If my friends could see me now!" Sometimes she hardly believed it herself. She who had never had any self-confidence with her peers found that she enjoyed meeting and helping total strangers.

She thought the last passenger was on. "No," Margene told her, "there's one more coming on, and he'd darn well better hurry."

She was looking down the long, dim, hallway, impatiently tapping her foot. He came around the corner swiftly, his coat fluttering open, but he slowed to a deliberate walk when he saw her. Her hair was different. He liked it. Her face was older—more make-up, more sophisticated. He didn't know if he liked that. Her eyes were the same, only more expressive than he remembered. He almost laughed, for disbelief, astonishment, panic and pleasure all showed in her eyes. She was struck dumb, staring at him. Paulo stopped before her and smiled with satisfaction.

"First class, please."

She couldn't answer him. She was too astounded. He gave her his ticket. She looked down at it numbly, and saw his hand touching hers. She looked back up at him, full into his warm brown eyes. Her heart was pounding as it had last June when she saw him for the first time on the balcony of the hotel. She felt as though she were falling from a great height.

Carefully she tore the ticket. "Step in to your left, sir."

His smile was calm and satisfied. "You made it," he said.

"So did you, sir . . . barely," Margene said pleasantly, taking charge of the situation. "Right this way, please."

He stepped inside and Shielah closed the door after him. She bolted it securely, then moved into the coach section to give the oxygen mask demo and the evacuation instruction. Paulo sat in the back row of the first class section where he could see her through the open curtain. He watched her intently, his enjoyment never faltering. She stumbled slightly on the instructions, advised them of "no smoking until after takeoff", and sprang toward her seat by the back curtain, hastily sitting and buckling up for take-off. He was behind her. She couldn't see him, but she knew he was just behind the curtain. She could feel him, and she could feel his thoughts holding her. Once she moved the curtain just a bit so she could look at him. He glanced over his shoulder and saw the curtain move.

Why did he have to come? she asked God, in the silence of her heart. If you want me for Stephen, you shouldn't have let him come. I thought I had everything worked out. Stephen is the one I want to marry. Who is this man? Why has he come into my life . . . twice now? What am I going to do?

The flight was not long, just two hours into Chicago's O'Hare. It was long enough, however, for Paulo to insist that she sit down for a minute beside him.

"I can't. We're not supposed to fraternize with the passengers."

"You can be polite and accommodate a customer can't you."

She glanced toward the galley. "Maybe, after I serve drinks."

She knew he watched her every movement while she pushed the cart and mixed drinks, handing them to the passengers. She tried not to look at him, though she knew he had no such reservations.

The more he watched her, the more pleased he was with what he saw. She had changed. No longer unsure of herself, although he had flustered her badly, she did her job quite competently, even graciously. She smiled more than she had in Hawaii. He knew it was required, but it was good for her. When she got to him, he flustered her even more.

"I didn't think you could be any more beautiful. I was wrong. That smile becomes you. Sit down, won't you?"

"Really . . . I shouldn't."

"Do anyway." She still hesitated, so he asked, "Shall I ask the head stewardess for permission?"

"No!" she replied, always careful to keep her private life to herself.

"Just for a minute," he repeated.

She glanced around. Everyone was busy. Her own assignment was done. The curtain was closed. She sat down. Immediately she wished she hadn't. She was overwhelmed with the nearness of him, and embarrassed with the strength of her feelings.

He was so natural with her that she felt like a little girl in comparison.

"You do it all very well. Do you like flying as you thought you would?"

"Yes, mostly." She was nervously tearing up a napkin in her lap. "I can't believe that of all the flights to Chicago, you got on this one. I didn't think. . . . " She stopped, afraid to say too much.

"You didn't think you'd ever see me again. Was that how you wanted it?"

She steadfastly refused his eyes. They had too much power over her. "Yes," she admitted quietly.

"I was afraid of that. But that wasn't how I wanted it."

"I got your flowers," she said, abandoning all pretense.

"Good. I hoped you'd guess who they were from."

"You're a thoughtful man."

"Persistent too. Have dinner with me tonight."

"I can't."

"Why? Are you flying right back?"

"Yes," she lied.

"Really?" He could see right through her.

"I have things to do."

"Nothing better than a delicious dinner by the lake."

"No, I can't. I just can't."

"I know a beautiful spot. You can see the lake from the windows, and the food is perfect."

"I have to be up early for a six a.m. flight."

"We won't be late."

"Can't you take 'no' for an answer, Mr. D'Agosta?" She was becoming exasperated.

"Not where you're concerned. You have a temper, Miss Sorensen! You surprise me."

"Yes, and it particularly flares around presumptuous people."

"I'm not presumptuous and you know it. I just want to have dinner with a beautiful blonde tonight, and I don't have a date yet. Have you?"

She couldn't help it. She had to return his smile. Once before she had softened . . . his knee touched hers and she jerked back.

"We'll be landing soon. How long will it take you to get off after the passengers leave?"

"It takes about an hour. We have to check all the seats and compartments. But I'm going straight to the hotel afterwards."

"I'll wait for you at the top of the escalator down."

106

"Don't. I won't be there."

"I'll wait."

"You'll be disappointed."

"I'll wait."

It was inevitable. She came.

The drive out to Pierre's from O'Hare was not as much of an ordeal as she had anticipated. He asked a lot of questions about training school, and she found herself talking, telling him all about it, then about Brandy, and even the Danilov incident. In fact, they were at the restaurant before she realized it, and he helped her out of the Hertz rented car.

Opening the door, he put out his hand to her and she put her smaller one in his. With the slightest bit of tension, he pulled her to her feet. The easy talk slipped away. No smile came between them. They stood looking into each other's eyes, seeing all. He wouldn't have let her look away if she had wanted. But she didn't. Looking at him so directly was a pleasure she hadn't allowed herself. She saw his love, and he saw her ambivalence—wanting, yet not wanting.

"I won't press you, Shielah."

"Good."

"Can we go on that basis?"

"Maybe."

"Someday you'll want me to love you. That's the only way I'll have it . . . if you want it too."

The moon slipped from the grip of the clouds and shone dazzlingly on the lake for a few minutes. It also shone brilliantly on her face. He was close enough. One small movement and he could kiss her. The desire was almost overwhelming, but he watched her eyes. He thought he saw a softening. Then she dropped her gaze and her mouth trembled, but he turned away. No, she would have to want it too. And she would have to admit it.

She didn't admit it until she had finished her prayers that night and lay awake between cool sheets. Then she whispered softly to herself. "How can I want him so? He touches me and I turn to jelly. I can't see him again, ever. He is the most dangerous man I know."

Ah, but danger . . . she knew nothing of it yet.

Chapter 6

*D*ear Shielah,

I thought boot camp was bad! Actually it wasn't *that* bad, mostly just getting us into shape. I couldn't believe how soft I'd become during my mission and college. I had a sergeant who told us that if the government had wanted college boys over here, they'd have sent Yale to teach us Freud. If he knew you had been a student, he really poured it on. So I was the lucky recipient of double duty most of the first month. After he saw that I wouldn't complain or drop, he gave up and treated me like all the rest, merely rotten!

I tried to call your Flight School in Orlando, but you were already gone. They must clear you out fast. I didn't know, of course, but instinct— faith— whatever, something told me that you passed and were on your way to the future. I got your last letter about your friend Brandy, just before we cleared out too. She must be good for you. I approve.

I've received a couple of letters from Buck. What a shock! I'd better save them and frame them—they could be worth money someday on the 'rare object' market. You don't know how much it means to get back to camp after a patrol and to find a letter from home waiting. It's the only normalcy of life over here. I sometimes wonder if Spanish Fork really exists, and the Main St. Movie and the Frostee Freez. Maybe they are just a dream and I'll never get out of this reality. I'm sure a long way from the Frostee Freez.

I'm not going to tell you about life in the barracks. After censoring, there wouldn't be enough to fill a half page, and uncensored . . . well, you wouldn't want to read it. Only the beautiful Vietnamese people make this at all bearable. Most of the guys can't see it like that. All they see is the jungle, the war, but I try to keep in mind that I am here for these people.

And they are worth it! They are tiny (at least compared to me), and delicate looking. But that's just looks. Boy, are they tough! They bend, they sway, they adjust, but they don't break. They can exist on the smallest amount of food you can imagine. And food like I wouldn't give my dog back home. All the good food is saved for the Americans. The restaurants buy it for the GI's. The Vietnamese people get the old produce, and souring meat. And when the fellas from the barracks go into Saigon, they act like kings. Of course that is how the people treat them. 'Sir this', and 'sir that', the best food, the prettiest girls, and right-of-way on the streets. What a mixed-up world! And the Americans are too young and dumb to realize that those are privileges, privileges accorded them by people whose right it is to dominate their own city. It is due to their courtesy that twenty-year-old boys are treated like kings.

Well, I've pounded my soapbox enough. I'm sending this to Clarksville, trusting Buck to forward it to you. By the way, I suppose you know that the girl he met in Hawaii is over at BYU now. Buck says he thinks he's fallen in love. That's something new. Never thought the bug would bite him. She sounds like a pretty straight arrow. Maybe she can do something with him.

I wanted to tell you on the phone that night how much I miss you. But there were too many listening ears. I wish I had a picture of you, a current one. I do have one in my wallet, but you would die if you saw it. It was of you and Buck when you were about fourteen and he was just graduating. If you don't want me showing that around, you'd better send me a more recent one.

Miss you,
Love you,
Stephen

Grandma had forwarded Stephen's letter and sent one of her own, confirming that Bridget was indeed at BYU and Buck was spending so much time dating she was afraid he wouldn't graduate in the spring.

Shielah looked up from her letter. Brandy was home, for a change, at the same time she was. She was doing her nails, humming along to the radio, and occasionally breaking out in a throaty voice to join in on a Neil Diamond song. I made the right decision, Shielah thought. College would never have given me this.

Then her eye caught on the red roses on her table. Of course, I also wouldn't be in this pickle if I had gone to college, she mused. Paulo would have quietly faded out of the picture. It was two weeks since the trip to Chicago, and she had been too busy to see him. The crew desk kept her hopping. Paulo didn't give up, though. The flowers came twice a week, and the last bouquet had a photograph of her enclosed. It was one of the few he had taken at twilight. She studied the picture minutely, reliving the memory of that day. He might cherish it, but she didn't. The temple part, that was good, and even the waterfall and dinner. But whatever had possessed her to go to that beach and dance for him . . . and then to be discovered by Buck, of all people! Her face hardened as she thought of it and the argument that followed.

Well, he was wrong, wasn't he? Life had not torn the pretty little wings off the butterfly. The china doll was still quite intact. She grew up thinking he petted and pampered her because he loved her. She hadn't guessed it was because he pitied her and thought she was incapable of standing on her own. She was not a cripple and she was determined to prove that to her own satisfaction, if not to his. A sudden realization dawned on her—anger is the great revealer. Love is too kind to be a friend. It hides the truth. It cushions, where the truth is painful. It will protect you from reality as long as it can. But anger—it's a cruel friend, it tells the bitter truth. It may be painful, but sometimes it is necessary if you are to survive and grow.

Two weeks later she got another letter from Stephen.

Dearest Shielah,

Patrol is over and I am ready to drop. Even if you don't get shot at, the tension takes all your energy. Tonight was quiet on our Eastern Front. This place would be gorgeous if it weren't for pint-sized terrorists hiding in the villages and bushes. No smog. There isn't even a Vietnamese word for smog. The closest they can get is 'dirty.' It's humid, heaven knows, and the air sometimes feels so heavy I can hardly breath. I'm too much used to the thinner mountain air. But the green of this land is unbelievable. You think the Salt Lake Valley greens up in the summer. It's still a desert by these standards. The foliage here is so thick that you often can't see the black earth beneath your feet. You push your way through a sea of green and come out into a clearing—surrounded by more green. Sometimes I swear it rains green drops.

Someday, when this asinine war is over I'd like to come back here, and walk through the villages without being afraid of being blown up. I'd like to hold a little black-haired kid on my knee and not wonder if I killed his mom or dad in the last skirmish. This is not my bag, Shielah. I was born to love the wilderness. I guess my dad passed that on to me. And that love serves me well over here. But I was not born to kill God's children, whatever their color or whatever their crimes.

I'm sick tonight! I need to think of you and that day on the mountain.

(Then further down the page in small, wavering handwriting) Did I tell you I love you? I do . . . I do.

Stephen

Tears filled her eyes. What did he look like now, in his dirty, army uniform? Did he wear one of those gray-green hats? Did he still walk with that easy, rolling, long-legged gait? Tears spilled over onto her cheeks helplessly. It wasn't fair. He shouldn't have been the one to go. He was such an idealist. War needs hard-headed practical men, but it takes the idealists too.

No one was at home today besides her, and she dropped down beside her bed onto her knees. Her prayers, when she remembered to say them, hadn't been very fervent lately. Life was fast and she had adjusted to the pace. Things were coming more and more easily to her. She was beginning to get better flights. New York beckoned and she followed, falling more and more in love with the excitement and variety that existed here. Prayers were no longer as necessary to her daily ability to cope. She thought sometimes of what Grandma had said about remembering her prayers, but they had become perfunctory.

Today they were not. She realized with shame that she had not been praying for the right person. She didn't need any more "please bless me's". Stephen was in danger and she rarely even thought about it. Her love for him was sure and steady, and it flooded over her with such a sweetness. Tears ran unrestrained down her face and dampened the coverlet of the bed. This love she did not fight. It was unthreatening and as natural as breathing.

The door opened and Brandy came in with Jeri.

"Hey Shielah . . . oops. Sorry!" They backed out of the room.

She got up from her knees. "No, it's all right."

"What's wrong?" Brandy did not pussyfoot around.

Shielah handed her the letter. Jeri read it over Brandy's shoulder. They both finished at the same time and looked up at her together. Their sympathy brought the tears again and the three of them sat down on the couch together.

"That's gotta be tough," Jeri said.

"I've been so selfish," Shielah confessed.

"How have you been selfish?" Jeri asked.

"I'm just a dutiful pray-er. Do you think I've been praying for No! I've been praying mostly for myself. 'Help me make it through this day.' How silly! He is the one in danger of not making it through the day. He's not just battling subway crowds. He's battling for his *life*. I have no idea how many people he has had to kill, but I can tell it's eating him alive. I don't know how he is going to handle it. He believes, just as I do, that these are all . . . even the communists . . . children of God. That makes them brothers and sisters, and he's supposed to kill them. I don't think he had ever even killed a pheasant before he went over there. It isn't fair! It isn't fair!"

The girls looked silently at each other. Reality was very close now and the pretties of the inviting city seemed rather paltry.

"Life isn't fair," the black girl offered at last. "Who ever said it was?"

"I don't know. Life has been good to me," Jeri countered. "I can't remember anything really tragic happening. And it looks OK up ahead too. Maybe there's such a thing as 'the breaks' and you can't question why."

"I think you *make* the breaks," Brandy said.

"I think you endure them," Jeri replied.

"I don't believe in enduring. I believe in *living!*" Brandy was determined.

Jeri gave a short laugh. "I believe in one step more. I believe in loving."

Shielah had been quiet. Now she spoke. "I hope Stephen believes in all three." She looked back and forth at her friends. "What if the breaks don't go his way?" The girls were silent. They didn't know how to answer her fear. They couldn't refuse the pleading in her eyes when she asked them, "Will you pray for him too?"

They knelt beside the couch and she helped them to pray. Neither of the girls had said prayers since they had been youngsters. Both were very self- conscious, but they had also come to love Shielah and they knew she needed them now. Jeri doubted God would pay much heed to her prayer, they hadn't been very conversant for a long time. Brandy thought He'd have to be impressed that she was praying—actually praying—for a white boy. Someday she'd tell Mama and her mother would be proud. It was a moment of closeness that Shielah rarely shared with anyone, but the old walls of self-protection had crumbled more and more in the last few months. She had gained a new security within herself and was able to open up in ways she never had before.

It was the end of October before Paulo saw her again. All his calls had been answered with "Shielah's not home." He was suspicious, but there was nothing he could do. When the phone rang Tuesday morning, Marci was still in the shower. Shielah had to get it. It could be the crew desk for Marci. Shielah had three days off, so it wouldn't be a flight for her.

She recognized his voice immediately.

"So, you do live there!"

"Only sometimes. Most of the time I'm suspended in air."

"I believe it. I've heard 'Shielah's not home' so many times I wondered if we were talking about a ghost. Don't you ever get time off?"

She was cautious. "Sometimes."

He guessed, "Are you off today?"

Reluctantly she admitted, "Yes, I am."

"And I'll bet you're hungry."

"No, actually not. I get by on just one meal a day."

"Don't tell me you've already had it."

She chuckled, "No, not at seven a.m. I'm not even out of bed yet."

"You're going to sleep on your only day off in two months?"

"Well, I thought I'd sleep a *little.* That was before I was so rudely awakened."

"I won't apologize. Get dressed, we'll go to the museum. Have you been to the Metropolitan Art Museum?"

"No, I haven't done too much sightseeing. They keep me hopping."

"You'll love this place. It takes two days to go through it. Everything strange and beautiful and wonderful in art is there."

"I really just planned a nice, sensible day of shopping. Staples, you know, like food and toothpaste."

"How dull! The Met is more fun, and you're only a few minutes from it. I'll pick you up in two hours. It opens at nine. We need to start early if we're going to see much."

"Paulo," she interrupted him in exasperation. "I can't keep seeing you."

" 'Keep' seeing me. You sound like it's been a regular occurrence."

"Well it can't *get* to be a regular occurrence."

"It's been almost a month since the last time. Next time we can make it only a week, and then it certainly won't be regular. Come on Shielah, stop being so afraid of everything. I'm not going to bite you. And, regrettably . . . I'm not going to seduce you. I promised you that in Chicago."

She yawned. "Don't you work?"

"Not if I have something better to do."

"Don't you have any sympathy for someone who does?"

"Not an ounce. Get up! I'll be on your doorstep in two hours."

He knew all the museums in town worth knowing, and he was on the board of directors at the Met. He walked her legs off there. He had warned her it would take two months to properly see it all, and he was right. They ate lunch in the Museum of Modern Art, which was across the park. Later in the afternoon he took her to the Guggenheim. She was not very well versed in art, but she liked almost everything she saw with the exception of extreme modern art. Even Paulo couldn't explain it to her satisfaction. But Renoir and Monet, they were her favorites. She lingered there until he pulled her away.

He was as good as his word. He didn't press her. He didn't stand too close. He didn't touch her, except as a courtesy when opening doors and helping with her chair. And he was so adept at putting her at ease. It was a cool November day and the wind was nippy, but not unpleasant. They walked along, window shopping and talking. He told her about his childhood days on the West End and made her laugh. Then he went on to his first attempt at skiing, when they moved out to the country. He was the most entertaining when he talked about Mama and Maria and memories of his Papa.

Later they stopped at Giorgio's for a late lunch. "I'm not sure Papa would have approved of you . . . at least not for me. He thought only Italian or Portuguese girls were beautiful, or so he said around Mama. But Mama, she is ready to palm me off on anyone who comes along. She constantly reminds me that I decided *not* to be a priest. So when am I going to bring home a nice girl for her to meet?"

113

"I'm sure there must be plenty of nice girls for you to take home, Paulo."

"There are. I confess, I haven't been a priest."

She looked down at her dinner plate. He was studying her. "Maybe someday you'll meet my mother. She's a delight, even in her crotchety old age. And she still rules the family with an iron hand. I go home as often as I can, but it's never often enough for her. 'Paulo' she says to me, 'why dona you stay home and runa that busy-ness of yours from a decent family house?' " He imitated his mother's Italian accent perfectly.

Shielah smiled. "You have a place in the city?"

"Umm hmm. It's not too far from yours. I have a view of Central Park. How do you like your place?"

"I like it. It's convenient. The doorman leaves a little to be desired though. He's supposed to be there for our protection, but he's drunk half the time. The strangest thing about our neighborhood is the children. I've never seen children go to school in suits and ties, carrying briefcases."

He laughed. "You're right in the middle of Preppieville, the young-executive-on-his-way-up land. Don't worry about them. Those kids will grow up to have long hair, sunglasses and bum around on the beaches of the world. Don't you know how the inverse reaction principle works?"

"Maybe you're right. I started out in my brother's cast off jeans and tennis shoes, and here I am in the most sophisticated city in the world."

He was smiling broadly now, and she wondered if he knew something she didn't. "You haven't seen the others. Get a flight into Sao Paulo or Copenhagen or Paris. Then you'll have something to compare. Deluth and Detroit just aren't on the same scale."

"I'm sure. They cleared me to fly overseas last week. In another few months I should have enough seniority to bid a line of flight that will take me to some of those places. That's what I've been waiting for and working for. I try on each flight to be the best, the most efficient, the most pleasant attendant on board."

"If you get a flight abroad, let me know and I can tell you what to look for in some of the cities."

"You've traveled a lot, haven't you?" He was fascinating to her, she who had spent her youth climbing mountains and hiding from life. He had seen and done the things she imagined. Her eyes were sparkling, her elbow on the table, and she watched him intently.

"As much as I've wanted. Before I got into Vista Color I traveled with Roberto. He runs the business and used to take me with him to Milan. That's the design capital of the world now. All those fashion shows in Paris—the garments come from the designer factories of Milan. I met cousins and family on my mother's side who had known my mother when she was a girl. 'How's America?' they asked me, as if I were on intimate terms with the whole country. Then I went to work for Vista Color and we got some international contracts. I enjoy the traveling. There are still some places I haven't been. Some I don't want to visit. I'd really love to go to South Africa. The photography opportunity there must be incredible."

He looked at his watch regretfully. "Do you work tomorrow? We'd better get you in."

She shook her head. "No, I have three days off now. Sometimes they call me on my day off and I always go. But, if all goes well, I shouldn't have to work tomorrow."

He was helping her up. Hand under her elbow he guided her through the crowded dining room. "Even so, it's time to go."

He hailed a cab and they sat silently in the back seat. Shielah was lost in her thoughts, trying to sort out the day and why she enjoyed her time with him so much. He had his way. And it was direct and quietly commanding.

He was sitting apart from her, not touching her, nor watching her as he frequently did. "Paulo, aren't you ever uncertain about things—what you want, what's right, what to do next?"

He looked at her with interest, his eyes sweeping her face, his mouth pursed as he tried to hear the hidden meanings of the question. "Everybody's uncertain at times. That's no shame. The trick is to make a decision, even in the face of uncertainty and go with it. Choices can be made and unmade. The thing is to act."

"My grandmother has a sampler in her cedar chest. It was made by her mother, and it says, 'We may not know until the last heartbeat of the universe what effect one single choice has upon our lives. But it is true that the sum of all our choices determines our exaltation or damnation.' I've always read that and wondered about it. If that's true then . . . then. . . . "

He finished her thought for her, "Then life is terribly frightening, and the responsibility of acting is awesome."

"Yes," she confirmed.

Now he studied her face, while he contemplated the quote. It struck a familiar note in him and he wondered if he had heard it before. No, he was sure he hadn't. Still, it seemed as though, when she spoke it, he already knew the words. He wanted to touch her, to hold her, to show her all he had learned in the ten years difference between them. He saw how much she had matured in the last five months, and he saw the woman she would become. She resembled the woman of his vision even more now, at least in confidence and determination. He focused on her long blonde hair and tried to picture her as he had first seen her, with the red light shining on her. Everything else was perfect, the intriguing child she was, the woman she was becoming. He wanted that woman to be his, more than she knew. But he would not press her.

"I've heard that before," he said. "At least it sounds familiar. It's a profound saying. Terrifying almost. But it needn't be. One wrong choice can be negated by a good one. That's what life is, it seems to me, a process of learning to make the right choices. If you look toward a God, or life after death in some kind of a heaven with Him, then you must also believe certain choices will put you there and certain choices will not. How do you know how to act . . . when to act? I'm not sure for anyone else, but something inside tells me."

"We call it 'the still small voice.' " Shielah said.

"That's a good description. Only it isn't so much a voice, as a warm impression. When I pay attention, it's always right. When I don't, I get into trouble."

Her eyes began to sparkle, and she was flirting with him. "I can't imagine you in trouble. You handle everything so beautifully."

"Not you. You are beyond my power."

His eyes were dark and warm and entrancing. They seemed almost a caress.

She held his gaze for a minute, then looked away. She wished it were true. They didn't speak again until they said goodnight at the door of her apartment. He didn't try to kiss her.

Kennedy Airport was a national disaster the day before Thanksgiving. People and baggage were strewn everywhere. The counter lines were so long and unwieldy they became tangled and confused. Buses and limos and cabs were beeping and honking outside, and every few minutes announcements were made over the loud speakers in the terminal that this flight was cancelled, or that flight was late. It was snowing on the day that half of New York was trying to leave for a place somewhere else, called home. Children were crying and lying on the floor, squirming in their misery. The telephones were kept busy with unlucky travelers reporting the dilemma.

Shielah had a flight out at 6:30 p.m. to Salt Lake City. She fretted over the traffic snarls, afraid she would miss the flight. Even leaving her apartment two hours early hardly helped. But when she got there, and waded through the melee, it was only to find that her flight was delayed. It would be another two hours at best. She wandered around the airport, looking at magazines in the little magazine booths, reading the paper to kill time.

Grandma was expecting her tonight. Shielah had called last Saturday when she was sure she could get on the flight to Salt Lake.

"Is this Shielah? Is this long distance? We'd better not talk too long, honey, it's too expensive."

"Grandma, I think I can get home for Thanksgiving."

"Oh, that would be wonderful, just wonderful. I'll tell Maddie. She'll set a place for you. We'd better say goodbye now . . . this will cost you a lot of money. Are you being a good girl?"

"Yes, Grandma, I'm being good. We don't have to say goodbye just yet. We have three minutes. I wanted to know how you're doing. Are you feeling well?"

"Oh my, yes, as fit as a fiddle. Don't get much sleep at night any more though, insomnia the doctor says. Goodbye darling. Be careful now, on that airplane. We'll see you Thursday."

"Wednesday, I'll be in Wednesday night at 7:30 p.m., your time. Can Uncle Will pick me up or should I take a cab?"

Grace was shocked. "A cab! I should say not! I don't know if they even run out here. A cab, imagine that! Will can come out, or Buck anyway. Now you'd better hang up. This is costing all your money."

"Not Buck, Grandma. I . . . I'm sure he's busy with Bridget. Send Will or else Drew. Goodbye. I love you. Goodbye." Grace had already hung up, anxious over the high cost of a telephone call from New York City. Shielah shook her head and laughed. "A cab, I should say not!"

She looked at her watch. Nine-fifteen. She'd have to stay overnight in Salt Lake. It would be too late for anyone to come. She hoped they had called the airport and hadn't just trusted the schedule. She tried to call home on the employee line from New World's crew desk complex to warn Grandma, but all the circuits were busy.

The city was caught with its snow pants down. No one expected the cold front that turned the drizzle into snow, and no one expected the blizzard that ensued. The snow flurries of the afternoon whipped themselves up into a perfect fury of screaming snow, and winds howled like banshees down the manmade canyons of New York's downtown section. By dark anyone who wasn't where he desired to be, decided he had better make himself comfortable right where he was. Parked cars were swiftly snowed in, and traffic came to a stop in the Lincoln Tunnel. It took days to clear out the mess. The fire department and city police ran rescue missions to get people out of stalled cars. The airport started turning incoming flights back about six o'clock. A few stray flights got off the ground before they shut the airport down at nine o'clock. Visibility was so bad the air traffic controllers refused to bring anything in or out.

The windows were lined with children watching the snow, while disgusted parents sat on their luggage, or the floor. It was impossible to find a seat. Those who had seats guarded them like prized gems. If someone left, for any reason, the floor became his home when he returned. The only good thing was that people were talking—usually to each other, sometimes to themselves. Oh, they were complaining, of course, but they did it together. People who wouldn't dare speak to a stranger on the New York streets were chattering like neighbors, while they were stranded in the airport for Thanksgiving.

In one waiting area, a middle-aged man with red face and booming tenor voice stood up, raised his arm, and began singing and leading the crowd in an old Thanksgiving song. "Over the river and through the woods to Grandmother's house we go." A voice from the floor spoke up, "Aww shut up, we ain't goin' nowhere."

The booming voice continued, "The horse knows the way to carry the sleigh through the white and drifted snow-o."

Several voices now called out, "Shut up, for crying out loud. Knock it off!"

He was not disturbed. "Over the river and through the woods, Oh how the wind doth blow." He wrapped his arms about himself and shivered convincingly. A big, fat man, sitting uncomfortably on a suitcase, pawed the air in front of him. "Aww, nuts to you, Mr.," he said disgustedly.

The bellowing tenor voice soared. "It stings the toes and bites the nose as over the ground we go." With that, the would-be opera star swept his hat off his head and made a gracious bow to the crowd. A few applauded. The teenagers cheered and laughed. Children stared, big-eyed. He lifted a bottle high in the air and called out. "Here's to Thanksgiving. Here's to Grandma, whereever she is. And here's to us—we deserve it!" He took a big swig and passed the bottle on. It was quickly finished and tossed away, but others began passing around bottles of Seven-Up, champagne, wine, and even cans of soda pop. Later, Christmas carols started up and spread down the concourse. At one end of the long hallway one group was singing "Jolly Old St. Nicholas," and at the other end a different group caroled, "The First Noel."

That lasted until about midnight. Then depression and fatigue set in. Women lined the walls, leaning against them, with children's heads in their laps. Children fell asleep on the floor or in their mothers' arms. Unconcerned with chivalry, businessmen and college boys alike sprawled out in the chairs, trying to catnap the night away.

Shielah went into the lounge for New World employees. The crew desk was located in a large complex of rooms. It boasted a large, airy lounge with couches and chairs and a make-up room for the flight attendants, besides the office where calls went out from the crew desk. All the couches and chairs were taken, but at least the floor was carpeted and not dirty. She too leaned against the wall, talking at first to some of the other attendants there, then finally falling asleep on the shoulder of a girl she had flown with to St. Louis.

Morning came in slowly as if afraid to awaken anyone, afraid to show them what the night had done to their city. The same crowds that drifted off to sleep, hoping they could get out the next morning, awoke to find themselves snowed in. The coffee shops ran out of sweet rolls and coffee. The restaurants ran out of salads, sandwiches and liquor. The runways were deep in snow. No vehicles were moving, and the snow plows were inaccessible by virtue of the fact that the crews couldn't get to the airport—or once there, to the hangars where the snow plows were stored. And it was still snowing—lightly, but nevertheless, still snowing. Now there was no singing. The people were rumpled, hungry, with cricks in their necks from a poor night's sleep. Children were grouchy and demanding that mothers manufacture food from thin air.

Shielah felt particularly sorry for the older people trapped there. They were not equipped to handle these conditions very well. Many of them seemed quite miserable and a little dazed. She pictured Grandma in these conditions, trying to be patient with all the noise and short tempers around her, with no sleep or food. Shielah found one little lady with a rose-colored hat askew on her head, wandering around the concourse aimlessly, quite lost. She thought she was at the United terminal. She took her into the employees room and sat with her, talking and drawing out all the information she could on where the lady lived and where she was going.

Word came through about noon that subways were running, if you could make it the three miles to the nearest entrance. Shielah was more

118

prepared than most. She had packed her snowboots, anticipating what she thought would be colder weather in Utah. She took them out of the bottom of her carry-on, put on two pairs of socks, then the boots, and stowed her carry-on in a small locker. After giving her old friend into the keeping of another attendant Shielah stepped out into the fluttering snow to walk to the subway entrance.

It was a walk she would never forget. Buses and cars were covered with huge, fluffy snowy domes. Buildings loomed through the white mist like great ghosts. The snow came almost to the tops of her boots on the flat places and she knew it would be to her knees in the drifts. She was not the only one walking. There were a few other hardy souls, all struggling quietly toward the subway entrance just beyond the long, lead-in entrance to the International Airport, now impotent and still. Three miles is a long way in the snow. She was glad when she finally descended the stairs down to the subway below the snowbeaten streets. Her nose was glad too. And her toes were starting to feel rather happy to find a warmer environment. The subway came on time. Dear old Grand Central Station! This was one time she had kind thoughts about it.

From the subway exit to her apartment she had only two-and-one-half blocks to go. She walked them slowly, unwilling to give up the experience. Most remarkable—beyond the unconquerable skyscrapers and miles of buried cars—most remarkable of all was the quiet. New York City had caught a cold and lost its voice. No honking, no whizzing automobiles, no airplanes overhead, no heels clicking and tapping on the sidewalks. Nothing at all moved or made noise. It was as quiet as a temple. She took a deep, startlingly cold breath and whispered, "God could come right now."

Her hair and shoulders were covered with snow when she came to the door of her own building. It stood as silent and immutable as the others. Not a soul was coming or going. She hated to go in, but her ears spoke sense to her and she went in to give them relief. The telephone was ringing when she opened the door to her apartment.

"Hello," she answered, twisting around to see if any of the other girls were there.

There was a momentary silence, then Paulo's voice, "Shielah? You're home! I've been trying all day. I almost hung up. Where have you been?"

She laughed. "Walking."

"Walking?" He was astounded.

"From the airport."

"What?" He almost shouted it.

Again she laughed. "I had to get home and I couldn't wait for the city to dig me out. They'll be days. I walked from the airport to the subway entrance. It was only three miles. The subways are running nicely. So here I am, a little frost-bitten, but otherwise just fine."

"The airport must be a mess."

"It is."

"Were you there last night? I heard there were riots. The cops had to break them up."

119

"Not where I was. In our terminal, people were singing Christmas carols and passing the bottle."

"Really?" He was incredulous.

"I slept in the employees waiting room with my head on someone's shoulder."

"Wish it had been mine," he said enviously. "So you just got in?"

"This very minute. The phone was ringing when I opened the door."

"Happy Thanksgiving."

"Oh, that's right. Happy Thanksgiving to you too. Why aren't you up in Albany?"

"Couldn't get out, naturally. I was going to drive up last night, but by the time I was ready to leave the office, traffic was already stalled. I called Mama and told her I'd come whenever I can."

"I'd better try my Grandmother again," Shielah said. "The family was expecting me last night. I'm sure they're aware of the problem by now, but she'll still be worried."

"Are your roommates there?"

"No, no one is here but me."

There was a silence on his end of the line, then he said, "Me too . . . alone, I mean."

Another pause, on her end this time. Then she said slowly and deliberately, "Can we get together?"

"I hope so."

"Do you like walking in the snow?"

"If I'm dressed for it. But you must be tired of it by now. You've walked a long way in the snow."

"Not so long. I've walked a lot farther than that back home. I'm used to snow, remember? Let me take a hot bath, and then we'll meet midway, and I'll show you your city as I like it."

They met on East 54th Street and walked seven blocks along the silent streets back to Paulo's place on East 61st. Night was coming on, but the sky was still light with the reflection of the white earth in the misty skies. Street lamps came on, glowing with golden halos in the mist. Apartment buildings began to light up— a window here, a window there, and colored neon lights in the shops along the streets. It was a ghostly amusement park, made just for them.

"This has been one of the happiest days of my life," she said as they walked arm in arm. "I'll never forget this sight as long as I live. I feel that Heavenly Father handed me this day, this night, on a silvery platter. He did it all for me, I'm sure."

"Aww, what about all those poor people who didn't get home for Thanksgiving?"

She smiled mischievously at him. "That's the breaks. One selfish wish, and that's the breaks."

He laughed. "Is this a hidden talent you have, turning disasters into unforgettable, silver-platter gifts?"

"If it is, it's been hidden from me too."

"Have you considered you may have many talents that have been hidden from you?"

"My only talent I know of, is the talent of working hard. *That* I'm sure of. I believe in hard work, and I believe it's the only way to make something of your life. I'm living proof."

"Let me look at this living proof of hard work," he kidded her, and stepped back to look her up and down.

She blushed and grabbed his arm, hurrying him along. "Why don't you like me to look at you?" he asked her.

"Because it makes me self-conscious."

"Why should it? You should be pleased. I think you're beautiful and you won't even let me tell you so. Can't you give a poor man a break and let him feast his eyes on a work of art?"

"Feast them on the lights of the city. This is what we went walking to see."

"Oh, is it? I forgot." She started to protest, so he quickly added. "But I remember, I remember now. Right! The lights of the city! They *are* lovely . . . so's the snow . . . so are you."

She looked warningly at him and he laughed. "I'll be good. I don't want to make you self-conscious. Heaven forbid."

Paulo's apartment fit him perfectly. Small and cozy, with one bedroom and a tiny kitchen, the main space was given to the living room and his bedroom. The carpeting was deep, rich brown and very plush. Shielah's stockinged feet burrowed into it, and she sighed with pleasure. The whole room was a mixture of thick carpet and shiny dark wood, the focal point a red brick fireplace, elegantly topped by a mahogany mantle. Against one wall was the bookcase, overflowing with books—many of them photography books. Shielah stood thumbing through them while he made some coffee for himself, and apologized for not having hot chocolate for her. "Orange juice is all I have. Will that do?"

"It's fine. Now, if I can just get my feet warm, I'll be all right."

He came in and took her by the shoulders, pushing her gently toward the fireplace. "This is the way, young lady, to toasty toes. Sit! I press a magic button, and . . . Voila! instant fire. Now, if you'll just wait a minute, I'll add a small but effective Presto log, and your feet should have instant relief."

She stretched her legs out toward the fire, and he took one of her feet in his hands, and began to rub. "Ouch, your feet *are* cold."

"Always," she conceded.

"Always? That's no fun."

"Well, not in the summer. But as soon as the weather cools."

"You should wear warm socks and sensible shoes like men do."

"Right! Wouldn't I look nice?" she laughed. "Besides, I have had on snow boots, the same as you, and look what good it did."

"Give me the other one. How can you go skiing with frozen feet like that?"

"I really haven't considered it."

121

"So, consider it. Let's go to Albany tomorrow. You can meet Mama, Roberto, Ruth—that's his better half, and I do mean better—and Maria. And, *and* we can go skiing."

"I don't know, Paulo." She pulled her foot away. "Thank you, I think my feet will be fine now. The fire helps a lot."

He stretched out on his side next to her, leaning on one elbow, and sipping his hot coffee. He stared into the fireplace. "You don't want to go to Albany?"

She was looking into the fire also, trying to think of an excuse.

"You don't ski?" he guessed.

"There won't be skiing tomorrow, at least, not unless Albany has had snow before this."

"Maybe you're right, but that's not your reason for not going."

She turned and looked fully at him. He was only inches away. "Maybe. And it's not *your* reason *for* going. Do you really ski?"

"Of course," he replied. "But, you're right. That's not the reason for going. I want Mama to meet you."

"Why? It isn't fair to her for us to pretend there is anything serious between us."

He was looking into space beyond her shoulder. He had a wry smile for a moment. "She wants so much to see me settle down and get married. She's afraid for me. She thinks I won't ever get married. I know she thinks I'm not trying very hard to find a girl. If only she knew." He focused on Shielah's face. "Family is very important to Italians and Catholics. It's almost a sin not to get married. Parents look forward to the time they will be grandparents, and then great-grandparents. It's very important to carry on the family line. So you see, I am the reprobate. No girl! No marriage! No kids, no babies for Mama to dandle on her knee, to rock and spoil. She tries to be patient with me, but lately she has been threatening to pick out a girl and arrange the wedding herself, then invite me when it is time."

"Family is very important in my religion too. I understand." Impulsively she reached out and brushed his dark hair with her fingertips. He glanced up, surprised. She never touched him voluntarily. She sighed long and deeply, then deliberately put her hand on his cheek.

"You should be married, Paulo. You deserve a wonderful wife and a dozen kids."

"I've been hoping."

"You'll be . . . such a loving husband." He saw how hard it was for her to admit the truths she had been thinking.

"That's true. I will. Love has been waiting in me a long time. I was ready ten years ago." He interrupted himself. " . . . has it really been ten years? That's a long time. I've been consciously looking for ten years. Can you understand why I was so pushy in Hawaii?"

"Yes. I understand. Everyone needs love so desperately. Most of us are lonely forever in our hearts. No one meets our expectations. No one knows our needs, our dreams, our hurts. I think love is rare—real love, deeply caring love! There's a lot of duty that passes for love, and a lot of passion, but neither of them is satisfying. Maybe that's the real signal of love, when the soul is satisfied." The firelight engulfed them in it's warm magic.

"That's a lot of philosophy for such a young woman." He was careful not to move, for fear the spell would be broken and she would jerk her hand away.

But she left it on his cheek, moving her fingers slightly to touch his hair. And she looked at him quizzically. Her barriers were all down now. "Are you . . . terribly lonely inside?"

"Are you?" he asked quietly, reflecting her question.

She didn't reply for a moment, just looked at his hair, at her hand, then finally at his eyes, "Yes." It was a whispered confession.

"For a long, long time?" he guessed correctly, seeing her as if in a dream.

"Yes. So long that I can't remember how long."

"You don't have to be." Now he moved, ever so slightly and slipped his hand behind the shining fall of golden hair. "Let me love you," he whispered. Her lips moved and she closed her eyes.

It wasn't far, those few inches from his mouth to hers, but he felt as though he had crossed an immense barrier. She was quiet as a sleeping kitten and just as soft. He had promised he wouldn't press her, and he didn't. That moment was only gentle, and so tender he could hardly breathe. He took his lips away just for a moment, and she opened her eyes, deep blue and shiny with welling tears. Her arm went around his neck and her lips searched for his. Ahh, he could breathe again, and the darkness around him shattered into a million, searing spears of light. "I love you," he whispered against the sweetness of her mouth. "I love you."

She fell asleep eventually beside the fireplace, and Paulo covered her with a blanket. He sat watching her for a while, wondering what it would take to win her, to penetrate the reserve she had with him. He sensed her physical response to him, and knew also that their spirits were old together. Where or when they had known each other he could not say, but soul recognized soul. If he could only get her to admit it.

Chapter 7

*T*he next morning they took the train to Albany. Pulling out of an unusually quiet Grand Central station, the long, dark tunnel was replaced with brilliant sunlight on snow when they were out of Manhattan. The train windows framed picture after picture as they rocketed past a countryside draped thickly in white, snow dropping precipitously from loaded branches, and houses generously frosted. Now he held her hand as they jostled along with the clickety-clacking wheels. She didn't protest. The night before had breached an unspoken barrier. At Albany Paulo kept a black Fiat which they drove for another half-hour to reach his family home in the Catskill Mountains.

"Rip Van Winkle should never have slept through twenty years of this," Shielah said with delight at the picturesque landscape. "This must be the location for all those Christmas scenes of Courier and Ives. The ones that are supposed to look like the ideal cozy villages."

"Does it look like the ideal village?"

"It's beautiful," she admired. "If you've lived in the Rockies you can hardly call these mountains, but . . . what beautiful hills! Look! Over there! Look at that church! That steeple! I feel like I've stepped back two hundred years. Isn't Betsy Ross or Johnny Tremain going to wave as we go by?"

Paulo laughed. She was excited over something he had taken for granted.

"It does seem like another world apart from New York, I guess."

She turned away again to look out the window. "This has a gentle, peaceful loveliness, with those rolling hills all covered in snow. Oh, Paulo, it's wonderful. It's dear! Thank you for bringing me."

He held her hand and was content. She was responding to his world just as he had hoped she would. Now for the family.

Carmella had fussed and fumed all day. What had happened to Paulo? Maria tried to remind her that he was snowed in. Still the mother fumed, "I know, I know, but can't he at least come home for Thanksgiving? A family shoulda be together for Thanksgiving. Do I cooka his favorite food so he can stay in New York?"

Roberto and Ruth had slept overnight in the family home, and Ruth tried to console Mama too. Mama agreed with everything they said. "Yes, Paulo woulda come home if he could. Yes, I'm sure he woulda rather be here too. I know he musta be lonely." She wiped her eyes. "My boy shoulda not be lonely on Thanksgiving. Maybe I better calla him again. Roberto, you calla up that place where he lives."

Roberto was calling for the third time that day, when the black Fiat pulled up in the circular drive, and Paulo walked around to help Shielah out. Maria saw them first.

"Mama, Mama, come quick. Paulo is here, and he's brought a girl."

"Roberto, hang up, so we won't have to pay for a call. Paulo isa come home. A girl! A girl! What girl?" She came jiggling and puffing into the sitting room, pushed back the sheer white curtains so as not to have the slightest distraction studying this girl her boy had brought home. She looked at Maria. Maria smiled up at her and laid down the stitchery piece she had been working on. Carmella burst into a grand smile and said gleefully, "She isa pretty one, eh?"

Paulo and Shielah had not reached the door yet when Mama burst it open and clasped her son in a satisfied hug. "So, the biga shot comes home, at last! How come it takea you so long? Who is this pretty girl that drives alla the way up here with a bada boy like you?"

"Be careful, Mama. I've been trying to convince her I'm a good boy."

Mama hugged him again and wiped her eyes, "A gooda boy, yes."

"Mama, this is Shielah Sorensen. We met last June and then . . . "

"Last June, and you justa bring her now for me to meet!" She took one of Shielah's hands and held it up. "Paulo, now I be angry with you. She is too pretty to hide for yourself. Come in, both of you. Why do we standa in the cold? Paulo, she willa catch a cold out here. Take her into the house."

Shielah was laughing in spite of herself. "You're very nice, Mrs. D'Agosta. Thank you. What a beautiful home!"

"Oh, it isa too big, too big for just Maria and me. I told Enrico that when he bought it. Of course, the boys were still little ones then and he said they needa lot of room. Too mucha room. He wouldn't listen to me. What do I know, eh? He want it. He buy it. Justa like a man. Now I have to live with it and pay some young girl to keep it up. My owna house and strangers keep it up!"

The D'Agosta home was, indeed, too big for Carmella and her invalid daughter. When she and Enrico had first started out in America their tiny flat had only two bedrooms that accommodated themselves and five children. But her husband was determined that his children should have advantages he never enjoyed, and when the clothing business made him a wealthy man, he moved away from the streets of New York and bought an old run-down mansion in the Catskill mountains north of Albany. Set on a hillside, with one long road straight up the hill ending in their circular driveway, it was a home that overlooked a small village below and the mountains of two other states. With six bedrooms, each as large as the living room in Paulo's apartment, a dining room that accommodated twenty guests and a large party room that opened off it, it was a home designed for entertaining. Carmella did little of that anymore, but Roberto and Ruth had the run of the house as often as they liked for entertaining. Consequently, Roberto saw that the home was kept in immaculate and lavish order at all times.

The kitchen was Mama's. She permitted maid service for the rest of her oversized home. She wasn't capable now anyway with the bursitis that constantly bothered her and her recent heart trouble. But the kitchen was all her own. From it she turned out the best Italian linguini, fettucini, and spaghetti that could be found in the state. Today, however, the house smelled distinctly of turkey, and Ruth was busy setting another place for the unexpected guest.

Maria wheeled herself out from the sitting room, and Paulo knelt beside her wheelchair. "There's my angel! Hello, sweetheart, been chasing any cars lately?" He kissed her on both cheeks and half lifted her out of the chair with his hug.

Shielah stood smiling and watching, amazed by the outpouring of family affection. Roberto was in the vestibule now, waiting for his turn at the bad boy who hadn't come home for Thanksgiving. The brothers embraced and thumped each other on the back, kissing on both cheeks as they always did. And Ruth stepped up, cocked her head and said, "You almost missed dinner again. Where's my kiss?" He kissed her and swung her around, and ended up facing Shielah, one arm around Ruth and one hand on Maria's dark head. His face was all alight when he proudly said, "This is my family!"

Shielah smiled and smiled, employing every bit of training she had received from the airlines and from her grandmother. Dinner was delicious—and noisy. Turkey and stuffing, potatoes and apple pie, cranberries and hot, sourdough rolls—all preceded by a small dish of minestrone soup and another dish of Mama's perfect pasta. Wine was liberally poured at every place, and they were all too busy talking and laughing to notice she didn't drink hers—everyone, that is, except Carmella. She noticed. She noticed everything about Shielah— what she wore, what she said, what kind of manners she had, how much she ate, and most of all how she looked at Paulo.

Not much conversation was required of Shielah, the overjoyed family supplied most of it. Holidays were made for families and the D'Agosta family took advantage of every chance to be together. Shielah felt enveloped in a warmth and happiness that she envied. Roberto sat at the head of the table with Ruth on his right. Beside her sat Maria, with the beautiful, long black hair, thoughtful eyes, and crippled legs. On his left, sat Mama. Usually Paulo would have been next to her, but the guest was

126

not to be left out. Tonight, Shielah sat between Carmella and her favorite son, and Shielah little realized how much the older woman saw.

Carmella saw Paulo drink part of Shielah's wine so there wouldn't have to be explanations. She saw the pride with which he looked at this blonde girl and she saw a becoming modesty in Shielah. The girl was not flirtatious, nor self-centered as many of the girls today were. Carmella also saw that Paulo was not presumptuous with this girl. No arm around her, no patting a knee under the table. He was solicitous of her needs, but didn't presume too much. That was good. She was proud of him. Her boy should be a gentleman. His father was. Of course—and she warmed at the thought of it—of course he had always liked to squeeze her knee under the table. There has to be some of that. Perhaps it's too soon with this girl. But, what's to squeeze? She is too skinny, thought Mama. Papa would not have approved. Skinny girls don't make healthy babies. My pasta will cure that. Would their babies have blue eyes like hers? Such blue eyes she had only seen in those fashionable magazines. Stop it, she told herself. This is Paulo's friend. That is all, he said. Who knows if they are in love? But she had seen her son with other women, and she saw him now with Shielah. A small happy sigh escaped her. He is in love . . . at last.

Roberto saw it too. Paulo didn't look at Elaina like that.

"You are from New York?" he asked Shielah, between the courses of minestrone and spaghetti.

"Yes . . . that is, for now. I'm a flight attendant for New World Airways. My home is in Utah." She was self-conscious under his gaze. If possible he was even more Italian than Paulo, whose finer features reflected the Portugese blood of his father. Roberto was taller, his features bolder, his skin darker and his eyes more demanding.

"Ahh," he nodded in acknowledgement. "Utah. You are a very long way from home. Do you like flying? No, that's a silly question. Of course you like it. What do you like about it?"

"Seeing new places, different places, living in New York. I've adopted the city. And I like the people I meet flying. They're always friendly . . . well, usually.

"You like New York?" Roberto's eyebrows went up. "Most people find it too crazy and unfriendly. Paulo's the only one I know that really likes it."

"Oh no! It is crazy, I guess—cars, people, and all that—but there's such a sense of excitement and life there. I live near the U.N. building and on my days off, I love to see representatives of all the nations of the world going in and out. It will be a long time before I tire of the city."

Ruth said, "I couldn't live there a week. We go down to the city for shopping at Christmas. I like that, but to live there . . . "

"Perhaps you like it because it is something new for you?" Roberto guessed.

"Yes. It is."

"Utah, is it wide open spaces like the cowboy movies show?"

She laughed. "In some places it is. But there are cities too."

"You live in Salt Lake City? And is there a salty ocean?"

"I live in a small town outside of Salt Lake—like the village at the bottom of your hill. And yes, the Great Salt Lake is an inland ocean, and so salty you can't sink in the water."

Mama made an exclamation of surprise. "Isa that so!" She looked around the table, then laughed and jiggled her hefty frame. "I could sink!"

Shielah laughed with the rest. "I don't think so, Mrs. D'Agosta."

Roberto quizzed her again. "You and Paulo have known each other a long time?"

Shielah looked at Paulo quickly. He interceded, "Just a few months. We met first in Hawaii, last June." He smiled at her. "She was my vacation. Then when she came to New York we met again. Shielah was caught in that blizzard at the airport, trying to get home for Thanksgiving. Obviously she didn't make it, so I invited her to spend the holiday with us."

"It's about time you brought her here to meet us," Maria smiled at her. "Just because she isn't Italian doesn't mean you have to hide her."

"I haven't been hiding her! I'm just not a fast mover." Paulo apologized.

"So I've noticed," Mama rejoined.

Maria clearly liked the guest. Shielah could feel warm signals from Paulo's sister. Mama apparently approved of her also. In fact, Roberto was the only one who seemed to put her on trial. She had a sixth sense from years of feeling unaccepted, and she detected an aloofness. He made her uncomfortable, and she reached under the table for Paulo's hand. It was warm and reassuring. He squeezed her hand slightly, smiling at her, obvious pride in his eyes.

Today there was no maid. Mama wanted the house all for the family and had told the girl from town to spend the holidays at home. The women all worked at clearing the table. Even Maria wheeled her chair back and forth, carrying dishes. Paulo got up to help, but Roberto pulled on his arm.

"Sit down, Paulo. Tell me how Vista Color is doing."

"We've got two men on that new design now. It's just a question of time. Welsch is like a cat on a hot roof. He wants it now. I just hope we can beat the Japanese."

"When are you going to have another show of your own?"

"I don't have time to put together another photo show. I'm an executive now, and you know how that is. They don't have time for anything, even the business."

Roberto was twisting his wine glass. "You have time for a new girl."

Paulo knew he would get to that. "We haven't spent as much time together as I would wish."

"Why not."

"She's hard to convince. And she's gone a lot."

"You like her?"

"Yeah. I like her."

Roberto sat back and studied his brother. "So she's pretty, and she's blonde. How old is she? She looks a little young."

"Twenty-one," Paulo lied, then said, "Almost."

Roberto shook his head. "She's twenty! Well, I didn't realize you were looking for a blonde . . . and one so young."

Paulo was getting irritated by his second-degree questioning. "Knock it off. I met a girl, a pretty girl, a nice girl. She happens to have blonde hair, and I like her. Don't make a federal case out of it."

Roberto leaned toward him. "You've *never* brought a girl home before. You think that doesn't tell me something. Tomorrow night is our annual holiday party. I invited everyone that can do us good and that includes the Marettis. What do you think Elaina will do with this piece of news?"

"I don't give a damn what Elaina will do. You're the one who's been pushing that match. I told you a long time ago—Elaina isn't my type. I don't like her family business."

"What's wrong with furs?"

"Nothing. They go great with designer dresses, right? But Vincent Maretti has his fingers in other pies too, and they're too hot for my tastes. Roberto, you'd better watch it with him. Don't be in debt to him in any way."

"You're a fool! What do you know?"

"I know who his friends are. Do you?"

Roberto didn't answer. Paulo asked again, "*Do* you?"

"What Maretti does is his own business. He's square with me, and he's damn good for our business. He knows all the best designers in Milan and he looks out for my interests. But then, of course, he thinks that his daughter is going to marry into my family, if my little brother will ever get out of his priestly robes."

"Maybe you'd better disabuse him of that belief."

"Why don't you?"

"Because I've never led him to believe it. You have, and you'd better stop trying to live my life for me." Paulo's temper flared. The two brothers were glaring at each other when Carmella came into the room. She took one look at their faces and set mouths, and promptly thumped both of them on the head.

"Stop it," she said in a loud whisper. "This isa a time for happiness, not quarreling. And we have a guest. How you makea her feel with all sucha bad talk?"

Paulo looked away from Roberto, and his eyes softened as he looked up at his mother. "Sorry, Mama. You're right. How's she doing?"

"She isa doin' beautiful. Thata girl can wash dishes I tella you. A wonderful help ina the kitchen. Can she cook?"

"I have no idea," Paulo said.

"Well, you leavea her with me for a week. I will teacha her to cook like a dream."

Paulo got up and put his arm around his mother's shoulders. "No one will ever cook like you, Mama."

Roberto still sat looking down at his wine glass.

Shielah had brought no clothes for a party. She was embarrassed to admit to Paulo that she was not prepared and said she had best go on back to New York. He could put her on the train from Albany. It was a pleasant ride and she wouldn't mind. But Paulo wouldn't hear of it. This holiday party would bring all the family friends to his home. He had never had a girl there before to show off, and he wanted most anxiously for Shielah to be with him that night.

Carmella had an instant answer. In her trunk of precious memories was a delicate, creamy-white lace dress Enrico had given her many years before, when she was as lithe and thin as Shielah and only slightly shorter. She had worn it only on a few special occasions, then tucked it away for memory's sake when she became too ample to fit into it. She had hoped to pass it on to Maria, but her crippled daughter had never worn it. It lay in the depths of her trunk, as beautiful and delicate as it had been thirty-five years before.

Ignoring Shielah's protests, Mama slipped the dress over her head and fastened the rows of buttons and loops in the back. She turned her around, clucking over the picture Shielah made in the dress.

"Ahhh," the older woman breathed. "Isa beautiful. Enrico, he knowsa good quality. 'Only the best, only the very best for you,' he woulda tell me, even when we were poor. This dress he givea me when Roberto was born. He was my second baby. Jean was the first, but Papa, he hada no money for dresses then, hardly enough to feed us. I worka in the produce market, sorting tomatoes and cabbages and zucchini. He worka in the factories with the biga machines, but they don'ta pay him much. So, he had no presents for me and the first baby. But when Roberto isa born, my Enrico, he work at night too, cleaning out the factories. What do I know? Nothing! I just thinka he is trying to earn more money for another baby. But no. On the night I givea him another baby boy he givea me this dress." She was wiping her eyes again, and smiling tenderly at Shielah.

"Mrs. D'Agosta, I can't possibly wear this dress. It's much too precious for you to let a stranger wear it."

Mama became insistent. "No! No! It isa wonderful to me to see it again. It isa too many years I have it locked in my trunk. Please, wear it for me. Please! I willa never wear it again." She laughed and pinched her round middle. "Looka, see! I am much too fat. But you are madea for that dress. I woulda be so happy to see you wear it tonight, and I willa tell everyone. 'Looka, see how beautiful I wasa in that dress of my Enrico's.' "

Shielah looked into the shining, twinkly old eyes, then impulsively hugged the Italian woman. "You were much more beautiful than I. I'm sure Mr. D'Agosta would have thought so. Are you sure he wouldn't mind?"

Mama waved her hand in the air, "No. No! Papa, he woulda want to see that dress again too. Come. I show you something." She took Shielah's hand and led her into her own bedroom. There, on one wall, beside the delicate lacy, curtains was a portrait of a dark-haired young girl in a creamy-white, lace dress.

Shielah stared appreciatively at the picture. Obviously it was Carmella, but it looked so much like Paulo she could hardly believe it. The same dark, languorous eyes, the same delicately contoured mouth. He looked more like his mother than either of her other two children did. No wonder he was her beloved one.

She turned to the older woman who was gazing with so much pride at the picture.

"I was right. You were much more beautiful in this dress than I am. Your black hair was such a rich contrast. And your eyes . . . oh, Mrs. D'Agosta, you were truly beautiful! And Paulo looks so much like you!"

Mama laughed. "Yes, he isa pretty boy all right." Then she looked at Shielah seriously. "But he isa good boy too. He makea good husband, like his Papa. He will adore his wife and give her everything. I know him. He is generous, too generous."

Shielah blushed, feeling uncomfortable under her intent gaze. "I'm sure he is. I haven't known him long, but I can tell that generosity runs in his family."

Mama smiled then, and patted her back. "You are a gooda girl too. I bet you havea nice mama. Now you willa wear this tonight, no? And Paulo will be so proud."

Shielah told Paulo only that Mama had found something for her to wear. They spent the day wandering through the house, Paulo showing her all his favorite hiding places as a kid, and later snowshoeing over the nearby hills until almost dark. After being out in the snow for hours, Shielah spent an inordinate amount of time soaking in the hot bath. Mama prepared it for her, complete with bubbles and a slight film of bath oil that left her skin silky. Carmella asked her to wait to dress until she could come upstairs to help with the heirloom garment.

Shielah spent her time employing every make-up technique Danilov had taught her, and put her hair into an upsweep, with curls clustered in the back, falling from the crown of her head down past her shoulders. Little tendrils of curls framed her face. She was just finishing her make-up when Mama came in.

Shielah was in her slip. Mama admired her, "Whew, you are beautiful justa like you are. Paulo woulda be lucky witha you. Does your family havea lots of children?"

Shielah laughed and shook her head, "Just my brother and me. My mother and father died when I was ten. But my aunt and uncle have seven children."

Carmella caught her breath in admiration. "Seven! How very happy they musta be." She lifted the dress tenderly and carefully. Shielah stepped into it. It slid easily up over her slip. Mama began buttoning it up in the back. "You lived with them when your Mama and Papa died?"

"No," Shiela answered. "Well, yes—for one year only. Then my brother and I lived with my grandmother."

"This grandmother. She musta be a good woman. She raise-a you to be polite, to be modest, and not to use that nasty tobacco. You love her very much?"

Just for a moment gentle but insistent questions brought back memories. "Yes," she replied, her voice breaking. "Very much. She's an angel."

131

Carmella was finished. She kissed Shielah's cheek then turned the girl to face her. "So are you, my dear," she said. "Now you go down to my Paulo, and be his angel tonight."

Shielah had never been so completely, so warmly accepted, and so quickly. She stood smiling at Paulo's mother, unwilling to break the loving spell. Then she returned her kiss and whispered, "Thank you. Thank you for being so kind."

Paulo started up the stairs to see what was taking Shielah so long. People were coming in a steady stream, and he wanted her by his side. Carmella opened the bedroom door, and Shielah walked out and immediately down the long, curved staircase. Had Cinderella felt like this the night of her ball? Would she lose a slipper and it all be over? Paulo backed down the stairs, giving her the full length to model in. She smiled at the expression on his face. He had not expected this, obviously. His face was a mirror of incredulity and adoration. She descended the stairs slowly, carefully; she would not risk damaging this dress. Roberto started past, toward the dining room to check on the food but stopped beside Paulo. There was also incredulity on his face, but it was quickly replaced with barely disguised anger. Shielah was unprepared for that, and it made her pause a few steps away from them.

Paulo was speechless. He simply held out his hand to her. Roberto was rarely speechless.

"I haven't seen that dress in a very long time," he said. "It's a family heirloom, you know."

"I know," she apologized. "Your mother insisted I wear it. It's really much too priceless for me, but she insisted. I'm sorry . . . I hope . . . "

"Shhh," Paulo put a finger to her lips, but she still looked at Roberto. "You are stunning in that dress. I'm glad she insisted. It is perfect for you. She's beautiful, isn't she, Roberto?" he asked, never looking at his brother.

The older brother did not attempt to mask his feelings even though he knew her gaze was on him. He answered, "She certainly is." But his eyes were narrowed and the tension in his face revealed his displeasure.

She didn't look back as Paulo took her arm, leading her into the entry way to meet the guests. Roberto watched them for a moment, his lips pursed and a frown furrowing his brow, until Ruth came up behind him and spoke.

"Don't be such a grumpy old man. Mama obviously gave it to her to wear. Let's go check on the dining room before we let people in."

Roberto looked at his wife. Ruth was tall, almost as tall as he, and she rarely missed when she guessed about his thoughts. She knew him well, but not as well as she thought. Papa had been happy when Roberto had announced his engagement to Ruth. A good Italian girl. She will give you many sons, he had said. And she was willing. But it wasn't fashionable to have a lot of children these days, and Roberto didn't want her slender figure ruined while she was still young. In a few years they would have children. There was plenty of time. Roberto kissed her quickly.

"Of course you're right. I'll go check. You go back to the guests."

The dining room was laden with food on silver platters, crystal platters, and in silver bowls. In the center of the table was a huge ice sculpture of Santa Claus, and clustered about his feet were chocolate covered, ice cream bon bons. Small round tables, set up in corners and covered with holiday cloths, boasted small, bite-sized morsels of layered chocolate and wafer-thin pastries frosted green and red.

"Where is the punch bowl?" Roberto asked the caterer.

"I don't know, sir," the young boy answered as he hurried back into the kitchen. "I'll get Rocky."

Roberto was impatiently looking at his watch when the head caterer came in. "I thought this was all to be set up by eight o'clock!"

"Yes sir. It is, sir. Our only problem is the champagne. Catskill was sold out completely and we had to send to Albany for more. The runner is due any minute."

"*Any minute!* My guests are here now, and I can't serve them yet."

"The punch is ready sir. We have brandy, hot toddies, martinis, almost everything but the champagne. I think we can begin to serve right now."

Roberto was icy. "Oh, you think so? My parties always begin with a champagne toast to the holidays and to good cheer."

The young man was extremely apologetic. "I'm sorry sir, I really am. Just a few more minutes. I'm sure he'll be here."

"Five! And then he'd better be here or you can walk to Albany and get it yourself. After five minutes, I cut your fee in half every five additional minutes. When I pay for service, I *expect* service." He turned and strode out. As he closed the door and stepped into the throng of guests in the library, he became the model of holiday cheer.

Shielah and Paulo were standing before the library fireplace. Clustered around them were guests wanting to be introduced to Paulo's date. He was having a grand time persuading people she was an American duchess, only twice removed from the crown of Sweden. She was earnestly denying preposterous lie, and Paulo was having the time of his life.

Elaina Maretti swept in from the dark cold night on her father's arm and in her father's sable coat. Her mother came in behind them. Roberto greeted Elaina and Vincent. Maria greeted Gina Maretti. Elaina heard the laughter from the library and moved slightly to see where it was coming from.

Vincent boomed out as he pumped Roberto's hand, "Lots of laughter already. I can tell it's going to be another memorable party. You seen the last shipment of furs? Not so good, not so good."

His dark-eyed daughter squeezed his arm. "Papa, you promised no business." "What's going on in there?" she asked Roberto, nodding toward the library.

"I don't know exactly. . . . " He was reluctant to tell Elaina about Shielah.

Maria was not. She smiled innocently up at Elaina. "I know. It's Paulo and his date. I heard him telling everyone she was a duchess. Then he said she was a model, and she keeps trying to get him to stop it. She's actually a flight attendant, though she's pretty enough to be a model."

Elaina's eyes had gone blank at first. Paulo never brought a girl home. Of course he had dates, other girls besides herself. She knew that. It didn't bother her. None of them had ever meant anything to him, any more than other men had to her. But that he would bring a girl home with him, on the weekend of the party—that was a mistake. She would be embarrassed in front of their friends who knew that Paulo D'Agosta was marked by Elaina Maretti.

When she looked at Roberto again her dark eyes smouldered and were hard as coal. "Well, I suppose I had better meet this 'duchess.' Introduce us, Roberto."

Vincent whispered to him as they moved toward the library, "Who's this girl Paulo brought home?"

Shielah saw Elaina before the Italian girl saw her. Elaina was tall, as tall as Paulo, with jet black hair, and large dark eyes, wide-set and angled slightly upward. When she wanted to make them appear so, they could look just like cat eyes. Tonight she wore a red dress that clung to her hips and waist and fell softly about her arms. The hemline was uneven, with triangular sections of cloth overlaid, the tips pointing down, and when she walked one could sometimes catch a glimpse of thigh. She was completely stunning. Shielah stared at her appreciatively, as if at an object of art.

Elaina stared at her in animosity. Roberto didn't have to introduce them.

"There you are," exclaimed a short, tubby man. "I've been waiting for Elaina Maretti all my life," he said to nobody in particular. At the mention of the Maretti name the other guests turned, and a path opened directly to Paulo and Shielah.

Paulo was unperturbed. He had known Elaina would be angry. She had long considered him her property. He also knew she could be a witch. Tonight she certainly looked bewitching, but his arm tightened around Shielah's waist. He smelled the soft scent of her, and was content to brave the witch for her.

"Hello Elaina." He smiled as he reached to take her hand. "And Vincent. How nice to see you again. I saw your latest line of furs at Sak's last week.

Vincent Maretti couldn't help admiring Paulo's taste in women. He liked looking at beautiful young girls. Sometimes he did more than look, although in the last few years he had grown to care more for money than for women. Then he became aware of his daughter beside him. She was as stiff as stone. He chuckled inwardly. A fly in the ointment! Elaina wouldn't like that. Tonight should be amusing.

His daughter wasn't amused, although she smiled. "The long lost brother is returned! And with such bounty! Paulo D'Agosta, you surprise me every time. They say you've brought us a duchess." She spoke only to him, never favoring Shielah with a look. Of course, she knew from Maria that Shielah was by no means a duchess, and she wanted her rival to have to protest.

Shielah fell into the trap. "No, no. He is being ridiculous. And he's embarrassing me. I'm just a flight attendant for the airlines. That's all."

Elaina was still smiling at Paulo. Roberto and Vincent were watching Shielah. "I've missed you." Elaina went on speaking to Paulo as though no one else were around. "I thought we had a date last week."

"Really?" He knew she was lying. "I'm sorry, I didn't have it on my calendar or I would have called."

She put her hand on his sleeve, and purred. "You would have done more than that. I know you. Let's set it for next Wednesday, since you forgot last week."

Paulo moved his arm, reached out and grasped another guest by the hand, with a smile and a warm hello. Then he turned back to Elaina who was still intent on his face. "Sorry. I'd love to, but I've got a busy week. Shielah, do you remember Jim Polanski? That's him coming through the door."

Shielah was so uncomfortable she could hardly speak. The party atmosphere she had been enjoying had become charged with venom and animosity. She could understand why Elaina Maretti should hate her. It was obvious that Elaina wanted Paulo. But why should Roberto dislike her? She was confused and felt herself slipping back into the cocoon she had shed in the last few months.

Roberto checked his watch, then backed out of the group and headed toward the dining room. Ruth stopped him just before he opened it, and spoke to him. He turned to the crowd and spoke above the voices and the laughter.

"Friends! Friends! We're glad to welcome you into our home for our traditional party. There aren't many of you here who are new to this group, so let's not be shy. The dining room is open. I'll propose the first champagne toast." With that he threw open the doors. On the other side there were eight waiters with champagne glasses on trays. They quickly made their way through the crowd, until everyone held a glass. Roberto raised his high and put his arm around Ruth. She smiled and raised her glass as well.

"Here's to good friends and old friends," he said smiling. "Here's to good business and prosperity. And here's to many years to come of happy holidays."

There was a chorus of affirmations and "Hear, hear!" People were clapping each other on the back and sipping their champagne. Jim made his way toward Paulo. He recognized the blonde girl by his friend's side as the one Paulo met in Hawaii. So, he thought, the plot thickens. He also recognized that while the rest of the crowd drank their champagne toast, she discreetly did not. Then, just before he reached Paulo and Sheilah, he saw a woman in a red dress turn around. He stopped and stared. It was Elaina Maretti. She was the reason he was here. He recognized her from the pictures on the society pages of the paper. He had come to meet her, for all that Paulo warned him away from her.

She stared at him rather uninvitingly as long as he looked at her. Then, the challenge taken, he broke into a grin, cocked his head and quickly shoved through to her side. Standing directly in front of her, he spoke. "I propose a toast to the most beautiful girl at the party." Her eyes narrowed and traveled up his six-foot-three frame. Then she smiled slowly and said, "And who might that be?"

"Only you," he assured her and lifted his glass.

Paulo caught the exchange and frowned lightly. Then his eye rested on his sister Maria, and he walked over to the wheelchair and looked around for his mother. People were still making toasts and drinking champagne. Mama was not to be seen, so he raised his voice and his glass anyway.

"I propose a toast to the most beautiful girl at the party."

All eyes were on him. Some of the guests looked quickly at Shielah, some looked at Elaina, but Paulo looked down lovingly at Maria and said, "To Maria, my sister, whose worth is more than gold, and whose beauty exceeds this world." Tears started in Maria's eyes. He bent to kiss her cheek and, at the sight, something sharp stabbed Shielah's heart. Unwillingly, her thoughts went to Buck, her brother, and regret knifed her. Buck! It had been four months since she had seen him. He had loved her once like Paulo loved his sister. That was before she had disgraced herself in his eyes, and before he had humiliated her. His true feelings had come out at last. He didn't trust her, didn't respect her now, even if he had once.

The guests began moving into the dining room, filling their plates with the delicacies Roberto had arranged for. The cost of the lavish party meant nothing to him. It was the cost of his image, the price of success. He was a thoughtful host, seeing that everyone had enough to drink, enough to eat, and felt bountifully welcomed. Ruth was under instructions to be particularly solicitous of Vincent Maretti and Edward Ciardi, a new member of the group and a friend of Vincent's. He was in the diamond business.

Carmella D'Agosta watched Shielah descend the stairs to meet Paulo at the start of the evening. She saw the adoration on his face and she knew she had been right about the girl and the dress. This was the girl he wanted? Fine! This was the girl she would help him win. However, she also saw Roberto's face, though she couldn't hear his words to Shielah. She was not stupid. Old, perhaps, but not stupid, she vowed to a silent Enrico. Roberto wants Paulo to marry Elaina. I'm glad he does not favor her, Papa. She shook her head reflectively. Too much wishy-washy, funny— and not so funny—business going on in that family. Gina Maretti was too blind to see anything her husband did, but that Elaina, she was not blind. She knew her Papa's business. Carmella had asked questions and collected all the bits of information she could about Vincent Maretti. She had even written her family in Milan and asked discreet questions. The answers convinced her that he was mixed up in the Mafia. How much she didn't know. Could you be in the Mafia just a little? She doubted it. She and Enrico had been so careful in the early beginnings of their business not to take investment money from anyone they didn't absolutely know to be clean. The last thing they wanted was to be indebted to the Mafia in any way. They wouldn't hire anyone who might have Mafia connections. Once, they had been threatened by some punks who had demanded a payoff. She and Enrico and their thirteen-year-old Jean sat up for three nights in a row, waiting with shotguns for the punks to come back. If they gave in once, only once, their family would give forever. Word went out all over the neighborhood, the D'Agosta's would fight! And the punks never came back.

Now Vincent Maretti and his daughter had become a part of Roberto's life. She tried to warn him. He laughed at her. He couldn't laugh at her veto on the board of director's, however, and she had consistently refused Maretti's being named to the Board. She had pored over the stock distribution of the company, and discovered that he owned fifteen percent. Too high for her tastes. She put out a moritorium on his buying any more stock.

Carmella zipped up her best white silk dress, turned once in front of the mirror and chuckled. Then she descended the stairs and quietly melted into the cheerful clamor of the party.

Try as hard as he would, Paulo could not stay by Shielah's side all night. People kept dragging him off to talk business, or to pry, or to ask favors. Determinedly he kept going back to her. He knew she would feel ill at ease after the confrontation with Elaina, and he wanted very much for this to be a good experience for her. Elaina could rip anyone to shreds if she chose, and he knew Shielah would be a prime target for her.

Jim successfully monopolized Elaina's time most of the evening, and Ruth stayed by Vincent Maretti's side as much as possible. However, about midnight Ruth was called away by the head caterer, and Vincent made his way to the blonde girl Paulo had left with Maria.

"Are you enjoying the party, young lady?" he asked her innocently enough.

"Yes, I am. How kind of you to ask," Shielah reluctantly broke away from her conversation with Maria.

"I've heard so many rumors about you I hardly know which to believe." He was smiling, his eyes bright with the liquor he had already consumed.

Although she was uncomfortable, Shielah did not detect any animosity. She laughed to convince him of her good humor. "What rumors have you heard?"

"I've heard you are a model, a movie star, a duchess and even," he leaned forward, whispering in her ear, "even a high paid call girl."

Shielah started back from the heavy smell of martinis and the tickling of his breath on her neck. Her laughter was gone. Embarrassment was quickly overshadowed by indignation. Her cheeks were flushed but she looked him straight in the eye. "You heard wrong on *all* accounts. I stated once before, I am simply a flight attendant for the airlines."

He smiled in unconcern for her offense. "Yes, I remember. But isn't that what pretty, young stewardesses do for *real* money?"

"No," she said shortly. "You are mistaken." She turned back as though to talk to Maria. Paulo's sister had been watching the exchange intently. She didn't know what Maretti had whispered to Shielah, but she guessed it was something off-color.

137

"Mr. Maretti," Maria spoke to him sweetly. "I have finished my drink. I wonder if you would find a waiter and get me some more punch." She knew he could hardly refuse his host's sister.

He took her glass, still watching Shielah, his smile turned now into a smirk. "It's too bad to waste such beauty on flying. I could arrange an excellent paying job for you."

Shielah didn't acknowledge his remark. She spoke to Maria and excused herself. Then she made her way to the restroom. She knew her cheeks must be flaming, and she felt hot and dirty all over, just from the man's look. Threading her way through the crowd was rather like trying to thread a rope between stitches of a tapestry. She was stopped several times. She was offered hors d'oeuvres, drinks. She was asked for a dance, though there was no band. She was asked for a date by three different men whom she already knew to be married. She wanted to escape.

Everyone had had too much to drink. Even Paulo and Mama had gotten high on the wine that flowed so freely. She had hoped he would not go along with the crowd. He hadn't meant to. Only two drinks all evening, he promised himself. But before he could finish a drink and set it down, someone would refill it. And he began to get very happy. To Paulo, everything was almost perfect. The only thing better would be if tonight were his wedding night and this his wedding party. He looked around for Shielah and reminded himself not to drink anymore. Where was she?

She only meant to go to the bathroom, but afterwards she could see she was not missed in the melee. It was very warm in the house, and she needed to clear her head, so she quietly opened the side door in the sewing room that let her out onto the patio. She could see outside from the window, and everything was icy and ghostly beautiful, covered in snow. The sudden rush of cold air was most welcome. She knew she couldn't stay long because of the cold, but just a few minutes would help clear her head.

As she opened the door and stepped out, she lost her balance slightly in the blast of cold air and teetered to her right. The door slammed behind her, and she fell against the rough cold shoulder of Roberto, standing in the shadows. Snuggled inside his suit jacket, with her lips inches from his, was Elaina Maretti. All three of them started in surprise.

"I . . . I'm sorry. I didn't know I'd disturb anyone." She was fumbling with the door handle. "I really didn't think anyone would be out here."

He put his hand over hers on the door knob. "But someone was! Miss Sorensen . . . that is your name isn't it? I've forgotten. I'm sorry you found our party so dull that you wanted to escape."

She shook her head. She desperately wanted not to have seen what she *had* seen. "No. It isn't that. It's just that it was hot inside and I wanted a breath of fresh air. I'm going back in now. Excuse me, please."

Elaina laughed. "I think she's embarrassed, or frightened. Are you frightened, Miss Sorensen?"

"No," Shielah answered softly. "I just want to go back inside."

"Then she must be embarrassed. Don't people kiss where you come from? Don't they wish one another happy holidays and steal a friendly kiss?"

138

Shielah didn't answer. Roberto's hand was still on hers, and he would not open the door. She shivered, but not from the cold.

Roberto's voice was low and smooth but with a warning edge to it. "Perhaps she should go back where she comes from. In Utah, I hear people don't drink or smoke or cuss, or kiss each other's girlfriends. Out here, no one minds. Not even Paulo. Not even Ruth. Isn't that right, Elaina?"

"Completely. Only one thing we mind, actually. That's when someone comes in from outside to mess up our plans. And we have plans for Paulo. Oh, they're very good plans. He'll be very happy with me." She smiled meaningfully at Roberto. "I can keep several men happy at once."

Shielah tried to open the door. She didn't want to hear any more, or see any more. She was sick. She was afraid of what she might say. She was afraid she might cry. That would be even worse. She heard a sound from the village down the hill, a clock was striking twelve. Cinderella's night at the ball was over.

"You're messing things up, Miss Sorensen." Roberto said to her averted face. "We have a family arrangement for Paulo to marry Elaina. Our two families would be very good for one another. I hope you won't get in the way. You don't belong."

Anger and nausea were hardening childish tears. She turned back to look at Roberto's handsome, dark face. "You're right. I don't belong with your crowd. I didn't want to stay. And as for Paulo. If he knows your plans and wants . . . her," she jerked her head toward the Italian girl, "then he is welcome to her, and to whatever comes with her."

"You were wrong, Roberto," Elaina reproached him. "She is not a scared rabbit. Perhaps she's a hawk." She reached out to grab the dress Shielah wore.

Shielah twisted in an instant, wrenched her hand from beneath Roberto's, and grabbed Elaina's wrist. Her grip was solid and tight from years of grasping the reins of a horse. She twisted ever so slightly, and the dark-haired girl flinched. "Don't touch this dress. It's not mine. It belongs to Mrs. D'Agosta."

Roberto looked from one girl to the other. He hadn't banked on the hidden steel beneath the softness of the visitor. Elaina didn't give easily, and always got the best of her adversary. It would be interesting to watch them in a contest for his brother. But it was too dangerous to allow. His own future in business depended on Paulo's choice.

He opened the door. Shielah let go of Elaina's wrist slowly, their eyes still locked. Elaina had the last word, as usual, as Shielah backed through the door. "Paulo knows he can get what he wants from me, and I intend to get what I want from him."

Shielah had heard enough. She started back through the crowd of people to find the stairway. Carmella met her just as she closed the door to the sewing room.

"You are cold," she said in surprise.

"I just . . . went out for a breath of air." But she kept her eyes averted from Carmella.

"What isa wrong?"

"Nothing. I guess I stayed out too long. You're right, I'm cold."

Shielah turned back to her before starting up the stairs. "Mrs. D'Agosta, you have been very, very kind to me. Thank you. If we don't . . . if we don't see each other again . . . for a while, I want you to know I'm grateful." She kissed the older woman's cheek, then climbed the stairs to the guest room at the top.

The party lasted two more hours. Paulo saw her climb the stairs and thought of going after her, but he couldn't get away. As soon as he extricated himself from one conversation, someone else grabbed his arm.

Elaina made her way through the people, amusing the men and antagonizing the ladies, as usual. Jim Polanski finally cornered her by the closet door and backed her into it.

"Hey," she challenged him, "Watch it!"

"Watch what? Watch you? That's what I've been doing all night. Or didn't you notice?"

"I noticed." She answered his stare boldly. "And do you like what you see?"

"Enough."

Her eyebrows raised, "Only 'enough?' "

"Enough is a word that is used to indicate nothing has been left out, everything is accounted for, the cup is full." He was grinning at her. "Can I say more?"

"You might say what you want from me, and what you mean by backing me into this closet."

"I'll bet you don't have to be told."

"Maybe not, but I'd like to be."

"Wouldn't you rather be shown?" Jim knew he was right about her. She was fully wise, and irresistible in her sophistication.

He thought she was about to give in to his suggestion, when she did an about-face, stiffened up and said imperiously, "Not really. Let me go. I have better things to do."

He continued to block the doorway, but pulled her up against him with one brawny arm. "You don't have *anything* better to do, Miss Maretti. I'm the best there is." He lowered his lips down to her own full, red ones, and tasted the lipstick she wore. He had been right. She didn't protest. Still he kissed her and she didn't move. Then he moved his lips and she pressed herself to him. It was easy. He had known it would be.

"When can I see you?" he asked her.

"Have you *seen* anything else tonight?" she asked coquetishly.

"No. But I mean later . . . another time—alone. Next week in New York?"

"I'm not in New York next week. I'm in Connecticut. The week after that I'm in Chicago, with Papa. The week after that I'm in Paris for Christmas shopping."

"When are you in New York for me?"

She chuckled. "You're conceited."

"No. I'm just hopeful. I want to see you again. Alone. When?"

"Do you ski?"

"Of course. Have you ever met a Pole that couldn't ski?"

"Next week, in Connecticut, I'll be skiing all week. There'll be some friends but we could get away for some time alone. Bring Paulo."

He jerked back. "What for? What I have in mind doesn't include him."

She soothed him with a kiss. "Silly. I know that. I just thought a foursome might be fun."

"I don't. I want you alone," Jim insisted.

"Conceited . . . and forceful."

"Next week, let's say Wednesday or Thursday."

"OK. Any day is OK. I'll be there 'til Saturday."

"Give me your address and directions before we leave tonight. I'll be there Thursday."

Elaina pushed her way past him and trailed one hand on his neck. "I won't forget," she promised.

Within minutes she made her way over to Paulo. She had purposely waited all evening to go to him. She wanted him to have a chance to see her with other men. She waited to see if the blonde would go to him after coming back inside. She hadn't. So Elaina knew her secret romance with Roberto was safe. She also felt certain Roberto would insure that it remained safe. Not that they meant anything to each other. They were both just bored, and Elaina was angry that she was not wanted by his brother. So, she consoled herself with Roberto. It was delicious revenge on Paulo, even if he didn't know it.

Paulo was turning away from Edward Ciardi when she came up behind him and slipped her arm through his, encircling his waist. Paulo knew immediately who it was. What he really wanted was to go upstairs and into Shielah's room and lie down beside her on the bed and . . . and rest, he told himself.

"Three wishes. The fairy godmother will grant you any three wishes tonight." Elaina laughed at him bewitchingly.

"Three, huh? Let's see. I know I'm supposed to wish for more wine, more time, and tomorrow never coming. I'm afraid, though, I'm partied out. I would have to disappoint you and wish for no more wine, no more time, and no hangover tomorrow."

"Ohhh, party pooper. Should I broadcast that treasonous wish? I might keep it a secret for a small wish of my own."

He should have known better, but he asked, "What's that?"

"I wish we could be alone for just a few minutes. You've spent all night with your cute little stewardess, and I've spent all night trying not to be jealous. I thought you were more of a gentleman than that, trying to make me jealous."

"I wasn't trying, Elaina."

"Well you did a good job for not trying."

"Why should you be jealous? You could have almost any man here, even the ones you shouldn't have because they're married."

"Does that include you?"

"I'm not married."

"Then, that's my wish. That I can have you. Are you granting wishes tonight, fairy godfather?" She was very kittenish at the moment, but Paulo knew she could change into a bobcat at any moment. Be careful, he told himself.

"I'm not worth it, my lovely."

"I like to throw myself away."

"That wouldn't be fair. You deserve the best."

"I'm looking at it." She stared intently into his eyes, and Paulo saw the unmistakeable look of love. He felt sorry for her, and kissed her softly on the forehead.

"I like that. How about once more, with feeling."

"Elaine, be good. This is not the time and you know it."

"Anytime, any place. I'm always available for you." Swiftly she kissed him and whispered against his lips, "you're the only man I want."

"Shh. Stop saying that. You don't know. There are dozens of other men who would kill to hear you say that. Go find Jim. He claims to be the best."

"He found me already," she pouted. "He wants to come see me in Connecticut next week. He wants to see me . . . alone." She watched him to see the effect of that news on him. There was none.

"Be careful. He's broken just as many hearts as you have."

Elaina stamped her foot. "Oh, stop being such a damned gentleman. When we were kids you used to think I was the prettiest girl around. I can remember a few cozy times in the old treehouse over the hill, even if you can't. What happened, Paulo? At first I was afraid I was losing you to the church. Then, just when you decided not to be a priest, you became even more celibate than before. When are you gonna grow up, and look at me."

"Oh I look, all right."

"But you don't touch," she said sarcastically.

"The gems are too rich for my money."

"Don't believe it. This ruby is free to the right customer."

She stared hopefully into his face. "You haven't found him," Paulo said softly, shaking his head.

She swore and stalked away. In moments she was swallowed up by the dozen men or so who still lingered at the dying party. Paulo watched her, not surprised that she hugged and kissed them each in turn, as if trying to show him something. She showed him, all right. He shook his head.

Within half an hour the party-goers all left, Roberto paid the caterers, turned off the lights, and Paulo started up the long staircase. He paused at the top. Directly across from the stairs was the guest bedroom. Shielah was asleep in there. He knew she wouldn't like the smell of wine on his breath, or the smell of smoke in his hair. Maybe she would be asleep then he could sit for a moment and watch her. He looked around. The light was off under

Mama's door. Roberto and Ruth had closed theirs. He stood, undecided, in front of the room for a moment, then softly tried the door knob.

Shielah was not used to locking her door, and consequently had not thought to do so that night. Paulo's eyes were already adjusted to the darkness. He had climbed the stairs in the dark. When he opened the door, the brightness caught him by surprise. It was the moon, brilliant through sheer curtains at the window. It fell across the room like a sheet of silver, engulfing him. He closed the door behind him and stood, looking at the still figure beneath the blankets. Longing coursed through him. This should be his wedding night! He had waited, so long, too long! He wanted her now. He wanted her softness and her sweet love. Something caught in his throat as he gazed entranced by the golden hair that lay in disarray on the pillow. Then she turned her face toward him. Smoothly and silently, he crossed the room to her bed. He knelt down beside it and longing overcame him. He bent down and touched her lips with his own. Her mouth answered his in a way she never had before. With her eyes closed, her head tipped back, he forgot everything and started to move to lie down beside her.

Still half-asleep, she whispered, "Stephen?"

Paulo jumped as though shot.

Shielah's eyes opened wide and she sat straight up in bed. "Who is it?" she whispered, frightened. Then her eyes adjusted. "Paulo!"

"I'm sorry," he answered, hoarsely. "I. . . . I didn't mean to waken you. I just looked in to make sure you were all right, and then . . . then I. . . . " he turned away, struggling with the lump in his throat. "Go back to sleep. I'll lock your door. I'm sorry."

Shielah still stared at him, hardly aware of what had happened. She had been standing on the hillside, in the moonlight with a man. Which man? She didn't know. But she knew he loved her. Love seemed to be all around her. Then he had kissed her, ever so tenderly, and the only name she had for such love was "Stephen." She watched Paulo lock the door from the inside, then slip out and close it. Still she sat up in bed, staring at the door. Stephen! But it had not been Stephen. Indeed, she could barely remember his face, so much had happened to change her life and herself since she had seen him. It had been Paulo who had emanated that intensity of love in her dream, and his lips that she had awakened to. And she had hurt him immeasurably, even in her unconsciousness. Would it always be so, she wondered?

Chapter 8

*D*ear Shielah,

 I won't be writing again for a few weeks, so don't expect a letter from me. They are sending some of us into Cambodia on a special mission to find out where the commies are getting all their weapons. There is a steady stream of them down the Ho Chi Minh trail, and we've got to stop them if we are ever going to stop the war. Progress here is slow. The boys are discouraged. Some of them have turned to pot and even harder stuff to endure the daily expectation of death. We've all seen our buddies die. We all wonder if we'll be next. (I shouldn't write this. Maybe I won't even send it. I know it will just make you cry.)

 Let's see if there is a more cheerful note. Ahh, yes. I have found another Mormon. He's a returned missionary too. His name is Greg Bryant, speaks wonderful Japanese. Wish that did us some good. But it does me good to know I'm not the only 'goody-two-shoes' in the crowd. On Sundays, if we're both at camp together, we go for a little walk in the safety zone, and very unobtrusively give each other a blessing. It helps. I can't tell you how much. Our blessings are not so much to help our fear, they're to help our hate.

 It's hard not to hate when you see the misery of war. I see fear in the eyes of even the tiniest children, and always in the eyes of the women. If they are not afraid of death, or the soldiers, they are afraid for their children. Whenever I crave revenge, Greg reminds me that the sweetest revenge of all would be to convert every last one of those commies as well as the Vietnamese. But how do you do that when you can't even speak the language?

 Vietnamese is nothing at all like Scottish. But I am learning Vietnamese. I am determined to carry on my mission here. I can see no other earthly reason why God might have sent me here. There is a little six year old girl who is my tutor. She teaches me everything I know and some things I don't want to know. I have to be careful. Swear words are a natural part of her vocabulary. She hears them constantly from the GIs. I'm making some headway. When I come back from Cambodia I will start to teach her family. One thing about these people, they are so amazed if you make even a small attempt to learn their language that they bend over backward to help you. Sometimes Hekai giggles at me, but then she is immediately sorry and apologizes profusely. She and Greg are the brightest spots in my week. Except for your letters. They are the best. I have them all. I keep them in my pillowcase, all except for the latest one. That one I always keep in my shirt pocket.

Is it fair to tell you I love you at a time like this? Probably not. I ought to keep my feelings to myself. I don't want you to feel responsible for them, or for me. But my emotions are too raw lately to be able to hide them. I cry easily now, over silly things, like a sunset over the ribbon of river, a little child with a balloon, or a starving dog with a morsel of meat. (Then in very tiny writing) Sometimes I . . . cry . . . for you.

Goodbye for a couple of weeks, my love. Tune in again next month, same time, same station, for tales from the Ho Chi Minh trail. I'm sorry. I guess I'm stupid. But I love you.

Stephen

The letter was waiting for her when she got home from Catskill. She studied it a long time before she could put it down. Brandy studied her.

"Your boy? Is he all right?"

Shielah flung down the letter. "Oh, I don't know. I don't know anything any more. Nothing is easy, Brandy."

"That's the truth, Sugar," Brandy replied philosophically, doing her nails.

"Things used to be easy. At least it seems so now. I hated my teenage years. I hated all those smart aleck boys who thought I was homely, but I didn't have any real, life-shattering problems. When you're a kid, you just go to school, year after year, cope the best you can, and wait to get out and get on with life. Now things aren't so simple. Paulo is in love with me and is quickly convincing me that I am in love with him. Stephen is risking his life every day in Vietnam and writing me these gut-wrenching letters. I was in love with the boy with the laughing eyes and the easy smile, who climbed up a hill to find me. I'm afraid I wouldn't even know him if I met him again. He's not the same boy I fell in love with."

Brandy eyed her wisely, "He sure isn't, honey. He's a man now."

Shielah looked at her silently, comprehending. "Yes," she said after a minute, "He is a man now. And I'm sorry . . . if that's what it takes to be a man."

Brandy unfolded her long legs, got up and started hunting beneath the bed with her toe to find her shoes. "Come on, young lady. We are going to you some fun. You need to forget all this heavy stuff, all this business about Paulo loving you to death, and Stephen loving you into the insane asylum. We are going into Harlem and I will show you some kind of fun."

Some kind of fun it was! Shielah ignored all the graffiti on the buildings, and saw only the flashing white teeth of Brandy's friends. On 118th Street they ducked into a semi-respectable joint, run by Ruby and Howard. It was a small, modest room filled with smoke, a pool table, a card table, a juke box, and a dance floor as tiny as a postage stamp. The whole place seemed packed with black swinging arms and hips and stamping feet.

"There's my gal. Brandy gal, where you been?" Ruby hailed them as they came in. Howard, behind the bar, looked up smiling, but his eyes lost their sparkle when they picked up Shielah's white face. Then the hood on her coat fell back and her hair fell down her back. In the sleazy light it looked reddish gold. Too gold for her good, Howard thought. He frowned. Blondes, they always brought trouble. Why'd Brandy bring her here?

As if to answer his silent question, Brandy took Shielah's arm and urged her over to the bar. "Howard, I'm gonna give you the biggest treat of your life and introduce you to my special friend. This is Shielah. She belongs to me, hear? She mine!"

He heard. And he knew what she meant. The girl was all right people. Well, good! He hoped she didn't bring no trouble, anyway.

"What 'chu want, honey?" Ruby asked Brandy. "Some namesake?"

"I ain't drinking tonight. My friend, she don't drink, so I don't. We together. We just here for some fun. But I will take some ice-tea. Shielah, what 'chu want?"

Shielah was amazed. She stared, dumbfounded, around her. It was another world, and fascinating. It was also amazing how Brandy's accent, so carefully educated in public, lapsed into a thick drawl amongst her own people.

"Just Seven-Up," she replied, watching the dancers on the floor. The music was deafening, and both men and women were bouncing, dipping, and jerking to the hypnotic beat. Lights were flashing over the dance floor, and the dancers seemed in ecstasy with their music.

Howard served her without a word, just a nod of his grizzled, gray head. She and Brandy went exploring.

"What are they doing?" Shielah whispered in Brandy's ear.

"Ain't you never seen pool before?" Brandy stared at her incredulously.

"No. I've never been in a pool hall before. Tell me how you do it!"

A gigantic black man overheard her. He was easily six-foot-eight, and thin as a rail. He grinned easily and his smile was a blinding flash of white, if uneven, teeth. He leaned over Brandy.

"Your friend want me to show her how it's done?" he asked, raising his eyebrows. "Just watch this."

"First you take your pool cue, sweet and tight. Then you swing it to the left, then you swing it to the right." He leaned over the pool table, and wiggled his skinny hips in both directions. In the dim, flashing light he lined up his shot. "You step around the floor, kind of nice and light." And he was wildly gyrating as his shot knocked the opponent's ball into the pocket. "And you twist around and twist around with all yo' might."

The lanky black man grabbed Brandy by one hand and twisted her, swirling her out into the dancing crowd, then grabbed Shielah's hand and did the same to her. Both girls were laughing at his antics.

"You throw that old pool shark down on his face, you fill up his pockets with such style and grace." Now he had his cue behind him, shooting through the space between his arm and waist. "Snake that old cue out," he shot with deadly accuracy. "And then you bring it back." He turned to face them and bowed imperiously before them. "That's a little bit of pool hall ball and the Jack."

Shielah and Brandy were laughing and clapping, and he was grinning from ear to ear. "Jack, I want you to meet my special friend. This here is Shielah. We live together."

His black, long fingered hand shot out. "Lay it in there, babe. Pleased to meet 'chu. Brandy's my gal, right shug?" He kissed her, but she turned her face so he only got her cheek.

"Wrong, boy. I ain't nobody's gal. I'm my own gal. Anybody wants me's gotta have more to offer than a basketball."

"I thought you must be a basketball player," Shielah smiled at him.

"The best, chile, and don't you forget it." He pointed a finger at her.

"The best, huh? You an' Meadowlark?" Brandy cocked her head at him and teased him with her smile.

"He's my little brother. Man, I teach him everything he knows."

"Right!" Brandy said sarcastically. "Jack you're full of . . . full of it," she ended decorously.

Jack laughed. "Your special friend don't 'low you to cus, gal?"

"Only when I do," Shielah said in mock soberness.

"You ever seen a card shark at work?" Brandy asked her as he pulled her over to a table lit only by a dim, yellow light.

"No, I never have".

"Honey, you are gonna be ed-u-cated tonight. This is better 'n college for you."

Nobody spoke as they moved up. "Don't stand directly behind anyone or lean over their shoulder." Brandy whispered. There was one player with his cards laid down, obviously out on that hand. They stood a few feet back of him. Shielah didn't see how the other five men could concentrate on anything with the deafening din of the jukebox. Words were sparse.

"Raise you, twenty-five."

"See you. Raise you another twenty."

"Call you."

"Damn! Thought you were bluffing this time."

Mighty Joe Young—as everyone called him—shook his massive head. "I never bluff," he said in a rich, gravelly voice.

147

Brandy leaned over and whispered something in his ear, then said loud enough for everyone to hear, "That's a bunch of bull-oney. You always bluff and you knows it."

His stomach began to shake, a smile twisted itself onto his pursed mouth and he reached up to grab her by the neck. "Sweet stuff. Here's my shug. Hey, shug, where you been so long? I'm missing you. You my luck, and my luck's been running out."

"Not me, Mighty Joe. I never run out on you." Brandy vowed with her eyes rolled upward and her hand held high.

The old man, with the paunchy belly, and the pile of chips in front of him gurgled a laugh.

"You lyin' woman. You run out with every Erastus, James and Rufus in Harlem. I know your type. You sweet talks me for a drink, then you goes and drinks it with some young buck. Who's this purty child you got here?"

His eyes narrowed when he looked at Shielah. She knew instinctively he wasn't any more thrilled about her presence than Howard had been. She smiled at him and tilted her head charmingly. "Just a poor, white child she pulled up out of the gutter, Mr. Joe. She fed me and clothed me and now I'm her slave forever."

She won him over easily. He began to gurgle again at that, nodding at her appreciatively. "You be careful with her, shug."

Brandy knew what he meant. It was night, and it was Harlem, and a white girl was often not welcome. So far the place had accepted her presence. Everything was going on as usual. She had Jack and Ruby to thank for that.

Mighty Joe Young squinted up at them. "You in for this hand?"

Brandy laughed, "Play against you? I ain't that crazy. I just wanted Shielah here to see a real card shark in action. Show her your stuff." He nodded and began to deal. Brandy took her arm and pulled her back. Then someone else also took her arm and pulled her further. She turned around. Jack had already claimed Brandy and was jiving to the music. Another young black man, shorter, and coal black was asking, almost timidly, for a dance. Shielah was embarrassed.

She partially shook her head. "I'll slow you down. I can't dance like you do."

"I'll show you," he volunteered softly.

"I warn you, I'm a slow study."

He smiled. "It's all right. Like this." He took small steps in a little circle, bouncing and jerking to the beat of the music. She tried it and laughed at herself. He laughed softly with her. "Come on. You OK. Like this." His hands were clasped behind his back, his knees seemed out of joint, but his movement was poetry.

Shielah had forgotten all her burdens. Who could think of Vietnam, or rich brothers who cheated on their wives, or Paulo with his unflagging love. She copied the young man as well as she could. She forgot about caring if she looked silly or did it wrong. The cocoon was totally forgotten and she was a shining, soaring butterfly. They danced until almost two

148

o'clock. Jack taught her to shoot pool, and Joe taught her to play poker. At last, the spell of the music and the fun was overcome by weariness.

Finally she told Brandy, "I'm not going to make it much longer. Do we go home, or do your friends, Ruby and Howard, have a cot for me to collapse on?"

"We'll go. I didn't realize what time it was. Get your coat. I'll be there."

They thanked Ruby for their night of fun and the drinks that were on the house. Then they headed for the subway.

The subway entrance wasn't far, just two blocks. Shielah could hardly wait to get home and cast her weary body into bed. The snow was mostly melted. What was left over from Thanksgiving was an occasional pile of slush and mud. Still, it was cold, and the wind was whining down the streets. At first the cool air felt good after all the dancing.

"Brandy, that's the most fun I've had in forever. I can't remember ever having more fun than tonight. It was wonderful. I'm jealous. You get to do that all the time."

Her black friend laughed. "Well, I'll tell you what. You let me go in your place to some of those swank parties of Mr. Paulo D'Agosta, and I'll let you go in my place to Ruby's anytime."

Shielah laughed out loud at the thought of Brandy waltzing into Roberto D'Agosta's ritzy party. She'd love to see it. And Brandy would be more than a match for Elaina Maretti. How she'd love to arrange it. Brandy had been right last summer though, and Shielah knew it. The black people accepted a white girl much faster than the whites would a black one. Brandy had only to speak the words, "She's OK. She's mine," and Shielah was accepted. Shielah shook her head over the injustice.

Brandy looked down at her wrist as she put her dime into the turnstyle. "Rats! I still have Jack's watch. We'll have to go back. I don't want this. He'll pester me for a month to get it back. That's just why he made me wear it, so he could call me every day for a month of Sunday's. I've got to go back."

"I'll just wait here." Shielah said.

"Oh, no you won't. Not at two o'clock in the morning. Come on."

"No, really, Brandy. I'm tired. I don't want to walk clear back. There's absolutely no one around. I'll be all right."

Brandy shook her head no and tugged on Shielah's arm.

"Now, I'm not a baby," Shielah said impatiently. "Everybody tries to keep me from going out onto the street alone, like I'm a 'babe in the woods' or something. You come and go anywhere you please, and so does Jeri, but I'm not allowed to do boo without someone with me to 'protect' me. Would you quit? I am not going back. I'm too tired. I'm going to sit right down here on the steps and wait for you."

She was out of her mind. Brandy stared at her. "You nuts?" she asked. "What'll you do when some gang of niggers comes by here and starts harassing you?"

"Why did you call them that?" Shielah asked incredulously.

"Because I can! They're mine. I can call them niggers if I want to." She laughed and stuck her elbow in Shielah's ribs. "But you can't. What'd you do anyway, huh? You be scared spitless. In fact, I'd be. Come on. Probably wouldn't be a bad idea to get Mighty Joe to see us home."

"Oh, Brandy, don't be ridiculous. No one has ever 'seen us home' before. Just hurry and go give him his watch. I'll wait right here." She sat down on the steps leading to the subway.

Brandy looked down the street. She could see Ruby's place down there. It wasn't very far. She could be back in two, well, maybe five minutes. She could see that Shielah meant to be stubborn. She glanced around. There was no one else out. In five minutes, what were the odds? She started down the block half running. What were the odds? Never good!

Shielah sat with her forehead resting on her locked arms, her knees pillowing her face. She was cold and uncomfortable, and her feet felt like fire pokers, but she was warm clear through inside. It had been an unforgettable evening. What would Stephen think? No, she wouldn't think of Stephen tonight. Then she smiled to herself. What would Grandma think? She would probably be appalled. Her granddaughter had danced the night away with ten different black men, she who had never seen a black person up close until last summer when she met Brandy.

She was indulging in memories of the summer when she heard laughter and shuffling feet, fingers popping, and a strange, spoken gibberish she couldn't understand. The feet started down the stairs, sometimes sliding, sometimes tapping. She still sat with her face buried, praying for them to go on by. She knew they couldn't see her blonde hair. It was tucked under the hood of her coat. She knew they couldn't see her face. Maybe they would think she was an old lady and leave her alone. How long had Brandy been gone? At least ten minutes.

"Ey, what dat?"

"Man, who knows. Come own!"

"No hurry."

"I tired, boy. I going home. You coming?"

"Shore." The footsteps were almost past her, to the turnstyle, when a voice spoke next to her ear. "Boo!" Shielah jumped, and her head jerked up.

"Whooo-ee. Jackpot! See what I got."

He was young, no more than sixteen, Shielah guessed. But his friends were older. Three young black kids had had too many beers and were heading home to sleep it off until next week.

"Graffiti, graffiti, graffiti," the boy in the long gray trenchcoat called out, then whistled, long and low.

"She wasn't gonna say 'hello', you know it?" the boy who had scared her asked his friends incredulously.

"How come you not say hello, honkie? You on my turf. You can at least be polite and say hello." Shielah didn't speak. She didn't think she even spoke English right then. The only thing in her head was disjointed sounds that didn't make whole words.

The three of them surrounded her. "She ain't as ugly as some of those honkies," the oldest boy taunted. "Only she's dumb. You suppose she's deaf and dumb?" he asked the other two, his eyes wide open.

"Dumb at the very least. She don't know 'hello.' Let's teach her. The three leaned down, their faces in her face, their beer breath nauseating her. "Hell . . . o." They said. They didn't wait for her response. "Hell . . . o." They said it over and over until she thought she would scream.

She closed her eyes to block out the twisted, leering faces, and prayed once more for Brandy. Then she heard them taunt, "I think she's gonna cry."

"You suppose if black's tears are white, honkies's tears are black?"

She opened her blue eyes and they were dry. This was exactly the slice of life Buck was sure she could not handle. She was badly frightened now, but the china doll wouldn't break for them either. "Leave me alone and go home," she spoke.

"Ooh," they drew back in mock surprise.

"The dumb lady speaks. But is she nice? No, she ain't!" The youngest boy seemed to have to prove himself. He was the nastiest of all, and his language the filthiest. His nose wrinkled up as he shoved his face back just inches from hers.

"We don't like your 'hello', honkie lady. Give us a sweet kiss instead."

Shielah stood up and started backing up the stairs, holding onto the rail beside her. "Go away. I'm not hurting you. I'm just waiting for someone."

They hooted at that and followed her slow ascent up the stairs. "Your honkie boyfriend, or your black lover?" They were having their fun with her, dancing up and down the stairs, flinging their arms around like they might hit her.

"Just my friend, Mighty Joe Young." She didn't know why the name came out, but it did, and it had an effect. They stopped for a second and looked at each other, disbelief on their faces. They stopped gyrating and became serious. "Joe ain't got no honkie friends. You lie, lady."

The oldest of the group grabbed her wrist and twisted it behind her back. The youngest jerked off her hood and whistled as her hair fell out on his hand. He looked up at his other friends and rubbed its softness between his fingers.

"Pretty! Mama's got pretty hair!"

Shielah fought down her panic, and remembered the few defensive moves Buck had taught her. Tensing all her muscles, she turned toward the boy who had twisted her arm. Forward, down and turn, and he was off balance when she shoved slightly. He fell back, knocking one of his friends with him.

"You boys just funning this lady a little, I see!" The voice was low and gravelly. They all looked up to see the great expanse of Mighty Joe Young at the top of the subway stairs. Brandy was beside him.

"She yo' friend?" the young boy asked in a new voice, this one was whining.

"She is dat! For a fact! You not causing her no grief, boy?"

They were easing toward the turnstyle. "No sir, Mr. Joe. No, sir. We just goin' home. It's late, you know. Our Mamas, they waiting up fo' us."

Joe pulled something out of his pocket, and smashed it down on the ground at their feet. A firecracker went off and they started like scared rabbits. "Don't you never mess with my friends, niggers, or that be buckshot in yo' tail. Git on home to yo' Mamas, befo' you mess them diapers." Shielah had never enjoyed a gurgling laugh so much. He waddled on down the stairs, and Brandy was wrapping her arms around her.

"Gees, I'm sorry, Shielah. I was afraid. I warned you. Why are you so stubborn, girl? You OK?"

Joe put his hand timidly on her coat. "Those young 'uns hurt you any, missy?"

"No, sir," she answered, respectful of the power he commanded in his circles. "I'll admit they scared me a little."

"Looked to me like you was getting the best of them," he chortled again, his belly heaving.

Brandy was standing back now, admiring her friend. "I'll say. I'd never have thought you had it in you."

Shielah smiled at her shakily. "I know. You thought I was a baby."

"No, but I . . . well, anyone would have been scared. I'm sorry."

"I am too. For being so stubborn. Next time I'll walk with you, even if my feet are like wood."

Joe Young waited with them until the subway came, and then he waved them goodbye. "Come see us again," he grunted. "We'll take better care of you next time." Shielah leaned forward, at the last moment, and gratefully kissed his forehead. "You took good care. Thanks."

She thought she saw the black man blush, then his squinty eyes grew big and round and a wheezy noise came out of him. The doors shut and he stood smiling and waving goodbye until they were out of sight.

Brandy looked thoughtfully into her friend's eyes for several minutes, then jerked her head up and down in one quick, affirmative motion. She grinned and said, "You mine!"

In November she bid a line of flight for December that would give her Christmas off. She hadn't been home since last July, and she was beginning to be homesick. Not desperately. She had come to love New York in three short months like she never had Clarksville. But she did miss her grandmother, although she would not permit herself to think of Buck and include him in those longings for home. But when the December list was posted, again she hadn't enough seniority to get what she had bid for. She was still on standby.

It was easy not to see Paulo that month. She was flying almost constantly, working up her hours for seniority. She deliberately flew four days on, two days off, and volunteered to sub even on those few days she had off. She didn't want to see Paulo. She didn't want to dig any deeper into the relationship. She had been frightened by her intense response the night he came into her room and kissed her. He was confusing her. She had always loved Stephen. She reminded herself often of her own vision of him before he went on his mission. She wanted to marry Stephen. It would be so right. They would marry in the temple, her sons would hold the priesthood because of their father. If she married outside the church, even someone as fine as Paulo, she would have to fight all her life to raise her children the way she wanted them raised. Her sons might never hold the priesthood or go on missions. They might grow up to be like Roberto, heaven forbid. She shuddered at the thought. No, there was too much to lose. She would put him out of her life.

But Paulo would not be easily forgotten. Roses still came once a week, and with them, occasionally, small perfume bottles, or, most recently, Christmas ornaments. Her roommates were envious. If not for the vision of Stephen, she knew she would have succumbed to Paulo's adorations. He was everything she wanted in a man, almost. Everything but religious. Was she a fool to make so much of it? She knew Jeri thought she was, and so did Marci. Brandy wouldn't comment.

In December she went through a prepared landing. Flying into Baltimore, the winds were so severe the plane was tossed around like feather. Passengers were moaning and throwing up, frequently in their laps or in the aisle, instead of the airsick bags the plane provided. The flight attendants were strapping everyone in, as well as themselves, praying for a safe landing. By some good luck, just before they hit the runway, the crosswinds calmed, and they only bounced twice before the pilot gained complete control and brought the plane in to a gentle stop.

That time she wasn't scared. She was too busy up until the last minute to think about crashing. Two weeks later she had a real emergency landing and the senior attendant froze up. She lost her nerve and Shielah gave the orders.

A fire broke out in one of the engines. The passengers saw it first and called the senior over. When she saw it, she ran up the main aisle. Shielah stopped her in the galley.

"What's wrong?"

The girl's face was white. She had been flying two years longer than Shielah but had never had a major problem to handle. "There's fire in number one engine."

Shielah expected orders but the senior was blank.

"I'll go to the cockpit" Shielah said tersely, "and find out how much the pilot knows, how bad it is, where we can put down. Nancy, you go tell the passengers that the pilot is aware of it and is taking steps to control it."

She went forward and knocked on the cabin door. "Joan, we got a problem," the pilot spoke as she entered. Then he glanced back and saw it was not the senior attendant. "Where's Joan?"

"She . . . uh . . . she's calming down the passengers. She sent me."

The pilot frowned, then said. "Engine number one is on fire. It's not bad, but I'm putting down in Quincy. Small airport, but they said they've got the gear to help us. Fire equipment is ready. Tell the passengers that we have everything under control. Make sure they know how to do a jump and slide, and remember to get all glasses and high heels, anything that would tear the slides. I've shut down that engine and all the auxiliary power in the cabin. Just try to keep those passengers calm and get ready for a quick exit."

"Yes, sir." She backed out of the cabin. "How much longer?" she asked before she closed the door.

"Four minutes to landing," he replied.

Joan was still standing in the lunch station. Shielah said, "Get all that garbage stowed, and all the glasses and dishes. We're doing a jump and slide landing. Fire trucks are already there. We'll all take our assigned exits. Let's get all the loose objects stowed, all sharp objects removed, even high heels." Then the six attendants went back through the airplane touching people on the shoulder, calming them with a soothing voice, telling them that in four minutes they would be on the ground. From their individual responses, eight people were chosen to act as aides in getting the other passengers to the exits as quickly as possible.

"When we land, we'll help you out," she promised all the passengers. "Just follow our instructions and move quickly. Occasionally we have an engine malfunction. That's why we have three others. To insure your safety. Your pilot has a perfect safety record of fifteen years with the airlines. He's a whiz. He really is. Remember, just let us help you. There'll be a rubber slide at each exit. Line up at the exit closest to you, grasp your flight attendant's hand and jump and slide." She started back up the aisle, trying not to look at the flames streaming from the engine. She was not the only one. All eyes were glued with horrified fascination to the faulty engine. Some of the passengers were crying, some of them praying.

The pilot actually got them down in three minutes. Fire trucks were on the runway, squirting the plane the moment they touched down, and Shielah stood in the blowing wind and directed the jump and slide exit from the right wing. It went as smoothly as could be expected. One elderly lady had to be carried, and went down the slide off the left wing in the lap of a forty-year-old businessman. Six big rubber slides went from the exit doors, down the wing and down to the ground. Airport personnel stood at the bottom and broke their slide, helping each one regain his footing. Paramedics were there to help the passengers once they were off. The flight attendants called out, over and over, "Jump and slide, jump and slide," grabbing each passenger's hand and throwing them into the rubber slide, for many of them were afraid to go.

They had all the passengers out in two minutes. Too long, Shielah thought. In flight school they said it had to be one-and-a-half minutes.

But John Sheppard, the manager of the Quincy airport, didn't think it was too long. He had nothing but praise for the operation, and Joan, to her credit, reflected the praise to Shielah.

"You really came through when I was scared spitless. Thanks. It would have been different without you."

Shielah shook her head, "No, you'd have done it just fine. Everyone gets scared for a few minutes. So did I. I'm a big baby about fires. It's my worst thing."

154

"Well, no one would have guessed it," the older girl said appreciatively.

The pilot stopped by and added his comments. "You did OK. You can fly with me anytime. You've got a cool head."

Shielah tried to smile. "Maybe just empty. You are really the hero of the day."

He shook his head, "Nope. I don't think so. Good job. You wanta go get a drink? You deserve one."

But Shielah shook her head. She only wanted to be alone, to lay her weary body on a soft bed.

It was only afterward that she began to shake and tremble. In the hot, foamy bath in the airport hotel, she grew weak and could hardly get out of the water. When at last she lay between the cool sheets, she shook and stared at the ceiling for hours, afraid to go to sleep to the same nightmares of fires that she haunted as a little girl. Tears slipped down past the corners of her eyes and wet her hair. Finally, unconsciousness came but, blessedly, no nightmares.

She knew she couldn't go home for Christmas so she made Christmas in New York as much fun as possible. She and Jeri went shopping at Bloomingdale's and Macy's three days before Christmas. The redhead bought presents for her five brothers and sisters and parents, until Shielah's arms as well as her own were overstuffed. Finally they took a cab over to Rockefeller Plaza, plopped themselves down at a table by the ice rink and ate a late lunch.

The Christmas tree at the plaza was mammoth, certainly the largest one Shielah had ever seen, and strung with thousands of lights. Couples and youngsters were blythely skating around and around the rink. It was another day that Shielah would later remember with nostalgia.

"Maybe I'll call Grandma tonight. I hate to tell her I won't be home. I've been putting it off, buying presents for her, and hoping to relieve some of her disappointment. But I know she's going to be really sad. She never did understand what happened at Thanksgiving. I mean, she knows there was a blizzard and all, but she still thinks I should have been able to make it home for at least a day. I can hardly stand to tell her I won't be home for Christmas. In fact I don't know if I can stand it for myself. This will be my first Christmas alone. I don't even know where I'll be—probably home alone."

"Umm, well, you'll have it better than I will. I am flying the commuter flight from New York to Buffalo, to Albany, to D.C. and back. It should be swell."

"Do you like being an attendant, now, Jeri?" Shielah asked her friend.

"Yeah. After three months of crappy schedules, hands creeping up under my skirt, smiling and saying 'pardon me' to some cigar-smoking joker—yeah, I still like it. I've met some nice men on the flights, too. One or two I've dated, discreetly, of course. But I like the excitement, never knowing who you're going to meet, a movie star, or a sports star, or a politician, or Mr. Wonderful. Do you like it?"

That was easy. Shielah loved it, for all the reasons Jeri had mentioned. She also hated the same things. But most of all, she liked what she had learned in becoming a flight attendant, the first-aid readiness, the grooming and poise, the pleasant conversations, and the sense of accomplishment she felt. She liked discovering that she could handle emergencies, face danger without panicking, and mix with diverse people. Her job was a diamond with millions of facets and she loved almost all of them. And best of all, she was beginning to like herself, to respect herself, and to have a sense of her own worth.

But Christmas Eve day Shielah got her call from the crew desk at four p.m.. She was to fly into Montreal, Canada. It would be her first flight abroad, and normally she would have been very excited. But flying on Christmas Eve was the worst. Almost everyone on board the plane was going home or to loved ones in Montreal. There were a lot of French-speaking Canadians on board, so she had a chance to use her high school French. It gave her a great sense of satisfaction. After three hours in the air, she found her herself fairly conversant. Any other time the practice would have been a lot of fun.

"Le cafe, monsieur?" she asked in her best French.

He chuckled at her accent. "A very good try, mademoiselle," he replied. "Oui, avec la creme, s'il vous plait."

These passengers were in the mood for Christmas carols and requested inter- cabin music of carols. They sang almost every one with the music, drank hot toddies, and cheered each other liberally. It was a boisterous crowd, one that Shielah was reluctant to try too hard to calm down. When they disembarked, many well-toddied men kissed her cheek. Cleaning up afterward, she became more and more glum. It was Christmas Eve! Grandma and Buck were at Aunt Maddie's. Uncle Will's family was, no doubt, out tobogganing, at least until they became too cold. She could picture, in her mind, the cozy farmhouse front room with the great, tall Christmas tree that Uncle Will cut, and the children trimmed with popcorn and construction paper chains and candy canes.

The more she reflected, the more her eyes began to fill. Stop it, she told herself. This is your job, and you love it! One Christmas away from home isn't going to kill you. Where was Stephen? Was he in the cold barracks on Christmas Eve? Maybe he was spending it with that friend Greg somebody or other. Where was Paulo? No, she wouldn't think about him. There, the cabin was finished. She would go to the hotel and take a long, hot bath and go to sleep with the Christmas carols playing on the radio. It would be almost as good as going to sleep in front of the Christmas tree, as she had done so often in her childhood.

The Hotel Pierre was a lovely, old brick and stone structure of Georgian architecture. It was immense and very impressive. The flight attendants for New World were always treated to the best wherever they went, but this was elegant beyond her imagination. Mahogany walls and banisters, and old fashioned dark, floral carpets. In the lobby, over by the huge stone fireplace, was the hotel Christmas tree. She and the other girls said goodbye in the lobby. Two of the girls were from Montreal and were meeting family. The other attendant was determined not to be alone on Christmas Eve. She went to mingle with the guests standing and talking in the lobby. Waiters wandered in and out, offering cocktails on the house to all the guests. Shielah stood on the threshold of the great room, looking for a few moments at the tree and the knots of people laughing by the fireplace. The other girl had quickly been drawn in. Shielah smiled. A gentleman passing by thought she was smiling at him and paused to tip his hat, saying something in French, but she turned away. "Pardonez, pardonez moi," she murmured and moved toward the elevators. There was only one couple on the elevator. They were cuddled up, arms about each other, faces beaming. Shielah tried to smile at them in answer to "Joyeux Noel." But she couldn't. Self-pity overcame her.

How Buck would laugh now. The china doll was falling apart, just as he had said. She had survived a mugging in Harlem, the subways of New York City, and an emergency landing with a fire in the engine. But now, with Christmas carols playing in the elevator and down the halls, the china doll was breaking. The butterfly's wings were drooping, and she just wanted to get to her room quickly so she could throw herself down on the bed and indulge in a good cry.

The elevator seemed so slow. She was trying desperately to hold back the tears. With her little flight bag in hand, she half ran down the hall, found her door and forced the key in. The door opened smoothly and she rushed in, making for the bed.

There, in the middle of the room, stood a Christmas tree. Not large, but not small either. It stood on a little nightstand, and with that, was as tall as she. It was decorated with red birds in tiny nests, and white, ceramic doves. The tiny lights that winked at her were inside white ceramic angels, and the whole thing was covered with pink angel hair. It was the most beautiful tree she had ever seen. Certainly the most welcome. She forgot everything else and walked toward, it entranced. Did the hotel do this in every room? she wondered. On its branches was one small, white envelope. All at once she knew!

"Do you like your tree?"

She whirled around at the sound of his voice. Paulo stood in the doorway, his face all smiles at her surprise. Now there was no holding the tears, they came in great gulps, and she threw herself into his arms.

"Oh yes, oh yes. I love my tree, your tree, whoseever tree it is. It's beautiful. I was so lonely. I've never been alone on Christmas. I thought . . . I thought . . . how'd you know I would be here? My roommates? Which one told you? I don't care. I'm glad they did. I'm so glad you're here. I'm so glad you came."

Her face awash with tears she beamed at him, then kissed both cheeks, then wiped her own, and cried some more. He closed the door, and sat in the overstuffed green chair, holding her on his lap. She put her head on his shoulder and they sat for a while listening to the Christmas carols piped into the room. He turned off the light so that the Christmas tree lights were the only bright spots in the room, shining through the pink angel hair.

After a while she asked again, "How did you know? Did my roommates tell you?"

"Nope. I have my ways."

"I don't think it's coincidence anymore that you seem to turn up wherever I am going. Who's your source?"

"Can't tell. Does it matter?"

"No," she said.

"How long are you going to try to kick me out?" he asked.

"What do you mean?"

"You know exactly what I mean. Ever since Thanksgiving you don't answer calls, you don't return calls, you obviously don't want to see me. Did I so offend you that night in your bedroom? If I did, I'm sorry!"

She drew away from him and looked into his face. She sighed, and shook her head. He had become so beautiful to her. Now she saw not only Paulo when she looked into his eyes, she saw also Carmella and Maria. They were all beautiful. Only Roberto spoiled it. She wondered if Paulo suspected anything about his brother.

"You didn't offend me. You scared me. At least, I scared myself."

"What are you scared of?"

"Wanting you. Loving you. Giving up my life for you."

He smiled at her tenderly. "Isn't that what women do—have always done—give up their lives for the men they love?"

"I suppose," she answered. "But I don't think I'm ready to, or even want to."

"What will you give up? Is being a stewardess so important to you?"

"It is. It sort of . . . defines me . . . if you know what I mean. It has become my identity. I never had one before, at least one I liked. I like this new Shielah Sorensen. She is competent, she is capable, she is respected by her peers. That means a lot to me."

He nodded. "I understand. That's important."

She went on, "But that's not the most important thing to me." He waited. "The most important thing I would give up is my whole system of values, morals, standards, goals, all of that. It's all wrapped up in my religion and my belief system. So far it's been the only support I have had to rely on. I am afraid to throw it away. And I don't know if I ever really could, because I believe it. I really believe it."

"I wouldn't ask you to throw it away."

"You wouldn't ask, but life with you could not possibly include my religion. What, you would go to Mass with Mama and Maria, and I would go to Sacrament Meeting and Sunday School alone? That doesn't sound like much fun to me."

"Sunday is only one day out of the week."

"My religion is every day."

"So is my love." And he kissed her to stop any further protestations.

"That's not fair. I wanted to say something else."

He kissed her again, longer this time.

158

"Paulo, you can't stop a discussion with . . . " He took her head between his hands and kissed her until she was breathless. When he had finished and she was quietly resting on his shoulder, enjoying the feel and the smell of him, he whispered softly. "Yes, I can."

Never was anything so clear to her. This was love, here in Paulo's arms, feeling soft and warm inside from the sight of his face, the feel of his body. She had known since the first that he loved her but hadn't admitted that she loved him. She hadn't wanted to know, not really. Her life was planned with Stephen and there was no place for a stranger with a different way of life. But tonight told her surely. He was no stranger. That uncanny sense of having recognized him at first meeting—she understood it now. Whatever her vision of Stephen meant, some time, some place, she must also have had a strong bond with this warm, loving man. And she felt safe tonight, without having to apologize for wanting to be safe. She had no need to appear strong with Paulo, for he never accused her of being weak. He seemed to understand her without explanations, and to love all of her, without demanding that she be different in any aspect. He had loved her before she loved herself.

"Paulo, can we go to your church for Mass? One of the other girls said that St. Anne's is a beautiful cathedral and has a lovely midnight Mass on Christmas."

He drew back and regarded her, slightly surprised, but pleased. "Of course. I wouldn't have suggested it for fear you might think I was pushing. Have you ever been to midnight Mass?"

"No, never. I've never been to a church other than my own."

"Then how do you know that your's is the only true one as you so often claim."

"That quiet little voice you talked about once. You know, the one that keeps you out of trouble if you listen to it."

"Yes, but you have to know the alternatives."

"What is the alternative to eternal marriage?"

He paused a moment, thinking. "You want me to say 'non-eternal' marriage, don't you? 'Temporary' is the word you're looking for."

"I don't know any other words for it, and it sounds awful to me. I may be insecure, or I may be selfish, but if I love someone enough to marry him, I want him forever, not just temporarily."

He pondered that. After a moment she said, "We are the only church that teaches eternal marriage. And there are other doctrines I also believe, which no other church has. I may not have been inside their doors, but I know what I believe anyway."

"Come on," he said. "Let's go to St. Anne's."

St. Anne's was in the very old, very European section of town. Shielah had expected Canada to be much like America, but this city was strictly European. The streets were cobblestone. Everything was written in French, although English was also spoken. There were outdoor cafes, empty now in the bitter cold of December. St. Anne's was not a massive cathedral, not as imposing as some, but brilliantly lit. The stained glass windows were glowing, the open doors were streaming light, and people were standing everywhere. They left the cab a block away and walked, the ferocious cold biting their ears and noses. Winding their way between the spectators, they were able to just edge inside the door. The altar was ablaze with candelabras and beautiful poinsettia displays. An almost lifesize statue of the Madonna and Child held the place of honor, just below the priest's pulpit. It was lit by one single, powerful beam of light. The rows of pews each had a small bouquet of flowers attached, with silvery streamers flowing down to the floor. And it smelled like Christmas. Burning candlewax and pine scent hung in the air, mixed with the scent of thousands of perfumes worn by the patrons.

Shielah studied the people. They were an indiscriminate mixture of lower class—with old, faded scarfs bound securely beneath fleshy chins— and the more affluent, sporting stylish, lacy scarves simply pinned on. Shoulder to shoulder with a man in dirty, ragged overalls and an old sweater was a fashionable woman with a full length fur coat, expensive bag, and high heels. No one seemed to notice their differences. That same fashionable woman leaned across her neighbor to embrace and kiss on both cheeks another woman with high- topped men's working boots and chapped, red hands.

The ceremony was beginning. The sound of Christmas carols was faint, but growing louder. Shielah thought the choir would come from a side door and line up across the altar area. But everyone was watching the open doorway in the rear, and soon the choir made its entrance. They had started two blocks away, walking through the streets, bundled up against the frigid wind, singing of the birth of the Christ Child. People had flocked along their path, singing with them, tears streaming. They came in slowly, very slowly, moving only one step every four beats, lining both aisles, and remaining there to sing two more songs, before they moved into the traditional formation at the front of the church.

"Un flambeau Jeanette, Isabella. Un flambeaux couron au berceaux." Their blend was rich and mellow, their faces reflecting the joy of their message. "Ah, ah, ah que la mere est belle, ah, ah, ah, que l'enfant est beau."

Then came the children singing "What child is this, who laid to rest on Mary's lap, is sleeping." There were twelve of them, and they each carried in a candle and took their places solemnly in front of the older choir. They were earnest and their voices high and pure. Tears started and fell unnoticed down Shielah's cheeks. Unnoticed by all except Paulo.

A tiny smile played across his lips. He knew it would affect her that way. She had no idea what a midnight mass would be like. She expected something strange, something she could politely pick apart later in a discussion of their religions. She didn't count on being spiritually touched in his church. Paulo shook his head slightly, as he watched her enrapt face from the corner of his eye. No one would guess that this girl beside him,

160

caught up in the beauty and sweetness of a Catholic Mass, was a solid, sensible Mormon girl.

But he was not prepared for the response of his own heart. He had stopped going to Mass several years ago. His father had not gone to mass regularly, only on Easter and Christmas. Roberto never went. And Paulo was sensitive to the mock title of "Priest" given him by his brother and a few friends. Besides, he knew the Mass forward and backward, having memorized it at age twelve. Only occasionally did Paulo go into his cathedral in New York, and then it was never at Mass time. When he was particularly upset or concerned, he went there to pray. There was a comfort about the solid structure, grand and solemn. His mind would clear after a while, and he would kneel to cross himself and thank God for His goodness. It never occurred to Paulo that God might require him to go to Mass regularly to prove his love. The great Creator, if He knew all, knew his heart, and knew that Paulo loved Him. That was simple and reasonable to Paulo.

Tonight he found a responding chord in his own heart for the beauty of this ceremony. He looked around the cathedral. People lined the balcony as well as the main floor. Good people, people who loved God, his people. To his astonishment, a great full feeling began to expand inside. As the choir began to sing "Oh come all ye faithful, joyful and triumphant," Paulo opened his heart and his mouth and began, in a deep, resonant voice, "Oh come ye, oh come ye to Bethlehem."

Shielah turned to him in amazement. There were tears also beginning their slow way down his cheeks. She slipped her hand into his, brought them both to her lips, and kissed the back of his hand. Then she joined him. "Come and behold him, born the King of Angels." Others around them began to sing as well, and by the second verse, the whole cathedral resounded with thousands of voices singing, "Oh come, let us adore Him, oh come, let us adore Him, oh come, let us adore Him, Christ the Lord."

Much later Shielah questioned Paulo about the litany, sung in Latin, and what it all meant. But tonight she simply watched and listened respectfully. She learned something she had never known before. She finally understood the scripture, "God is no respecter of persons." His spirit was as strong here as it had ever been in her own congregation at home. In fact—she hardly dared let her mind breathe the thought—in fact, it was stronger. Christmas programs in her ward at home had rarely reflected the warmth and effulgence of joy that this Catholic celebration did. Later she would think about that and try to understand. But now she simply let it flow over her, and responded to the love of good Christians for the Babe of Bethlehem.

Afterwards, they braved the icy weather and walked quietly to the warm, quaint Inn at the end of the block, each of them lost in thoughts of the beautiful spiritual experience they had shared. The cobblestones and street lamps seemed to put them into another world. And in this world, they two were the only ones who mattered at all.

As they stopped in front of the heavy black wrought iron gate, Shielah spoke first. "I'm sorry, Paulo."

"What are you sorry for?"

"For implying in all our conversations that only my religion has merit. For implying that I am the religious one, and wearing that title proudly, like a silly banner. It finally occurred to me tonight I have yet to learn the depths of your soul."

He squeezed her hand. "How you have grown up since Hawaii!"

"I feel a million years older."

"Thank goodness, you don't look a million years older." He stopped and tipped her face up to his and searched her eyes. "However . . . I have noticed one or two tiny wrinkles beginning right about here."

"Oh, stop!"

"Yes, and a few—a very few mind you—brown hairs amongst the gold."

Josephine's was an ancient alehouse dating back to the seventeen hundreds. Over the doorway was a cast iron sign that would stand ten more centuries. The wallpaper, once undoubtedly elegant, had obviously seen grander times, and the wooden floors were well polished—and well worn. But, beyond the creature comforts it afforded on this hoary night, it also had a certain charm—quiet and old, a place where countless other lovers had met and pledged themselves. The innkeeper discreetly put them in a tiny alcove, tucked back in a corner, out of the way of the few other patrons warming themselves with a Christmas toddy, and promised to call a cab for them in a half-hour.

"Have any of your fears been answered tonight?" Paulo asked after a little while.

"Some." she admitted. "I have a lot to think about."

"Let me give you something else to think about. Question: If I love you, and you love me—of course that point has yet to be cleared up—but supposing that hypothesis to be true, isn't it reasonable that we should get married?"

She stopped sipping the hot cider they had been immediately provided. He looked across the table at her, her eyes wide and deep blue in the dim, golden light, her scarf still covering her hair. She had never been more beautiful. She didn't answer him.

He went on, in a light voice, "I mean, that's what most 'moral' people do, and we certainly do intend to be 'moral' about the whole thing. Marriage, Shielah, is an honorable act to commit when you love each other." His voice grew more serious, and he took her hand in his and brought it to his lips. "Of course, there's that point to be cleared up. Just that one small point. You know how I feel about you, but I know nothing about what is inside of that gorgeous head of yours."

Still she was silent. Tiny, tingling rivers streamed through her as he gently drew her hand across his lips.

162

"Once when I kissed you," now all smiles were gone, and his eyes were intense and direct, "another name came from your lips. Or maybe from your heart. Tell me now. I have to know. Do you love me . . . at all . . . ?"

This moment she could lose him forever, before she was certain of anything. And yet, she had only just admitted to herself a few hours ago how she felt about him, and had not had time to really understand it completely. Certainly she hadn't thought of the implications of loving him. How she could love him as well as Stephen didn't make any sense. But she couldn't say that to him now. He was so vulnerable at this moment, she could kill him with a word.

Mentally she asked Stephen's forgiveness, then looked into Paulo's eyes. It was so hard for her to say that she could only whisper the answer he wanted. "Yes . . . I . . . I . . . love you." Words of love came not easily to her. She had never practiced them—she rarely used them. Then too, she was not yet fully sure. Nor did she understand how this love was to fit into her life. But she couldn't deny it any longer. "Paulo, oh Paulo, yes I love you. I didn't want to. I've tried not to. But I do. I can't help it. I love you."

The next moment he pushed back his chair and knelt beside her, crushing her to him, not caring who might see them. He held her locked in the joy of his heart, afraid to try to talk, afraid to even kiss her because he could taste his own salt tears. Had it been ten years? It seemed like only yesterday that he had been nineteen and seen a vision of a girl whom he knew was his. The years between then and now were gone, melted into eternity as though they didn't count, had never mattered. They hadn't. Only this mattered. His love, and the knowledge that he had won her's. Fear was not a part of Paulo's nature, but now that she had finally answered him, fear struck him. What if he had not been able to win her? What if she hadn't loved him?

She felt him shaking in her arms and knew he was crying. She also knew that her own tears were dampening his coat. But she was crying for him, that he should love her so, that she should have such awful power to make him happy or miserable. It was a terrible honor, one that she still was not sure she wanted. Yes, she loved him, but all was not said, the final count was not in. She put reservations aside and devoted herself to making him happy.

She wiped his tears with her fingers and kissed those that were on his lips. "Now I will tell you something," she whispered to him, "You always tell me how beautiful I am, but I have never told you that you are beautiful to me. Of course I am supposed to say 'handsome' because you're a man. But 'handsome' seems just a surface word to me. You are beyond that, you are beautiful as well."

"Ahh," he said, brokenly. "Then we are both lucky. "But I am the luckiest of all."

Paulo bought an engagement ring the next week. He meant to give it to her on New Year's Eve. That day, while she was dressing for the gala affair with Paulo to be given at the Waldorf Astoria Hotel for contributing patrons of the Metropolitan Art Museum, a telegram came from Buck. It said simply, "Stephen is Missing In Action."

Chapter 9

On the eighteenth of December, Stephen went out on a hit with his patrol. There were fifteen Americans, all experienced, all very wary, all working as a team. Covering Stephen's back was his friend Greg Bryant. They had become fast friends and constantly bouyed each other up. Stephen's patrol had lost three men from a previous raid and this time, Greg had been pulled in to fill in the ranks. They were gone five days, penetrating deep through the humid green jungle of the Delta, to find a camp of Viet Cong who had been systematically wiping out villages. It was on their way back to American lines that the patrol saw the B-52 bomber burst into flames overhead and crash into the dense undergrowth a mile or so away.

The men looked at the Lieutenant. "What're you looking at? Come on, get going. Our mission's over, we're going in."

Stephen spoke for the others, "Sir, we should check for survivors."

"We wouldn't have any survivors if we did that. You think you wiped out all the Cong on this little raid? Hell, they're thicker than flies on our back! I'm taking this patrol in."

They had gone only a few yards when Stephen and Greg looked at each other and read the other man's thoughts. They both moved up behind the Lieutenant.

"Let us go back for them. If they're alive, they are gonna need help."

"And if they're dead?"

"Wait for us. Give us just an hour."

He swore. "Git! You got one hour."

They disappeared in the undergrowth in a moment, zigzagging as they ran, crouching low and barely ruffling the great, green leaves. They could see and hear the fire spout flames from five hundred feet away. The plane was down in a fairly open spot and was torn in two like a rag doll. The back section was roaring with flames. The front section was shattered.

From fifty feet away, still hidden in the bushes, the two men watched for any movement. One body seemed pinned by the cabin door. It was not moving. Another body was lying a few feet from the wreckage, and after a couple of minutes they saw it stir.

The two friends looked at each other. They both knew the Viet Cong frequently used one hurt American soldier as bait for the others. The Cong didn't understand the brotherhood that made the foreigners risk their lives for each other but they knew of it. The VC might be watching, just as they were watching. On the other hand, with their raid just completed, they might be gathered some place else to plan their next attack.

Running low and fast, they sprinted the forty yards to where the wounded co- pilot lay. He was moaning, but not bleeding profusely. A small cut on his forehead was dripping blood in his eyes. He was trying to sit up when they reached him. He wiped the blood off his eye with the back of his hand and broke into a wobbly smile when he saw the American fatigues!

No VC fire! So far, so good! They each grabbed an arm and half-carried, half-dragged him between them back to the underbrush. It was just five feet before the jungle that the VC broke cover, running and firing as they came. Stephen was hit in the leg, and another bullet slammed through the shoulder of their rescuee. They fell and rolled with the force of the impact. Damn, Stephen thought, my arm too. His left arm snapped when the pilot fell on him.

Greg quickly hoisted the wounded pilot over his shoulder. The man was over six feet and outweighed little private Bryant by fifty pounds, but no one would have known it. Adrenalin had taken over. Bryant carried the big man and half pulled Stephen along. It seemed an eternity to Stephen before they stopped and bandaged his leg. He felt like a boy running a three-legged race at the State Fair. Only, he wasn't having any fun! They stopped to listen. At this point they didn't know where the VC were or when they might run into the middle of them in the dense, mat of a jungle. After ten minutes of listening and emergency bandaging, they calculated their best chances.

It was a foregone decision for Stephen and Greg. Their best chance started with a prayer. They took a few precious moments, bowed their heads, and to the bewilderment of the groggy pilot offered a prayer for their safety. It took only a second for him to overcome his amazement and join them. More slowly now that the adrenalin had worn off and the two men were in great pain, they made their way back to where they had left their patrol. In the massive undergrowth, it was often hard to tell where a certain spot was, though you might have passed it a hundred times. Stephen swore the trees were alive and kept changing positions.

In any case, whether they lost their way, or whether they simply exceeded the hour stipulated, the patrol was nowhere to be found. They did find a good hiding spot where the bank broke off, and they could hollow a spot behind the undergrowth into the small hill. There, they did a better job of bandaging and ate some rations and drank some of their canteen water. They discovered that Kurt had some internal injuries—at least two cracked ribs. When they felt a little renewed strength, they moved on toward what they hoped were the American lines. But it was to be twenty-two days before they made it back.

No one expected them. They had been given up for dead after the first week. No one survives in the jungle, hurt and weak, and hungry for twenty-two days. Stephen and the co-pilot did. Greg Bryant was not so lucky.

The first concern was for their wounds. They had some first aid supplies with them that they had taken on patrol. For days they lived off the few rations they had left from their patrol duty. Then they gave out, and the men went for a day and a half, growing weaker and hungrier, wounds inflamed. They came upon a Vietnamese village. They watched for hours to see if there were VC around. At last, assured that it was safe, they sent Greg in to beg food for them. He came back with a paltry bit of cold rice, two fish—which they ate raw—and the roots of some medicinal plant which an old, toothless lady had given them. She showed him with signs how to scrape it and put it on wounds, as well as how to eat it.

The village helped them as much as possible for three days. On the fourth day they awoke in their dugout hiding place to the sound of machine guns. The Viet Cong were repaying the village for its aid to them. At the sight of women and children gunned down as they ran to huts, Greg lost his senses. They still had ammo themselves, having purposely reserved it in case of ambush. He grabbed the ammo and his gun and ran toward the patrol of Viet Cong, taking down three of them before they stopped him with their fire. Unfortunately he wasn't dead. Had he realized what they would do, he would have shot himself then.

Stephen and Kurt, the pilot, were helpless, wounded and without ammunition. They could do nothing but listen to the screams of their friend as the Viet Cong had their sport. They tied him to a tree and tortured him until he lost consciousness. Then they waited until he came to and had some more fun. The two Americans lay sick and filled with hatred for the VC, for the war, and most of all for themselves, their incapacities and their lack of action.

In the next ten days they tormented themselves with recriminations and questions which always led back to the obvious answer that they could have done nothing; they were both too weak from hunger and loss of blood and infection. Stephen had learned what plants were edible, and he succeeded in catching a few fish and eating them raw. Sometimes Kurt became delirious, his fever raging. They used carefully the medicinal plants from the Vietnamese woman and scrounged others like it in the jungle. Stephen called upon all the power his priesthood promised him to bless Kurt to live. He prayed constantly. He ceased to ask or to care if it were God's will. He had to keep Kurt alive. It was a recompense for not rescuing Greg, or at least dying with him. Finally, it was the hardiness and indomitable will of his wilderness ancestors that brought him to the American lines.

Dragging Kurt with his good arm, blood soaking the leg of his fatigues, he came out of the jungle just a few feet away from the barbed

166

wire encampment. American guards rushed out to help them in. He would have collapsed with his unconscious friend, but his pride kept him on his feet until he had given their names, ranks, and reported, with tears streaming down his face, the murder of Greg Bryant.

When he awoke in the sunlit army hospital, a gentle breeze was blowing and a nurse was bending over him. He immediately demanded to see Kurt. He was told he was not to move for at least one week. His leg wound was deep, almost clear through. Infection was severe and widespread, even in lesser wounds. His blood was so thin they were having trouble getting it to coagulate. And his arm had to be rebroken and set correctly.

The nurse told him as gently as she could, "It's really no use to see your friend now. He has been in a coma for days. The doctors don't expect . . . it's not good."

But Stephen was stubborn. "Where is he?"

"In the intensive care, down the hall, but it's no use for him, and you'll only hurt your own chances."

When she finished her administrations and left, it was six o'clock. Stephen raised himself with tremendous effort, pushed himself to his feet, and stumbled out into the hall, looking for the intensive care door. What did the doctors know? What did any of them understand about life or what he had shared with Kurt and Greg?

Kurt seemed dead when Stephen found his still body under the oxygen mask in the intensive care unit. Nurses tried to get Stephen to go back to bed. He shook them off and grew angry. Tears coursed down his cheeks, as he told them, "For this man I am almost dead, and my best friend has been tortured and killed by the Viet Cong. He can't die. Can't you understand that. I won't let him die! I have a power promised me from God to bless and heal, and I must keep him alive."

The nurse and young intern respected his need, and moved back, shaking their heads. Stephen was trembling so badly he could not stand without leaning on Kurt's bed.

"Do you have a small bottle of oil?"

The nurse brought him one. Stephen bowed his head over it and silently offered the simple consecrating prayer. Then he put a few drops onto his friend's head, and laid his hand over them. He prayed over the man for almost half an hour. Once, when the intern tried to take his arm and pull him away, Stephen shook him off, and resumed his silent blessing. He would not let him die, or what was it all for? What was Greg's life given for? What was the priesthood given for? It was an obsession with him now. His whole belief system hung in the balance. He gave every possible ounce of strength he had to steal Kurt away from the grave. Finally, reluctantly, he took his hand away. The nurse pushed a wheel chair under him, and in the moment it took for him to turn away, Kurt died.

It was January twentieth when Shielah called home to talk to Grandma. Paulo had been pressing her to marry him. Out of respect for her feelings over Stephen he had not given her the engagement ring he had purchased for New Year's Eve. But he continually talked about life together and marriage as though it were the next, simple step.

Shielah wanted to go home. It had been six months since she had seen Grandma and swung in the old porch swing, where she had so often reflected on life. Her head was reeling with impossible complexities and she wanted to run from it back to her childhood home. Once you grew up, did you always have to be an adult? With Grandma she could be a child again, if only for a few hours. She would tell her about Paulo. Grandma would know how to counsel her.

She thought she was going mad. She would be with Paulo, her head on his shoulder, he would be talking about marriage and where they would live, and she would see Stephen's face. Not as it was on that graduation day, but as it must be now, covered with dirt and bruises, his gray-green helmet shoved down to his eyebrows. And in his eyes, an unbearable pain.

"Hello, Grandma," she plunged in at the sound of a faint hello. "This is Shielah. I'm coming home. I think I can get some time off next month. I bid on a line and got it and it gives me a week off. I'm coming home."

There was a small silence, then a man's voice, "Grandma is taking a nap. This is Buck."

"Oh," she said, her excitement dissipated.

"I'm glad you're coming home. We've all missed you."

She didn't respond. He continued, "I have some good news for you, too. Stephen's mother got a telegram yesterday that he is in the army hospital in Nam. He's hurt, but at least he's not dead. When he is better they will decorate him for bravery above and beyond the call of duty. It sounds like Stephen, doesn't it?"

"Yes, it does," she admitted. "Will they send him home? How badly is he hurt?"

"Broken arm, reset twice because it wouldn't hold. Left leg shot out from under him, infection through his body, and twenty-two days of no medical attention while he was running from the Viet Cong. They'll release him and send him home when he is strong enough to stand the trip. Probably another month at least."

"But he's alive."

"Yes, barely." Buck had tried to keep his voice matter-of-fact, but bitterness crept in now. "I could have gotten him out of it. I know I could have."

She remembered the conversation between her brother and Stephen last June when the draft notice had come. "Buck," she said in reminder, "that was not Stephen's way. You know he would never have gone with you on a dig to escape the service."

"I know. But I can wish he had."

"Maybe he wishes he had, now. Well, this changes things a little. I'll wait to find out what is happening with him. If he comes home next month, I'll come too. If it's longer, I'll wait. Will you let me know as soon as you get word?" She hated to ask him a favor, but in this instance she had to.

"Sure. What else?"

"Thanks. How is Grandma?"

"Old. She's getting weaker lately it seems to me. She misses you. Doesn't say much, but your picture is on her dresser next to Mom's and Dad's and she looks at it a lot."

"I'll be home. Just let me know when. I'm scheduled for February twenty-first, a seven day vacation."

"All right. Grandma will be glad. I'll keep you posted."

She hung up. That was the first she had spoken to him for months. She felt defeated—just when she should have felt the happiest. She knew Paulo felt that way, happy, optimistic. But Shielah felt pieces falling in her life. She scrambled to keep them put back together. Just when she had one piece in place, another fell down. Where did Stephen belong; where did Paulo belong? And Buck could mess the pieces up more than anyone else, just by acting like her big brother—so darned competent, knowing everything, keeping her ten years old forever.

Stephen wasn't ready to come home in February. His body had healed enough to release him, though they kept him on medication. But his mind was even more in need of help. They kept him for two more weeks under a psychiatrist's care. At times he wasn't clear about who he was, Greg, Kurt or Stephen? He seemed to go through their deaths, experiencing what they had felt, and not quite understanding that he was still here and they were gone. It wasn't unusual, many men who felt responsible for a friend's death went through a period of non-reality. But his had gone on a little too long. Finally, the middle of March, the psychiatrist released him to be sent home. He could do no more to help the soldier. Maybe his family could.

"Paulo, I bid a line of flight that will allow me to go home next month."

"When?"

She looked him in the eye, "On March twenty-second, the day before Stephen comes home."

"Oh," he said, noncommittally.

He didn't ask, but she felt she had to explain. "He's still sick. Not so much physically, but emotionally. I don't know how bad it is. I don't know if he will even recognize me. They say he has been through hell. I'm not sure I ever want to know how bad it was. But I know I have to be there— I made a promise once."

Paulo just sat and watched her across the table. He had talked marriage. She had not talked marriage. He knew why. It was Stephen, of course. He knew about her experience of seeing this fellow in a spiritual moment, just as he had seen her. He had never understood it any better than she did. But he understood one thing. If she went home, he would lose her again. There was no doubt in his mind. Here she had an identity that

169

had become comfortable to herself and to him. She felt free to decide her own feelings and fate. Back in Utah, with her childhood all around her and a wounded, old love touching her tender heart, he would lose her. He had only one hope.

"I bought you a little present the other day."

She didn't want to talk about presents. She had no thought for anything lately except Stephen. "What is it? Why are you giving me a present now? Christmas is over."

"I know. But maybe you'll like it anyway."

He drew from his pocket the small box he had carried with him for days. She guessed what it was as soon as she saw the box, but hoped she was wrong. She was not. Inside the box in a little case was a beautiful, glittering diamond ring.

She looked up at him. She was at a loss to know what to say. This was not the time. Surely, as tuned in to her as he usually was, he should have known that.

"You don't have to say anything." She couldn't avoid his eyes. "Just put it on."

Instead she put it down. "I can't."

"I want you to."

"I know, but I can't." He held her gaze for a moment then looked around the restaurant and hailed a waiter.

She put her hand on his sleeve. "Paulo, it's not because I don't love you. I do. I wish I could put everything and everyone else out of my mind and be happy with you. I know we'd be happy together. You make me very, very happy. But, I am not there yet."

He leaned toward her, his mouth tight, his eyes growing angry. "Shielah, what's going to happen when you get back to Utah? Are you going to turn into the poor little princess again with the ragged clothes, sweeping soot from the fireplace? Will you throw away all Cinderella's beautiful things from the ball? Will you let them persuade you that Utah is your home, and the big bad city is corrupting you? You don't have to tell me, I know! I know exactly what will happen! See, I'm a prophet. I have visions too! The answer is "yes". Yes to all of the above. And what's more, your wounded soldier boy will need you. Right? That's what you think, isn't it? Right! You'll play mother and savior to him and mistake pity for love. So you loved him when you were a little girl. So you had a vision of him and you. Maybe all you saw was yourselves that day on the mountain. Maybe that's all the vision was, a deja-vu kind of experience. It doesn't have to mean that you spend the rest of your life with him. Love isn't something that happens in one bright vision. Haven't you found that out? I have. I saw a golden girl that I looked for for ten years. And I found a golden child. Over these last six months, that beautiful child has turned into a beautiful woman. And I love her, really love her, not just because of the vision, but because I have watched her grow and mature, gain strength and competence. Now, damn it, act like it. Don't regress on me now."

She had never seen him angry. She detested anger in people, even herself. It frightened her. But she wasn't frightened of him. She saw

170

through it. She saw his fear. She put her hand over his on the table. "Paulo, don't be angry with me. It won't work. I have to go and I will go. Hopefully I've gained enough strength to be a woman instead of a child again, but you need to help me believe in that, not doubt myself."

He sat back, the anger slowly subsiding, and he was surprised. She was wiser than he had thought. "Will you keep the ring?"

"I don't know. It's beautiful. Your mother told me you would be a generous husband. She was right. *Too* generous."

"Will you keep it, at least until you are ready to wear it?"

After a moment she rose, leaned over and kissed him, though the waiter was standing by his elbow. "I'll keep it," she smiled.

She was glad she did. The week before she was to go to Utah, she had two days off. While she was drying her hair the phone rang. It was Roberto D'Agosta. He asked to meet her for lunch. He had something to tell her that she would be interested in. She was reluctant. It was about Paulo. Just a quick lunch. He, Roberto, also had another appointment.

They met at a cafe across from Central Park. She was repulsed as soon as she sat down. He was smiling. Neither of them spoke until the waitress took their order.

"You are going home?" he asked.

"Only for a vacation. I'll be gone a week."

His lips pursed. "I see. Are you sure it's only a vacation? Wouldn't you enjoy living closer to home, flying, let's say, out of Denver or Salt Lake City?"

She didn't answer him. He waited a moment. "I could arrange it."

"I'm sure you could, Mr. D'Agosta."

"Perhaps the pay would not be so good, nor the opportunity to fly abroad so nice, but I could make it worth your while!"

She played along. "What do you mean?"

"Oh, a little subsidy."

"What *exactly* do you mean?"

He was growing impatient. Shielah wanted him to have to spell it out, although she had already guessed what he meant.

"Exactly? I had in mind about half again your regular pay."

"Let me see if I understand. You are willing to pay me to leave New York and not come back. Is that it?"

His face was hard now and unsmiling. "You put things rather plainly."

"I'm a plain person, as I'm sure you'll agree. I like to know what we are talking about precisely, so I know how to respond to the offer. Now, was that it?"

"Yes," he said tersely.

"I'm curious. Am I really such a pain to you? Am I messing up such wonderful plans? Why do you care who Paulo marries? He isn't in your business. How can he possibly help you with marriage to Elaina?"

"That's my business. It doesn't concern you. In Italian families we look out for one another. Elaina has everything to offer a man. You have nothing." She thought she saw one edge of lip curl up. "Beauty," he said distastefully. "Beauty is common. But Elaina is a beautiful woman, and she has money and influence besides."

"She is not Paulo's choice." Shielah said serenely.

"She was until you came on the scene. She will be again when you leave."

The waitress brought the food. Shielah stood up, opened her bag, slipped Paulo's ring on her finger, and drew her hand out from her purse.

"You are too late." Roberto was staring at her hand. "Paulo is a big boy. He has the right to choose his own wife." She gathered her purse up, and started past him toward the door.

In one slight, swift motion he had her wrist, and she was forced to stop and look at him. His face was not handsome now, and he bore no resemblance to either Paulo or Carmella.

"You make a mistake. You will not be happy. I will see to that. And eventually he will also be miserable and come to hate you. Go home! You don't belong here. I can make life comfortable for you or—I can make you sorry."

"I am sorry, Mr. D'Agosta. Sorry that you ruin a fine family with your presence. Sorry for you, that you hate. Take your hand off me and don't ever touch me again. I am not a prostitute that you can buy off with your money!"

She was gone. He threw the money down on the table, and stalked off, both lunches untouched. He took a cab to Maretti's Imported Furs on Fifth Avenue.

They saw each other two full minutes before they could get close enough to touch. People were hard to move. "Excuse me's" went unheard. Stephen was jostled several times, and Shielah could see his eyes flinch with the pain. She saw something else there also that she couldn't read. In fact, he seemed almost as much a stranger as she had feared. Still, there was an unseen bond between them—like a powerful magnet that pulled them together through the crowd. Finally, she almost dove for him through the last few people.

It was their moment. Just like the others, they didn't hear the "excuse me's". He tried to smile at her in his old way, but it never reached his eyes. They were too full of hurt to let anything else in. Stephen reached out to touch her hair after a moment of letting his eyes wander over her face. Then, with his good arm he pressed her to his chest, roughly at first, trying to keep the tears in check, then more tenderly as he decided it was no use. Still, they didn't say a word to each other. She found herself stroking his unruly blonde hair, trying to wipe out all the horror with her wholeness, mourning for that tranquil summer day they had sat together on the mountain and discovered their love. After a few minutes he managed to get some words out.

"I was afraid you wouldn't be here."

"I'm here," she said. "I'm here. Remember, I promised."

They only had those few moments before they were encircled by others who loved him. Shielah moved away respectfully as his mother reached out for him, tears streaming down her face. Cam was right behind Mary. He put his arms around both his son and his ex-wife. The three heads bowed until they were touching and they wept. All bitterness was forgotten for the moment, all reproaches silent. There was only relief and gratitude in their reunion.

Shielah looked over the heads of the crowd and saw Buck waiting at a respectful distance, just behind Stephen's brother and sister. Where was Grandma? She knew Buck was watching her, but she didn't meet his eyes. Where was Grandma? Hadn't she come? Then Shielah moved around a cluster of people and saw Grace sitting in one of the airport chairs. She was waiting for Shielah. She had not come for Stephen, though she was glad he was home safely. No, she had come for her granddaughter.

Shielah had flown in the night before and stayed at the Hotel Utah with the other attendants, rather than go all the way home and then back again for Stephen's nine o'clock arrival. She had, of course, gotten to the airport before any of them and down to the gate first. She looked back over her shoulder. Stephen was hugging his brother and sister now, trying not to let the pain show so much in his face. Buck was waiting just past Tami's shoulder. Buck's eyes got wet and in another moment he was locked in Stephen's good arm, the two of them trying their best to talk instead of cry.

"I missed you, buddy," Buck choked.

"Me too. But I can't say I wished you were there."

"Nope. But I sure wish you'd been here."

"I'm gonna be all right."

"I know it. I know you will. You were always tougher than me. I just didn't let you know it." They both chuckled over that, hastily wiping their eyes.

Buck thumped his friend's chest lightly. "They've got you fixed up like a Fourth of July parade."

"Yeah. It's silly. Doesn't mean a damned thing!" Stephen spoke with uncharacteristic vehemence.

Tami had her arm around her brother's waist, looking up at him. She was surprised. "Stephen, they decorated you for bravery."

His jaw worked for a second, "Not for brains though."

Cam spoke to change the subject. "Come on, son, let's get you home. You must be tired from the trip."

Stephen looked around for Shielah. He saw her sitting beside Grace, holding her grandmother's hands and wiping the old woman's eyes.

"Let's wait for Shielah," he said.

Mary looked meaningfully at Cam. He had heard nothing of his son's serious attachment to the Sorensen girl. Mary would fill him in later. Right now she went back and put her hand under Grace's arm, wanting to help.

Shielah saw that Cam was looking at her and realized for the first time how much Stephen resembled his father. She smiled up at Mary, feeling the older woman's thoughtful concern for Grace.

"Shall we go, Grandma?" Shielah asked.

"Are you ready?"

"I think so. Everyone's waiting."

"Oh," said Grace, and looked around in confusion. "Why are they waiting?"

"For us to go with them. We'll all go back home now."

Grace saw Stephen then, "Oh, the boy is home. Buck will be so glad. I guess you will be too."

Shielah's eyes met Stephen's. "Yes, I'm very glad. It was time for him to come home."

Seven precious days! How quickly they flew. Mary Gailbraith had a hard time understanding that Stephen would spend this first week with a girl. She hadn't realized how much Shielah meant to her son. Like his father, he hadn't talked about his feelings. Mary didn't understand that. She spent all her professional time counseling people, listening to their problems, their needs and worries. It was her forte, or so she prided herself, but her children and Cam rarely let her inside. That night she asked Stephen if he and Shielah had been writing.

"Yes," he replied.

"And are you serious about each other?"

"We were. A lot has happened, Mother. I don't . . . I don't know where I am now . . . with anything or anyone. I'm not even sure I'm here, this minute, with you. Maybe it's all a dream. Maybe I'll wake up back in the jungle."

They were sitting on the couch, turned toward each other. Mary reached out in one quick, impulsive motion and drew her son's head down to her shoulder. In a moment, the tension went out of Stephen's body and he put his arms around his mother's neck and wept, while she rocked him as mothers do.

Stephen slept most of the first day. That left only six. He explained to Mary that he wanted those days with Shielah, because she would be gone soon. Then, later, there would be time for others. Mary fought down her feelings of motherly jealousy, and relinquished her son to another love.

For Shielah it worked out just as it needed to. Stephen slept, and she sat with Grace, not caring to go anywhere, or see anyone else. She made dinner, against Grace's protestations, and served her grandmother. After dinner, she washed the older woman's white hair and fixed it with curlers and soft waves.

"I look just like I've been to a beauty parlor."

"I should say you do. You look beautiful."

174

"Not beautiful, but as good as these old wrinkles will let me. Now, Shielah my baby girl, I want you to answer something for me."

Shielah smiled. Grace had become more and more childlike in the last year. Some things were confused in her mind, but that which was clear she stated simply.

"What's wrong between you and Buck?" Shielah started to protest, but Grace would have none of it. "Don't tell me it's nothing. I know that isn't right. You and Buck have been fighting ever since last June when you went to Hawaii. I thought you'd love that trip over there, but instead you came back mad and left home. I want to know what's wrong between you youngsters or I'll not rest."

Shielah was trying to sort out how much to tell her. "We had a little fight over there. Well, maybe it was a big one. I found out some things that hurt a lot, and he found out some things about me he didn't like, I guess. Anyway, we agreed to disagree."

Grace pursed her lips and made a raspberry sound. "Tell me something true now."

Shielah couldn't help laughing. Her grandmother was painfully direct. "We just had a fight and haven't resolved it yet."

The old woman shook her head as she blew her nose delicately in her handkerchief. "That's not good. Carrying a grudge is not good. Just cankers. I want you two to forget all that old business and be good to each other again. It worries my mind."

"I'm sorry." Shielah knelt beside Grace. "I try to be good, but it's not easy." She was grinning at the serious look on her grandmother's face.

Grace chuckled. "That's right. I try to be good too, but it isn't any easier when you're old and crotchety." They both chuckled.

Shielah looked up into her grandmother's dim, blue eyes and said fervently, "I love you, Grandma. I have never told you that very often, only once or twice, maybe. I'm not good at finding words for my feelings. But I sure love you."

Grace's eyes filled up with easy tears, and she whispered in her granddaughter's ear, "Then love Buck. He needs you."

But loving Buck was not easy to do. The first two days she spent with Stephen, she also spent with Buck and he could say nothing right. The first day, he brought Bridget and the four of them took a drive into Salt Lake and back through the canyons on their way home. Bridget had not changed, except in her understanding of Buck. He was no longer a mystery to her, but she still loved him. They are as different as night and day, Shielah thought. She is as straight as a Mormon ruler, and he is an outlaw. Why does she love him?

"Tell us about New York." Buck commanded.

"Do you love it or hate it?" Bridget asked. "I know people have completely different feelings about it."

"I guess I belong in the first camp," Shielah answered, feeling Stephen's gaze intent on her. "I loved it from the minute we first were sent there. Of course, there are some things I don't like. I can take a tissue and wipe soot off my face after being outside an hour. That's awful! I don't like

175

the graffiti or the wind in winter. It's really vicious. It will blow you over if you don't hold onto something."

"I can't imagine your liking New York City after growing up here in the mountains," Buck put in.

"It's different. You can like things that are different."

"What's to like?"

"Harlem," Shielah said. "Sak's Fifth Avenue, the U.N., the bag ladies, the music on a hot summer night, the people."

Bridget looked back at her in surprise. "The people? I thought New York was the most impersonal place in the world. Why do you like the people?"

"Because they don't like each other."

"That doesn't make sense," Buck challenged her impatiently.

"They're too crusty to like each other, so I just have fun enjoying their crustiness."

After a minute, Buck said, "You're just saying that to be smart."

"No," Shielah answered. "It's true. You can like people who don't like you."

Buck looked at her in his rearview mirror. "That's a new philosophy for you isn't it? I seem to remember for years you hated the whole town because a few boys were obnoxious."

She blushed at that. He sent her right back into her cocoon with that reminder. Paulo's words flashed through her mind, "Are you going to let them turn you into the poor princess again, sweeping soot from the fireplace." She was silent. Her favorite refuge.

Bridget spoke to ease the tension. "People can change. Shielah has grown up a lot."

Stephen squeezed her hand. "That's enough. OK, you two?"

That day was a trial for Shielah. She wanted to be alone with Stephen. It was impossible to explore her feelings for him or to discover his hurt and help him with Buck in the way. Still Buck persisted. He drove them everywhere and reminisced about old times until Shielah wanted to scream. Old times hadn't been so hot!

On the third morning she awoke early. It was five-thirty. Buck and Grace were still asleep. An idea came to her and she rose immediately, bundling up against the early morning chill. Shielah started down the road through Clarksville, walking the mountain road to Stephen's home at the mouth of the Spanish Fork canyon. It was dark, but she didn't mind. She knew the dawn would soon be breaking and it felt wonderful to stretch her legs. Sometimes she jogged, sometimes she walked. The railroad tracks, running beside the river, brought back memories of childhood adventures with Buck. The song of the river was loud in the stillness of early morning. The air was exhilarating, and she admitted to herself that she really missed this clean air when she was in the smog of New York. There was something

176

comforting about coming back to the mountains of her childhood. They had always been her friends, even when the other children had not. I will have mountains in my worlds, she thought. If I ever get to be like God and make worlds, I will definitely have mountains, and I'll sit on them and wiggle my toes in the lakes.

She could see herself as a child, walking through these hills, and for the first time, she felt a great tenderness for that child. She might have been different if . . . if things had been different—if life had been different and Mother and Dad hadn't died. What would I have been like, she wondered, if I had had a real family? It took years before Shielah was to realize she had always had a "real family".

The sky turned white for a few minutes, and then the sun broke over the rim of the eastern hills behind her. She spent ten minutes walking forward and looking back. As she jogged the black asphalt, it occurred to her in a sudden rush that most people spend their lives doing just that— running forward, but looking back. Certainly she had. Tears sprang to her eyes at that thought, or perhaps at the brilliant spears of light rays piercing the sky in all directions. She lifted her face to the light. The throne of God must be like that, she thought. I wish I could show this to Paulo.

She reached Stephen's home just before seven o'clock. Mary Gailbraith was just leaving for Salt Lake and her job. Mike was beside her. She would drop him off at college.

"Am I too early? Is St . . . is everyone still asleep?"

Mary looked at the girl intently. She had certainly grown up from the silent, skinny girl she had been a few years ago. She wondered just when romance had sprung up between her and Stephen. "Tami is up, she has school. I think Stephen isn't ready for company yet."

Mary couldn't help but see the difference in her son when Sheilah was around. His face softened, his body relaxed, and his eyes lost some of their hurt look. Mary had not been used to the thought of sharing Stephen. He had always been her right hand man, even when he was an adolescent. She could see, however, that she must learn to let go, and as she watched Shielah, the thought struck her that neither of them had ever seemed like children. Both of them had suffered a terrible loss. Losing her parents had catapulted Shielah out of the golden days of childhood and divorce had done the same to her son.

"Well, maybe I can wait and cook him breakfast when he does get up. I'm sure he needs his rest, so I won't bother him." Shielah saw the reservation on Mary's face. "I'll sit out here on the porch until he wakes."

"No, no," Mary protested. "Don't be silly." She patted Shielah's hand reassuringly. "Go on in. You can talk to Tami. She's dying to find out how to do her hair like yours."

Shielah laughed, "Like this?" She tugged at her windblown tresses. The car was pulling out of the driveway. She waved goodbye to Stephen's mother, then went to the door and knocked softly.

Tami was just sixteen. After informing Shielah that Stephen was still asleep, the first thing she asked was how she could set her hair to make it look just like Shielah's. I wouldn't be sixteen again for anything in the world, Shielah thought. So she helped the younger girl with make-up and hair until the bus turned the corner and Tami ran out to catch it.

Shielah wandered around the house looking at the pictures and the magazines, trying not to be impatient. The house revealed Mary Gailbraith's personality. It was very clean and austere, except for a small, ornate bookcase packed with books on church doctrine and on psychology-related subjects. There was a fireplace at one end of the room, rarely used. Besides the bookcase, Mary's feminine love for beauty was indulged only in a crystal hanging lamp. A few family pictures hung on the wall, none of Cam, one of Stephen taken at boot camp with his brand new uniform on. Shielah studied it. That was the face she remembered. The face he wore now was older, often blank, and often tense.

"Don't look at that!" He spoke right behind her.

She was startled and whirled around quickly. "What? Why?"

"I'm going to take it down."

"Why?" she asked again. He was staring at the picture.

"Because it's a farce. It's not true. That's not how soldiers look. What are you doing here? So early, I mean?"

"I came to cook your breakfast." She smiled at him, but there was no answering smile.

"How'd you get here?"

"I walked."

"Ten miles?"

"Eleven, remember?"

"Yeah." He looked at her silently and she held his gaze. It was the first time they had been alone. Then he remembered and glanced down at himself. He had awakened to sunlight streaming in the window on his face, pushed himself out of bed, and staggered to the bathroom. After brushing his teeth and shoving his fingers through his hair twice, he was going to the kitchen. He saw her through the open doorway. He had on only his pajama bottoms, and the sling that he still wore to hold his broken arm in place. He wore no temple garments.

"I'll bet you don't look this awful when you get up in the morning," he commented without breaking a smile.

"I hope not," she replied.

"I'll get cleaned up and see you in a minute."

"What do you want for breakfast?"

"Nothing."

"You'd better, because I'm going to make something and you'll have to eat it. So you'd best put in your order now."

"You're getting bossy since you went to New York."

"That's right. I've become used to bossing the poor passengers around. What'll it be coffee, tea, milk or . . . "

"You," he finished, then slowly he began to smile.

"I'm not on the menu."

"Then how about some juice and honey-butter toast."

"I'll try."

178

Stephen came out of his bedroom, dressed and cleaned up, and was sitting down to his good country breakfast, when the phone rang.

"Hi Buck," he said, looking at her. "I don't think so. I have plans today. No, all day. Can we make it tomorrow? Sure I'm OK. No, I'm not spending the day alone just brooding. I told you, I have plans. I'm all right, really. Quit worrying about me."

There was a long silence from Stephen as Buck talked. Shielah was leaning against the sink watching him. After a couple of minutes, Stephen glanced up at her and spoke into the receiver, "Don't worry about her, either. She can take care of herself. Tell Grandma she's all right." Then, unwillingly, he added, "She's with me. She walked. I'll see she gets home. See you tomorrow."

They contemplated one another silently while he ate. It was as though they were starting over. Relationships had never been easy for Shielah, and she wasn't sure she was glad she had come. She had hurt Paulo and risked their love in order to come to Stephen. Now, all the letters he had written were forgotten. There was no softness, no love in his eyes. She bit her lip. This was wrong. She didn't know what to say. He didn't need her as she had thought he would. He was a stranger.

"It's time we were alone." he said.

"Is it?"

"I wish we could climb your hill today. Maybe this summer I'll be completely well and we'll go hiking."

"That would be nice."

"Does it make you uncomfortable? That I limp, I mean."

She was surprised. "No. Not at all. Why would it?"

"It makes my mother uncomfortable. She won't look at me when I walk."

"That's not because she's embarrassed. It's because she's your mother. Mothers hurt with their children."

"Where'd you learn that?"

"I don't know. It's a known fact, I guess."

"What else do you know? What did you learn in Harlem?"

Memories of Mighty Joe, and Jack playing screwball pool, and dancing in a sea of black faces flashed past. They were quickly interspersed with seeing herself on the steps while three black boys harassed her.

"In Harlem I learned that I am not afraid, and that I like black people."

"Really? That's a lot to learn all at once." She didn't reply. He moved, adjusting his weight and winced. She wondered how bad the pain had been before he was well enough to be sent home.

"You've changed, Shielah."

"I suppose. I meant to, you know. I didn't like myself very much the way I was."

"I liked you."

"Do you like the new me?"

"I think so. I think I would like you almost any way you decided to be."

She blushed and looked away from his intense gaze.

179

"Can we go outside?" she asked to change the subject. "I like to be out in the open where I can get my fill of looking at the mountains. I miss them in New York."

"I'll bring my pillow."

They sat in the white wicker patio chairs. The pillow supported the arm that hung uselessly in a cast.

"Now," he said, settling comfortably in the chair. "Tell me all about your job as a stewardess and your life in New York. I'm a little jealous. I feel like it has taken you away from us."

"I guess it has. I can feel the ties growing thin. Grandma is really my last real tie here to Utah."

"Do you mean that?" he asked.

"Well . . . "

"I can see you do. What about Buck, what about Maddie and Will, your family. Don't you own them anymore?" He paused a moment, "What about us, about me?"

"I don't know about us. I don't know where you are. I can't feel for where you've been or what you want from me. Do you want something from me? You're so silent and . . . and distant. I came because I thought you might possibly need me. But now I don't know."

"My feelings for you haven't changed. But, where I've been, you don't want to know. And I don't want to remember. Don't ask me to tell you. It drives me crazy when I think about it. I don't want to think about it now. I want to think about you. Thinking about you was the only thing that kept me alive in the jungle. I had your letter the day I went out on patrol, and I read it over and over those next three weeks while I was dodging the VC and trying to get back to camp. I thought about you, and the day on the hillside, and what you told me there. Do you remember that?"

She couldn't look at him. They were strangely new together, but speaking of things that only lovers do.

"I remember."

"You were so beautiful to me, and so shy. I was afraid you'd run away from me if I got too close, but you didn't. Then I was afraid you'd run from me if I tried to kiss you. But you didn't . . . Would you run now if this crippled stranger tried to kiss you?"

He had only one good arm. It reached out for her. He stroked her hair and cheek and slowly tipped up her face. "Are you still shy with me? Has it been too long?"

He didn't wait for her answer. He drew her toward him and murmured against her lips, "Don't run from me. I need you now, more than ever."

He buried his face in her hair at the base of her neck. She felt him shaking. She started to speak, to reassure him, but again his lips touched hers and they were trembling. She felt the world dissolving. If the earth had moved away from under her, she wouldn't have known it. There was only his strong arm holding her and the rest of the world was swallowed up in their kiss. Was there sunlight? Were there mountains? What had happened to time and space? In quick succession she was seven, ten, twelve, fifteen,

180

and his face changed with hers, dear and precious as a little boy, beloved as a young man. Her hand went up to his face, her fingers caressed his cheekbones, his forehead, his eyelids and finally the corners of his lips on hers.

A sound struggled up from the depths inside him. It was a half-cry, partly her name, partly a plea to heaven. It was much like the sound an animal makes in a trap.

"Do you hurt so much?" she whispered against his mouth.

His answer strangled in him. He could only nod his head. She held his forehead next to hers. "Can I help you?"

"Just love me. Just love me. No one can help me now, not even God."

She waited while he struggled to put into words the greater pain he was carrying.

"I'm not wearing my temple garments, Shielah, and I don't know if I'll ever put them back on. I thought I knew all about it—life, God, everything. But I knew absolutely nothing. Ever since I was twelve years old and was ordained to the priesthood, I believed in the power of that priesthood. Over in Scotland I used it constantly, daily. I blessed people; they got well. I prayed for answers and they came. It was like magic. My own special powers given by the great magician. I thought that was the answer to life—the priesthood, the Church. Then I went to Vietnam."

"Buck said serving in a war wasn't like serving a mission. Oh, boy was he right! So right!" Stephen paused a moment shaking his head. "It's literal hell over there. If any place on this earth is hell, it's Vietnam. And you want to know what effect the priesthood of God has in that hell? None. It's a drop in the ocean, that's all. You can maybe save the life of one or two children. They later get killed in a Viet Cong raid, or end up pushing heroin to the American soldiers. So many of the guys turn to dope over there. Why shouldn't they? It helps them stand the terror, the constant nightmares, the shells going off in the middle of the night. I can't blame them. I can't handle it anymore myself. I've been on morphine since I hit that army hospital. Maybe I'm a dope-head myself. I don't know. I don't know if I can live without it even now."

He had pulled away from her. Now he pushed himself to his feet and started a limping pace of the patio. The words came on like a torrent unleashed.

"You know they gave me a silver star, and a purple heart for bravery. You know what they were for? One guy who didn't live more than five days-Greg! I got him killed, convinced him to help me rescue a survivor in an airplane crash. Damn it, Greg wasn't even hurt. He wasn't even the one hit. He was carrying Kurt and pulling me along. He was a Mormon, Shielah. The one I wrote you about. He was a Mormon, and they tied him to a tree and tortured him to death. The silver star was for Kurt. Why they gave me that, I'll never know. I dragged him through the jungle for twenty-two days. I gave him six blessings to keep him alive. I wanted him to live." Tears were distorting his words now, but he leaned his head back and looked into a sunlit, peaceful sky. *"God, he should have lived!"*

She felt so completely helpless to comfort him. There was nothing to say, until he had said it all.

He stopped pacing in front of her and looked down. "But he didn't. He died. He died! After six blessings! What good were they? What did I spend twenty-two days in the bush for? What did I get myself shot up for?" His voice rose and rose to a strangled shout. "*What did Greg die for?* He died so we could live. He ran out there in that clearing to make them think he was the only one the village was giving food to. All those people, all those villagers, the children, the old people, they died for giving us food! Just for feeding us. Greg took the rap for us, and they caught him and tied him to a tree and cut him up alive. I feel like a murderer!"

He was sobbing now, and she reached for him, but he moved away. "And what good did it do? Kurt died anyway. I kept him alive for a while on sheer will power. We had hardly anything to eat or drink, and we were hunted the whole time. When we made it to the lines—our lines—they put us both in the hospital. I passed out. I don't know for how long, but when I came to, Kurt was dying. That's what the nurse said. I got some oil, and consecrated it just like we're supposed to do. I blessed him. I blessed him and prayed over him for hours. He should have lived or else everything was useless. And he died as soon as I took my hands off his head. That's how much good my blessing did! And they gave me the medals! Greg and Kurt both died, and they gave *me* the medals."

"It isn't fair," he cried out at the blue sky and the blossoming trees. "It isn't fair, and I want no part of a hoax. When we need it the most, the priesthood fails; God doesn't listen. I don't think He even cared. How can He stand to see the horror of war and not help us when we try with all our souls to do something decent? I don't know Him any more! I don't know Him."

This is it, she thought. If he won't let me help him now, if he won't come to me, it's all lost. Her prayer was silent, her eyes closed. Please, let him come to me now. Please.

Stephen stood with his back to Shielah, tormented by the screams of Greg, the body of Kurt, until he thought the blackness inside his soul would swallow him alive. Then, after what seemed an eternity, he felt something else. It was like a soft, summer breeze. Maybe it was the spring day coming to life. It touched his hair and it touched his heart. He turned around. There was Shielah waiting for him, praying for him. He dropped down beside her on one knee and put his head in her lap, crying unashamedly. She sat stroking his hair for a long time while sobs wracked his body. She caressed him. She tried to enfold him within herself, to heal his wounds with love.

They spent the rest of the day lying on a blanket beneath the blossoming peach tree. Sometimes they held each other without words. Sometimes they talked. He told her more about Greg, some of the happy times they had shared. She told him about Brandy. He talked about the Vietnamese children, learning to speak the language, and how they would giggle behind their hands. She told him about flight attendant school and her emergency landing, about Harlem and the Staten Island ferry and the picturesque hills of upstate New York. But she didn't tell him about Paulo.

When Mary came home she found them still on the blanket under the tree. She sensed a closeness between them that she couldn't help but envy. Mary stood behind the kitchen sink watching them bend toward each other, seeing Stephen play with Shielah's fingers and kiss them from time to time. Happiness for his happiness sprang up, but along with it, a deep longing that she had long tried to deny.

Mary Margaret Gailbraith put her hands to her face and, behind the tears, her eyes saw the young face of Cam Gailbraith. It was a gentle face, kind and adoring, a lot like Stephen's was right now. Then quickly the picture changed, and she saw his lined, tired expression the day he had walked down her steps for the last time. Defeat seemed to pervade his body. Where had it gone, their young love? Why had it gone? Was she so hard to live with? A sense of failure turned her stomach into a hard knot.

Mary heard Tami at the front door and hastily wiped her eyes with the dish towel. But Tami went down the hall to her bedroom. Quickly Mary regained her iron composure and reminded herself for the millionth time that love does not conquer all. She and Cam were simply universes apart in their needs, and they were both better off now. But neither of them had remarried.

After dinner, Shielah and Stephen took her car and drove up to the lookout point on the hillside above the new homes. The valley was serene and twinkling with soft lights.

"You are good for me," he said, kissing her most willing lips.

"I hope so."

"Did I shock you today?"

"No. I think I can understand just a little. You've been through hell and come back. You would be unnatural if you weren't angry and hurt and puzzled."

"But will I get over it? I don't know."

"You'll get over it. You'll remember all the things you used to understand about God and the priesthood."

"What things?"

"That the priesthood is not some supernatural power by which we dictate to the universe and to God. It's His power. He only uses it through you. You don't control it."

"Then why wouldn't He use it to keep Kurt alive? I tried so hard, Shielah. Was it so wrong to want him to live?"

She shrugged slightly. "Is this such a great world to keep him in? Suppose he had lived a paraplegic? Suppose he had lived but been a vegetable mentally? Would you have been happy with that? There are worse things than dying."

"I know that's true. But you haven't seen your best friend tied to a tree and tortured to death for you."

In the dark, she looked out at the blinking lights below. Just for a moment, her eyes glazed over with tears as the answer he needed came to her. "There was another man who was pinned to a tree and died so you could live. Greg gave his life willingly so you could live physically. Another friend, perhaps your very best friend, gave His life so you could live . . . spiritually. You hurt now because this time you witnessed the pain of a devoted friend. Jesus' pain we rarely even think about. Now you will think about it, perhaps even comprehend it a little. Stephen, people give each other their lives all the time in one way or another. Every time we go out of our way to help someone in need, we give a part of our lives. Every time we love each other, and cry with each other, and rejoice with each other, we give our lives. That is what we are supposed to do, give our lives for each other. 'He who would lose his life for my sake shall find it.' "

"I also remember Jesus said, 'Greater love hath no man than this, that he lay down his life for his friends.' He was talking about us. We are the friends He meant. And Greg did that for you. He actually played the role of a savior and gave his life for your sake. What a gift, what an honor! Don't refuse it because it was hard for him to do. Take it reverently. Cherish it and use it. Make that gift count for good, for great things, so Greg will know it was gratefully accepted. You can't bring him back. Maybe you shouldn't even want to. That act of unselfish love probably won him his Celestial crown. Just make him know his sacrifice wasn't wasted on bitterness."

Her eyes were shining and her face aglow with a light beyond the moonlight on this spring night. He studied her and pondered her words. She willed them into his mind, his spirit. As they struck home, he buried his face in her soft hair.

"I hear you," he said. "I hear you."

"Not me. Him. Father just gave it to me to say for Him."

After holding him for a few minutes, Shielah spoke, "When is your birthday?"

"Why?"

"Just tell me when it is."

"It's already past. It was February fifth."

"Oh, I missed it. But I have a present for you anyway. Even if it's late."

He looked at her curiously. She put her finger to his lips and said, "It's a pair of temple garments. Will you wear them?"

Stephen sat looking into her face, trying to lay hold on the words she had spoken. To accept a gift so painfully given as Greg's was hard. To reject it was unthinkable. Shielah's face glowed with the conviction of what she had been teaching him. How could he disappoint her? "I'll wear them," he said.

The night before she left for New York should have been a happy one. Buck and Bridget, Shielah and Stephen all went out to a movie and dinner in Provo. Buck had been strange. She told herself he was just jealous of Stephen preferring her company over his. But surely even Buck should be able to understand that. He loved Bridget, didn't he? It would have been a happy, comfortable evening. Stephen was beginning to laugh occasionally, and to relax into his old good nature. He hadn't by any means worked through his feelings about Vietnam, but a good start had been made, though he wasn't yet wearing the new temple garments Shielah had bought him. But Buck had something on his mind.

"I guess you'll be glad to get back to the big city."

"I'll be sorry to leave," she answered, looking at Stephen.

"Why don't you stay?" Buck asked casually.

"I can't. I have a job. You can't quit a job just like that."

"Oh. Well, so give them notice and come back home in a couple of weeks."

"And live where? With Grandma? And do what? Work at Mike's Hamburger joint?"

"There are other things than that. You could go to college like Bridget and get an education you can use for the rest of your life."

She looked at her brother intently. Why was he pressing her?

"I like what I'm doing."

"Even if it takes you away from Stephen?"

Stephen started to protest, and Bridget laid a warning hand on Buck's arm.

"If it is right between Stephen and me, it will work out," she said calmly. "He's still got a lot of things to sort out for himself, and I still want to do what I'm doing. I love flying. I really do."

"Is that all?"

"What do you mean?"

"Is that all you love? Flying?"

Their eyes locked and held. She knew what he was driving for now, and she warned him silently, but he wouldn't back down.

Buck spoke again, "Isn't there something else you love about New York? Maybe someone?"

Bridget almost exploded, "Buck!"

Stephen looked bewildered. Shielah was rigid with anger. Buck held her eye. "He's got to know," he said.

"Are you God?" she challenged him acidly.

"What are you two talking about?" Stephen asked.

"Nothing," Bridget said, trying desperately to brush it aside.

"Hasn't Shielah told you about the one thing that really ties her to the big city?"

"No, what?" Stephen was still puzzled.

Buck waited. Shielah didn't speak. At that moment she hated him ferociously. He had totally humiliated her in front of Paulo in Hawaii. Now he was determined to torture her in front of Stephen. And Stephen didn't need this. Didn't he at least care about his friend's feelings, even if he didn't care about hers?"

"You can't force me, Buck. If you want it said, you'll have to say it."

Buck slid his chair back and put his palms flat on the table. He looked at no one but his sister. "Paulo D'Agosta."

The name came like a bomb in their circle. Stephen looked at Shielah. Bridget got up and left the table for the restroom. Shielah wanted to scream, no, no, not now, not yet! Why are you doing this to me?

Buck waited for her response. So, he had been right! He had just been playing a hunch. Shielah had not written anything home about the Italian. But he had long ago put two and two together. It was his city. Buck had been sure D'Agosta would find Shielah. Obviously he had, or she would have passed off his name casually. Did she think she could play with Stephen? She had become calloused and hard in the year since she had left Clarksville. The man from the big city had turned her head. Stephen had a right to know about his rival. She would certainly never tell him, just play both men at once until she satisfied her ego. He hated the things he saw in her now. He had loved her softer self for years, protected her and ached for her when he saw her unhappiness. But she had changed, had thrown away her childhood, him, her life in a small town, and affected a big city personality, complete with fickleness.

Stephen looked from one to the other until his eyes rested on Shielah. She still stared at Buck, and what he saw in her face he didn't like.

"Who's Paulo D'Agosta?"

She answered, still looking at Buck. "A man I met in Hawaii, and a man I still know in New York."

"Is he a problem?" Stephen asked her.

"He's a fine man, a true gentleman, and Buck wants you to know that he loves me."

"Oh. I see. Thank you, Buck. I needed to know that."

Buck answered him, "Yes, you did. Shielah wouldn't have told you of her own choice, but you can't build a relationship with unknown ingredients. I want to see you two together. I happen to love you both, although Shielah doesn't believe that. But, I do. And I especially love and respect you, Stephen, too much to know that my sister is playing games with you."

"You always thought you knew everything, Buck." Shielah said wearily. "If you only knew when to shut up. I'm not playing games with Stephen or Paulo."

He leaned across the table to her. "Then who are you in love with?"

"Buck! Buck! Don't do this! You always push me too far. Do you want me to hate you forever?"

"Why won't you answer that question?"

"Because there isn't any answer. I love Stephen! Of course I do. I've loved him since I was a kid, tagging along after you two. And," she looked at Stephen sorrowfully, "and . . . I love . . . Paulo. He's . . . he's . . . a wonderful man," she finished lamely.

Stephen was still. He just looked at her.

"Are you satisfied?" she asked her brother. Angry tears started up. He had been determined to spoil everything, to ruin their last night. He wouldn't wait to let her tell Stephen in her own way. He had to win. Win! That's all he cared about, controlling and winning. She stood up and pushed back her chair, starting away just as the tears began to fall.

Buck jumped up and ran after her. He caught her just as she went out the front door. He spun her around and tried to put his arms around her. She flailed out and pushed him away.

"Shielah, you had to tell him."

"Not now, not here, not this way. Stephen is hurt, all over, but mostly inside. Maybe you don't realize that, but he is. I meant to tell him. I would have told him, when he was better, when he could understand and not be hurt. When I had sorted out my own feelings. Why can't you stop trying to run my life? All you do is ruin it."

"I don't mean to. I love you. Why have you changed? You're as hard as nails now."

She was amazed. "What? Not the china doll anymore that you so despised? Didn't you want me to be strong and tough, like the great Buck Sorensen? You can't be tough and tender too. You've made me hard, if that's what I am. But one thing's for sure, this china doll doesn't break. I told you she wouldn't, and she hasn't. Now, if you don't like me the way I am, then *leave me alone.* You make me crazy!" And she shoved him and ran.

She called a taxi and scandalized Grace by coming home in a cab. Shielah would have packed her things and left that very night for the Salt Lake Airport but Grace begged her to stay. She was glad she did. Late in the night, after everyone had gone to sleep, Shielah heard a tapping against her window. In the moonlight, his blonde hair glistening, Stephen stood beckoning to her.

"You ran away too fast."

"I couldn't help it. I'm sorry. I hate Buck for making me hurt you."

"Don't hate him. That will really hurt me."

"He loves to torture me, and control me."

"No, he just loves you," he put his finger to her lips to stop her protests, then kissed the spot his finger touched. "Yes, he does. He wants you back home, and he wants things to be like they used to be, you and him and me." His eyes were smiling in their old way, crinkly and amused. "I don't know about him, I just want it to be you and me." And he kissed her again. His body was warm and comforting.

She pressed her cheek against his shoulder. She was happy here, at peace with herself and she wished things could be just as they used to be— at least as they were that one, splendid week before Hawaii. "I . . . I . . . I love you, Stephen," she whispered, and she was surprised at how easily the words came.

187

Chapter 10

Summer found Brandy and Shielah moving. Jeri had quit the airlines. She was pregnant. She told them she was going home to Indiana to her family. They hoped she did. Marci eloped with a wealthy Texan she met on one of her flights.

Brandy looked at Shielah. "It's just you and me, babe." And she grinned.

Shielah laughed and hooked her arm through Brandy's. "Come on. Help me with these boxes. You wouldn't think just the two of us would have so much to move."

They found a cheaper place, but much more fun, over on West 72nd Street. They were just a few blocks from Central Park. Shielah loved that. At night they would sit on their fire escape and listen to the city. It was Neil Diamond's city, and his music was everywhere. Harmonica lovers played it. Guitarists played it. "Kentucky Woman," "Shiloh," "Solitary Man," and "Forever in Blue Jeans." On warm summer nights, the sounds of honking horns, tires whizzing past, fellows calling out to girls, and snatches of music could entertain the two friends for hours.

On West 72nd, they had no drunken doorman, just a buzzer at the door and a walk-up flat on the third floor. They didn't care. It was cheaper rent that two of them could afford, and they had more disposable income. Shielah saved hers. Brandy squandered hers generously. They no longer cared about associating with the lawyers, bankers, and up and coming executives of East 48th Street. They had enjoyed enough of that. Here, the people were mostly blue collar workers, and artists—dancers, singers, painters. And they all watched out for one another. As soon as the girls moved in they were told about the neighborhood watch. They were not to walk home from the subway alone at night. Call Jedediah. He'll see someone comes to meet you. And if you are expected on the train at a certain time, you better be there, or call, because the neighborhood will be worried.

They enjoyed every moment of it. They had a hundred Jewish mamas and they could hardly get the sniffles without chicken soup appearing on the doorstep.

One night while they were doing their daily facial cleansing routine they got the silly giggles, looking at the weird concoctions they used on their faces.

"Did you ever think we'd have to look so ugly, just to look beautiful?" Brandy asked, dying of laughter at the green, minty masque Shielah had just applied.

"We could sell this masque for Halloween," Shielah agreed. "Help me get this thing off. I think it's going to peel my face."

"Shielah," Brandy quizzed her. "What would you think if I went out with a white man?"

"I'd think you might be kind of uncomfortable."

"Lots of blacks and whites going out now."

"I know. Do you want to?"

"I have!"

"Oh. Did you have fun?"

Brandy stamped her foot, "No. I didn't. I wished I had. This man was the smoothest. He was a CPA, dressed to the hilt, pinstripes and all that fancy stuff. He was good looking too, an Italian like your Paulo, and a good dancer for a white man. Leastways he was smooth. None of this bouncing around like Harlem boys. But heck, it wasn't fun. He asked me out again, but I turned him down. How about that, Brandy turning down a white man. And he had money too. You could tell it. It showed all over him, like a pig with measles."

She sighed and started rubbing cream into her feet. "But he was too sad for me. Sad-sack I call him. Didn't crack a smile all night. You can't have fun with a man like that. You didn't tell me what you think?"

Shielah sat down beside her on the bed. "Are you asking for a moral judgment?"

Brandy looked at her friend with her head cocked sideways. "I guess maybe I am."

Shielah put an arm around her friend's shoulder. "You're testing me."

"Naw."

"Yes, you are. Why?"

"I don't know. You seem to accept me and my people so easily. It isn't natural."

"Why not? It seems to me that prejudice is unnatural. Babies don't have it."

"Yes, but most grownups do."

"That's because the blacks are taught to resent the whites, and the whites are taught to feel guilty about the blacks, and it's a truth, that you don't like people who make you feel guilty."

"Don't you feel guilty, whitie?" Brandy grinned.

"No. Should I? Can't I just like you? Do our grandfathers' relationships have anything to do with ours?"

"Most of us are just like the Hatfields and the McCoys. We hate the people our fathers and mothers hate, even if we don't know them."

"Now I want to ask you a question," Shielah said.

"What is it?"

Shielah held her arm up next to Brandy's chocolate one. "Do you ever wish you had white skin?"

Brandy looked at her in astonishment and broke out laughing. "Does vanilla wish it were chocolate? Does Vodka wish it were gin? Does a flower wish it were a tree? What you saying, girl? There is no way I could hate my own skin."

"I didn't mean that. It just seems that having black skin makes things harder for you."

Brandy sobered up. "That's for sure. But it hasn't ever made me wish I was white. I hate to offend you, you being my best friend and all. But I think my color is much prettier than yours." She held up her leg. "Look at how rich and pretty that color is. You've always looked a little washed out to me. Much better with a tan. You know, just a little closer to the true color."

They laughed at each other, then Brandy looked straight into Shielah's eyes. "I never thought my best friend would be a white girl. It gives me hope for the human race."

"Me too." Shielah answered.

Brandy got up to put on her nightgown. "Now that we've got all done with that foolishness, I got something good to tell you."

"Such as?"

"Mr. Benjamin D. Mitchell, the fourth! Yes, the fourth. Mr. Benjamin D. Mitchell the fourth is a black gentleman of respectable family. Mr. Benjamin D. Mitchell the fourth hasn't never had no chitlins, no clabber with syrup. I suspect he hasn't never had no real, true hushpuppies. He's a Northerner. But just to show I'm not prejudiced, I love him anyway!"

Shielah was fascinated. "Tell me more. Tell me more. Benjamin D. Mitchell, the fourth. That's wonderful. I love it!"

Brandy was "do-wopping" around the room. "Mr. Benjamin comes from the very best black family on Forty-First Street. He has made his money in the stock market, although engineering is what he does for a living, and he is spending that money on me at a scandalous rate. Isn't that *fine*! I tell you I have never been lunched, brunched and dined so well. And he has never had his shoes danced off before either." She stopped and turned to Shielah. "I expect a ring any day now, and it won't be puny. Speaking of rings, do you still have Paulo's?"

"No," Shielah admitted. "I didn't think it was fair to keep it and not wear it. I gave it back to him. He didn't want me to but I did. I don't want him to think I am committed to him."

"How you gonna make a decision?"

"I don't know. I don't think I have to right away at least. I haven't had my fill of flying. I am a senior attendant now, and I'm mad for power," she laughed. "I'm not in any rush."

"Neither am I," the black girl agreed. "Let's just enjoy our freedom while it lasts. When you commit yourself to a man, whoo-ee, say goodbye to freedom."

Shielah dragged her weary body up the three flights of stairs and stuck her key in the door. Her feet hurt. No, her legs hurt. No, her back hurt. No . . . oh give up—everything hurt, even her baby finger which she had squashed in the door at the lunch counter. She had just finished four days on, and about seventy hours of hard work. They were only supposed to work thirty—they were only paid for thirty, but the reality was more like seventy, counting all the time spent preparing, washing uniforms and ironing them, traveling time to and from the airports. This week she would only be paid for thirty-three hours. It was counted from block to block, the time at which the ground crew unblocked the wheels of the airplane for take-off, and when the destination crew blocked them on arrival. All the time spent getting people on and off or, as in the case this week, waiting at the gate with irate passengers because of the slowdown in tower control, was never included in the pay. Yet it was the hardest work. She was going to sleep until Sunday!

The first thing she saw when she opened the door was the window wide open and the curtain fluttering in the breeze. Brandy must be home! She called out expectantly, but interrupted herself in the middle of the call. The room was a shambles. Brandy wouldn't have made this much mess. Books and papers were strewn everywhere. The open door of the closet revealed all the clothes piled in a heap on the floor, some of them tossed across the room. Drawers were open with clothing falling out helter-skelter. Pillowcases and pillows were separated, and the mattress was cockeyed on the bed.

Shielah gasped. She dropped her flight bag on her foot and never noticed. She stood stock still for a minute, looking around the disheveled room, then turned and ran.

"Mrs. Ramsey, Mrs. Ramsey, someone has been in our room!" she burst out when the landlady opened the door to her furious pounding.

"I don't believe it! Let me take a look. There ain't been no noise up there a-tall, and I checked your door to see if'n it was locked when Brandy left yesterday. I'll get my broom." She snatched her broom from beside the refrigerator and puffed up the stairs after Shielah.

Shielah didn't want to go back in. Suppose the intruder were still there. He could still be there! She stood out in the hallway, leaning against the wall, while Mrs. Ramsey clucked and "tisked" over the state of the room. The good woman held her broom in both hands while she checked out the bathroom, behind the shower curtain, under the bed, finally in the closet—although it was plainly empty.

"Ain't nobody there, honey. I ain't been broke into since we started the neighborhood watch. Jedediah's gonna have to tighten up his program. We can't have you girls scared to death and your things stolen. I'm gonna call his missus right now." She started down the stairs huffing and puffing and called back over her shoulder. "You can go on in. Ain't nobody there now. I know that kind—do their dirty work and leave somebody else to clean up after them. Tsk, Tsk."

It was several minutes before Shielah could make herself go back into the room. Even then she felt spooky, and jumped at every strange sound. She pulled the window down and fastened the latch, even though the summer breeze felt good. She looked around the room in despair. She was too tired to deal with it now. She was too tired to deal with the fear as well.

"Paulo?" she said when he answered the ring.

"Yes. What's wrong?" he asked hearing the tremor in her voice.

"I . . . my . . . there's been . . . someone broke into my room."

"When? Were you there? Are you all right?"

"No I wasn't here, and yes, I . . . I'm all right. I hate to be a scaredy-cat, but I . . . " her voice broke and she didn't finish.

"But you're scared and that's all right. Where are you?"

"In the room."

"Don't stay there. Go down to your landlady's. I'll be there as soon as I get a cab."

It was easy to let him handle it. He was good at that, taking care of things. She let herself be taken care of. She was too tired to even help in the clean-up. He sat her in a chair in the corner, and began systematically putting the room in order. She fell asleep while he was remaking the bed. Through a drowsy fog she felt his arms around her.

"Come on, beauty, your bed is ready. You must be beat."

"Seventy hours this week."

"That's unholy. They'll kill off their best girl."

"You don't have to clean everything up. I really didn't call for room service. I just needed a little comfort." She started to lie down, but stood back up and put both her arms around him, burying her face in his chest. "I'm scared, Paulo. Suppose he comes back?"

"He won't. Probably just a kid getting his jollies. He didn't even take anything that I can tell. Your clock radio is still here. Brandy's fur coat is still here. Besides, the whole neighborhood is on the alert now. These people have got a better security system than my office building."

"Will it be all right?" she begged, looking up at him.

He kissed her and patted her hair. "It'll be all right. Get some sleep. It won't seem so bad in the morning."

But he was wrong. She awoke to the same feeling of dread and wariness she felt the night before, only slightly less intense.

Perhaps that was what colored her perceptions. She began to look over her shoulder frequently when she was walking, or waiting in the subway. Even in the crowd and noise of the airport, with her companion attendants on both sides of her, she seemed to hear specific footsteps behind her, and to feel an eerie presence. For the first two weeks after the break-in, she wouldn't walk alone to the subway entrance three blocks away, even in the broad daylight. Mrs. Ramsey became impatient with her and she knew it. After a while, she forced herself to calmly walk alone. She occasionally succeeded in forgetting the footsteps and enjoyed the children playing in the water hydrants. But the haunting footsteps always returned. She told Brandy about them, and Brandy was sympathetic at first. After she continued to mention them for a month, her friend gently told her she had become paranoid. Maybe a good counselor could help her deal with her fear. Shielah brushed the suggestion away, and determined to deal with her fear herself. She didn't tell Paulo for that reason. She just endured, scorning herself and waiting.

In late August she and Brandy went shopping together, she mostly window shopping, while Brandy splurged in Lord and Taylors. They were fumbling with packages and trying to open the door when Brandy realized that the door was already open.

"Didn't you lock this door when we left? You, the scaredy cat?"

But her teasing smile quickly disappeared. The room was in an even greater mess than the first time. She had never seen it like that. Paulo and Shielah had cleaned it up before Brandy returned from her flight. Her packages slid to the floor, and she stared, wide-eyed around the room.

"I'll be damned!" she said softly.

Shielah screamed. Not once, but three times she screamed. Mrs. Ramsey came running up the stairs, hollering at the top of her voice. "What's wrong? Who's that screaming? Who's hurt? What's wrong?"

Brandy grabbed Shielah by the shoulders and locked her in a tight hug, reassuring her constantly, "It'll be all right. It'll be all right."

Mrs. Ramsey took it personally. The girls had never heard the older woman swear. She tried to be a model of decorum with them, but her vocabulary was quite colorful. Brandy started to giggle a little as the plump little hen of a woman ran on. Mrs. Ramsey wasn't at all amused. Her other tenants might become nervous about their own security when the word spread that there had been another break-in. She helped the girls clean up the mess and swore them to secrecy, saying she would have Jedediah see that her building had round the clock watchers. Timidly, Shielah asked, "Could it be any one in the neighborhood? You know, someone even Jedediah wouldn't suspect?"

"I suppose it could," the woman said doubtfully. "We are strictly careful who we rent to though. Most of the tenants around this neighborhood have been checked on as careful as if they had asked for a million dollar loan."

"I'm sure they have, Mrs. Ramsey," Brandy consoled her. "You sure gave us the third degree."

"I'm sorry girls. Guess we'll have to tighten up even more."

Nothing seemed to be missing this time either. That's what they both thought, until the next morning after Shielah showered and was dressing.

Rummaging through her drawers for underclothing, she could find not a piece, bras and panties were all gone.

Determined to be calm, she asked Brandy if her underclothes had been put in with hers during the cleanup. Brandy looked and sorted her things. No, there was nothing of Shielah's in her drawers.

Shielah sat down on the edge of the bed, staring at her friend. A horrible, creepy sensation of perversion about to strike, paralyzed her. Brandy stood across the room, staring back at her. Then Shielah lay face down on the bed with her head buried under a pillow, and there she stayed until evening when Brandy finally got her up and out for some dinner.

Shielah had not been looking well for several weeks, Paulo observed. She seemed nervous, and frequently lost her train of thought. At times he wondered if she heard him.

"Have you been to a doctor?" he asked her as they strolled, hand in hand along her favorite path in Central Park.

She replied as though jerked back to the present. "No, why should I have been to a doctor?"

"You just seem, a little, well a little, nervous. Maybe you're not feeling well. And my discerning, lover's eye detects some dark circles under your eyes."

"I'm not sick."

"Are you tired?"

"No more than usual." Behind them a little boy lost his balloon to a bush. At the loud pop, Shielah jumped and spun around.

Paulo watched her reaction. "When do you have your next four day layover?"

"Next week."

"Mama's been asking after you. 'Wheresa that nice-a girl? That pretty one you bringa home one time? You never bringa her back. She doesn't like-a your family, isa that it?' " Paulo imitated his mother for Shielah's smile.

"Thatsa not it," she rejoined.

"Let's plan a couple of days in the mountains. Mama really is asking for you. You stole her heart as well as mine."

Shielah was watching the path. "Will Roberto be there?"

Paulo frowned. "You didn't like him, did you?"

"He didn't like me."

"How do you know?"

She pushed her hair back from her eyes, "I can feel things. Especially things like that. I have a sixth sense."

"Are you sure you don't imagine it?"

She looked at him, quick tears filling her eyes, "Don't you start that too."

"Shielah, what are we talking about? What the hell is going on? Sometimes I think we are talking about different subjects."

She jerked away from him and walked ahead. She didn't need his anger. She simply couldn't deal with it. She could barely contain her own emotions. She didn't want to tell him about the footsteps. She didn't want to talk about it at all. She wanted them not to exist, and at the same time she wasn't really sure they did. They walked that way for several yards, her before, and him a few feet behind. Then she became aware of Paulo's footsteps and listened carefully. They were solid and even. The others— they were stealthy, quick, syncopated almost. She turned around to face him, struggling to keep her eyes from overflowing.

"I miss your Mama too. Let's go home."

The next weekend spent on Paulo's family estate was simply idyllic. The fear left Shielah when she settled into Paulo's Fiat. The drive through the hills was as beautiful as it had been last Thanksgiving. She had been wrong to stay away from Paulo's family so long. She was starving for love and peace, and his home was rich in both. This time it was she who watched him as they drove. After all this time, and constant dating, she still was not used to the long-lashed brown eyes. They could melt her resolve with a look. She put her hand on his shoulder, surveying his body. Solid strength combined with grace. Why hadn't she married him this summer? He had asked her a hundred times. The airlines had just changed their ruling on stewardesses. She could now be married and still fly. She would be safe with him. Why was she so stubborn? But she knew the answer—she kept seeing Stephen beckoning to her in the moonlight.

Carmella was visibly and effulgently happy. She thumped Paulo on the chest.

"You shoulda not keep her so long to yourself. Papa willa say you are a bad boy." She giggled, "So willa I." She enfolded Shielah in her soft fleshy arms and held her in a long, satisfied hug.

"So!" she said, looking from one to the other. "So, you are still lovers, yes?"

Shielah colored slightly. Paulo gently tried to explain as he took his mother's arm. "Mama, we are in love, but we are not lovers. You'll embarrass Shielah. Lovers are for when you are married!"

"So whatsa wrong with that. If you are in love, you get married and you are lovers, right?"

Paulo grinned at Shielah. "I told you so."

Carmella patted Shielah's arm. "Don'ta you tease her. She isa my friend. She willa marry you, big shot, when she is ready."

"I hope so. I'm gonna marry my office desk if she doesn't hurry up."

Carmella gave Shielah her first cooking lesson in chicken cacciatore that afternoon, and, later that night, in real Italian noodles. Shielah and Paulo spent most of their afternoon walking across the hills. Paulo showed her the tree house he had built when he was nine. That day she never looked over her shoulder once. The view before them was too exquisite to miss. Rolling hills stretched as far as she could see—mound after mound of green, patchwork earth. Carmella had planted banks of flowers along the hillside and around the home. Shielah lay back on the warm grass. Peace at last!

But for Stephen there was no peace. Summer came and he was still not well enough to hold a full-time job. The army was paying his salary, and he lived at home, so money was not a problem. But he was idle. Stephen hated to be idle. He registered for summer quarter at BYU and began taking classes in business management. He had been away from school for almost four years with his mission and the service. He hadn't the foggiest idea of what he wanted to do with his life as far as a career was concerned. He envied Buck, and Shielah too for that matter. They both knew what they wanted.

Buck had graduated with a degree in physical sciences that spring. With his diploma in hand, he headed to Mexico immediately to join his professor friends at the dig site. Archaeology was his first love, his true love. He had wanted to marry Bridget right after graduation and take her with him to Mexico. But she would not budge. He would marry her in the temple if he loved her. If he didn't, he might as well ask her to simply live with him. They were two immoveable objects on that important point. Buck would have nothing to do with the church. Bridget would have nothing *but* a temple wedding. He was clever in his arguments, but she was implacable. Everything was black and white to her. To Buck, everything was a kaleidoscope.

"You just enjoy stirring the waters," she accused him.

"Somebody's got to. Still waters go stagnant."

"Don't you have *any* religious faith?"

"Yep. I believe in love! Let's get married."

"Show me your temple recommend."

He threw her back against the couch and kissed her soundly.

"That's not it. It's a little piece of white paper that says you are worthy of me."

"Oh, that." He scrounged a grocery receipt from his wallet and on the back wrote, "Buck is an OK guy and worthy of Bridget's love. The question is: Is she worthy of his, and what about . . . Naomi?"

"Who's Naomi?"

"How should I know! I just made her up to make you jealous."

"Buck, this is not a temple recommend."

"It's a person recommend. And I recommend me."

"How can I love you?" she said in exasperation.

"How can you not?" He grinned.

196

She loved him enough to let him go to Mexico and think about her. She went home to Hawaii, and did not reapply to BYU for the following year. It was over for her until, and unless, Buck came back to the church. She loved him, she adored him. She dreamed about him at night, and longed to feel his arms around her, to see the gleam in his brown eyes. But she would not marry outside the temple.

Buck said his last goodbye to Stephen. Bridget was already gone. He gave his car to Stephen for the summer or until he came back. Stephen drove home from the airport and the summer stretched before him, long and empty. He had written to Shielah asking when she could get another vacation and come back, if only for a few days. She had called him. She missed him too. But the facts were tough. It took most of a day to fly home and another to fly back. She would only have one day there. Her next four day layover came at the end of August. Maybe she could come home then.

Stephen was wearing the temple garments. He was also spending a few hours a week talking with a religion professor at the college. After a week he stopped that. The man had never been outside the U.S. He had never seen a man shot and killed. He had never seen a baby die from starvation. He had never seen an eight-year-old prostitute. He didn't know life as Stephen had seen it. He knew his own, safe, American God.

Stephen was still tormented. His understanding of Greg's and Kurt's death was coming slowly, but his hatred of Vietnam and the war was growing. It sometimes consumed him until he could hardly enjoy the warm, Utah summer, the peaches, the apricots, the smell of canned fruit in his mother's kitchen. He could be sitting with his family, eating fresh corn from his mother's garden, and a vision of barbed wire with dead bodies before it would flash through his mind, and his stomach would turn over. He would dash outside, afraid he would vomit, then walk until his leg hurt.

One day, late, when the sky was already pink and rose, he walked for two miles and found himself on the main street of town. Over his head was a sign, 'Jones Drug.' He could see a counter through the window. He walked in.

"Do you have slurpees?" he asked the man behind the counter.

"Nope, got some cherry coke from the fountain or a lemon squeeze."

"I'll take the lemon squeeze."

The man held up a lemon and squeezed it into the glass.

The doorway back into the kitchen simply had two strips of leather cloth hanging down. In the crack, Stephen could see a slight figure in jeans and a huge shirt. It looked like a child scrubbing the floor. When he had enjoyed half his drink, the figure slipped between the leather cloths and approached the man who had fixed the drink.

It was a Vietnamese girl. Even at such close range Stephen could not hear her words to the man. But he heard the same lilt in her voice, and the same gentle, musical tones.

Contrasted with her quiet voice, the owner sounded like a fog horn, "If you've finished with the floor you can go. Nine o'clock tomorrow."

She nodded and backed up. The owner was perturbed, "I told you not to do that. Don't bow to me."

197

"Sorry," Stephen heard her say.

She disappeared into the kitchen for a few moments, then reappeared and slipped around the edge of the counter, and was quickly out the door.

The next day Stephen came back and the next. The third day, when she came through the door, he spoke to her in her language. Her hand flew up to her mouth, and wide eyes stared at him a moment, then decorously dropped. He spoke again. Between the fingers of her hand she replied, "You speak Vietnamese?"

"Just a little."

Her perceptions were swift. "You were a soldier there."

"Yes," he affirmed.

Her eyes seemed to look into his spirit. "My country was beautiful once."

"I'm sure it was," he said.

"It is too bad you had to see it so ugly."

"Only the war was ugly. Your people were wonderful. How long have you been here?"

She counted silently, "Two years."

A voice called her from the kitchen. She quickly turned and ran, not looking back at him. The next day he came at sunset again. And this time, when she slipped out the door to go home, he was leaning against the building next door.

"Hello," he said.

"Hello," she looked studiously down.

"Are you headed home?"

"Yes," she whispered, "My work is over."

"Do you mind if I walk with you?"

She stole a quick glance at him. "I am not supposed to be alone with a man."

"Oh. Will you get in trouble if I walk with you?"

She seemed to struggle with herself. After a few moments she shook her head and replied, very softly, "I am in America now. Here it is permissible. I will talk to my father. Perhaps he will understand."

"You said you have been here for two years. You speak well."

"I am going to college" she said proudly. "That is why we came. My teachers in Saigon say I must go to America to get an education. They cannot teach me any more."

"You must be a very good student. Are you going now? During the summer?"

She giggled, "No, now I work. I work hard all summer, then I go to school."

"I see. How old are you?" It was almost impossible to tell age amongst the Vietnamese.

"I am twenty years old."

He studied her and shook his head. She certainly did not look twenty.

"How did your family come here?"

"We were lucky. An American Colonel sponsored my father."

"You *were* lucky. Many of your people are not so lucky."

198

"I know this," she said, watching the ground as they walked. "Many are dying. My uncle and my aunt, they are dead now. We talk of this often. And we try to bring others of our family."

"What others?"

"My sister and her husband and baby."

It wasn't far to the tiny garage they called their home. It was behind an older brick home, a detached garage rented to the Vietnamese family by an old man who lived alone in the house.

"Your name is?" he prodded her.

"Li-ly," she answered, pronouncing the 'i' with a long 'e'. "My father chose it after we were here one year. He says it means beautiful flower, the same as my Vietnamese name." She was blushing now and staring hard at the ground.

Stephen looked down at her. Her head did not reach his shoulder. She was as delicate as a blossom, and she made him think of all the lovely flowers of Hanoi, hanging around in nightclubs, waiting for the American servicemen. He had hated that. He had wanted to make it all better. But, of course, he couldn't. He was glad she had escaped.

"Lily, I wish you much good luck. You will be happy here, I hope."

Now she dared a look at him before she went through the small side door. He was very tall, even for an American, and his hair was light. It picked out the moonbeams and caught them. She hoped he would come again to the store, but he seemed to be saying goodbye.

He meant to say goodbye. But the need to talk was strong. A week later he sat at the counter and watched as she wiped off the glasses, the counter, the sinks, the griddle. She refused to look at him but she spoke once in a whisper.

"You were thirsty tonight?"

"Yes." After a few minutes he asked, "How long before you are finished?"

"Twenty minutes."

Twenty minutes later he was waiting outside. This time she smiled at him when she saw him there. She is quite lovely, he thought. Her black hair hung straight to her waist, unadorned and thick. She was so fine-boned that she looked as though a summer breeze could blow her over. Her slight figure was completely concealed in a voluminous man's white shirt.

They walked a block without speaking. Then Stephen asked her, "Do you miss your homeland?"

"Yes, of course."

"Would you go back if you could?"

"If the war was over, yes."

"Do you remember the war?"

Her eyes searched his face. Quietly she admitted, "Yes."

"Do you remember it *all?*" he asked pointedly, wondering if she had seen the horror he had seen.

She did not flinch. "Yes," she replied, still looking fully into his eyes.

All at once his eyes filled with tears and he shook his head. He took her arm and said, "Let's sit on the grass."

They sat down. Only a few inches separated them. Stephen put his forehead on his arms for a minute. She sat watching him. Neither of them spoke.

At last Stephen said, "I remember the war."

"Too much?" she guessed.

"Yes, too much! All the time! Everywhere, every day!" His anguish could not be concealed.

In a moment, a gentle touch on his arm brought his head up. She was watching him, her head cocked slightly, pity in her eyes. "You have not left the war."

"I guess not," he admitted, wondering how she knew.

"You must leave it."

"How did you?"

"I live today."

"I live yesterday."

"Then you will always stumble."

"It's not easy to forget."

"No, it's not. I did not forget in a day. I cried many nights. I feared many nights. My father, he taught me to live today."

"Teach me," he pleaded.

"Only one who is whole can make another whole."

"Teach me," he asked again.

Then she rose up on her knees and began singing a soft, lyrical song. He couldn't understand the words. They didn't matter. Her hair lay in a dark fall past her cheek, and her hands were folded decorously in her lap. Gradually she began mixing English with Vietnamese and he began to understand that she was making up the song. It was a song about blossoms lying in the mud, children sleeping in their mothers' arms, and the quiet of a heaven where no harsh sounds destroy the senses. She crooned to him as to a baby, the same song her mother had crooned to her on many a tearful night.

After a time, she sat back on her heels and smiled expectantly. "You are better?"

He nodded, afraid to speak and break the spell.

"There is hell and there is heaven. That is what my father says, Stephen. Sometimes they both exist side by side. Sometimes they both live inside you at once. You must find the heaven."

He stretched out on the grass and put his head in her lap. Then she looked up at the stars through the tree limbs and smiled.

Stephen's leg healed faster than his faith. By July he could walk without a limp. He practiced that. It was important to rid himself of the limp, as if that would rid him of the war. As he grew stronger he needed to work, to work hard. He found a job with a journeyman carpenter, and he learned how to put in a nail straight with four strikes of the hammer, how to find a stud, and how to walk on very narrow beams eighteen feet up. It was not especially satisfying work, but at least it left him too tired to think. He took no joy in the work. Stephen swung a hammer relentlessly, nailing frustrations and memories with his strokes.

Only Lily brought out the smile that had made him so well-liked by his friends in school. She had strange names for everything. A bird's song would be a "whistle-jim" and the white clouds overhead she called "cradle-snow." Stephen became "Sailmaster" and when they parted, she would touch his chest lightly with her fingertips, stretch to touch his forehead, then her own, and whisper "Sail far, Sailmaster." She did it mostly to make him smile, but the words seemed to hold special messages to her. It was as though she spoke in her own heart code.

He never knew how she had convinced her father to let her spend time alone with him. He knew the Vietnamese customs of proper behavior between men and women were very strong. She only told him that her father was very understanding and very sorry that Stephen was hurt inside.

Sometimes Stephen doubted whether she was truly twenty years old or really only thirteen. She was as open and unaffected as a child. She sang to him frequently. She told him long stories of ancestors and magic bushes where enchanted birds could heal you with their music. She could sit for hours cross-legged and listen with no expression while he retold the heartaches of his war, for it had become that. The pain all belonged to him, the loss was his own. Every death in his platoon was his own death, and every failure a victory for evil. There was no separation in his mind between Stephen Gailbraith and the dark night of death, the screams of the wounded and tortured. He spoke above them, and the world around him heard his words, but in the reality of his own private world only the screams existed, and they were interrupted by cries of tiny children.

This he told to Lily, and he named the names and described the places of death. He painted his word pictures of the children, the old people, the grief and the hatred. She listened hour after hour, week after week. But she never wept with him, nor did she show any sorrow at all for the horror he voiced. When he would cease his recounting, he would focus on her eyes. They were usually lifted above the treetops, or, if they had driven up the hill, focused on the white sparkles of the water on the lake. Invariably she was smiling.

Stephen grew impatient with her one day. "Sometimes I wonder if you hear me. Do you listen to me, Lily, or are you lost in your own world?"

She looked at him in surprise. "It is not I who am lost, Stephen Gailbraith. I hear your words. It is you who are lost, living in another world," she sighed. "I am merely amazed that you choose it."

He had thought she understood, she who had experienced the same horror of war. "I'm sorry if I burden you with my grief for your country. I don't choose it. I didn't ask for the privilege of serving in Vietnam. I wish I had taken Buck's advice and gotten out of it. But I am surprised that you seem to leave it behind so easily and forget the condition of your own people."

"I will suffer with you, my friend, if you want me to." She looked at him quizzically. "Do you want me to?"

"No, of course not. No one should have to suffer needlessly."

"But you do. And your friends continue to suffer even though they already did once, and died for peace." During the summer she had grown so that she could look at him when she spoke. Now she gazed steadily into his eyes. "If I did not know how kind your heart is, I would say you are very cruel—to make them suffer still. To make yourself suffer still. And now you want me to also suffer, and to weep while the sun shines. Do you care for me so little?"

Stephen looked away. He couldn't stand the clear depths of those dark eyes which showed, even as she spoke, no reproach and no hurt. Somehow the pain had all been wiped from the pages of her mind, and she refused to take it back. How could she do that? How could he?

"I care for you more than you know. You have been my friend. You have listened to me and seen me cry and you haven't judged me for the tears. I don't want you to suffer. Of course not. I am simply trying to find a way out of my own pain."

"Would you give it to me? Or would you give it to your dead friends?"

"No."

"But you are!" she said simply. "If you want to abolish the pain for all, you must give it back to the universe. You must let it go back into the blue of the sky. Out there, beyond the clouds that hang over the lake, beyond the light, loose the pain. Part as friends and say goodbye with no regrets. You are friends now, and pain may someday visit you again, for Life is the door through which it enters. You must greet it always as a passing friend. Do not close the door on it. It will either break down your door, in order to enter, or you will trap it inside if you close the door."

Almost inaudibly Stephen said, "Why? Why must it exist at all?"

She touched his shoulder lightly so that he looked at her again. "If you will banish pain, you will banish joy. If you will banish hate, you will banish love. They all walk the earth hand in hand. Some have tried to live only with one or the other, but Life itself is then diminished. You have been living only with pain, and Life has fled from you. There are men who live apart from the world, so as to live only with love. Life also flees from them, and, in order to live without pain or evil, they cease to give love to anyone else. That is not you, Sailmaster. You are not meant to give up Life so easily. You can master the two friends. When evil stands at your back, give goodness before you. When hatred spreads around you, give love as the potion to heal. When pain and grief strike, beckon gentleness to make her home with you. As long as there is Life, there will be two friends, dark and light. Do not hate the dark or it will consume you. Only love the light . . . and it will transform you."

Stephen sat staring into her eyes, now transformed with a radiance, as she taught him the knowledge of her fathers. That she lived her own words was clear. The light had transformed her and he hungered for it. She took his hands. They were twice the size of her tiny, delicate ones, and she held them firmly.

"Do not look at me, Stephen. Look across the lake. Do you see the sunshine? Can you open your door and let the darkness disappear in that sunlight? Now, can you feel the warmth and the light coming in?"

"*I am the light of the world: he that followeth me shall not walk in darkness, but shall have the light of life.*" Even as he spoke the words of St. John of the New Testament, a chill ran through Stephen and he experienced both the joy of understanding and the fear of ignorance.

"*He that ascended up on high, as also he descended below all things, in that he comprehended all things, that he might be in all and through all things, the light of truth; which truth shineth. This is the light of Christ. As also he is in the sun, and the light of the sun, and the power thereof by which it was made. And the light which shineth, which giveth you light, is through him who enlighteneth your eyes, which is the same light that quickeneth your understandings.*" The words he had studied from the Doctrine and Covenants—words he had wondered over and cherished and memorized in Scotland—became, in that moment, his answer, finally understood.

Then there ran through his mind one more scripture, "*Behold, here is the agency of man, and here is the condemnation of man; because that which was from the beginning is plainly manifest unto them, and they receive not the light. And every man whose spirit receiveth not the light is under condemnation.*"

Never had light flooded Stephen's consciousness so completely. He had refused the light. Lily was right. He had preferred to dwell in the darkness and so he had indeed been condemned. Not by God—by himself! Darkness was so antithetical to the light of his own spirit, a light that had come from Christ. And he had closed the door, holding the darkness in, choking his own light and denying the light of Christ surrounding him.

Comprehension was swift, complete. Humility followed and with it a tremendous desire to flatten himself upon the earth, to be one with something greater than himself and to give himself up to the light, and transcending feelings of freedom and relief. Lily saw the change come. She had listened to his words, memorized, but spoken as if for the first time.

"This is your Jesus Christ?" she said.

His eyes were wet, and he was unashamed. "Yes and also *your* Jesus Christ."

"A good man? A monk? A prophet?"

"More, the very light of which you spoke, and the Life also."

"One man?"

"No. Eternal existence given flesh—that is Christ!"

"If all eternity is embodied in his flesh, then eternity must cease at his death."

"He gave the light to the world at its inception. And he gave his light to the earth at his birth, so we could understand all. *And* he gave his light to the world after his death—for he proved to men that death does not end their existence, it only modifies it. He showed us resurrection. He showed us that it is the *fulfillment* of life in light."

"This Jesus Christ is your English word for Life?"

"Yes, and for love and light and joy."

"You forgot him too long, Sailmaster. The darkness has left with his name. I see a light in you that was dim before. It . . . it—how can I say—it breaks through your skin."

Stephen smiled at her, holding back the tears. "Yes, it is His light combining with my own, and it consumes me! Oh Lily, my heart will burst today. I cannot hold it!"

When he stretched out upon the grass and sobbed with ecstasy and relief, she tiptoed away from him and sat by herself. In the time that followed, she saw him rise to his knees and remain there a long time, and finally slump back to earth as though in deep sleep. She was not afraid. Her father was a quiet man, not given to tears or ecstasy, but she understood that Stephen was just learning the secret of Life—the joy of existence despite evil—and she was glad for him. She also hoped that once he had returned from his journey into eternity, he would remember her.

For the first time in a year Stephen slept without fear. It was remarkable to him that in one year, he had forgotten all he had once known. And as the light returned, it touched all parts of his conscious and subconscious. He saw that his mother's concern for him was translated into criticism and sharpness. He was able finally to be patient with the lack of understanding in his country about Vietnam. He also saw Lily as a person, instead of a country, for the first time. He saw the shy, hopeful tenderness in her eyes when she looked at him. Gratitude made him gentle.

One night he took her to a movie and afterward walked her home. Neither of them were anxious to arrive. They walked slowly, stopping often to talk. He talked continuously of his new understanding of the war and all he had learned. He spoke of his wish to grow closer to Jesus in love, so he could help others who suffered as he had.

"You speak much of love, Sailmaster."

Now he stopped and looked down into her eyes. He studied the soft curves of her face. "Yes. Perhaps I lived so long with hate that the other friend is anxious now to receive the attention."

"How will you give this love?"

"I'm not sure. Maybe I can counsel others and help them as you and Christ did me."

"Will you go away to do this?"

She was looking into his face, searching for something. Stephen was not sure just what.

"No, I think my place is here, but there are lots of veterans who come home as I did. I am going to Salt Lake next week to talk to the people at the Veterans Administration. They have a counseling service."

"When you are so busy giving this love to them, perhaps I will not see you so often." He could tell that was hard for her to say. She had struggled with the words and now was looking down. He put his hand on her head.

"Maybe not. But Lily, you have helped make me whole. Can't you be happy for me?"

"Oh, I am happy for you! I am happy for you. For me I am sad."

He felt his way carefully. "You will miss me?"

"Yes. I will miss our talks. I will miss being in your life."

"You will always be in my life. I can never forget you."

"But can you . . . love . . . me . . . a little, with all that love you are ready to give away?"

A thrill of sadness ran through him as he understood what she meant. He bent to kiss her forehead. "I do love you, I always will. You have taught me so much."

Her slender arms went up around his neck and she pulled his head down to kiss not her forehead, but her lips. No, he did not want it this way. It was a different kind of love. But his arms went around her anyway, and he had to confess to himself that he loved her. She was dear to him now, precious for what she had done for him. His soul was always at peace in her presence. A kinship existed between them, a kinship in the love that she had helped him re-discover.

"Stephen," she whispered. "You touch my spirit. I know you will sail now far beyond the dark shores that held you fast. I would come with you if you wanted me."

He stood looking down into her delicate face. He ached from the sweetness of that kiss and for the need that it awakened in him, the need for a woman's love, for that kind of sweetness to be his, moment by moment, day after day. He hadn't realized how much she had become a part of his thinking. Each new insight that came to him he wanted to share with her. Each lovely thing he noticed he saved to describe to her. The flowers he saw in tidy lawns and gardens made him think of her and he frequently picked one for her hair. Then, quickly, his arms tightened around her, lifted her from her feet and pressed her to him. In the starlight he held her, rocking back and forth. When he put her down he sighed deeply, sorrowfully at the reality he had to face.

"Lily, there is love and there is love." She looked at him quizzically, sensing that their moment of being lovers was over. "I will love your spirit forever. You are the loveliest of women, the sweetest of flowers. But . . . but . . . I cannot give . . . my life to you. And I wouldn't want to deceive you. I wouldn't claim your love, if I couldn't return it in kind."

"Now you will tell me that you love another," she spoke softly, sadly.

"Yes. I could wish it were not so. Sometimes this summer I have. I could give my life to you and be very happy, I think, if it were not for another woman who claimed my love years ago."

"This woman, she is good for you?"

"Yes. We are, I think, soul companions."

Lily's defenses rose. "She did not heal you."

"No. She began the healing. I think no one could have made me whole but you."

She nodded slowly. "I am my country in your heart. You wanted to love me because of that. But I am more than my country, Stephen. I am a woman and I wish to love you, as much as to heal you. Now that you give up your anger and your hate of Vietnam, must you also give up the country?"

"I do not give up the country. I have good memories now that I keep. And I don't want to give you up. You comfort my heart. I love you."

She moved away from him and shook her head. "That kind of love is over. You do not need me anymore for that. And I need you in a different way, a way you will not share."

"Lily, I . . . I can't stand to hurt you."

"I know. But still . . . " Her words ran out with her tears. He walked her home, and they did not speak again until they came to her door.

"Goodnight, my friend," he said. He wanted to hold her again, to comfort her as she had so often solaced him. But he knew he couldn't. It would only hurt her anew.

She touched his chest, then his forehead and last of all her own. "We will be friends—if we can bear to be. Goodbye, Sailmaster, sail far."

The next week Stephen left for New York.

Chapter 11

Shielah and Paulo drove leisurely home from the mountains. Paulo was reluctant to end it and go back to the reality of weeks and weeks without her. He had asked her again, this weekend, to accept his ring and to set a date they could plan for. She had looked at him thoughtfully, played with his hand, and reluctantly told him she wasn't ready. He had been afraid he would lose her when she went to Utah in the spring, but even though he had sensed a distraction in their relationship, it was plain she still wanted and needed him.

She was silent the last hour. The deeper they drove into the city, the deeper her silence became. He looked at her from time to time and she seemed almost morose. He asked her several times what was troubling her. She answered only that she was tired.

Paulo was lucky to find a car just pulling out and parked the Fiat in front of the apartment building, intending only to be gone for a few minutes. They walked up the steps, Paulo searching for an answer to Shielah's silence. He wanted to believe it was having to say goodbye, but he doubted that was the reason. Shielah put her key in the lock, turned to kiss him goodnight, and the door swung open slightly. Brandy was talking to someone. Stephen sat by the open window.

Surprise and an instant rush of happiness sparkled in the sad face that Paulo had been watching for the last hour. "Stephen! Stephen! I can't believe it! What are you doing here? When did you come? Why didn't you call and tell me you were coming? How long. . . . "

Stephen had crossed the room to her. Paulo stood in the doorway watching Shielah's face light up. She had forgotten him momentarily. Stephen was looking directly at him but spoke to her. "Wait. I haven't answered the first one yet. What is this, a quiz show?"

207

Quickly Shielah remembered her manners. "Paulo, come in and meet Stephen. This is Stephen Gailbraith. He's a childhood friend of mine and a returned vet from Vietnam."

"Shh," Stephen countered before Paulo could acknowledge the introduction. "Vietnam is a bad word with the American people. Sometimes they don't think too highly of their soldiers who fought over there." He put out his hand to Paulo and smiled. "Hello, you must be Paulo D'Agosta."

"That's right," Paulo affirmed. "I've heard a little bit about your time over there. I guess you were glad to get out."

"I was lucky to get out—alive. Sometimes I haven't been so sure I was lucky, but lately I've decided I'm glad after all."

Shielah's face was all alight, watching him. A pride which Paulo had never seen before seemed to shine when she looked at the tall, boyish-looking young man. Paulo assessed him—lean and broad-shouldered, confident but not overbearing. His all-American good looks belied the maturity in his eyes that signaled challenges met and matched. Paulo looked at the two of them, standing side by side, smiling and very much delighted in each other's company. All at once it was painful for Paulo. He seemed to see them as Shielah had described seeing them, alone together on a hillside, both dressed in white, and Eternity stretching behind them. The vision stabbed Paulo. His hand went involuntarily to his head to ward off the pain. He wanted very much to leave so as not to see her happiness with this young man. On the other hand, he didn't dare leave.

Stephen was intent upon Shielah. "Let me try to answer those questions before you bombard me again. What am I doing here? I'm talking with Brandy." Shielah pushed at him in mock exasperation. "No, actually I'm here to see New York. I needed a vacation. I deserved it and I came. I understand stewardesses make wonderful tour guides."

Her face fell. "Not when they have to fly tomorrow."

"I know. Brandy already told me. Thank goodness she isn't as cold-hearted as you. She has promised to guide me around while you're gone. When did I come? What was it Brandy, about one o'clock? And why didn't I call?" He shrugged. "What can I say? Too expensive? Too impulsive? Maybe it's a flaw in my character that I just like to surprise people."

Carefully, Shielah didn't look in Paulo's direction. She was standing between them, one on each hand. "Well, you sure surprised me. It's too bad I'm flying all week." She was trying to bring herself down for Paulo's sake. She was acutely sensitive to him and could feel his silent dismay.

"Not all week, is it?"

"Four days on and two days off."

"Oh, you mean they actually make you earn your keep and work like regular folks?"

He was teasing her again. She knew already that he had come a long way from the mental state in which she had left him. She laughed. "You should work so hard!"

"Absolutely not! I'm on vacation."

Paulo spoke, "Well, I'm not. I have to go to work tomorrow, too. I'd better say goodnight."

Shielah turned with him back toward the door. He took her hand and drew her outside, into the hallway, for a moment.

"When will I see you again?"

"I . . . I don't know."

"Next week?"

"I'm not sure. I work four and two next week again."

"Dinner next Tuesday."

"Paulo, I can't promise. I don't know my schedule or how tired I may be."

"I'll call you Monday and check on it."

For a moment they were both silent, looking at one another. Finally Shielah could not deny him any longer. "Alright. I'll talk to you Monday night."

"Whenever you get in."

"OK. Goodnight. I loved it. It was therapeutic for me to be there with you and your family."

"Right." His voice was tight. He hated being civil. Damn, why should he be. He kissed her but she pulled away too quickly. "See you next week." She watched him walk away, and she felt guilty for some unfathomable reason.

"What time do you leave in the morning?" Stephen was at her side. She turned back, putting Paulo out of her mind.

"Early. Six-thirty. I take the subway and then the bus out to Kennedy. I haven't looked at my schedule for a few days, but I think I won't be back until about seven thirty or eight."

"Suppose I ride the subway with you. That's kind of a new kick for me, and it will give us a some time together we wouldn't otherwise have. Shielah, I know I should have written or called or something. It was really a spur of the moment decision. I've had a lot happen, and I needed . . . I needed . . . you, to share it with. Is it all right? Do you mind?"

What was it on his face? A kid with a secret he couldn't wait to tell, some intense kind of happiness he was barely holding in. She put her arms around his waist. "Of course, it's all right. I'm glad you're here. I've missed you and thought about you so much. You look . . . wonderful . . . happy."

"I am happy. I don't know if I can wait til Friday to tell you about all this. You might get it piecemeal."

"That's OK. Where are you staying? Do you have a hotel?"

"I thought about getting a hotel, but your soul-sister in there talked me out of it. We took a walk down the block and found out that Mrs. Moriariti has a room she hasn't been able to rent. She said she'd rent it to me for the week. She warned me she would have to show it if a renter came, but I don't intend to be in it much anyway, just long enough to lay my head at night."

"I'm going to be jealous, knowing you and Brandy are having such a great time while I'm working!"

Brandy had sauntered over. "You should be jealous, gal! If it wasn't for Mr. Benjamin T. Mitchell the fourth, I would steal this beautiful young man from under your nose like *this*." And she snapped her fingers in Shielah's face.

"Oh, she's hard to resist." Stephen shook his head and put his hand over his heart. "She promises me hushpuppies and pool, Harlem and the Statue of Liberty."

"Wait a minute," Shielah objected. "I want to go with you to the Statue."

"You'll be flying, honey, you'll be flying," Brandy reminded her. "This poor boy got to do something besides mope around for you. Mitch-4 will chaperone us if we go anywhere too exciting."

Shielah stood with her arm around Stephen as though they had never been apart and no one else existed. "How long will you be here?"

"I planned a week. Wish I'd planned better. But I will be content with four nights and two days. It's better than I would have had if I had stayed home. You're not as soft over the telephone. Brandy, do I have your permission to kiss this pretty lady?"

"Permission given, soldier."

"Then you have my permission to go out for pizza, a banana-split, or whatever you please."

Brandy grinned broadly. "Where's my quarter? My brothers always got a quarter from my boyfriends!"

Stephen dug into his pocket, but she had closed the door laughing before he fished anything out.

Before she would kiss him she went to the window and drew down the yellow shade. Then she turned back to him, suddenly shy.

"You don't like to be on television?"

"Not much. In the summertime people are pretty free around here. You see lots of hugging and stuff on the fire escapes and on the streets. But I like privacy."

"You do? Already thought that one out?"

She blushed.

"I see why Buck wanted me to know about Paul D'Agosta. He . . . uhh . . . let's just say he makes me nervous."

"He's good to me."

"I'm sure he is. Obviously he is very intent on you. Does he love you?"

"Yes."

Stephen still stood across the room from her. "So do I."

She colored even more. "You look tanned and healthy. Have you been working this summer."

"I don't answer questions yet." He moved toward her and held out his hand. She took it from across the couch and he drew her to him. "I'm not here to talk about work. I only came for one thing," he held her lightly in a circle of his arms. "To kidnap you and run away with you, leaving no ransom notice or any way of tracing us. You will wake up tomorrow morning in a small tropical hut in Porte Vallarte, and I will inform you that you married me last night, even though you can't remember a thing due to

210

the amnesia pills. Then I will persuade you to make mad, passionate love to me."

"Wait, wait," she laughed. "You forgot the deaf and dumb houseboy and the little fat smuggler, who flies us in and out of the country hidden under a sack of illegal silver trinkets."

"I was just getting to that . . . but I got stuck in the thoughts of the mad, passionate love. That's my favorite part. Let's go back to that."

"I didn't know you were so impetuous."

"I've grown that way after years of waiting. The thoughts of you have driven me most out of my mind, Scarlet my jewel. If I'm a rogue, it's all your fault. I die for your kisses."

"Do you?" she tucked her head and looked up at him from the corner of her eye.

"I do. Indeed I do." Then his eyes lost their smile. "The last time I held you I only had one arm to use. I like two."

"So do I."

Then the easy banter was gone. They were alone and they held each other, savoring the wild, wonderful feeling. His fingertips traveled up and down her shoulders and back, pressing her more tightly every few moments. His lips rested on her temple, and he breathed in the soft perfume she wore. Time turned back.

"Remember your senior dance, and how long every dance seemed? I remember holding you and smelling your perfume, until I thought I would go nuts. I wanted to kiss you so badly."

"Why didn't you?"

"I don't know. You were so shy, and you were my best friend's sister."

"I kept hoping you would. In fact I didn't think of anything else after about the third dance. Then I was afraid you'd see what I was thinking if I looked at you."

"Is that why you kept your head down all night?"

"Umm hmm. I was embarrassed over my thoughts."

"My goodness. I didn't know you were so crazy over me."

"You were blind."

"So were you. Did you really think I came over every day just to see Buck?"

"I couldn't presume."

"You can presume now. Buck's not here."

"I'm not hiding my head now."

His fingers climbed up under her hair and around her neck. Still he held back, looking, just looking, letting his eyes caress her face and touch her lips. Finally she couldn't stand it anymore.

"Please. . . . "

"Please what?" he asked.

"Kiss me."

His eyes sparkled again. "I thought you'd never ask." And then his lips closed over hers and they both forgot the world. They didn't hear the noise of the street or the sounds of music floating up from the corner hamburger joint. Stephen held her and they swayed to their own music, the songs they had danced to two years before, and touching was as unbearably beautiful to them now as it had been then, when everything was yet unspoken.

"I'm going to love you a long time," Stephen whispered against her cheek.

"I have loved you a long time, already."

"Can you stand any more?"

"I'll try."

"Come with me to Porte Vallarte," he said.

"The ends of the earth?"

"No, just Mexico will do. I'll serve you cool, delicious drinks, and you can swim in your bikini while I watch and savor."

"I don't own a bikini."

"Religion has ruined you."

"I suppose. Would you want me to wear a bikini?"

"Uh huh. But only with me."

"Silly."

"Where are you going tomorrow?" he mumbled, still nuzzling her.

"St. Louis and back."

"I could go with you."

"Without a ticket?"

"I could stow away."

She giggled as he kissed her on the neck. "You'd look funny tucked up in one of those compartments we stow things in."

"I could hijack the plane."

She squeezed him. "Don't talk about that."

"I could! I have a deadly banana I always carry in my coat pocket. I could demand ransom for the airplane—one stewardess with long, silky blonde hair. I'm a depraved Buddhist Mormon monk and I want her for my love slave."

"How long have you been like this?"

"Like what?"

"Depraved and deranged?"

"Years really, ever since I first saw an eight-year-old, skinny girl tagging along behind me."

"So! You had your lustful eye on me even then."

"Right. I was twelve. I thought you'd make a marvelous child bride."

"If only I'd known."

"We'd have both been in trouble. I love you. Did I tell you that last year?"

"Once. Tell me again."

"I love you. I'm going to sit around and watch your apartment all day while you're gone, and pray for the night to come."

She shivered, remembering that someone else had apparently been watching her. "Don't say that."

"Can you stand me for a week?"

"I'll try. It'll be hard but I'll try. Only, don't have too much fun with Brandy."

212

"She's everything you said she was. She did say she'd show me around Central Park and the U.N. tomorrow. I guess her boyfriend is going to join us on Tuesday. I think she was concerned about him being jealous. But I'll be at the airport to meet you every night. I want you every minute I can get . . . in more ways than one."

Paulo sat alone in his apartment. He meant to go to bed. He had turned off the lights. But still he sat in his favorite chair, alone in the dark, staring into the cold fireplace and seeing Shielah and Stephen together, shining with a light he rarely saw. Despair paralyzed him. For over a year now he had been totally wrapped up in his relationship with Shielah, watching her grow and mature, falling more and more in love with her as she blossomed into the confident woman he had known she would become. His whole focus had centered on winning her love and her future. There were times he thought she loved him and that they would certainly be married eventually. This weekend had been one of them. She obviously adored his Mama and sister, Marian. But this! How could he fight that instant connection she made with Stephen? What had he seen as he watched them together? Was it truly one of his visions? Or was it just his fear that made him imagine things?

Two glasses of wine had made Paulo very tired and accentuated the weight of sadness that seemed to crush him. At last he put his wine glass on the hearth and rested his head in his hands. He was monstrously tired of being alone. It was foolish. He didn't have to be alone. There was more than a few women whom he knew would help him ease his loneliness. But his heart said "No." Why? Why? Why couldn't she be his? Why did he see that vision of her so long ago if she was not to be his? Anger and pain welled up and he stood up quickly, kicking the wine glass to pieces against the stone hearth, slamming his fist against the bookcase and spilling out a dozen books onto the floor. The blackness around him seemed to mock his anger. Who was to care? Who was to see or care how he felt? The pain of being alone was suffocating.

Paulo stumbled to the doorway of the bedroom and flung himself across the bed, deep groans breaking from his lips. Eyes staring wide in the darkness, he seemed to see in suspended animation, Shielah and Stephen dressed in white, holding hands, smiling and shining with a brilliance like the sun, and blue infinity stretching round about them. He closed his eyes. Still the vision would not go. "No," he cried, hoarsely. "No, no, no, no. It's not so. *It's not!* I love her too much," he cried. "No, please dear God, no. If You haven't forgotten me completely, don't let it be."

Mercifully sleep came quickly, but even still the pillow beneath Paulo's head was damp when unconsciousness overcame him. For the first few hours it was a restless, fitful sleep. He tossed and turned, curling up, clutching the pillow to his chest. Finally, after he had been sleeping a few hours he seemed to sink into a deeper, almost trancelike slumber. And in that deep unconsciousness Paulo dreamed a dream.

There was a meadow, cool and covered with wild flowers and berries. A small stream formed a little pool, and beside that pool walked a young woman. At first she seemed very far away, tiny, and unreachable. Then she turned toward him and grew suddenly very close. She smiled. It was Shielah. No, it was not, but she looked very much like this young girl. The girl had red hair, like a polished copper, and freckles stood out across her nose and cheeks. He was instantly lost in her eyes. They possessed him and he fell into their depths, grey and green at the same time. She teased him with a willow-wand, twisted away as he reached for her, flounced her long skirts, glanced coquettishly back at him over her shoulder. And he turned in every direction she moved, hungering for the sight of her. Oh, but she was beautiful! And something about her satisfied the longing of his soul.

Then the bright meadow changed, as dreams will do, and he saw her lying beneath an enormous oak tree, a horse at her side. Lightning crashed around her and rain pummeled her body. He stood above her and willed her to arise, to protect herself from the elements. Then he felt an impending sense of horror and danger. He watched as a hideous figure of utter evil laid a cold hand upon her shoulder and bade her come with him. All at once, Paulo felt a glowing power within himself blaze out and challenge the wraith of darkness. A battle followed, a battle of wills for the woman lying beneath the tree. Paulo would not suffer that the power of evil should possess her. In that dream she had become too precious to him to allow anything to destroy her. It was imperative that she survive. He used every ounce of energy and power of his soul to protect her. And at last, the figure of evil turned and crept away into the shadows of the night.

There followed a swift panorama of her life. Paulo watched as though on a screen, yet followed her, almost by her side. He saw her life, her children, another man she called her husband. He saw her agonies, her tears, her turning to God, and he saw her lying upon a bed as an older woman. She was separated from him only by a thin veil and after a moment it parted and she rose and came to him, holding out her hand. She came into his arms, a beautiful young girl again—the girl he had seen in a vision more than ten years ago. This time she did not fade as she had then. He seemed to feel the warmth of her body, to bask in the glow of her spirit. He held her, wrapped in his arms, and the comfort to his heart was healing. When morning came, the dream had faded into just a dim memory of a girl who looked like Shielah. But the comfort remained.

In the week that followed, Paulo left Shielah and Stephen to each other, submerging himself in office routine, waiting until he knew Stephen was gone. He did not allow himself to think about them together, nor the impression he had had at seeing them together in Shielah's apartment. Twice during the week he went out with Jim, but when the evening was over and Jim took a girl home, Paulo went back to an empty apartment— alone.

On Wednesday morning when Shielah left Stephen at the concourse, he didn't turn and go straight back into the city. Instead, he took a seat and a paper. He turned the pages every so often; he looked down, but he didn't read. He listened, and carefully watched. Three times he moved from one area to another, and then to the furthest table in the coffee shop. He left the money on the table beside the paper, sauntered into the men's room, and purposely stayed for twenty minutes. During that time, two men came in. The last one wore black patent shoes. He was a well-dressed Italian and quite young. Stephen noticed his shoes and the slight tapping they made on the floor. Stephen slipped out when the young man's back was turned and was quickly lost in the crowds. Stephen's money supply was not large, nevertheless, he rented a car and got lost only once trying to drive to Shielah's apartment building. When he finally made it, he parked the car across the street, down at the end of the block. Then he sat all day and watched the people on the sidewalk. Brandy was flying the rest of the week. He wasn't really there for sightseeing anyway, so he just sat and listened for the footsteps he had noticed behind him and Shielah for the last two days.

He didn't drive the car to pick Shielah up when she came in that evening. He slipped out of the car, joined a stream of people passing by, then took the subway to Kennedy. She was very tired, even though she arrived an hour earlier than the last two days. It had been a bumpy flight. One businessman had gotten sick. She had spent the day apologizing and soothing other people's nerves. Her own were a frazzle. But the sight of Stephen's smile when she walked into the concourse cheered her.

"Why don't we stay right here and have dinner, and let you rest awhile before we brave the crowds," he suggested. That was fine with Shielah.

Again he chose a table at the very back of the room and sat with his back to the wall so he could see the entire dining room. They hadn't had much time to talk in the last two days. The subway was noisy, and she had been getting in later. He had been waiting for the right time to tell her about Lily and how she had helped open his eyes. Over dinner he told the story from the beginning. Shielah was quiet, listening, feeling the struggle and the resolve. He couldn't read her reaction.

"I am happy for you," she said when he had come to the end. But she did not smile.

"I think it was the only way I could have been freed. It took all summer long to work through those feelings of anger and futility and hate. Lily was so perceptive for someone so young. She said her father taught her. I'm almost inclined to go sit at his feet and learn."

"Why don't you?"

"It was very plain to me that day that we have the same knowledge available to *us*. The scriptures are full of the mysteries of life. We only have to open our minds, question, visualize, and draw the analogies. What is amazing is that the other religions actually teach much the same concepts of life and living. They just use different words and analogies. If I thought he would actually let me in his life, I might even still go to him to glean. My guess is he wouldn't open up to me though, even if he had the time between working two jobs. Lily says one job is for his family here, in the U.S., and one is for their family still in Vietnam. He is saving to bring them here. I hope he gets them out before it is all blown to pieces."

"I think you'll never really be free of Vietnam. Your thoughts still revolve around it, even though your bitterness seems to be gone."

He looked at her in surprise. "I didn't want to be free of Nam. I wouldn't want to be free of Scotland either. They are both an intimate part of my mind and heart now. You're right, I'll always think about it and hurt for the people. But I am free. Free to love and appreciate that which I never could before.

She was silent.

They finished dinner silently. But Stephen was not one to let things go unsaid. "You're awfully quiet. What's wrong?"

"I don't know. Nothing, really. I'm just tired."

He sat regarding her thoughtfully. "I hoped you'd be happy for me, for us."

"I am happy for you." She reached across the table for his hand and, tried to smile.

"You're melancholy."

"Maybe just a little." He waited for her to go on. "I wish I had been able to stay last spring. I would have liked to help you."

"You did. I think you opened the door, that door that had kept all the hate and bitterness inside. I could not have let anyone in with that door shut so tightly."

"Perhaps, but I feel like I failed you when you needed me most."

"Shh. What's this talk of failure? This is supposed to be a talk of victory. You didn't fail me at all. When you met me at that airport, I've never been so grateful for anyone. I'd have been demolished if you hadn't come."

"I just feel that I did so little . . . by comparison."

"Who did what? You did this, Lily did that. Circumstances changed this. A good field commander looks at his recruits and uses their peculiar talents and abilities where he can, to the best advantage. That's what God did here. You could not be Lily, just as she cannot be you. She represented for me the whole, terrible experience and more, a serenity in the face of tragedy. But that doesn't change my love for you."

"Do I sound jealous? I guess I am a little."

He had been holding her hand. Now he brought it to his lips and kissed it. "No need to be. She helped to free me, but you're the one I have flown to. Someday I want you to meet her—yes, even if it makes you jealous. She's unique and she's part of me now." His grin was quick and challenging. "Besides, you introduced me to someone I wasn't supposed to be jealous of . . . even though he kissed you in the hallway, almost in front of my nose."

She laughed uncomfortably. Then she said very seriously. "Stephen, I'm afraid. I feel so uncertain of how this all will end. It's almost as though I am floating on a boat on a river and the current is getting swifter and

216

somewhere ahead is a large waterfall. I've actually had dreams about it. I go over the falls and it seems like I'm dying. And then I wake up."

"I understand. I've felt that same sense of being drawn toward my destiny and not knowing what I would face or whether I would make it." He leaned toward her, his blue eyes shining with conviction. "But I learned this. Do not be afraid. Two friends walk the earth—fear and faith. They walk together, and if one comes in your door, the other waits just outside. If fear enters first, it is possible to invite faith in and politely excuse the other. Only, be careful not to shut the door too tightly. The other friend is always jealous and will hammer on your door to break it down if you are too anxious to exclude him completely. Faith is a good friend. She will hold your hand and say, 'See, there is fear, my companion. But I will stay by you and nothing can hurt you as long as you hold my hand.' "

Shielah watched him and saw the glow of his conviction. "You learned this from Lily?"

"Partly, but I have thought it out and understand it for myself. Can you make it your own?"

"I'm not sure. I'll think about it. Could you do it if you were back in Nam?"

Now he leaned back. "That's a good question. I don't know the answer. I can only say I hope so."

They took the subway home. After Stephen had said goodnight, he slipped out a back door of the apartment, walked through the alley way, and down a block. Then he crossed the street and sat in the rented car, watching and listening to footsteps for two more hours before he went into his own room.

Friday was their day. They had stayed up late Thursday night since Shielah wasn't flying the next day. It was their day for sightseeing. They walked all over the city, through Central Park, through the Guggenheim Museum, then down into midtown. They walked Broadway together and Stephen was amazed at all the girls on the streets obviously selling their "wares." Shielah hated that and quickly directed their steps to the Rockefeller Center. They went up in the Empire State Building, and Stephen kissed her there. He said he wanted to kiss her at the top of the world. She was embarrassed but none of the people in the tour group paid any attention whatsoever.

"You can't even be an exhibitionist here," Stephen whispered to her.

About five o'clock he asked her, "Aren't we ever going to stop walking. You're the worst drill sargeant I've had since boot camp."

Then she became aware that his right leg was dragging just a little, and he was exercising a lot of discipline not to limp. "Time for dinner," she said. "Do you want Italian food or what? The city is famous for it's Italian food, and we could take the subway downtown. There are a dozen restaurants on every street corner. Well, maybe that's exaggerating just a little."

"Sounds good to me. Just let me sit down for a minute, will you Sarge? I'll do double time later."

After dinner in midtown at the Napolina, on the way back to the subway entrance, they walked slowly and casually. You could smell good things cooking, even from the sidewalk, and several different strains of Italian music floated around them. Shielah had twice started to talk, and twice Stephen had cut the conversation off. He walked with his head down, she also grew silent, aware now of tapping, syncopated footsteps behind. They began instinctively to walk faster. When they came to the end of the block, Stephen took her elbow and pulled her around the corner, then ran, half dragging her to the next doorway and shoved her down a dark stairway.

"Stay there, and don't move, no matter what. I won't be far away."

In seconds he had blended into the shadows of the tall, dark buildings. He pressed his back against the concrete and waited, hardly breathing. Then he heard the footsteps again. Tap, tap, quick step, then slow. He had heard them all week. They paused a moment, then started up again, quicker than before and not so syncopated. They were only a few feet away, and Stephen steeled himself.

He didn't see the man's face in the dark. It wasn't necessary. He knew it was the young Italian. Stephen's elbow came in with force into the solar plexis and the footsteps ceased with a heavy grunt. The youth was on his knees doubled up, his face still hidden, and Stephen was straddling his back instantly, one hand yanking up the head, his foot planted on the back of the knee. A long knife appeared in Stephen's other hand—since Vietnam it was always in his pocket.

"I don't like to be followed. And I don't like Shielah to be followed. Who are you, and what the hell are you doing?"

There was no answer, just groaning and ragged breathing.

"You got thirty seconds to talk." Stephen laid the knife against the man's temple. He had jerked the head back until the face stared straight up at him. The eyes were closed at first, then opened in fear when the knife blade touched his skin. He was a young kid, no more than eighteen, clean shaven, expensively dressed in pinstripe pants, black patent leather shoes and a wine-colored silk shirt.

"I didn't hurt her."

"You didn't answer my question, and I am not very patient."

"I'm just supposed to follow her around."

"What for?"

"For nothing." Stephen put a little pressure on the knife and drew blood. The kid cried out. "Just to scare her, that's all, just to scare her."

"Who are you?"

He didn't answer right away and Stephen bore down with his foot. The kid's knee cracked and he swore. Stephen was merciless, "How much do they pay you, and is it worth a broken knee cap, and a tic-tac-toe face?"

"Buddy! My name is Buddy Ciardi!"

218

"That's better. Who pays?"

The Italian boy was convinced now. His eyes were constantly on the knife, and blood was making its way down his cheek. "They'll kill me if I tell you."

"Maybe. I'll kill you if you don't."

The boy glanced up at the bigger man who straddled him. There was no trace of gentleness on Stephen's face now. He was scowling, his eyes narrowed and his mouth twisted in determined concentration. The tip of the long knife began to make it's way down the temple to the cheekbone and then over to the ear. The boy began to whimper. Stephen was relentless. "Who pays?"

In a whisper, the boy finally confessed, "Maretti. He set me up. Don't hurt her, just scare her real good, he said. A hundred bucks a week and all I do is follow her."

"Anything else?"

"Messed up her room twice, just to scare her, that's all. Swear to God I wouldn't touch her. Never touched her!"

"Say the name again."

"Maretti. Vincent Maretti."

Slowly, carefully Stephen released the pressure on the boy's knee, and dragged him to his feet. He twisted the boy's arm painfully behind his back. Stephen wiped his knife on the boy's silk shirt and held it down, slightly concealed, so Shielah wouldn't see it.

She had crouched on the steps down on the first landing. She hadn't been so aware of footsteps this week. Her attention had been on Stephen, and she had not realized he had heard them. She hadn't told him anything about the two break-ins, or her fear. She was almost convinced she was imagining the footsteps, but tonight they were there again. What Stephen would do she had no idea. She expected, if anything, sounds of a fight. She heard almost nothing, a cry once, then nothing. Then Stephen called her and she came hesitantly out of the shadows and up the steps, holding onto the railing.

"You've been followed."

Stephen stood slightly behind a younger man. The dark head was bent down in embarrassment and pain, blood dripping on his collar. Shielah's eyes were wide with amazement and fear.

Stephen asked her, "Did you know you were being followed?"

She nodded, unable to speak at all.

"You didn't tell me about your room being messed up."

She shook her head no, staring at the young man who had tied up her life with fear in the last four months.

"You know the name Maretti?"

Now she glanced up quickly at Stephen's face. It was set with determination and coldness. It hardly looked like the man she knew. "Yes. I've met him."

"He has something against you. He paid this hood to scare the pants off you."

Her voice was low and shaking. "He did a good job."

219

"He ever touch you, ever hurt you?"

"No. I never even saw him."

Stephen jerked on the already taut arm. "Good thing for you, *Buddy*! Now I'm gonna pay you off."

The kid began to dissolve. He was shaking and scared and trying hard not to cry.

"I'm going to let you go in exchange for a favor. You are going to tell Mr. Maretti that he damn well better lay off. The next one he sends won't walk back in his door. If he has a gripe with Shielah, he has a gripe with me. He wants to play hide-and-go-seek, I'm good at that, real good." He shoved the kid away from him, up against the dark concrete wall. "Now you get your butt out of here before I carve it up too. And I better not hear anymore footsteps. They make me nervous. Do you understand what I mean?"

"Yes, sir," the young hoodlum whispered. He inched along the wall and split suddenly, running and stumbling down the street.

Shielah stood silently looking at Stephen. After a minute, his face relaxed. A tentative smile appeared and she moved toward him hesitantly.

"You're very convincing."

"I intended to be. I've been aware that we were being followed since the first day I brought you home on the subway." He drew her against him, and held her head against his chest. "I heard the footsteps the first morning. He followed us to and from the airport. I was suspicious immediately but that evening when I picked up the sound again, there was no doubt. He has a very distinctive walk. He's been watching your apartment too. I got a car and parked it, just sat there and watched and listened for the footsteps. He passed me in the car probably four times. I don't think he went in the apartment this week. Why didn't you tell me about this?"

"I didn't want to concern you. Brandy thinks I ought to go to a psychiatrist. I wondered if I was imagining it too."

"What about breaking into your room?"

"He never took anything of value. The time that really scared me though was the second time, when he took my underclothes."

"What?"

"He took all my underclothes. I had to go out and buy new panties and things. Brandy started to believe me more then, but I think she and Mrs. Ramsey still thought the two break-ins were a fluke."

He sighed heavily. "I was afraid this joker was connected to that D'Agosta fellow." She started. "I know you like him. I know you think he loves you. But I don't know anything about him. How do I know he doesn't have some strange ideas about you. Anyway, I'm glad, for your sake . . . and for his, that it wasn't true. Who's Maretti?"

Shielah didn't know how much to tell him. She now knew the answer to the whole thing. "Vincent Maretti is a very wealthy furrier in town. I think he wants his daughter to marry Paulo."

"I see, and you're getting in the way. Well, that sounds like a good match, let her!"

"It's not me. He really doesn't love her."

Stephen kissed her forehead and hair. "Umm hmm. How could he, with you in front of him all the time? I wouldn't love her either."

"You haven't see her. She's gorgeous."

"Let's go home."

"I need to make a telephone call first. Can we stop in the subway station?"

"Sure."

From the telephone booth, with Stephen standing a few feet away, she called Paulo and told him the whole story. He was appalled, angry, disbelieving at first, then furious with Roberto.

"Shielah, are you really OK? I mean, I know you must have been scared for a long time. I wish you'd told me more, sooner."

"I didn't really understand it all. I had forgotten Roberto's threat, and I didn't connect it with the footsteps. I began to doubt my own senses and wondered if Brandy was right when she said I was paranoid."

"That's why you have been so jumpy and quiet lately."

"I guess so. I'm sorry to have to tell you all this, but I'm afraid now, not for me but for Stephen. I don't know how powerful Maretti is or how he'll take the news of what happened tonight."

"I'll handle it. Nothing will happen to your friend."

"Thank you."

"Shielah, don't go yet. I . . . I've missed you. I wish I could see you."

"Tuesday night for dinner, you said."

"Can you make it?"

"I'll make it."

"Honey, I'm sorry about this. What can I say?"

"I know. It isn't your fault."

But Stephen would never have understood and she didn't tell him anymore than she already had. It was over now. She stood next to him on the train. He held onto the grip with one hand, and kept the other protectively around her shoulders. She looked up and smiled at him.

"Do you want me to kiss you, here, with all these people around?" he whispered in her ear.

"No!"

"Then stop smiling at me and looking so beautiful."

But she didn't stop, and their walk home from the subway was delayed several times while he paused to make good his threat. Saturday was their day for the Statue of Liberty and Coney Island. They walked everywhere, arms locked around each other's waists, happy, at ease with each other, kids again and this time in love. What would she ever tell Paulo?

Chapter 12

Buck had been in Mexico since May. He had left Utah as soon as his diploma was in his hand, not even staying for the pomp and ceremony of graduation exercises. He only had two regrets about leaving, Bridget—she would not come with him—and Grandma—she could not understand that she would see him again. Grace had wept over him as she hadn't even over Shielah. He had tried to comfort her. He talked and joked and showed her pictures of the place he would be, the men he would be working with. She was not consoled. She peered at the pictures then swept them aside. She looked up at him.

"Will you be a good boy for me?"

"Grandma, you know I'm always a good boy. Didn't you teach me right? Of course you did. Any time I'm tempted to do something wrong, I say to myself 'what would Grandma think?' and I'm always a good boy then."

He earnestly wanted her to believe him. Even with her dim eyes she could see that. She gave a sort of laugh. "Buck, you're an awful liar."

"How can you say that?"

She pulled on a long curl in his hair. "Because it's true. You know it and I know it. And I know something else." Now she patted his cheek sorrowfully. "I know you're going away now and you're never coming back."

"I'm not! Grandma, it's not true. I'll make you a promise. I'll be home for Thanksgiving. You can count on it. No matter where I am or what I'm doing, or if the airlines go on strike or the next ice age comes, I'll be home for Thanksgiving and I'll stay with you through Christmas. Put that in your checkbook and bank on it."

Grace couldn't help smiling at him. "You are a good boy, Buck, and don't you forget it. You're an awful liar and an awful tease, but you're a good boy and I've always loved you. Ginny and Ed did too. Only one thing you failed them in. I know your mother would have wanted you and Shielah to be friends, close friends, and you have been fighting."

"I've been trying to make up, but she won't. She's really mad at me."

"Then you go apologize to her."

"It's not that simple."

"You make it right. You're the oldest and you're responsible. She loves you, I know she does. She always adored you when she was a little girl. Love like that just doesn't stop. You find that love again. It's still there."

It was a heavy burden to Buck. He suspected she was right. He was the oldest and probably responsible, although he had long tried to be *irresponsible*. "OK, Grandma. I'll try. I'll write to her. Maybe she'll make it home for Thanksgiving, or at least Christmas, this year. We'll work it out. Don't you worry."

She had held him tightly for several minutes before he left and waved to him from the doorway as long as she could see him. Then she went back into the bedroom, picked up the picture of Ginny and Ed and looked at it for a long time. After a minute she turned around. There, on the wall, next to her bed was the picture of her grandmother Charlotte. She walked over to it and studied the face for a long time. Then she whispered, "He's your boy. You make him behave!" And she lay down on the bed and fell asleep.

In Mexico, Buck was in his element. He spoke good Spanish from all the summers he had spent there. The hot sun, the bright colors the Mexican workers wore, the warm, starry nights spent talking with men that he respected—it was all as he had wanted it. Everything was perfect—if only Bridget had come with him. The Mexican government made sure their workers did the actual labor of the dig. Buck spent hours with Armand Marceaux mapping, overseeing the digging, making excavation decisions. The artifacts uncovered, they sent to a lab in Mexico City for cleaning and cataloguing. They were making progress. Often a large dig would require fifteen years to uncover and catalogue, depending on the size of the city uncovered. This particular site was hundreds of acres.

It was mid-summer before he even thought of girls, except for Bridget. The dig was almost a days drive south of Mexico City and in late July, Buck, Armand and some others drove into the city for a long weekend. They ate in a fine restaurant, saw an American movie, swam in the hotel pool, and Buck could have had his pick of the senoritas. They were not unattractive, and he hadn't seen a woman for two months. But they weren't Bridget. He excused himself, went into the hotel and placed a long distance call.

"Hello." The voice was faint on the other end.

"Is this Bridget? I want Bridget!"

"Yes, it is! Buck? Is that you?"

"Yes, but I can't hear you very well."

"Where are you calling from?"

"Mexico City! And the connection isn't very good!" He was talking very loudly in order for her to hear him.

"Do you like the dig?"

"What?"

"I said do you like the dig? Is it what you wanted?"

"Yes, I like the dig. No, it isn't what I wanted. I wanted you."

"Oh. Well, you know the answer to that."

"You want to get married in a temple?"

She was uncertain what he might be getting at. "Yes, you know I do."

"There's a temple down here. It's a Mayan temple. Very beautiful. Very old. What could be more traditional than that? Mormons believe these were Book of Mormon people. Their temples must be OK."

She wasn't amused. "Oh Buck, I miss you so."

"Then come over. I'll send you the money."

"Are you reading the Book of Mormon?"

"No, why should I?"

"You're working in Book of Mormon country. It seems like you'd be curious."

"I read it when I was little."

"No, you didn't. You cheated, and just pretended."

"How do you know? I read it. I didn't like the plot."

"You're older now, read it again."

"Bridget, I miss you."

"I miss you too."

"No, you don't or you'd marry me and to hell with religion!"

"That's not me. I am who I am."

"Me too."

After a moment she said, "I love you anyway."

"What?" he shouted into the phone.

"I said, I love you anyway."

"I can't hear you," he shouted again, smiling all the while.

"I love you. Can you hear that? I . . . love . . . you."

"Good. I was beginning to wonder. I have that on tape now, so there's hard evidence against you if I ever have to take you before a judge. I have to go now."

"Be careful. Be good, and read your scriptures."

"You sound like my grandma."

"We're in cahoots."

"I thought so. Goodbye, sweetheart."

He heard a garbled sound and the phone was dead.

After a few months of peering into the past lives of people who had lived and loved and melted back into the earth, one begins to ask questions. Buck began to ask himself some questions that summer. They found skeletons of men and women and children, locked in an embrace, apparently having decided to die together. They found evidences of their lives—cups, bowls, plates, urns, knives.

And this is all that lasts of human beings? Buck wondered. This is all that lasts of love and families and a woman's beautiful eyes on a moonlit night? These people have lived in this spot before me. Look at these tiny bones. They had children and probably spanked their behinds and kissed their tears, just like we do now. And for what? They have returned, dust to dust, as the preacher says. Perhaps my life and my loves will mean just as little. The thought made him melancholy. He pondered it for weeks. Finally he mentioned his thoughts to his French mentor, Armand Marceaux.

"It is a realization that we all have to come to sometime," Marceaux philosophized. "Our lives count for very little. Our loves count for very little, at least after we are gone. No one will know if we are scoundrels or saints. They will not know if we loved a woman or if we were loners, like you and me, and loved only our work."

Buck was pensive. "Somehow that doesn't feel right."

"There are only a few things that will survive that people will remember or perceive. One are the *things* we made—our tools, our structures, our roads, our religion." Armand Marceaux was puffing nonchalantly on his pipe, star gazing.

Buck looked at him strangely. "Why do you say 'our religion?' "

"Oh, because our little good deeds die with us, but the religion as a whole, pervades all our structures, the organization of our society, the art, the ceremony of death, the very way the cities are built. As you can see, the temples are the most imposing structures here. I suppose ours will be too, our temples to money—the banks—will probably survive the centuries. Our cathedrals—they are built to last. Movie theaters, football fields, radio wires, automobiles, they will all be gone. The earth will take her revenge on our vanity and cover all. Just the true temples will remain."

Buck was listening intently. His breath almost stopped. Marceaux had no idea what his philosophy meant to the younger man.

He went on. "Religion of one sort or another pervades every culture. Sometimes it accomplishes great things, sometimes it destroys, as it did the poor Inca civilization. I'll never forgive those pompous Christian fools for plundering that civilization. But, for good or evil, religion leaves its mark. And every man has one. Whether he knows it or not. A religion of self, a religion of love, of pleasure, of fear. Sometimes, not too often as I observe, a man may have a truly great religion that transcends our time and space. Rare, rare! Ghandi had it. Probably Mohammed and Buddha. Christ had it. I knew a Jesuit who had it, and a black nurse in Algiers. They all seemed to understand life and love in a way that cast out fear and ignorance. They actually transcended their circumstances and took other people with them, at least as far as they would go. Each person has his own self-imposed limitations. Some allow themselves to see and know and do more than others."

"Cave in! Cave in! Cave in!" The cry spread like dynamite through the vast dig site. "Cave in on site sixteen."

Armand Marceaux dropped his maps and ran. Site sixteen was half-way across the city they had been carefully uncovering. It was the pyramid site. They had been clearing rubble from the passageway into the inner chamber. They were hoping to find the sarchophagi of the king and his queen in the interior. Sorensen was supervising that site.

The Mexican sun in September was murderous. All the men worked in shorts and no shirts. Their skin darkened to varying shades of deep brown or honey. Now they stood in groups, questioning, gesticulating and trying to account for their men. Was everyone out? Had any gone directly into the crypt? It was too new. Too freshly uncovered, not secured yet. No one should have gone into the crypt . . . not until the site was judged safe. Was anyone missing? Marceaux saw immediately who was missing. He was not surprised. Sorensen had been excited about this find for weeks. It is rare to find a pyramid like this one where much of it was still intact. He had been too anxious to get his hands into it, too anxious to clear the doorway. And now, too anxious to know what was inside. He was missing—trapped, no doubt, in the crypt! The Frenchman shouted orders to the bystanders and the Mexican workers. They only had a short time to uncover that crypt again, before his air ran out. Marceaux's religion didn't often show, but it did allow him to pray silently. Buck had become like a son to him.

Yes, he had been stupid! Buck knew it. He knew it before he went into the wide, dark hole of the burial crypt. First order of archaeology—you never go into a hole, a door, that leads inside a pyramid until it has been deemed secure. He had known that for eight years. He had forgotten—on purpose—just this once. At the doorway they had uncovered the bones of a tall, well-built man, clutching a spear, with a huge knife at his side. Obviously a guard for the king's tomb.

Often there were remarkable artifacts inside those burial crypts—jade, jewelry, statues. Buck had seen some in an exhibition years ago. Now it was his turn to make the find. The coolness of the dark shadows was a relief from the savage sun above. He had inched his way further and further along a narrow corridor. When would it open into the main room? In his pocket was a small, slender flashlight. He took it out to penetrate the darkness. Then he cleared the corridor and carefully stepped into a large room where the sarchophagi lay side by side. He drew in his breath. This was the moment of a lifetime. He savored the moment, looking around in the dim light cast by his flashlight, and had the feeling that he was invading a personal relationship between two ancient people. He turned to go back to get Armand, and then the walls of the room moved, he heard a rumbling and instinctively swore.

"That's it," he said aloud as he was knocked down by the wall caving in.

When he regained consciousness he was surprised. He had expected, in that second of understanding, to die under the crushing rocks. He was lucky to have made it as far as the burial room. The corridor was blocked with large rocks and debris, but the burial chamber had not been damaged, at least as far as he could tell. His legs were buried under dirt and rocks. He worked for an hour digging himself out. He didn't seem to be broken, although he was badly bruised and bleeding on his upper thigh. He could hear nothing up above, but knew they would be gathered, beginning the rescue effort. How long would it take? It had taken weeks to clear this crypt before. He hadn't any idea how bad the cave-in was or if his supply of heavy, dry air would last.

He didn't want to lie down. It reminded him too much of dying. So he sat up, leaning against one of the walls of the burial chamber. When he turned on his flashlight he could dimly see the two coffins in the center of the room. He felt as though he were sharing their honeymoon suite instead of their burial chamber. There was a solemn, almost holy silence down here in the presence of two people who had wanted to be together in death. He switched off his light. He didn't know how long that would last either, and if he got really spooked he wanted to have some light available.

In abject blackness he sat. Even with his eyes wide open and straining, there was no seeing even his own hand as he held it up touching his nose. This is outer darkness, he thought, then characteristically chuckled in the silence, or "inner darkness", he amended. Then it wasn't funny. In the sacrament meetings and Sunday School classes Grandma dragged him to, he had heard the Mormon concept of life without the light of Christ—outer darkness, a total absence of light, the ultimate condemnation of the Sons of Perdition. He had never been able to comprehend it before. He had never tried. Now he began to ruminate on it. Could anything grow in this darkness? No, of course not! Could anything be accomplished? Only insanity. Could anything live in such blackness for very long? Even with a supply of air, the very blackness would crush you eventually. Outer darkness—was it true that Christ was the light of the world, and without him life would be like this? Forever? Buck shuddered. If he felt the air growing too thick and began to have a hard time breathing, he would crawl over to the caskets. He would not die here alone. He would die beside another human being.

Then, instantly, he realized how fantastic that need for companionship was. Another human being, even though dead, was somehow comforting, with death staring him in the face. Why should that be so? Why should we seek another human being? In death there was no longer any caring. His mind filled with the vision of Bridget, her remarkable, chiseled face, determined chin, and the soft lips he had often, casually kissed. It was a sin to be that casual about life and love! Then a thought crushed him as surely as if a boulder had fallen from the ceiling. It was not Bridget who had been casual. It was he! She had seen the importance of life and death and being together after death, just as surely as the ancient couple whose devotion he had interrupted. He could hardly breathe for several minutes. The understanding was too overwhelming. Her love was like theirs, beyond life, beyond death, joined for eternities to come. His love was selfish and short-sighted, wanting her right now and not caring, indeed not thinking, about the future. He wrapped his arms around himself, hugging his chest tightly.

"I understand," he whispered to her in the darkness.

The silence was as complete as the blackness. The whisper of his own voice was a shattering sound. As he sat there, hour after hour, his senses failed him. With no sight and no sound, the world became a dream. The only reality was his mind, his memory. So he used it. People he loved he saw and yearned for, as he never had before. Laughter and love—he clung to the memories, reluctantly letting go of one and then quickly moving on to another. Even his grandmother's little brick house, too small and old to be comfortable, seemed all at once precious and charming.

Then he remembered Bridget dancing in the native show in Hawaii, and immediately after saw his sister, also in a grass skirt, on that fateful night in Hawaii. He had been appalled. Now he saw the scene again in his mind and realized that he had never accepted her as an adult. In the blackness of the tomb of death, he gave Shielah her maturity and surprisingly was not sad to allow the sister-child to recede and take her place in the past. A lump choked his throat. Why do we cling so to the past? Are we so fearful of the passing years—of our own mortality? He went to sleep for a while and when he woke again, he had an unfamiliar panicky feeling that threatened him. In the abject blackness it was hard to tell if he were still a part of this world. He rubbed his legs, his arms. He ruffled his own hair and touched his tongue with a dirty finger in order to experience taste. He had to reaffirm life to himself. Then he disciplined his mind to go where he wanted it to go.

Start with my earliest memory. I may be here a little while. Earliest memory—I was three. Dad brought me home my first puppy, and it piddled on me. Again he chuckled, the sound hollow and foreign in the silence. His face, I remember Dad's face—light-skinned, and blue, icy blue eyes. He should have been a Viking. I must be as tall as Dad now. He seemed big, but I was so little then. Then quickly Buck's mind jumped to the day of the fire. No, I won't think about that. This is not the time to remember that. He forced himself to remember his mother smiling and trying to tell him a story. He kept making silly remarks, until she finally closed the book and refused to read anymore. In the darkness, tears wet his eyelids. He had loved Ginny. A boy wasn't supposed to love his mother so much. She was soft, like Bridget, and laughing most of the time. He could count on her to love him and understand even when he was naughty. He had overheard more than one conversation where Ginny defended him when his Ed despaired of his son.

Buck warmed all over at the vivid memory of his mother's laughter. Then another memory claimed him. He was fifteen. He had found an old cigarette lighter and rolled his own cigarettes for fun like some of the old timers in Bird's Eye did. In a corner of the barn he sat half-chewing on the end of the homemade contraband, puffing for all he was worth, trying to get the thing going. It was burning fitfully and the acid taste almost made him throw up, while the small breaths of smoke burned his lungs, choking him miserably.

"Children, come to lunch! Buck? Shielah? Come to lunch now." His mother was calling.

228

Crushing out the cigarette hastily, Buck looked around for a hiding place and quickly tossed the lighter in a corner of the barn, under the hay. He ran to get a drink and a piece of her fresh mint to chew on, so Ginny wouldn't smell the cigarette on him. His stomach was churning; it had almost made him sick.

The tape was relentless now. Buck couldn't stop it. In the blackness he saw the picture roll on, and he saw himself, taking his sister for a picnic. He had loved her too, fiercely, that was why he teased her so unmercifully. He could see her ten-year-old face, delicate and soft-cheeked, big-eyed and winsome as she wrinkled her nose at his teasing. Why hadn't he known enough to stop, and really look at her then, to hold her close and tell her how much he loved her, how precious she was to him? Because it would have made him cry, that's why. Crying was death to him at fifteen. Now the tears were blind beggars with no one, no one at all to notice. He had carried her, that day, when her feet got sore, and she couldn't walk as fast as he. He saw them both, hurrying piggy-back across the scrub-brush hills, with black smoke billowing from the direction of their farm. Then they came over the last crest and he dropped her. His worst fears were horribly confirmed. It was a fire! It was the barn! Oh dear Lord, not the house too!

Sobs began to wrack his body in the darkness and he was carried away into an ocean of grief and recrimination. "I didn't know. I didn't know. The lighter was out. The cigarette was out. I thought it was out. Mother, Dad, oh help me! I thought it was all out. I was careful. I tried to be so careful. Forgive me. If you can hear me at all, forgive me. I loved you. I really loved you both."

Then Shielah's face appeared before him, angry, hurt, suffering and accusing him. He tried to touch her, to bring back the love, to bring back the ten- year-old adoring eyes. But she moved just beyond his reach and still stared at him accusingly. He wept until he had no more tears, the blackness around him perfectly matching the desolation within. Then Buck pushed himself away from the wall, dragged the little flashlight from his pocket and switched it on for a few moments. He held up his hand so he could see his body, but it hardly seemed to belong to him. In the middle of the room, the caskets lay in perfect peace. He saw his own parents inside them. He saw himself and Bridget. Love does endure. Lovers have always known it regardless of what philosophers or theologians say. Buck reached out for that last comforting emotion, crawled over to the two ancient lovers, lay down at the foot of their caskets and gave himself up to oblivion.

Sometime the next morning a cool breath of fresh air awakened Buck and he heard Armand Marceaux calling his name. He crawled over to the spot of light down the corridor. They had cleared the manageable boulders, and dug out the loose dirt, making a hole big enough for him to crawl through. Armand put his arms around him and held him tightly, saying over and over, "Thank God you're alive."

"Yes, Buck answered, breathing deeply and squinting upward into the bright, welcome light. "Yes, thank God. I learned that much last night."

Shielah had made her bid to get Christmas off so she could spend it with Grandma and the family. Buck was in Mexico. She wouldn't have another scene with him, thank goodness. Thanksgiving was already planned. She and Brandy were both lined up for a flight to Stockholm, Sweden. If she couldn't have Thanksgiving with her family, she might as well go somewhere fun. She bid that line of flight in October and now had enough seniority to get it. The girls were ecstatic. They had rarely flown anywhere together. Now, after a year, they had more seniority, and intended to schedule more together.

The fall had been difficult. She had felt torn between Stephen and his weekly telephone calls, and the constant presence of Paulo. She felt like a traitor to both of them. And yet, she loved them both. She told herself it would all be simple if she could once put Paulo out of her mind and her life. She told herself she would try. It would have been easier if she were not affected by his presence, if there weren't that instant kinship between them. She had purposely spent one entire month without seeing him at all. Then November came and she went to his office unexpectedly. The secretary had let her slip in his door quietly. He glanced up and saw her, and they looked at each other for a full minute before he spoke.

"I needed a miracle in my day."

I'm not good at miracles but I can try."

"Just smile. That's all the miracle a man could want."

She smiled at him, shaking her head. "I missed you too much."

"Good. I was beginning to think you didn't miss me at all."

"I found myself hoping you'd turn up on one of my flights. You used to."

"Yes, but now you know where to find me."

"And I did."

"Yes, you did. And I'm glad." He walked around the desk. "Does that mean that you have time for dinner tonight?"

"Yes. I have three days off before the next block."

"Three days, that's tempting. However, I have a big project I'm working on now and I can't take three days off, if you are propositioning me. I can only see you in the evenings."

"I'll take it," she said, "Sold American."

He leaned against the desk, still several feet away from her. She moved closer and touched his tie. "I like your tie."

"Liar."

"You're right. Actually, I never even noticed it. I just needed an excuse to touch you."

Still he didn't move. His arms were folded across his chest, his feet crossed at the ankles. "Since when did you need an excuse?"

"Oh, I don't know."

"Let me help you, since a month ago when you last spent an hour with me."

She looked down, away from his steady gaze. Why did his eyes have to do that to her. They saw into her mind, into her heart, and they touched her soul until she could hardly stand it. "I'm sorry."

230

"I don't want you to be sorry. I just can't understand why."

"My schedule has been so. . . . "

"Huh uh! Don't use that. It's insulting." She didn't speak. Paulo sighed, then unfolded his arms and ran his finger down her arm. Finally, she looked up at him. He was studying her intently. Her eyes dropped to his mouth and that was what he had wanted to know. He didn't hold her. He didn't take her in his arms as he wanted to do. Just seeing her again made him realize how tender the wound had become inside. He merely leaned forward and kissed her lower lip just as she was starting to bite it.

She caught her breath. Resolve meant nothing when she was in his presence. Just the nearness of him made her forget that she intended to wind this romance down, to douse the fire until only embers remained. She had thought after a month she would be able to trade love for friendship. She had silently vowed to Stephen that she would do that. But she gave it all away when she looked at his lips. She was the one shaken when their lips parted. She was the one who searched his face for a clue. Why? Why? How can I love him? I love Stephen. How can there be so much between us? Why won't the strings break that bind us together?

They spent that evening together. They were both a little on edge. There were many long silences. There were questions he didn't dare ask her now. Such a long way since last Christmas Eve in Montreal. Would he ever recover the distance? He had to find a way.

The next night he cooked dinner for her in his apartment. It was cold for the first part of November, and even though it hadn't snowed yet, the first storm that blew in would undoubtedly blanket them. He had a fire already going when she came. The smell of lasagna greeted her reddened nose.

"Ummm. Smells just like Mama's."

"I take that compliment with some pride. Mama can make the best lasagna in New York. But the proof is in the tasting. Are you hungry?"

"Starving. I've been saving my appetite for tonight."

"Good, me too."

They ate cross-legged on the floor. Paulo had the table all set with silver and crystal, but they put down a blanket and moved it all, so they could sit before the fire. They talked late into the night about everything except their love. They reminisced at length about that Thanksgiving a year ago when it had snowed and they had walked through a quiet city. She made him promise he would go walking with her again in the first snow of the year.

The night slipped away, and Shielah lay cradled in Paulo's arms. With his body next to hers and his face just inches away, there were no thoughts of anything but him. To be so completely loved, so secure, so comfortable in another person's love for you . . . it was rest for her soul. This was why she came to him, she admitted to herself. She had felt a little estranged from the city, from the world, without him. With him, she was complete again, with no loose ends to disconcert her. Her arms went around his neck and they were locked in a long embrace. His lips moved from her mouth to her neck, just behind her ear, and then down to the base of her neck. He brushed her hair away and nuzzled her until she tingled. His hands were warm and they began, slowly to move, to press her closer to him. He kissed her until she hardly knew where she was. The room, even the fireplace, receded into shadows, leaving only the two of them and the sweetness of his kiss.

He would make her his own tonight. He had already decided that. It was the only way he could be sure of keeping her. She would marry him, if she had once slept with him. Of that he was sure. And so he was careful, he was tender, he was as gentle and patient as he could possibly be, bringing her slowly to want him as he wanted her. He had all night, and he would not rush it. He knew how to touch her and where to touch her until she trembled, as he wanted her to. He had never tried to seduce her. He had been afraid to break their bond of trust. And if he succeeded it might shatter her carefully cultivated self image. He had been a fool. He could have married her last Christmas if he had taken her love then. This last month had proven the danger to him, and now he was determined not to lose her.

Shielah was drifting into a world that only consisted of his mouth and hands and the joy of his body near hers. She had no defenses against him. She had never needed any. She trusted him implicitly, just as she trusted his love. Her blouse was unbuttoned and slipping down her arm before she realized what was happening. She blinked, as though awakening after a deep sleep. Beautiful, dark, deep eyes were only inches from hers. The eyes of a poet, she thought. His hand on her bare shoulder took her breath away. She blinked again and forced herself to whisper. "Wait."

He didn't answer. "Wait," she pleaded. "I . . . I . . . I don't want you to do that."

"Yes, you do," he murmured against her lips.

"Then, don't make me want it. Wait, Paulo. I'm getting confused . . . no . . . don't touch me any more . . . don't kiss me again."

He kissed her again.

"Please," she whispered.

"Please? Please what? Please love me? Yes, please do. You know I love you. For so long, for too long. I need you, I want you." His lips were on her neck, her shoulder. She tried, but she couldn't protest. "Please need me, my love, my sweet love."

She took his face between her hands and kissed his lips. Then she pulled away, just slightly, a question in her eyes. "Do you love me then, so very much? So much you would hurt me?"

"No," he whispered, stroking her shimmering hair. "No, I'd never hurt you."

She smiled trustingly, slipped her blouse back up on her shoulder, and buttoned it. "Good. I believe you. I didn't think you would. That's why I can love you too, so unbelieveably. I knew you from the first moment I saw you there in Hawaii. I looked into your face and saw a man I had known and loved somewhere before. If only I understood where and why and what we are supposed to be to each other."

He was leaning on one elbow, listening to her. The firelight reflected from his face. "I could tell you, but you won't believe me. I think we are supposed to be husband and wife. I think we are supposed to be lovers. You would never regret being married to me, Shielah. I will be a most loving husband."

Now she lay back again, secure and trusting, her head on his shoulder. "I know, Paulo. I know. I just have to figure everything out in my own mind. I believe in a grand scheme, and I want to know where we all fit, you . . . and me . . . and. . . . "

"Shh. You fit right here, against my shoulder."

"Will you be careful? If you kiss me like that again, I could forget every thing in my life but you. But there is someone else in my life. Someone I couldn't bear to betray."

He nodded, thinking of Stephen, but she read his thoughts and shook her head, "No, not Stephen, although he is also someone I love and feel committed to. But he is not the one I mean. As long as I can remember I have had a very close, loving relationship with Jesus. He is my Savior, my friend, my protector, my consolation, my mentor. I have a certain mental image of myself as He sees me and wants me to be. I have to be true to that. Being untrue to that would be like betraying my best self. I know you probably think I'm ridiculously old-fashioned. Most people don't understand that committment. They think it's dark ages stuff, but it's very current, very immediate to me."

He had known that. Her relationship with God was more personal than any he had ever observed before. To him God and Jesus were revered, respected, untouchable beings, looking down benevolently from a far away heaven. To Shielah, they were companions she knew on a daily basis. He admired that, envied it really, and he knew that if he seduced her, he would damage that relationship as well as her self-image. And he didn't want her that way. Not really. After half-an-hour, he took her home. When he lay in bed alone that night, he cursed himself for not risking it and following through. He wanted her, he loved her, he would make her the best husband she could want. He was a fool! How long would it be?

The night before Thanksgiving Shielah arrived home to find a short, terse note from Buck.

My dearest Shielah,

I have to see you tonight. Will be back at nine o'clock.
                                        Buck
P.S. I love you.

She read it and looked up from it to Brandy who was watching her, eyebrows raised. "He was here when I got home at five-thirty. You didn't tell me you had such a handsome brother."

"I don't want to see him."

"Why not?"

"He does nothing but upset me. We can't talk for two minutes without the boxing gloves. He's completely condescending and thinks I'm a little flower just begging to be trampled on. He'll never admit that I've grown up. To him I'm always five years old and he is my keeper."

"Hmmm. I didn't get that impression. He said he had something important to talk to you about, something about Mexico. Isn't he an archaeologist?"

"Yes, and I thought he was still down there digging. Why does he have to mess things up? I get along without him very nicely. Didn't he say why he has come all the way to New York from Mexico City?"

"Just said he had to talk to you."

"Well I don't have to talk to him, and I'm not going to. I'm going to shower and change and go to Paulo's for a couple of hours. Tomorrow is Thanksgiving and I want to say goodbye. I won't see him for a week."

Brandy cocked her head and looked at Shielah strangely. "Your own brother?"

Shielah began undressing and moved quickly. She wanted to be gone when he came. "My own brother causes me nothing but a headache and a messed up mind."

She disappeared into the bathroom and reappeared again in twenty minutes, fresh and determined to get out of there. She was reaching for her coat when the buzzer rang from downstairs. Brandy looked up questioningly. Shielah stood unmoving. She did not press the answering buzzer to let him in. In a moment the buzzer rang again. Still she didn't move. After a few silent moments, she stepped behind the couch and looked down to the street below. There was no one on the stoop by their door. She began to think he had gone already when she heard him knock. Someone else must have pushed the buzzer for him. Again Brandy looked at her friend. Shielah looked down at her as she sat curled up on the couch, a romance novel in hand. Shielah put her finger to her lips in a silent gesture. Brandy frowned and shook her head.

He knocked again, and she heard him softly call her name, "Shielah?" Never had she felt so horrible, so dirty, so cold. She stared at the door, not knowing whether or not to open it, hating the confrontation she was sure would come, rejecting the feelings of childishness and frustration that always came with talking to him. Let him go away, she prayed. Let him go away and leave me alone. I don't want him in my life. I don't want him in my mind.

Again he knocked and again, but the fourth time it was softer. He waited a few minutes and knocked one last time. Then a small white note slid under the door. Footsteps faded down the hallway and stairs. Standing beside her window, she could see him walk into the dark street. He paused, turned, looked around, then pulled his hat down against the cold November wind, ducked his head, and walked away into the night.

Tears sprang into her eyes and her chest hurt until she wanted to hit it. Oh Buck, where have we come from? I'm sorry, she cried inside. Come back and I'll let you in. *Ally ally oxen free, I see you, Shielah. I saw you all the time. I'll give you anything in my pocket for a kiss!* She wiped away the memories angrily. No! He shouldn't have come. I don't know why he's here, but I refuse to be tormented.

Brandy was watching her, disappointment showing plainly in her face. After a few minutes she said, "I don't believe you did that. Not you."

Shielah was defensive. "I'm sorry that disappoints you. You never saw what he has done to me on several occasions."

"What? He beat you? He beat up your guy? He called you names and kicked your fanny around the room? He's your brother, gal! He does all that because he loves you. Maybe he's a little jealous. Maybe he acts like your Lord and Master. Heck, he's just a boy, trying to be a man, and not knowing how. You never had a brother that did that to you I bet. He doesn't look like the kind. This man's got too much twinkle and kindness in his eyes to kick your butt. I ought to. Don't you know anything about family?"

She was standing now, her eyes flashing, and she really warmed to her subject. "Let me tell you about family. They can claw your eyes out and you'd kill anyone else for them. They can scream at you all night and call you any name they can think up that the garbage won't have, and when they fall and scratch their knee you pick them up and kiss it. What do you think blood is, gal? It's you! It's part of them in you. You hate 'em, you love 'em, but you never, never forsake them. Ain't no wall big enough, ain't no door strong enough, ain't no river wide enough to separate you from that family, that blood kin."

Shielah had the grace to be embarrassed for herself. After Brandy finished she was quiet for a moment, then said softly, "I think I'll go after him. Maybe he's not far. Maybe he even thought of coming back. I'll go look."

She hurried down the stairs and onto the street, hoping—and hating—to meet him. Brandy took the little white note and put it on the end table, beside the lamp. When Shielah came home several hours later, the lights were all off. She had not found Buck and had finally gone on to Paulo's to say goodbye to him until next weekend. She was bone-tired when she slipped in the door at one a.m. and she had to fly the next morning. Blurry-eyed and still yawning, she left the apartment at six a.m. for Kennedy. She had forgotten the note. It lay unopened beside the lamp in the apartment. They flew to Stockholm, Sweden, spent their thirty-two hour layover sightseeing and marveling over Tivoli Gardens. It was Monday morning before she sat down on her couch again and noticed the white note folded three ways. When she opened it, she screamed.

"Grandma died today," was all it said.

Chapter 13

*B*uck had gone to New York to make amends with his sister. He had been intending to keep his promise to his grandmother. He was going home for Thanksgiving. He had good news to tell her, news that would make her old heart happy. Since the cave-in, he had studied seriously. He read the *Book of Mormon*, he read the *Old Testament*, and he read a comprehensive book called *Man and His Religion*. Through all of it, he was impressed with one thing, that Christianity alone had two testimonies of two different nations that Jesus Christ actually lived and was called the Son of God. Not Buddha, not Confucius, not Mohammed— none of them had more than one group of people proclaiming them divine. Christ alone had more than the testimony of one people acclaiming him. The Jews wrote their testimony and the people in America, half a world away, spoke up and confirmed, "Yes, he is risen, for we have also seen him. He came to us too—the resurrected Christ!"

He had been anxious to get home as November came on. He was anxious to discuss it with Stephen. Grace would be so relieved. Then he had received a letter from her. In shaky script she had written, reminding him of his promise to her, not to come home, but to go and make peace with Shielah. So he left Mexico City Tuesday morning and flew straight to New York. He found her address easily, but no one was home. The girls were not due home until tomorrow, the landlady said. On Wednesday, he met her black roommate. They liked each other immediately. She told him to come back at nine. He went back to his hotel room by the Lincoln Center and from there he had called home. When Grace didn't answer, he called Will's place. He wanted Grace to know he would keep his promise and be home for Thanksgiving. Maddie had answered and given him the news. Will and Drew were at the mortuary. His grandmother had died that morning of a heart attack.

He hung up numbly. His heart hurt too much, too much. It wasn't fair. He had wanted to tell her. She would have been so happy to know, and now she was gone before he could share with her his new-found faith. But there was Shielah. At eight o'clock he left the hotel and went straight to her place. Even if she wasn't there yet, he would wait. But she was there, her light was on. He pressed the buzzer twice before she pressed it in return. He climbed the stairs heavily, hating to tell her the bad news, but anxious to share his own good news. He knocked, then waited. She didn't answer. He knocked again and still she didn't open the door. He called her name, puzzled. He could see the lamp light beneath the door. He was sure her roommate would have told her, or at least left a note for her. Still he knocked and still the apartment was quiet. At last he gave up in puzzled defeat, and walked back down into the windy November night. He felt very much alone. Grace had taken the place of mother and father to him. She was both parent and grandparent, and he loved her dearly. Now they were all gone and he was completely alone, with no one to share his grief. He went back to the hotel quickly, just to pick up his bags and pay his bill, then he went straight to the airport and took a standby seat to Salt Lake City. Shielah didn't make it for the funeral.

An old woman sat on the bench in Central Park. She had on ragged, men's shoes and black stockings that crawled up under her skirts only as high as her knees. She wore two skirts, one longer and brown in which she had split the seam in order to walk. The other skirt was black wool, and she had it pinned at the waistband. A short, gray jacket she hugged around her, keeping out the cold by sheer will. Around her were piled many bags, misshapen with her secret treasures pirated from the garbage of the city. She sat on the bench chewing on an unnameable substance. Out of the corner of her nearly closed eye, she watched the pretty, rich, blonde girl who sat at the other end of the bench. What can she have to cry about? the old woman wondered angrily. She's not cold or hungry and she probably has a fancy bed to lay her head on. Life was not fair.

And that was what Shielah thought too. Life was not fair. She had thought that for as long as she could remember. Only lately, in the last year had she started to even the score a little. After years of feeling homely and unloved, she had run eagerly after the reassuring love of Paulo and rejoiced in the happy love of Stephen. She had intended to go home for Christmas and to spend that time making her grandmother happy. Being away made Shielah realize how precious that old, wrinkled, soft face was to her. She remembered the velvet cheek she had kissed when she had left last spring. She had known Grace was growing older fast, but there were just three more weeks before they would have been together. Now she would never see her again, not in this life. It wasn't fair!

Shielah walked until she was lost, even though Central Park was one of her favorite places and she knew it well. Even crowded with people, it was one of the most private places in the world. No one there cared or even saw if you cried, if you died, if you had a baby on the grass. She could go home, but what good would it do now. The funeral was over, the casket in the ground, and she would never see Grandma's face again, not even to say goodbye. And, her conscience reminded her, it was her own fault. Hot tears scalded her reddened cheeks—tears of pity and of regret. If she had only let Buck in that night, she would have known and been there for the funeral at least. Now, she had lost Grandma and it was almost as bad as losing her mother and father. Her childhood was gone with Grace, and she could never be a little girl with anyone again. No one else saw her with eyes that remembered a pigtailed six-year-old. No one else had washed her skinned knees and bandaged them. No one else had knelt beside her in the night rehearsing the words to simple prayers. Even though she had grown much more capable and strong than the older woman in the last few years, the memories they shared and the soft pillow of love had comforted Shielah's heart. No comfort she knew could replace it. Her grief was soul-deep and relentless.

She sat on the park bench until the evening began to fall. At last she turned to the old, ragged woman near her. "Let me help you," she said softly to the woman, sorrow making her tender. But the woman was startled and scuttled away from the bench, looking over her shoulder as though the devil himself had spoken to her. Shielah cried for a few minutes over that and the futility of reaching out to others.

When the pain and grief became overwhelming, she roused herself, with a great effort. When she needed comfort there was only one place she could go. She took the subway straight to Paulo's apartment. It was after six when she arrived. She heard music inside as she knocked. After a moment the door opened. Elaina Maretti greeted her, black eyes dancing.

Shielah backed away. "Oh, I'm sorry . . . I mean, I didn't know . . . is Paulo? No, it's OK. I'll call later."

Elaina was never flustered. "Paulo is certainly here. He's cooking my dinner and . . . uh . . . my breakfast too, I suppose," she added. "That was the arrangement this time, anyway. Wait a minute, I'll tell him. . . . "

"No! Never mind," Shielah started down the hall. "I'm sorry to bother you." She had to get away. Her breath was coming too fast. She felt as though a crushing weight was pressing the life from her. She didn't want him to see her, to have to explain, to hear him tell her Elaina was just a friend. She couldn't support that now. She would scream and embarrass them all. Frantically she pushed the elevator button. But it was too late. Paulo stepped out into the long, cool hallway and saw her at the end of it. She turned her back, trying to hide inside herself. Before the elevator could come, his hand was on her shoulder.

"Shielah, come back. It's all right. Elaina just dropped in."

"Let me go. I can't talk about it now!"

"You can't leave like this. You're upset. What's wrong? I'm sorry she opened the door. I know what you must have thought, but it's wrong. Turn around."

"No, I have to go." She could barely get the words out. Ten years had rolled back and she was alone on the hillside, watching her mother die in a fire.

He forcibly turned her around and tried to take her in his arms. She pushed him away and ran into the open elevator. He followed her.

"Shielah! What on earth is wrong? I can't believe Elaina could do this to you. What did she say?"

She put her hands over her ears to shut out his voice. She couldn't deal with this now. She would lose her mind if he didn't stop!

"Stop it!" she screamed at him. "Stop it! I can't listen to you. I don't want to hear about her. Please go away and leave me alone. I'm sorry I came. I shouldn't have come. I just thought you could . . . never mind. Oh, never mind. I have to go home." She was sobbing and shaking now. "I have to go home," was all she would say when he tried to speak to her. She wouldn't let him touch her. When he tried to speak, she shook her head and said, "I have to go home."

The elevator opened onto the main floor. She dashed for the door. He ran after her and grabbed at her arm, pulling her up against him. She stared wild-eyed into his face. Paulo was scared speechless. He had never seen her like this. He had no way of understanding. Helplessly, he said her name, "Shielah?"

"Don't say that! It's *my* name! It's not yours to use! Don't ever say that. I came to you. . . . " Finally she blurted it out, using it to slap him. "My grandmother died. I thought you'd care. I thought you'd help me. But. . . . "

She wrenched herself away from him. His reflexes were off, he was so thoroughly surprised. "I'm sorry. Please let me. . . . "

"Let you what? Let you what? She'll let you. Go back to her, stay with her! Sleep with her if that's what you want!"

Now she succeeded. She smacked him right where it hurt most. He had loved her and been patient for over a year. He hadn't taken advantage of her, even when they both wanted it. And he had stayed away from Elaina Maretti even before meeting Shielah, knowing she was not the one for him. He could have slept with her many times, but he refused her open invitations.

"That isn't true."

"Isn't it?" Shielah was merciless now, hurting too wildly to care who she cut with her weapons. Life had ripped her open and left her bleeding and exposed, and she had no sense of any pain other than her own. "Dinner and breakfast she said! I'm not willing enough. A man has to have his needs met. Go meet them! She's your type, a fine Italian girl that the family will approve of. She'll cook you linguini and spaghetti and give you fat, bouncing sons. I can't stand it anymore! I'm going to lose my mind with all this. Let me go. Let me go! I'm going home! I'm going away."

Still he held her fast and then she used her last weapon. "*I . . . don't . . . love . . . you . . . anymore.* I hate your touch! Let me go!"

There, she was free. The night air was startling against her hot cheeks. She was startling to passersby—a young woman, dodging through the

239

crowds, her long hair tangled and flying, her face red and wildly twisted with some inner grief. Cars honked at her as she slipped between them on the street.

"Hey, you'd better watch out," a woman called after her.

She was going home. Which direction didn't matter. She saw it in her mind. It was just over the hill, beyond that block. No, there was nothing but a blackened ruin of a farmhouse. She stopped and turned frantically around on the street corner. There it was. If she could just make it to the highway, Buck would find her. He would be coming down the highway in his old car in just a few minutes, whistling like he used to, his elbow resting on the rolled down window. He would find her and take her . . . where? Where? Home was gone, burned down. Where would they go? She rushed on through strange streets. Then it came to her, Grandma's! They would go to Grandma's. Buck would take her there, and Grandma would put her to bed with a kiss and a prayer. She was tired. So very tired. She wanted to go to bed. She wanted to go home. But he never came. Buck never came whistling down the road. She was lost and it was dark—and she was all alone.

Shielah ended up standing stock still, her head bowed, in front of a Catholic church. It was not a cathedral. It was just a small, neighborhood church. It was open around the clock, and she walked numbly in. At the very front of the chapel a young priest, new to his ministry, was lighting candles. She walked up the aisle as though in a trance. He turned at the sound of her footsteps and wondered if he should speak to her. She seemed strange, wild, and dumb. But it was his duty to care for the flock. He walked carefully to her and stood directly in front of her. There was no recognition in her eyes. He asked her name, if she were ill. She made no reply. He asked if she would tell him where she lived. Then she answered at last. "I have no home. I am lost."

With gentle persuasion he got her to kneel down with him. He prayed for her and after the prayer he looked through her purse for some clue as to who she was and who he should contact. An identification card was in her wallet, and also Mrs. Ramsey's name and number. He called that number at midnight and gave the address of the parish. In a half hour, Brandy's dark face appeared in his church.

"Shielah, baby, come on shug. I'll take you home."

The blonde girl with the fair skin and far-away blue eyes looked up at the black girl and tears rained down her face.

She had come to the bottom of her chasm of grief. She had lost them all, Mother and Father, Grandmother, Buck and now Paulo. Her soul was desolate and she could not be comforted. She suffered Brandy's attentions, her care, her concern, but Shielah was sick, truly sick. Brandy called the company doctors and made an appointment for Shielah. A young psychiatrist saw her the next day, and spent all afternoon trying to pry open the cell door to her heart. He could not get in. She would not talk. She simply sat and wept, soundlessly. At length he signed a sick leave order and told Brandy to make sure she didn't experience any further stress or pressure. She was young, he said, and most likely would bounce back in time.

Brandy was reluctant to leave her friend alone, even to do her own flights. But Shielah seemed not to know or care if she came or went. Brandy would return to the apartment at the end of the day and Shielah would be lying in the same spot as when she left. There was no sign she had even eaten. Shielah would talk if Brandy sat beside her and forced her to speak. But the words were an effort and virtually meaningless to her. Brandy made an appointment with a psychiatrist. Shielah would not go. She knew within herself he could not help. Her soul was wounded and she was the assailant.

Over the years the tender, sensitive spirit had built up layer after layer of protection. Denial, rejection, hatred, anger, coldness, they had all done their parts in keeping her vulnerability protected. And she clung to them desperately, afraid of the exposure if she let them go. Afraid that someone would penetrate to her very center and devastate her. That was why she could not afford to forgive Buck. His assaults had only served to thicken the protecting wall. To forgive him was unthinkable. In order to do that, she would have to peel back the layers and offer him her tender places to hurt again. Love only made it more difficult. She loved him so intensely and identified so acutely with him that his every scornful word cut her. If she forgave him now, and he attacked her again, he would kill her. If she had ever been fragile, it was now. And she was holding onto her life gingerly, careful not to say a wrong word or to let in a stray word that would damage the already frayed threads.

For the same reason, she couldn't call Stephen or Aunt Maddie. One word of reproach, one question as to why she didn't come—it would ruin her tenuous hold on herself. The phone rang occasionally, but she never answered it. It didn't occur to her that it might be Paulo, after all she had said to him. If it were Buck or even Stephen, she didn't want to talk. Buck she couldn't face after turning him away. Stephen couldn't help her. He belonged to that old world, the world that had caused her so much loss and pain. And he would never understand why she had turned Buck away. She could never endure his censure. Not now. So there was no one to help her, no one at all.

At times, she told herself it wasn't true at all. Buck had lied in order to hurt her. Grandma was still alive and waiting for her to call. She would almost convince herself of that and reach for the telephone when the truth would insist, and she would lie back against the pillow, knowing that if she called, no one would answer. But he wanted to hurt her, her mind persisted. He could have told Brandy beforehand if he wanted her to know such an important thing. He could have gone to a telephone and called her after he left. He had surely seen the light on and known she was home. He wanted her to miss the note and the funeral and all. . . . but she couldn't hate him! His laughing brown eyes were always in front of her. He jingled his money in his pockets as he walked. And he didn't merely walk, he sauntered or skipped or leap-frogged as he went. He bought her that graduation dress with his own, hard-earned money, and other things—dolls and bicycles, ice cream and valentines, Christmas trees and Flexible Flyer sleds for the snow. He had rubbed her frozen hands between his warm ones when they had been out cross-country skiing all day. But he did not love her anymore! And she could not let him in to hurt her again. Shielah seemed to have an endless supply of tears, and now they slipped incessantly down her cheeks.

Sometimes she heard her grandmother's voice. Grace would reproach her for burning the cookies, then she would measure her for a new school dress. Shielah heard, more than once, her grandmother's voice leading her own tiny voice in evening prayer. How could she be gone? God wouldn't do that to her, take away her only comfort, her only memory of unconditional love. He had taken her mother and father. Surely He could not be cruel enough to take Grace and leave her totally alone. But He had, and, for that, Shielah could not forgive Him. She truly couldn't understand. If He knew her heart and mind as she had always thought He did, then He must know she could not exist without the support of love. It anchored her spirit. It was her safety net. She could go out into the world and make it on her own if she knew that safety net was there for her. Or she could fall squarely on her behind, if that net were only there. But without a back-up safety net, the fear of falling was so strangling she could hardly move or function. God could not do this to her if He loved her. But . . . if He did not love her, and He was God . . . then eternity was lost and she was nothing, nothing at all.

Those were the paths in Shielah's mind where Brandy could not walk, or guess or know. She was tortured on those paths a hundred times and suffered the most exquisite sense of self-hatred. It was almost a denial wish of her own existence, since she was so rejected by those she loved and, finally, by a God who is supposed to love all.

One thought nagged at her mind. She didn't remember all of that evening when she had run from Paulo out onto the streets. Much of it was lost, in her confusion. But she did remember the words between them. Her own words came back after a time, how she had accused him of sleeping with Elaina, and how she had told him she hated his touch. That was the worst. She had been desperate to flee, to be rid of all restraints. Her mind was screaming for home and he was holding her. She had to say something, anything to get him to release her. But oh, it had been cruel. And, she knew, unfair. That Elaina had lied was very probable to Shielah, even in her state of despair. The truth had not been a factor that night. Only the onrushing of insanity. But now that it was over, she knew how she had hurt him. And she wept for herself because he no longer loved her either. He could not love her after the blows she had so deliberately dealt him. He was a proud man, and he had been good to her. He would rightfully resent her for the things she had said.

That Paulo might forgive her didn't occur to her for many days. Why should he? How could he? She could never forgive him if he had viciously

242

hurt her when she was trying to help him. If he had said he hated her touch, she would certainly never venture to touch him again. Memories came of the Christmas Eve in Montreal. She saw him as he had been then, loving, gentle, almost begging her to love him. Why hadn't she married him then? He would have taken care of her and none of this would ever have happened.

Shielah spent two weeks lost in her world of fear and pain. One voice kept whispering to her something that finally pushed her up from the couch and out of her apartment. A voice inside her head told her over and over to go and ask forgiveness of Paulo. She didn't want to. She fought against the insistant voice. She didn't know if she could really do it once she found him. The words might not come. He might look at her with reproach or scorn or anger, and she would turn away without asking. She could not see the scenerio of Paulo freely forgiving her. She could not have done it and, therefore, she did not trust him to. But the voice would not let her rest. It forced her to go, even while she feared his rebuff.

It was ten days until Christmas. Great, feathery flakes had been falling off and on for days. That night they had turned into small driven bullets of snow. They stung her face as she walked. She didn't go to his apartment. She went, instead, to the office building of Vista Color. Why, she could not have said. Something seemed to tell her he was not at home. The sidewalks were still filled with Christmas shoppers at nine-thirty p.m. She reached the huge revolving doors and could not go in. Perhaps Paulo was up there in his office. Perhaps his secretary was too. She couldn't face him alone, much less his secretary. She backed up to the curb and looked straight up. There were lights on, clear up the building past where his office would be. She walked to the end of the building, then turned and walked back to the other edge of the mammoth structure. It wasn't pleasant. The wind was whipping her hair into her eyes, snow was building up inside her collar, and her feet and nose were totally numb. Still, she couldn't force herself to go up. She was trapped there. The voice within would not let her leave without forming the words, "Please forgive me." But her heart could not believe that he actually would. He would reject her plea and leave her as she had left him. And she knew that if that happened she would not survive it. All love was dead to her now, and she was only alive very tenuously. She couldn't bring herself to the task. So she walked to and fro, growing colder and more desperate by the minute.

At ten-fifteen the foot-traffic along the sidewalk had slowed to a trickle. The colored lights of the shops along the street were ghostly in the snow. Shielah alone remained, huddled close to the building for some shelter from the snow and wind. Paulo turned off the light in his office and locked his door. He had worked late because he couldn't bear to go home alone, to ride up in the elevator and remember that terrible scene with Shielah. He had no idea where she had gone that night. He knew he had failed her when she needed him most. He had called her place many times that first week, but had never had an answer. He presumed she must have gone back to Utah to Stephen and now she was lost to him completely. When he walked through the revolving doors, he glanced to the left and to

243

the right as was his habit. She was turned away from him. Her back was hunched against the cold, and her head was bowed and snow-capped. But strands of blonde hair waved wildly in the wind. He stood, staring at her, unbelieving. Then she turned and saw him.

She wanted to run. He could see it in her eyes. He must be very, very careful. He didn't make the slightest move toward her or away from her. They simply stood and stared at each other for minutes. Then he moved gingerly, slowly closing the distance between them. Still she didn't move or speak. She just watched his eyes.

When he was close enough to touch her, he spoke softly, "I'm glad you came."

A slight look of surprise and hope seemed to touch her face. He spoke again, careful not to say anything wrong. "I thought you might have gone."

She shook her head and neither of them spoke.

"You must be cold." She made no sign. "If you want, I'll help you get warm."

Still she did not move or speak. She just stood there—a picture of terrible misery—not even looking at him. He was running out of safe things to say.

At last he tried again. What could he say that would move that awful wall? "Let me help you." He put out his hand to her, not knowing if she would run or if she would take it. She looked at his hand, then opened her lips. They moved slightly, but he couldn't hear what she was saying. Quietly, he said, "You want to tell me something?"

Blue eyes looked into his, hollow and red-rimmed, hopeless and suffering. He hurt so badly for her he could have died. She whispered just barely loud enough for him to hear through the wind. "Please . . . please . . . forgive me. Can you ever . . . forgive me?"

The wind stung his eyes and froze tiny drops of water below his lids. He had been holding his breath. It all came out in one gush now and frosted her hair. His voice broke as he replied to what seemed to her an unimaginable request. "Shielah, when you love someone as much as I do you, it is a . . . privilege . . . to forgive—my privilege. You do me honor by allowing me that."

Now his tears came too hot and fast for the wind to freeze. Remarkably, she was dry-eyed. Mercurial emotions came and went across her face, disbelief, wonder, awe, hope, relief and finally rest. He reached out for her and carefully, gently, pressed her head against his coat. "Come, my sweet, I will take you home."

That night he healed her with his words and with his love . . . and with his forgiveness. She stayed with him all night, and they only slept toward dawn. She rehearsed it all to him, the night she had refused her brother, the terror of isolation she had been enduring, the questioning of God's love. It was the beginning of healing to simply give voice to the burden of guilt and the fear. But he completed the process for her.

After she had spoken all that she had words for, she took his hands and put them on her cheeks so that her face was cradled. "I didn't know if you would ever forgive me. I hurt you deliberately. I couldn't help it, but still it was deliberate so you would let me go. You had no reason to love me again after that, to care about me, to forgive me."

Paulo shook his head. "You don't understand. How can I put into words all that is in my heart?" He paused, looking into her pale, drawn face. "I have watched you for a year now, and seen the pain you suffer because you will not forgive, because you do not understand it at all."

"Forgiveness is the only true basis for happiness. And forgiving life for all its injustices is the beginning step. You want to be happy, but you can't. How can you? You haven't forgiven the fire. You haven't forgiven your mother and father for dying and leaving you. You haven't forgiven Buck for being just a boy and for not thinking of you. Your world still revolves around yourself."

"Stop it! Please! Now you're trying to hurt me."

"I'm not. I'm trying to *help* you. You want to be happy, and I want to be happy with you. But you've been most miserable. Why? Why? Because you've lost all the people you love, your parents, your brother, your grandmother. The last two you could have helped, but you wouldn't forgive. Your rigidness lost them and yet you blame them in your heart for your misery. When are you going to own your own problems. When are you going to forgive life for its unfairness? Hating life is like hating your own body. Unfair though it is, it nurtures you, cradles you, and gives you experiences. Sometimes they hurt. Sometimes they are sweet!" And he kissed her softly.

"It's OK for things to go wrong, for things to be difficult, even for people to be unfair, because it is in the definition of life. That's what it is, a series of experiences, good and bad, and we have to learn to deal with both. But they are life. It's a wonderful, fantastic gift, the gift of Life, but don't expect it to be fair or to make sense. It frequently doesn't. Good people get hurt, bad people go free. We have a divine sense of justice that is often outraged, but you mustn't walk around in a living death, rejecting all the wonder and capriciousness of life. When you forgive life for hurting, then you can forgive yourself, for you are simply a part of life. You can be a child and not hate yourself. You can be wrong and not hate yourself. You can be sorry. You can be unfair and admit it. In other words, you can be human and still be good. *You can be human and still be good."*

He was straining every mental nerve with the intensity of trying to make her see. "And when you know that about yourself, and don't expect life to be fair or consistent, then you can love God, because you are free to love—free from the guilt of disappointing Him, confident that He accepts your failings, and free from expecting a certain thing from the life He gave you. You are free to truly love Him. Not just talk about Him, not just study about Him, but love Him. Worship Him, trust Him, without the fear that he will direct your life a way you don't want it to go. Life will hold no fear for you, don't you see, for you will have learned to simply *let* it be what it is and whatever life brings you, you won't blame God, or yourself, or anyone else.

"But it hurts!" she persisted.

"Because you do not forgive . . . yourself and others."

"How can you forgive when they . . . hurt you?"

"You forgive because that relieves the hurt. You don't close up in order to protect. You *open up* in order to protect. With the forgiving . . . moment by moment if necessary . . . you are protected from the pain. It is as if you were an open window and if an arrow is shot, it goes through you and passes out, not shattering you at all."

"But if they are not worthy of your forgiveness?"

"Not so. In the first place every person is simply human and fallible as you are and struggling to learn. We are all worthy for we are all human beings. Everything that exists has worth, for it was handmade by God. He wanted it to be. We exist, we are divine creations, therefore we have worth. In the second place, you do not forgive them or yourself because of worthiness, you forgive in order to live free. We do not forgive them for their sake. We forgive them for ours. It is to your benefit to forgive as much as theirs. You do it for yourself as much as for them."

He was holding both her hands tightly. He raised them to his lips, kissed them tenderly, then quietly said, "And most of all, we forgive ourselves, for God's sake."

Tears overcame her. When she could get her voice again, she confessed. "If you only knew the terrible things I have accused Him of in my heart."

"I can imagine. But He can forgive you. And He does. He is the master of that program. But all His forgiveness won't matter if you don't forgive yourself. It will all be negated, just as though there were no forgiving God, because you won't let it be true for you. It is as though He held out the most priceless gift of eternity and you refused it."

"But I'm not. I'm really not worthy."

"Wait a minute. Whose child are you? Didn't you used to say you were His child. You've even gotten me to believe that now. If you're His child, doesn't that make you pretty dear to Him. And didn't He send His son to die for you so you could have forgiveness. What, are you going to throw that sacrifice right back in Their faces? Are you going to say 'It's wonderful that you would die for me; I appreciate the gesture, but no thanks?' And do you think He is any less forgiving than I am—me, a Catholic, almost a heathen." He smiled as he gently teased her.

She was exhausted with the awesome gamut of emotions and concepts she had been grappling with. She wanted to go to sleep, but she didn't want to lose the moment. It was the most enlightening moment of her life. Overwhelming gratitude filled her for this man who loved her beyond her comprehension. And gratitude for her Heavenly Father, whom she had doubted and now could also see His love.

"How do you know all this, my priest?" she asked him.

Paulo looked into her eyes for a moment. "I don't honestly know. I have never thought it through before. It is as though it were given to me for this very moment, and even as I speak the words to you I know they are true."

246

Peace had come to her now and she affirmed. "I know they are too. How awful to suffer so for knowledge."

"The knowledge that hurts the most is the knowledge we refuse to see."

"Of course that's it!" she exclaimed, light dawning for her. "Truth is so important that if you refuse it, it will knock you down trying to be known. We refuse God's eternal principles at the peril of our lives and mental health! I have been almost out of my mind with fear and warped, crazy assumptions. Let me hear those words again. I love them. Let me say my part and you say yours!" She was so eager. Paulo loved her as dearly then as he ever would.

She sat up on her knees and clutched both his hands. A tear escaped and trickled down her cheek, but her blue eyes sparkled for the first time in weeks. "Please . . . will you please forgive me?"

Love so sweet it pained him took his breath away for a moment. When he could speak, his voice was husky. "With all my heart. When we love, as I do so love you, it is . . . a privilege . . . to forgive." He kissed her hands that grasped his own. "You do me honor to allow me that privilege."

And they held each other and wept.

Two days before Christmas, her sick leave still in effect, Shielah flew to Utah. There would be no joy in this pilgrimage now, but there was need. Before she saw anyone else or did anything else, she had to go to the cemetery. Stephen picked her up at the airport and took her straight to Grace's grave, which lay in the tiny cemetery right next to the graves of Shielah's own parents. It was bitter cold that December afternoon and Stephen was afraid for her, afraid she would be inconsolable. Yet, she stood looking at the graves with not a tear. Only at the last did she show any emotion at all. She went down on her knees beside Ginny's grave, touched the headstones, and smoothed her fingers across the names. After a few minutes she was ready to go, and he took her to Will and Maddie's.

It was a different Shielah that Stephen met at Christmas, quiet like the girl he had grown up with, yet relaxed and peaceful. There was no easy laughter nor lover's play this time as there had been in New York. But neither was there the tension that had seemed almost an integral part of her personality. Peace had come in Shielah's door and remained as her friend. He knew that she would tell him about it when the time was right.

Will and Maddie opened their doors and lives to her just as they did more than ten years before. To them she never really left. They watched her grow up, worried over her as they might one of their own, hoped for her, and loved her, though she rarely accepted the offering. Now she accepted. They cautioned their younger children to remember that Shielah would be sad because of Grandma's death. The children tried to dampen their own natural excitement for the season, but they didn't succeed. A snowball caught Shielah right behind the ear. Everyone was amazed when she

247

straightened up slowly, turned with not the tiniest smile, then suddenly whooped and plastered her older cousin with her own snowball.

On Christmas morning each of her seven cousins came and placed a small gift in her lap. They were each handmade and precious because of it. Her Uncle Will's gift was the most valued of all. He simply handed her an envelope with a certificate. The certificate read, "Guaranteed—one grooming session with Sheba now, one afternoon of riding in the spring or summer, and the first foal she throws this year." She went to him and hugged him in appreciation. He reddened and patted her hand. It was nothing, he said. But it was something to her. Sheba was the golden palomino she adored, a sleek, shiny mare with near perfect conformation and the disposition of a saint. The grooming would be good therapy now, and the riding would ascertain Shielah's return in the spring. As for the foal, it was a pleasure Shielah could only anticipate with shivers. To have a wobbly Sheba of her own would be heaven.

The rest of the day was spent eating. Maddie's kitchen smelled of turkey and cinnamon. The two women worked side by side getting Christmas dinner on, while the children played with new toys and the boys went out skiing off the long sloping hill behind the farmhouse.

"I was sorry you couldn't be here for the funeral. I knew how much it would mean to you." Maddie brought up the subject hesitantly, yet feeling the subject should be out in the open.

"It meant everything to me. I was totally shocked when I came home from a flight to Stockholm, Sweden and found Buck's note."

"That's a terrible way to get the news."

"Yes," Shielah admitted. "I wish Buck were here. I'd like to see him."

"I guess he's happier right where he is, with Bridget. You wouldn't believe the change in him."

"What change?"

Maddie looked at her curiously. "I thought you'd know. Buck is active in the church and working for a temple wedding with Bridget."

Shielah stopped the electric beater and stared, open-mouthed, at her aunt.

"How did that happen? When did it happen? I knew he loved her, but I figured she'd have to be the one who caved in. I wouldn't have guessed Buck in a million years."

Maddie laughed. "Buck is not even doing it for Bridget. The only cave-in happened in Mexico. He was almost buried alive in one of those ancient, Mayan tombs. He said his whole life passed before him, and he didn't like the movie. Anyway," she went back to her work with the pies. "Anyway, he started studying and now you can hardly beat him for understanding the gospel. But, my, he does have a funny way of talking about it."

Shielah had still not gone back to work on the mashed potatoes. She was thinking. "I'm happy for him, for them both. I know Bridget loved him and I give her credit, she wouldn't marry him outside the temple. That's hard, especially when you think the man might never come around. She could have lost him completely."

248

"Yes, but she'd never completley have him anyway if they weren't married there."

"When will he be home?"

"I'm not just sure. He might not come home, now with Mother gone. He may be just intending to fly straight back to Mexico."

"I have to talk to him."

She called Honolulu that afternoon, not anticipating how strong her reaction would be at hearing his voice.

"Yeah, this is Buck here, who's this?" He knew someone was on the phone, he could hear little sounds, but no voice answered him. "Merry Christmas! Is this Stephen? Hey, whoo-oo, who's there?"

Finally, she got her voice to work, barely. "It's me. I'm sorry. It's Shielah. Buck I . . . I . . . I miss you. I'd hoped you be here this Christmas."

"Shielah! Merry Christmas, muffin. I miss you too. If I had thought you'd want to see me, I'd have stayed. Well, maybe. I have someone else right here beside me who was pretty anxious to see me too. Are you at Will's?"

"Yes, Aunt Maddie sends her love." There was silence on the line for a minute as Shielah's voice gave way. After she swallowed the lump in her throat, she finished. "I wish I could be with you to give you mine directly."

There was none of the usual banter in her brother's voice. "I'll take it anyway I can get it, across the wires even."

"I'm sorry . . . for . . . everything, everything! Please, will you forgive me?"

"I never held anything against you, so there's nothing to forgive. I'm the one who needs to ask you. I'm the louse in the family. But I never meant to hurt you, Sis, I just loved you too much and was too dumb to do it right. Do you forgive *me*?"

"With all my heart. Brandy, my roommate, taught me something. 'Ain't no wall strong enough, ain't no river wide enough, ain't no door big enough to separate you from your blood kin.' When will I see you? I have to see you."

"He paused a moment, thinking. "I'm headed straight down to Mexico, but I might be able to re-route. When are you going back east?"

"Day after tomorrow."

"Meet me in Arizona."

She laughed. "Arizona, why there?"

"Just selfish. I'm gonna go out of my way to meet you, and I just want to see if you'll go out of your way for me."

"I'll go to Mexico, if you want me to."

"Arizona's fine. I'll call you back and let you know when. Merry Christmas, Shielah, you made mine. I love you."

"I love you too."

Stephen picked her up at five-thirty on Christmas day, when the last light was fading. They drove to Salt Lake to the temple grounds to see the lights. She told him about her conversation with Buck, and he listened in silence, glad for them. Then, carefully, she began to tell him more, what she had been through since Thanksgiving and the death of Grandma. She didn't hide anything from him, and she also told him all that Paulo had taught her. She looked at him squarely, and said, "I know you'll never be able to appreciate him because of me, but you need to know that I love him. He's a great man."

Stephen heard what she wanted him to hear, and he realized she could not long vacillate between the two of them.

They walked through the open iron-bar gates into a fairy-tale land of tiny twinkling lights. The trees were great chandeliers, with elf-lights and ice winking from their branches. It was enough to take the breath away. The tabernacle stood solid and dark in the temple block, presided over by spires of the white granite temple that rose more than two hundred feet into the dark sky. Lights lit up the soaring spires, and atop the highest one stood the golden statue of the Angel Moroni with a trumpet that announced to the world that Jesus Christ is King. That trumpet was most appropriate tonight. On the open stretch of lawn, new snow blanketed the grass, and to the north of the tabernacle, a life-size nativity scene had been erected. The shepherds knelt at intervals before the rough manger, and wisemen stood with gifts of love and respect in their hands. The rich voices of the Tabernacle Choir resounded through the night, song after song of praise.

Shielah and Stephen walked slowly through the magic land. They stood looking up and up, at the regal spires over their heads, then turned toward the nativity scene. The music paused and a narration began.

"And there were in the same country, Shepherds abiding in the fields, keeping watch over their flock by night."

Tears started up in Stephen's eyes as well as Shielah's at the dear familiar words, and when they looked at each other, they smiled to see their identical reactions. All around them other couples stood, arm in arm, and families with children, "ooh-ing" and "ahh-ing" over the beautiful scene.

"Glory to God in the highest, and on earth peace, good will toward men."

At those words, particularly priceless to Shielah now, tears fell heedlessly. But she was not alone. Others who truly understood those words were together in their response. Peace had come to her this Christmas, the peace of forgiveness and the understanding of life. It was the most precious gift of all.

The narration ended and the music soared, a thousand voices filling the dark night with a triumphal song, "Joy to the world, the Lord has come, let earth receive her king." Shielah and Stephen walked forward to better see the manger and the babe. As they did so, they raised their eyes and across the field of snow, presiding over the entire scene of worship, the white figure of Christ stood with his arms outstretched. It was the Christus, the majestic white statue, standing on the second floor of the

Visitor's Center, with a wall of windows that allowed viewing from the temple grounds.

Her breath intake was sharp, the sight was like a blow to her heart, and she clutched her chest. Instinctively she wanted to kneel, and wished passionately that her own church might adopt the humble practice of Paulo's church. Stephen took her arm and helped her stand. He could see she was unsteady with emotion. Then they walked toward the Visitor's Center, their own pilgrimage calling. Around the circular ramp they walked, the rich blues and purples of a darkened universe painted on the surrounding walls. Then, they stood silently before the statue of the Lord of that Universe. There were no words; awe and reverence were their common bond. Shoulder touching shoulder, hand in hand, their devotion was as one. All that they were and hoped to be, all that they knew, the very foundation of their lives was represented in that statue of the man Jesus, of Nazareth.

The next morning Shielah was up early helping Will with the chores and the horses. She spent an hour with Sheba, currying the mare, feeding her, cleaning out the stall, and occasionally patting her round belly. The warmth, sleek flesh of the palomino was comforting to Shielah. There was a feeling of kinship and affection with the animal. It was curious to her that she often felt more at ease with the animals than people. The horses were intelligent creatures that responded to her commands as well as her love. Sheba would thrust her muzzle under Shielah's hand or under her arm, indicating a desire to be scratched or stroked. There were no uncomfortable barriers between them. Shielah never felt rejected or threatened. It was pure, soul to soul, affection and communication. Working in the huge barn was therapeutic for Shielah's still tender heart. In her jeans and oversized sweatshirt, bundled up in her cousin Drew's wool jacket and furry Russian hat, she was toasty warm and looked like another one of the boys.

Will was working in the next stall with a bay gelding that he boarded for a Salt Lake City man. Shielah had just finished scraping Sheba's hooves. She was still kneeling in the fresh hay, her back to the stall door.

"Looks like you've got a new hired hand, Will," she heard the familiar bantering tones of Stephen's voice.

"Yep, a good worker too!" Will replied tersely.

"Huh, looks like a softie to me." She knew he would be grinning from ear to ear when she turned around. He was. One arm resting on the top of the stall, one hand jammed into his pocket, Stephen was dressed as she was, jeans, boots, ready for a working day. With his hat clutched in his hand, his blonde hair was in disarray, slipping down over his forehead. She stood up and instinctively reached out and brushed it back for him.

Stephen caught her wrist before she could drop her hand. "I needed that," he smiled.

"I know! Are you here to help or make smart remarks?"

251

"Neither. I'm here to spirit you away from all this. What's a nice, city-slicker girl like you doing in a place like this? It doesn't smell like roses!"

"It smells like my friends."

"Great. Does that include me? Are you trying to tell me something?"

She glanced over the side of the stall at her uncle, studiously intent on his grooming of the bay. She looked back at Sheba and quick tears stung her eyes. "These are my friends . . . and I've missed them."

"We've missed you too." Stephen brought her hand to his cheek, twining his fingers with hers. "Wish you were home to stay."

Shielah brushed her eyes quickly with the other hand and shook her head. "I have no home now. Only my place in New York. With Grandma gone I'm just company."

She heard a soft growl from the next stall and her uncle's eyes appeared over the top board. "Don't you let Maddie or me hear that, missy. You're not too big for a spanking and company don't get spanked. You want me to prove you're not company here."

Stephen wiggled his eyebrows at her and tried, unsuccessfully, to squelch a smile. "I think he means it," Stephen said.

"Darn tootin'. As long as this farm stands and I pay my taxes, you've got a home. You would have been ours anyway all these years, but we let Grace borrow you."

Shielah turned back to the palomino and put her arm around Sheba's neck, fighting down tender emotions still too sensitive to keep under control. Stephen took his foot off the boards, settled his hat back on his head and held out a hand through the open gate. "Come on. I came to take you riding. It's too nice outside to stay cooped up in here. Besides, the air's better out there."

"Well, as soon as I'm finished helping Uncle Will."

A disembodied voice came from three stalls over. "All done! Gonna take a break myself. Git on outa here you two."

She saddled Sheba and Will led a seven-year-old paint quarter horse up for Stephen to ride. When they walked the horses out of the barn's sliding door, the brilliant cover of snow dazzled their eyes and the frosty air caught in their lungs. Down the slope, side by side on the long rutted driveway they rode, to the wire gate just at the little twisting road through the valley. This was only the third snowfall of the season, but it had been a thick one, and now, crusted over after five days, the blanket of snow was crystallized and sparkling like a sea of diamonds. Shielah looked at Stephen, easy and relaxed on the mare beside her. His breath was silver smoke. A rush of love flooded her, quickly followed by guilt. She loved them both now, Paulo and Stephen, and one was not before the other.

Shielah feasted upon the sight of the rugged mountains ringing the valley. They rose, massive and white, cutting the blue sky into a jagged puzzle, and the rolling foothills on either side of the narrow, paved road teased the eye with white shrouded shapes where fences, bushes and oak brush were concealed. How had she left this beauty so easily? This time the leaving would be harder. Her eyes seemed to be opened in a way they never had been before. The city, with its concrete and glass, suddenly ran a poor second to the peaceful majesty of the mountains. The white was so white it hurt the eyes. The sky was so blue she could almost see through into infinity. The tight, clenched feeling in Shielah's heart slowly relaxed and opened like the fist of a baby as it drifts into slumber.

Stephen saw her breathe deeply, twist around in her saddle to admire the full panorama of the valley. He saw her smile, watched her eyes soften and glow and sensed the opening up of her spirit. Good! It was what he had hoped for with this ride. He needed more time with her, time to talk about them and their future, lest that future belong to someone else.

"We'll make this a regular date, shall we? Every year, the day after Christmas, when everything is peaceful and quiet, we'll go riding together in the snow. How does that sound?" he asked.

"Like heaven. You prescribed the right medicine for me."

"I hope so. And the doctor says you need still more recuperation. Bedrest is prescribed, especially on a honeymoon!" She could see his eyes sparkling and a silly grin on his lips.

"Oh, stop! You are trying to tempt me."

"Exactly right. You tempt *me* every time I look at you. Aren't you tired of being a working girl? Wouldn't you like to be a 'kept' woman?"

"Would you keep me in a pumpkin shell?"

"Nope. I'd keep you in a rose covered cottage, with a white picket fence, and two or three little blonde-haired carbon copies of Shielah running around. When are we going to make that dream come true?"

She cocked her head thoughtfully and looked at him. Two years ago she would have thrilled to hear that invitation. But two years ago if she had married him it would have been as an escape from her problems, from herself. Now, many of those problems had been worked through and she still needed time to feel very solid about her ability to stand on her own. She still wasn't ready to give her life to a man.

"Are you ready for that? And are you sure it's me you want?"

"It never has been anyone else. Maybe those questions are for yourself."

"Maybe so." She looked away, off beyond the horizon. "What's that, up on the hillside there?" Shielah pointed to a tiny spot on the foothills across the road.

"Looks like a little lean-to. A cabin of some sort. Shall we go see?"

It took almost twenty minutes to reach the rough, log cabin. It was obscured at times by pine trees as they rode toward it. "I think this must be the hunters' cabin that Buck and Drew and Uncle Will sometimes use in the fall. I've only been here once, and I was so young I had forgotten until just now."

They tied their horses to a tall post that stood at the west corner of the cabin. "Do you suppose it's open?" Stephen asked as he tried the rusty old door knob. The knob twisted, but the door only groaned instead of opening. Putting his shoulder to the rough boards he heaved his weight against them, and reluctantly the door moved inward.

The cabin was simple, obviously built only for men. Two windows were boarded up and the one that was not was encrusted with dust and dirt. Stephen ferretted out an old red sock that had been carelessly left in the wood bin and wiped the window with it. Instantly, sunlight flooded them. The view from the window was the only decoration of the place. The valley lay serene and lovely below them. The road they had ridden was a narrow strip wandering lazily between gentle ridges.

"We could have a fire," Stephen ventured.

"Are there matches?"

"Yep. Here on the shelf." He was already stacking up the wood and stuffing the old scraps of a Sears catalogue in the crevices. Within a few minutes the tinder-dry wood caught and a fire was snapping in the fireplace. Stephen glanced around at the two cots lining the sides of the room. Then he pulled the old, lumpy mattress off of one and laid it on the floor before the fire.

"It's not the Waldorf-Astoria, but I guarantee you'll be warm as toast in a minute."

Shielah smiled at him, his long, slim body stretched out on the floor. He looked like the pictures of pioneer ancestors. He might have just ridden in from a Wyoming cattle ranch. There was nothing pretentious about Stephen. He was as open as the prairie sky. His natural self-confidence had matured into casual decisiveness. He knew who he was, what he wanted, and he didn't hesitate. She did sense, however, a certain shyness about him in this setting.

Almost reluctantly she moved to sit down beside him. He was right. Within minutes the chill was broken in the little room and after ten minutes she removed her hat and jacket. He turned quiet and hardly spoke, but sat watching the fire, jabbing it at times with the long poker. He didn't put his arm around her. In fact he barely looked at her the first twenty minutes they sat there.

"Stephen, what shall I do? I don't know anymore."

He shook his head silently, still staring into the fire. "Do you know that there are people on the earth who have never seen snow?" he said. "There was a little girl that used to come to the barracks, selling cigarettes and candy, and she had no concept of ice or snow. Just think how lucky we are. We have everything in the world we can conceive of or wish for."

His profile was strong, his arms long and hard-muscled. Shielah suddenly wanted those arms around her. She laid her hand on his right arm. "Is your arm all better now? The bones all knit properly?"

"I think so. It seems almost as strong as my left now. But then, I've been using a saw and lifting a lot of furniture these last few months. Did I tell you I'm working two jobs—one with a furniture moving company and another as an apprentice carpenter?"

"No, you didn't tell me." They were both silent for another few minutes. "I don't know when I'll be coming back, Stephen. With Grandma gone and Buck gone there really isn't much reason . . . "

254

"That's for you to decide," he cut her off. "If you need a reason to come back . . . maybe there isn't any."

"Well . . . I didn't mean it like that."

"What did you mean?

She could hear the irritation in his voice and knew she had offended him. "Only that, with Grandma gone and the house closed I'm just company wherever I go. I hate to inconvenience anyone."

He turned to face her, his eyes narrowed and his face set in intense concentration. "Shielah, you want me to tell you what to do. You want me to say 'come back, for me.' I won't do that. You know how I feel and I'm not going to beg you. If you have rejected your home, your family, that's up to you. I thought you had outgrown that, but if you are determined to be an orphan, I can't help you. There isn't really any doubt in your mind that Will and Maddie are happy to open their home to you. There isn't any doubt that I will make a home for you anytime you are ready. But until you are, I am stymied. I'm stuck. We can't go any further. You are investing all your time in the airlines and in Paulo D'Agosta, and that is the direction in which you are going to grow. It's your choice. I've been watching you make that choice for months. I hoped it would change. I hoped that if I asked you to marry me you would be as overjoyed with that idea as I am. But obviously, I was wrong. If D'Agosta has come between us, you are the one who invited him in and you are the only one who can put him out. I won't beg you to marry me, Shielah."

It had all come out in a burst and she realized it was painful for him. "Stephen . . . Stephen . . . I . . . don't look at me like that. I'm sorry. I don't mean to hurt you. I don't want you to be miserable. I'm trying, really I am, trying to decide what to do with my life. It doesn't mean I don't love you. I do. I love you just as much as I did before Hawaii, before Vietnam . . . "

"Before Paulo D'Agosta? As much as you did when you were a little girl? Sorry, Shielah, we're too old for that. If that is the way you still love me we'd better face it right now—it won't do! If that's it, then you really don't have any reason to come back again."

Now his pain had been transferred to her and her heart hurt intensely. Her breath caught. Tears spilled. "No, it's not like that. I love you—not like a little girl. I love you and I . . . I want you to love me!"

"Okay. Then what? How long shall we go on, calling for a few minutes a week, seeing each other twice a year? You want me to love you but you don't want me to marry you. Shielah, it will fail." He took her face between his hands and watched the tears trickle down. His voice softened. He kissed the streaks on her cheeks. "It will dissolve like spring snow. Is that what you want?"

"No." She struggled to get it out. "I don't want to lose you. Oh Stephen, I love you so. You feel so good to my soul."

A slow smile spread across his face. "How about your body? I hope I feel good there too." He drew her into his arms and kissed her lips.

She put her arms around his neck and clung to him tightly. "Don't be angry with me. Please. Please, don't talk about us losing each other. I feel as though I'd lose my whole childhood, my whole self, if I lost you. You have been a part of me almost as long as I can remember. Half of me would die if it weren't connected to you. Can you be patient a little longer? I'm trying to get myself straightened out, but it's been hard. I've had such a long way to come. This is the first time that, coming home, I haven't regressed into an insecure little girl."

She sat across his lap, her arms around his neck and her head resting on his shoulder. He held her, stroking her hair down her back. "I'm not angry, just disappointed. I wanted you to throw yourself into my arms and say, 'Yes, yes, yes! Of course I'll marry you. Let it be tomorrow.' That's what I want. Shielah, my sweet, I can't offer you fancy restaurants and fancy cars, world travel and flowers delivered every week. But I think I could manage a little house by a stream, a garden of flowers, maybe a couple of horses and, for whatever it's worth to you, a love beyond time."

This is what she had wanted all her life—a family of her own, love, Stephen's love, a love beyond time, which death and flames could not steal. Her heart responded "yes" but the memory of Paulo's voice saying, "When you love someone . . . as I do so love you . . . it is a privelege to forgive," held her bound.

"In the summer I'll come back and we'll decide then. Will you give me until then?"

"Be careful, my love. Be careful not to let someone steal our dream. I have great and wonderful plans for us. Someday I'll be a mission president and go back to Scotland, maybe even to Vietnam, and you'll be the most beautiful mission mother in the history of the church. With your sensitivity to people, you'll be the sweetest, too. We'll walk the little back roads in the hills of Scotland and you'll find out what it's like to see the gospel of Christ work miracles in the lives of people. Missionary work was so fulfilling, so exciting, even working with another elder. Missionary work with you by my side would be pure joy. Just think, no more peanut butter sandwiches and soup after a long day of knocking on doors!"

"So that's all you want me for—to cook for your enormous, insatiable appetite."

"Well, I wasn't thinking of your cooking so much as feasting on *you*!" He pushed back her hair and began nibbling on her neck and ear. "Umm, delicious! Much better than peanut butter sandwiches."

"Is that any way to treat a sister missionary?"

"They never had it so good," he mumbled against the base of her neck.

"I should think not!" she sighed, tingling with the touch of his lips. "You will be a wonderful mission president, or bishop, or . . . or father. Whatever you do you enter into it with your whole self. That's what I love about you, your zest for living. And your enthusiasm carries everyone else along."

"Does it carry you? Will you come along? I want so much to share my life with you, for us to work together, to build the Lord's kingdom together. It wouldn't be half as exciting without you. I could do it. But I wouldn't love it like I would if you were by my side." All the banter was gone now. He was perfectly serious. "I have discovered that I can endure and eventually triumph over anything . . . almost anything. But I haven't discovered how to live without you. I hope I don't ever have to. I'll wait 'til summer. I hope that's as long as I need to."

Silently, Shielah hoped so too.

Chapter 14

*I*n the winter and spring, Shielah saw Paulo every chance she got. They explored ideas together, relationships, emotions, concepts and religion. She was trying to come to a decision. She had promised Stephen she would. After a few months a common thread seemed to run through their discussions— prophets, authority, eternal marriage, and the nature of God. They began studying the Bible together and she occasionally read him a scripture from her Book of Mormon. It was very spiritual in nature, he gave her that, and it seemed to support the Bible, but it wasn't sacred scripture to him and he wouldn't accept it as authoritative. In fact, he didn't even accept the canonized Bible as completely authoritative. At times it seemed to contradict itself. Often it was obscure, and there were obvious errors—sentences started and never finished. Centuries of translation by the hands of priests under candlelight had obviously taken their toll on the accuracy of the Bible. Even beyond that, in Paulo's mind, the men who wrote the Bible were simply that, men, subject to misunderstanding and faulty concepts.

The discussions frequently ended with Shielah promising to study more to answer his questions. At first he did not press her on the question of marriage. He wanted to be sure she was emotionally stable before he threw another problem her way. Yet, he felt that time was running out for them. They had never been closer. She had never come to him more willingly or openly. But the current was running and he felt an impending sense of climax near.

One afternoon they were at her apartment. Brandy was flying and they were alone when the doorbell buzzed. Shielah pushed the answering buzzer and in a few moments a knock came at the door. When Paulo got up to answer it for her, a delivery man stood in the hallway with a oversized box at his feet.

"You Miss Shielah Sorensen?" he asked Paulo with a smirk.

"Right. You got it."

"I'm Shielah Sorensen," she said, joining the men. "Who is the box from?"

"You'd know that better'n me. Says Utah, Springville Utah."

She signed, then took a knife to open the box. On top was a letter from Aunt Maddie telling her they had disposed of Grace's things and had saved a few they felt she might want. In the box was a treasure of memorabilia—an old yellow, organdy Easter dress made for Shielah when she was eleven, pillow cases painstakingly embroidered, books that Shielah had bought and left in the bookcase, a silver dish her grandmother had promised for her wedding, and many other precious, sentimental items. Along the side of the box, well wrapped in foam, was the portrait of Charlotte O'Neill Boughtman that had hung behind Grace's bed.

Shielah carefully unwrapped it and tentatively placed it up against one wall. "What do you think?" she asked Paulo, who had been getting some glasses of juice from the kitchen. "Everyone says we look alike. Come see this picture of my great, great grandmother. Grandma Thompson said it would be mine when she died. I guess she told my aunt too. I'm surprised Aunt Maddie would let it go. After all it's her. . . . " She stopped rambling when she saw the look on Paulo's face.

He had come into the room, ready to hand her a glass and take a drink from his own. Now he set down both drinks on the endtable and was staring speechless at the portrait. He looked at Shielah; he looked at Charlotte. His face was white and he sat down on the floor leaning back against the wall. His hand was touching his temple. He rubbed his head absentmindedly, but his eyes never left the portrait.

Shielah looked at the portrait too, and after a minute said, "Paulo, are you OK? What's wrong?"

But he didn't speak. He couldn't put his thoughts into words. Indeed, the thoughts were more like impressions, none of them lasting long enough to identify. Over and over, like a scratched record, his brain registered, "It can't be the same one. It can't be the same one." But it was. He didn't understand it, and certainly he didn't want it to be so, but the truth was, it was that girl, in that very dress whom he had seen more than ten years ago. He looked again at Shielah. The same eyes, the same shape of the face, the same tilt of the head. Her neck was long and graceful, like the girl in the picture. They were close, very close. His breath had almost stopped and he felt himself getting dizzy. Paulo forced his head back against the wall and breathed carefully.

Shielah put down the picture and went over to sit beside him. He opened his eyes and met hers. He couldn't tell her what he was thinking. He couldn't even believe it might be true, that he might have made a mistake. He had grown to love her now, regardless of his youthful vision. She was his only choice for a wife, for a sweetheart. Suddenly he grabbed her and crushed her to his chest, burying his face in her hair, but with one eye he could still see the Charlotte's red hair. Shielah could feel him trembling and couldn't understand the problem.

259

"Paulo, please, what's wrong? Is it something I've said? Is it . . . is it the picture?."

He didn't answer, just held her, and stroked her hair, and kissed her face and forehead. She looked back at the picture, worry creasing her brow. "It is the picture. What's wrong, for goodness sake?"

"You . . . you . . . are very much . . . alike, aren't you?" He finally managed to speak.

"Everyone always said so. Why?"

"It's just very startling. I thought I was seeing double for a minute."

"Not *that* much. After all, she does have that beautiful red hair and I'm blonde. Her eyes are gray-green, mine are obviously blue. And she has that regal bearing I always wanted to copy. They say she was a very strong woman, but had a very unhappy life. I'd like to know her. Maybe someday—you know, in the next life—I'll get to meet her and know her."

A memory came back to Paulo, the memory of a dream. "When did she live?"

"Between 1827 and 1837, as nearly as we can figure out. We don't have all the records on her, especially her death record. Grandma has searched genealogy records for years so we could get her temple work done. So far, nothing."

They sat looking at the picture together. His subconscious yielded up to his conscious memory the dream of the girl in the meadow. All at once he could remember seeing her body beneath a towering oak tree and battling with strange spirits of darkness for her soul. After a few minutes he got up and walked slowly over to the portrait. After studying it a moment, he reached out, almost reverently, to touch it. "Who painted this picture?"

"Her daughter, my great grandmother, Annie. She had beautiful red hair too. She died the year I was born, 1953. I don't remember her, but Grandma had pictures of me, my mother, herself, and Annie, her mother. Maybe they are here in the box with the other things."

"Was Annie an artist?"

"No, not really. She was a nurse. But she always worried that when she died her mother's memory would disappear, so she went back to school when she was sixty-one years old to learn to paint. She was only interested in portrait painting, and once she had practiced enough, she began this portrait. It's beautiful, don't you think. I wonder if Charlotte really looked like that?"

Paulo stood directly in front of the portrait, touching it delicately, as one might a priceless art object. "Yes, I think she did. I mean . . . your great-grandmother seems to have been good at her hobby. She had real talent. What do you know about your great, great grandmother?"

"Not too much. Grandma said she was an excellent horsewoman. Her mother told her that Charlotte was a saint, an absolute saint. Of course, that's what we all think of our mothers, I guess. They seem bigger than life, so much wiser and more perfect than we. I guess she had an unhappy marriage. She left her husband and took her daughter Annie with her. Grandma said Annie didn't remember her father much except that she had been afraid of him as a little girl. It'll be interesting someday to be able to learn all about our ancestors." Shielah was still going through the box. She found a smaller box with old pictures in it and showed them to Paulo. He glanced politely over them, but always his gaze returned to the portrait of Charlotte, in the blue dress, staring relentlessly at him.

Paulo left soon after. He needed to be alone with his thoughts. That night he went to a cathedral and sat in the last row for a long time, sorting through his thoughts and feelings. Had it been Shielah he had seen that night in Denver, or had it been the woman of the picture, the girl in his dream? He could hardly tell. They were much alike. But he was frightened—frightened that he might have been wrong in Hawaii. That thought was terrible to him. Then he had loved a vision, and had been anxious to make it come true. But now, now that he knew Shielah, watched her grow and change and mature, wept with her and held her—now he had come to love her deeply. But, the recognition of the red-haired girl in the portrait was undenieable. He knew he could have told Shielah the story of the woman's life. It was all like a movie reel in his memory, and he could have recited every detail of Charlotte's life.

But, but . . . who was she . . . to him? She could not be the girl promised to him that cold December night in Denver. How could she be? She belonged to another century in time. Her life was over. She could never belong to him. Such a vision, such a promise, would be a cruel joke. How could he know her life as he did? Was it part of a strange spiritual gift he had never understood? Paulo thought back to Hawaii and the first time he had seen Shielah, now almost two years ago. He had been watching the waves crash in, then looked up casually, watching for Jim Polanski. She had been standing under a red overhead light in a blue dress, her head tilted slightly, her face transfixed with a far away dream. Paulo put his head in his hands to stop the pounding. Oh, dear Lord, they were just alike, just alike.

After an hour with his thoughts still in turmoil, a middle-aged priest approached him. The man wore his long, black robes and his hands were clasped serenely behind him.

"You seem to need a friend. Can I help you?"

Paulo looked up. "Can you explain the gifts of the spirit to me? Do people still have visions and dreams? Am I going crazy?"

The priest was silent, taken aback by the outburst. Then he sat down and they began to talk. Paulo told him everything about Shielah and then his dream of Charlotte. The older man listened quietly. When Paulo finished, the priest said, "I don't think God interferes too much in our lives, but when He does it's always for a purpose. You'll discover the purpose in all of this someday, I'm sure of it. You are either blessed or cursed, my son, and only time will tell."

"The greatest curse I can imagine is to lose the girl I love and spend my life with dreams. I thought of being a priest once. My family wanted me to go into the priesthood. But I want a family of my own. I want love here and now. I don't know how you do it, being always alone, I mean."

261

"Choosing between the love of an immortal God and a mortal family is not easy. Not every man is meant for the priesthood. If you love this girl, forget every dream of any other and make her yours."

It sounded simple. Perhaps it was and he was only confusing himself with strange dreams. Whoever the red-haired Charlotte was, she was only a woman of his mind. Shielah was the only thing important to him in this life.

"Shielah, when we are married we will read both scriptures, yours and mine, side by side." As their love grew stronger, so did their need to resolve their differences. Shielah felt a keen sense of owing Paulo her life in one respect. He had held it together when she had been coming apart emotionally. Where gratitude and respect left off and love began, she could not tell. " When they are correct, we will know it. When they are not, we will seek the truth," he said in an effort to reassure her.

"But will we? Or will you stop questioning and reading and asking when we are married. That's what I'm afraid of, that all the progress we have made together will dissolve into the work-a-day world. We'll be fat, lazy and happy."

"What's wrong with happy?"

"Nothing, if it lasts!"

"It will last, I promise."

"Not wanting to hammer on the subject, she looked at him in silence. Then asked, "How long, this life? Today? Tomorrow? Until we have a child that dies like your brother? Until I die, or you? How long?"

"No one can tell that, not even your prophet."

"Yes, they can. Our happiness, our love will last just as long as we will it to. If we want it just for this life, that's what God will give us. If we want it forever, He has that available."

"And I would have to leave my family, my heritage, my church—that I dearly love as you do yours—to become Mormon."

She knew it was hard. She looked away. "Yes. You would."

"Will you leave your church for mine? If I tell you that our priest is the only authority on earth to marry us in the eyes of God, will you leave your friends and family and become Catholic in order to marry me before God?"

She didn't speak. He knew the answer. They sat for a moment not speaking, then he kissed her hair, lightly rubbing her shoulders and arms. "Don't worry. We'll work it out. There is a way. It will come. Don't worry. Right now it means more to me than you can imagine just to know that you love me and want to marry me."

But she also loved Stephen. This she never said to Paulo. But the conflict between the two loves was with her all the time. She shared with each one things that were precious. How could she make the choice? As the months passed with no resolution, Paulo began to get anxious. Then he began to press her to give herself to him. She would know from that intimacy how dearly he loved her. She refused. It was unthinkable to her especially after the intense study of the gospel she had been doing and the memory of her conversation with Stephen in the cabin. To Paulo it was the next best thing to a marriage. He would marry her tomorrow if she wished. He didn't want her to feel immoral. They could be married at City Hall and have neither a Catholic marriage nor a Mormon marriage. It was a perfect compromise. She was steadfast in her refusal. He couldn't understand her on this point at all. To Paulo, it was simplicity complete. You love, you marry. If there is a conflict, you compromise.

"If you love me but won't marry me, let's have the next best thing. 'Come live with me and be my love, for life is quickly passing,' " he often invited her. His logic grew harder and harder to refuse. His love grew intense and passionate, and, again, harder to refuse. After one particularly difficult evening, when Shielah hardly knew if she wanted to refuse or simply be swept along with the current, she told him she couldn't see him for a while.

"A week?" he asked.

"No."

"Two weeks, a month? Have I so offended you?"

"No, no! You haven't offended me. No one has ever loved me as you do, or taught me what you have. I am simply overwhelmed with the need to clear my head, to try to know what Heavenly Father wants me to do, and I can't hear Him with you whispering in my ear. Give me some time, Paulo. I don't know how long."

"Can I call you?"

"Just to say hello. I won't see you until I have worked this out."

"Then, fair is fair, no conversations with Utah either."

"I won't."

"How will I live? Without you, I mean. Even a week is hell!"

"Imagine eternity." She looked straight into his eyes meaningfully.

"Stop. I can't imagine tomorrow. Don't go. Don't go tonight."

"Shhh, please. Please, Paulo, don't ask me again. Your love is so hard to refuse."

"You don't have to refuse it."

"I have to make a decision for my life. Only God can whisper that to me."

She didn't see him for three weeks. They were long and difficult weeks. She fasted, one day on and one day off, for over a week. She was grateful for her work. It kept her mind active all day long, thinking of other people instead of her problem. The last week of April, she scheduled an overseas flight to Algiers. They were to fly into Madrid, then on to Algiers. She was looking forward to that. She had never been to Africa. Brandy said she was jealous, but, truth to tell, she was so involved with Mitch the fourth, as she

263

now called him, that she could hardly think of anything else. Shielah spent the night before she left pausing before the telephone trying to decide if she should call Paulo. It had been over a week since she had spoken to him, and even then the conversation was very short. She wanted to see him tonight. She still didn't have an answer, but she was beginning to despair. The heavens seemed closed to her prayers. On this question there was no one on earth to advise her, no one at all.

She actually picked up the phone once, then laid it down and went on with her preparations. She would not have long in Algiers, just twenty-four hours. She had arranged with another flight attendant who was flying in the week before on vacation, to take her flight home the next morning. Shielah wanted at least one day to see the sights and take pictures. She was keeping a picture scrapbook of all the interesting places she saw.

Excitement was high amongst the girls as they readied the plane for the flight. The others were jealous that Shielah would be able to stay for sightseeing the following day. "I want copies of the pictures," they all put in their requests. The DC 10 would take off at six-fifteen a.m. and land in Madrid at five-thirty-five p.m., European Standard Time. They would have one hour there and fly on to Algiers. Within a twelve hour time period, she would be on three different continents. The excitement was contagious.

The passengers filed in and Shielah spent her time in the back of the plane stowing parcels and hats, fetching blankets, and helping a white-haired little lady, with stickers on her bag from all over the world, find her seat by the window.

"Ladies and gentlemen, this is your pilot, Andrew Cameron. Welcome to New World's Flight 269 to Madrid, Spain. We will be flying at an altitude of three thousand feet, crossing the Atlantic Ocean. Below you now, off to the right wing of the airplane, we are passing over the Statue of Liberty. In Madrid at this time, there are scattered showers, but clear weather is predicted for our arrival at five-thirty-five p.m. That will be only twelve-thirty-five p.m. by your time clocks. Enjoy the flight. Our flight attendants are here to serve you."

Jenny, the senior attendant, assigned Shielah to serve juice and pastries in the coach section. It was one of the most enjoyable services she had ever done. The passengers were all excited about the flight, each had a story to tell about his plans for vacation in either Madrid or Algiers. Some had been before and told her places to go and see. It was eight o'clock before she was finished and could sit down in her seat in the galley for a moment.

"Shielah, sorry. I know you just sat down." Jenny was holding out a tray with a glass of juice on it. "A passenger changed his mind. Could you take this into first class? Seat eleven."

Seat number eleven belonged to Paulo D'Agosta. He was especially delighted at the total surprise on Shielah's face. He had not wanted her to know he was on board, so he had quietly slipped into his seat and waited until the initial work was over for her. His source on the crew desk hadn't needed to provide him much information in the last year, but Paulo pumped him a week ago to get Shielah's schedule. Immediately, he made a reservation. It had been too long. He didn't know if she ever intended to come back to him, and he had to keep trying. He hoped that she would respond as she always did to the chemistry between them.

He wasn't wrong. It had been three weeks, but it seemed like three months since she had been close to him. Instantly her body responded. The desire to touch him was indescribable. His flesh seemed to draw hers. His face, his shoulders, his hand, anything just to touch him. Memory of the last night they spent together came back in a flash.

"Why do you do this to me?" She had to speak softly.

"It's fun," he said. She could see he was amused at her reaction to his presence.

"I can't talk to you."

"Yes, you can. I already asked, and told Jenny that we are old friends. Stewardesses are supposed to be nice to the passengers."

He caught her there. Of course, he was right. "Sit beside me," he half-commanded, half-invited, knowing he had the upper hand.

"Just for a moment."

"I'm going to kiss you."

"No! Nice is nice, but that would be too much!"

"Not for me. Not enough for me."

"Do you have business in Madrid?" He shook his head. "In Algiers?" Again he signaled no.

"I just came along for the ride, just to see you."

"This is a very expensive date."

"I've been saving up. It's not nearly as expensive as the honeymoon I've been planning."

"Stop. I don't want to hear this. I've been trying to get my head sorted out. You promised you'd give me time to do it. Now here you are, confusing me with. . . . "

"With love," he finished for her.

"With talk about honeymoons before I've decided to marry you."

"It's easy to decide. Let me teach you a word. It's called yes. It's spelled Y.E.S. Very simple, very effective."

"Paulo!" She warned him with a look. "You're pushing me."

"Heaven forbid. I wouldn't push you. We've only been in love for two years now. Two years in June, my lady! That is when we met, and that is when we fell in love, even if you were too stubborn to admit it for six months. This is a terribly long engagement. Mama is despairing of grandchildren. Think how happy you will make her, even if you're miserable."

Carmella D'Agosta was one of the complications that made the decision more difficult. She adored Paulo's mother and the emotion was quite mutual. On the other hand, Stephen's mother . . . well, they hardly knew each other. But . . . she wasn't marrying their mothers. Then the understanding came to her, she was marrying their lives—the total picture, family, religion, values, dreams.

"I wish you hadn't come."

"I'm sorry. I'll stop. Really I will. We won't talk about marriage at all, or Mama's grandchildren, or the engagement ring I carry in my pocket. All right, all right," he said as she held up a warning hand. "Let's talk about you. You're beautiful. What do you think about that?"

"I think you're crazy. You've always seen me as something else. Someone I'm not."

"That's not true. I have seen you through the eyes of a photographer, an artist with a good eye for a picture. You're a gorgeous picture."

"I'm going back to the galley now." She started to get up to leave. He held her hand fast. She tried to pull it away, looking at him in exasperation. He only grinned at her and raised it to his lips. The touch of his lips made her shiver. He saw it and smiled even more. "I love you," he whispered.

Directly below were the Straits of Gibralter; Europe lay behind them and Africa stretched interminably before. She had been warned not to expect anything cosmopolitan, or even beautiful in the traditional sense. Algiers was a land of its own, mostly desert and rolling brown hills. The streets were often dirt except for the immediate city where they were uniformly paved with gray cement. The city itself was drab, gray or beige stucco buildings, flat roofs, few trees or shrubbery. Only the people made it colorful. They appeared still to live back in Biblical times and wore long flowing robes with colorful sashes and marvelous turbans.

It was eight p.m. in Algiers, but with the time difference, it seemed more like afternoon to Shielah. Only a little tired from getting up early and working for nine hours, she intended to go out that evening and wander up and down the main streets. She had expected to be alone. That was the way she wanted it, actually. Paulo was an intrusion, and although he was very tempting, she didn't want to be tempted. She wanted to make a sound decision. She had hoped it wouldn't take this long. She knew it was torture for him. His presence only brought back a sense of confusion, of being lost in a fog. She couldn't think clearly about him when she was with him. The sensuality about him, drawing her like a magnet, made it impossible to think.

The American Hotel was the best in the city. It was unique in Shielah's experience. Only at certain times of the day, the hotel clerk explained, would she have running water. No carpets graced the gray, concrete floors, no grass mats. They were plain, unadorned. The tapestries were hung on the walls as decorations. They were gorgeous, Arabic tapestries, larger than the commercial ones in the states. Her room was simple, one narrow bed and one dresser, antique with a mirror. No throw rug, no bathroom— that was down the hall. She left her luggage in the room and quickly went back to the lobby to meet Paulo. It was the dinner hour in Algiers.

The restaurant was fascinating to Shielah. A tall, turbaned African roasted a lamb on a spit at one end of the room. Directly above him, the

266

roof was open so the smoke wafted upward. Even still, the dining room was smoky and odiferous. The chairs and wooden tables were worn smooth with many years of service. Their whole attention was taken up by the multi-colored jewels of people in that room. Tourists were noisy. Algerians were dignified as they came in, then later they became flamboyant, gesticulating as they spoke, laughing with the huge joke of living, even dancing as the hour grew late.

Shielah would not talk to Paulo about their relationship. She told him about the last three weeks of flying. She talked about the country, the strange combinations of people in the restaurant, but she steadfastly refused to be drawn into a conversation about themselves. She also didn't tell him she wasn't flying back tomorrow on the return flight. She would fly tomorrow night, privately, to Madrid and go back as an attendant on the evening flight to New York. She was impatient at her involuntary response to him. She needed this time alone if she was ever to get things sorted out.

He was reluctant to leave her that night. Twice she said goodnight, and twice he pleaded for more time. They sat in the gardens beside the hotel, with just the dim light from the windows. Her face in the moonlight was his dream. Longing for her had become his way of life. He hardly knew if he could live without the ache. But she wasn't his. She kept pulling away from him, though he knew she wanted him. He was frustrated with the effort of winning her. How could he transfer that longing into action?

"We should do this more often."

"What do you mean?"

"Traveling together and seeing different cities. I know, I know. I won't talk about honeymoons. I just mean that exploring with you is much more fun than alone, or with Jim."

"This was one of the reasons I wanted to fly. I wanted to see these places. The world is so large and most people's lives so narrow. How can people in the world understand one another if all they know is their own villages, their own traditions? Sometimes I wonder if there is any hope at all for world peace and understanding. Just being here gives me a whole new understanding of these people and their lives."

"I'm glad I came with you. I feel the same way. I'd like to do it more often."

"Paulo, I . . . I can't say I haven't enjoyed being with you. But I feel an answer is so near and I have to be alone. Being with you is so hard. You're almost . . . undeniable. Please don't make it harder for me than it is."

"You think it's not hard for me?" He sat relaxed in the chair, wearing white pants and a pink shirt, casual but elegant. It was his style. Shielah loved it. She couldn't look at him.

"I'm sure it is. I feel guilty for hurting you. I don't do it because I want to. I love you. I truly love you. You must know that. I turn into jelly every time you touch me. But I don't believe our lives will mix. Yours is too important to you and I see why. Your religion, your family—they're beautiful. But mine is just as important to me. I went to the temple grounds with . . . with . . ."

"Stephen," he finished for her.

"Yes, with Stephen, last Christmas. There was such a sense of belonging. We would never share that, you and I, and I don't know if I could live forever without it."

There was silence between them. He was helpless. He had been struggling against it for months, but he saw now that he was helpless. Only she could decide. Nothing he did could make that decision for her. So, he gave in at last. The struggle was over for him. He left it for her to endure.

"I understand. I hate it, but I understand. I'm not sorry I came. I had to be with you, if only for a day. I'm going to bed now, and I won't bother you again. Not until you make your decision and come to me. I could love you with every cell of my being, but it wouldn't make you love me. I'm tired. The decision is yours. I'll see you."

She didn't stop him. She sat alone in the garden for a long time, her thoughts bouncing back and forth. She could come to no decision. Either answer was too difficult to accept.

Paulo rose early. He took an early morning walk and knocked on the door of Shielah's room about ten o'clock. There was no answer. He asked at the desk. The clerk did not know whether Miss Sorensen had gone out or not. The bill had been paid in advance. He took a beat-up, old taxi to the airport which lay to the north of the city, some fifteen miles. He was almost an hour early for the flight. When he got there he could see the flight attendants down the terminal, dressed in New World uniforms. They were headed down the concourse. He quickened his step and reached the last one who had been hanging behind.

"Was Shielah Sorensen with that group of attendants?"

"No, I don't think so. If she's supposed to be on this flight, she'd better hurry up or be docked. We'll begin taking passengers in half an hour."

He sat down in the waiting area and watched for her. She didn't come. The half-hour passed. Passengers were boarding. He went to the airport phone and called the hotel. No one had seen her that morning. Paulo grew concerned. That she might have a layover didn't occur to him. It was unusual that she would not fly the same plane home. He didn't check with Jenny, the senior attendant. He was nonplussed and sat watching the flights take off, wondering where she was. She might still be in Algiers somewhere. Probably she didn't want to see him. Should he continue to look for her? As he sat watching, pondering, her scheduled flight lumbered out onto the runway and began winding up for the take-off. Airplanes were fascinating to watch. Take-off was beautiful, graceful, remarkable in its advanced technology.

This take-off was not quite perfect, technically speaking. The plane lurched slightly at lift-off, and before it could clear the ground and soar, it shuddered, lurched again, stumbled and bounced with ripping force back down to the runway. Power failure turned the graceful bird into a dead whale, roiling on its belly. Paulo leaped to the window along with other spectators. Horrible fascination held him glued there. Momentum carried the monstrous airplane on down the runway, turning slow, torturous circles before it crashed into an old deserted maintenance building at the farthest end of the runway. The impact of tons of steel ripped the delicate, silver skin apart, and the center fuselage severed just above the tail section. By this time a siren was screaming, trucks and service vehicles were streaming toward the wreckage. The whole airport was in an uproar, clerks left the counters, as did prospective passengers. There was but one focus, the airplane, broken and shattered at the end of the runway. People crowded out of the doorways, some just to watch, several offering professional help.

"I have someone on that plane. I have to get out there." He pulled at the guard's arm.

"Not if it burns." A black guard held them back. "No one goes near the plane until we know if it's going to burn." It was common that when an airplane broke at the fuselage the slightest thing could cause a fire. If that happened, the passengers and crew had only seconds to get off.

An ambulance went screaming by. Airport service crews and fire trucks were rushing to the wreckage. Cries and occasional screams from the airplane drew them on. Finally, Paulo could see that the plane was not in danger of burning immediately, and he and two other men, both doctors, ran toward the wreck to help in the rescue effort.

"She's not there," he kept saying to reassure himself. Suppose she had left earlier, and the other attendants were merely trying to shield her from him. "No, she's not there. I know she's not there." But he didn't know it. Why wouldn't she be there; it was her job. "She's not there!" Then he was dwarfed by the side of the gigantic, manmade structure, cries and screams and sirens deafening his hearing, and he started the task of finding her.

Shielah slept late. She had been up late the night before. When she awoke, she thought she heard sirens far away. A vague, uncomfortable feeling disturbed her, but she took her time dressing, putting on her make-up, choosing comfortable shoes for a day of sightseeing. She was elated and anxious to get out onto the streets, to browse through all the tourist shops and pick out mementos. The sirens still screamed. When she went down to the hotel lobby, she stopped to ask directions from the clerk. The young girl stared at her.

"Aren't you the stewardess?" She spoke with a British accent.

"Yes."

"A man called for you earlier. He was on your flight to Madrid."

Something about her expression stopped Shielah's elation. "And? What is it?"

269

"It . . . the sirens . . . the radio says . . . a flight to Madrid crashed on take off."

Shielah screamed and ran. Paulo! That was all. There was no one else on that flight. Paulo! Now she had only one name in her heart, Paulo's. There were no taxis on the streets. She ran two miles toward the airport. An English boy on a motor scooter was on his way to the site. He stopped and gave her a ride. She couldn't talk. Her breath had all but stopped and her mind was numb. An ambulance streaked past, blaring its urgency as it transported bodies to the hospital, already geared for the influx of passengers from Flight 345.

She knew no prayer, no words but one—Paulo! They motored right out onto the runway, now a total chaos of trucks, ambulances, service vehicles, cots, stretchers, and white uniformed hospital attendants. The wreckage was horrifying. She had seen a very convincing replica of one in the training movie, but nothing could simulate the indescribable terror of reality. It had been a half-hour since the crash. The hot Algerian sun was adding to the problems of the rescue effort. People were moaning for water and help. With one hundred and ninety people besides the crew, it was taking a long time to get to each one. Some were pinned in the wreckage. A few were thrown out when the fuselage broke and the tail section separated. They were the worst cases. Shielah wandered in blank awe through the bodies and the chaotic relief effort. Algiers was a major airport and decently equipped to handle a major disaster. They were doing their best, but still it was awesome work. Doctors were continually interrupted in their work to answer questions from amateur first- aiders. They could hardly finish the care for one patient and get him prepared to be transported to the hospital without being pulled away to care for someone else in desperate need of medical expertise.

Where was Paulo? First class! How could she get up into the airplane to get into first class? The question was pointless.

"Are you a nurse?" a man in civilian clothes asked eagerly.

"I'm a flight attendant."

"You know first aid?"

"Yes, of course."

He pulled her toward a woman on the ground covered with a blanket. "She needs help."

She knelt beside the pitiful, straw-haired woman with a broken arm, fractured ribs, and a large gash on her hip. Her mind only knew one thing, Paulo!

"Can you help her?"

"We can stop that flow of blood, but we need bandages. Can you get me some bandages?" The man disappeared into the maze. The middle-aged woman lay staring stupidly up at Shieliah, whimpering. Her nose was broken and a massive hematoma had begun to spread down the side of her face and neck. Shielah sat with her, unwilling to leave her alone, but desperate to continue her search for Paulo.

The man returned with bandages he found in the back of the ambulance.

"Has anyone been killed? Have you heard of any deaths?" She asked him as she worked on staunching the blood flow from the wounds.

"Five so far."

Panic almost tied her hands. Then she worked even more quickly, packing, winding the bandages. She left him with instructions not to move her until the hospital attendants could get her onto a stretcher. Her internal injuries could be worse. She left him holding the hand of a perfect stranger.

A small moveable stairway had been edged into the melee, and people were going up and down it, carrying blankets, stretchers and first aid supplies. Frightened and reluctant to find him pinned, or broken, or even worse, dead— nevertheless, she was drawn there inescapably. The body of the airplane was like a foreign war zone to her. It was writhing with bodies, some moving, some not. The wounded were crying and moaning, intermittently screaming. The rescuers had to shout above the noise to make their needs known. Shielah was dumbfounded and moved as though in an awful dream. She never got to the first class section. A doctor grabbed her arm and handed her an infant.

"She doesn't seem to be hurt, but be careful of internal injuries."

Shielah looked down into a tiny face twisted in a weak cry.

"Please don't take her. Don't take my baby away," a young woman shouted in Spanish. The doctor continued cutting away her blouse to see the wound that was soaking her clothes with blood. "Just stay here, can you?" he ordered. "Keep that baby here until I can get her tranquilized." Shielah nodded and held the baby against her breast, hoping her body warmth would transfuse energy into the tiny body.

And so it went, one hurt and broken passenger after another was slowly taken off the airplane and transferred to the three-hundred bed hospital in Algiers. It took all afternoon. Shielah gave up her search for him. It was no use. Perhaps he had already been taken in. She could not get away from the moans and cries of the wounded. The attendants had fared just as badly as the passengers. Two of them were unconscious, and Shielah sat with them while the stretchers came. This had been her flight! And she had given this nightmare to someone else. Someone was hurting now because of her. And Paulo, he would not be here now if it weren't for her. The guilt added to the burden of the carnage.

It was late in the afternoon. She was exhausted from the emotional as well as the physical work. Her emotions were ragged and she wept easily and silently. She was not the only one. Even the nurses, as they bandaged and blanketed, wept at the sight of the misery around them. She was kneeling beside an old man. His eyes were closed, his breath was shallow, the balding place on his head showed a tiny pulse, very irregular. "Hurry," she kept saying to the doctor down the aisle. "Hurry, he's weak." She was holding his hand, willing him to live, talking to him softly, encouraging him to hold on, to be strong, the doctor was here and it would only be a few more minutes. She didn't even know if he understood her words. His clothing was distinctly European, he might not speak English. But he felt her concern and her young strength.

271

She felt a hand on her shoulder and she looked up. Paulo stood above her, his face was wet with tears and he didn't wipe them away. Then he was kneeling in the aisle beside her, holding her and sobbing while she clung to him for dear life, and to the old man's hand for his. Old eyes opened momentarily, saw their embrace and their tears, and just for a moment he smiled.

Over and over she said his name, shaking and sobbing and kissing his wet cheek. "You're here! You're here! And you're not hurt! You're not, are you?"

"No, I'm not. Are you? You must not have been on the flight. I waited. I didn't know. I kept looking for you. I was afraid you were pinned somewhere. Are you OK?"

"Yes! I thought you were dead. That's all I could think. I was so afraid." She ran her hands over his back, his shoulders, his arms, even down his leg. "Are you hurt at all?"

"No, just scared stiff. I saw it happen! I saw it crash! I thought you were on it. Don't ever do that to me again."

I'm sorry. I'm so sorry. I should have told you. I arranged to stay a day and go back tonight. I'm sorry."

"Oh Lord, Shielah, I love you. I was so scared. If you had died, if you had been hurt!" They couldn't hold each other tight enough, or stop touching and kissing each other. Each time Paulo thought he should stop kissing her forehead, her hair, the fear would tear him anew, and he would press her close and kiss her all over again. The rescue continued around them but they were only good for each other for many minutes. When they took the old man away from where Shielah and Paulo knelt, he squeezed her hand lightly and in a cracked voice, he whispered, "Mine esposa. Mine esposa." They looked into each other's eyes and Shielah said, "Yes."

They were both exhausted from the gut-wrenching effort of the day. They lay together on the narrow bed in Shielah's room, locked in a silent, unmoving embrace. They had fallen down on the bed together, and Paulo made his shoulder a pillow for her head.

"You're so tired. I'll leave so you can go to sleep."

"No! Don't you leave. I could never sleep without you here beside me. I would have terrible dreams. I may anyway."

He stroked her hair and she lay with her hand on his neck, feeling his pulse warm and constant beneath her fingers. "Are you hungry?" he asked.

"No, I'm not hungry. I just want to stay with you like this. I don't ever want to move. I don't want to eat, or talk or laugh or do anything else but lie with you."

"Is that an invitation?" But he already knew the answer.

Deliberately, she put everyone and everything else out of her mind. "Yes," she whispered against his neck. "Yes, it is. Stay with me tonight."

272

His arm tightened around her. After the trauma of the day, tears seemed to come of their own will. She felt the wetness on his cheek and rose slightly to kiss it.

"I didn't think I'd ever hear you say that."

"I know, but tonight is different. Tonight I know how much I love you."

"How much?"

"Enough."

"Enough for what?"

"Do you want me to say it?"

"Yes."

"Enough to sleep beside you tonight, to belong to you, to be a part of you always."

"Enough to be my wife?"

There was a slight hesitation. "Yes."

"I'm a selfish man. I want you too much, Shielah. If you offer I will take."

"Then take," she kissed his hand and held it against her face. "I'm offering."

Paulo made only one mistake. He kissed her until the world went away. He knelt beside her as she lay against the pillow, and carefully, reverently began to undress her. But, in the midst of their love, when he could have taken her and kept her for the rest of his life, he asked her a question.

"Will you love me forever?"

"Yes, forever and ever."

"Will you forsake all others and cleave unto me alone?"

"Yes, I will."

"For better or for worse, for richer or for poorer, in sickness and in health until death do us part."

Her eyes opened and stared into his. They filled up with tears and overflowed. "No, no. Don't say that part. Not, 'until death do us part'. I said I would love you forever."

"Shh, it doesn't mean anything. It's just the old traditional words."

"I know," she cried. " 'Until death do us part'. I can't stand it. If death had parted us today, I don't know what I would have done. How awful would it be if we were married and loved and lived our lives together. Oh, Paulo, please, please, for me, please see how terrible that would be."

"Darling, don't cry. I know. I know. I do see. It would be terrible for me too. We won't have them say those words. We'll make up our own ceremony, here, tonight. Just our own, and we'll say whatever you want."

Slowly she shook her head. "It won't mean anything."

"It'll mean whatever we want it to mean."

"But what will it mean in heaven? What will it mean to God? Nothing, because we haven't done it the right way, through the right channels that He gave us." She sat up and put her hand on his chest. Sorrow was a perfect masque on her face. "No. I love you. Heaven above knows I love you, but I won't make a farce of my religion. I won't marry you like that.

If you want me, take me now. I give myself to you tonight. But I won't marry you like that."

"Don't. Shielah don't. I can't stand it. I only want one thing in the world, and that is you and your happiness. I want you, I love you. Come to me and forget all this. It's not important. Just us, just our love, that is all that is important."

"I said I would." She lay back down in his arms, but when he kissed her it was different. There was no passion, no oneness. After a few minutes of trying to recover what they had lost, he pulled away. Slowly, he rose up and sat on the edge of the bed. "And will you cry when it is over?" He didn't look at her.

She didn't look at him. "I don't know."

"Will you regret it all tomorrow and be ashamed?"

"I don't know."

"Will you resent me for it in a few weeks and feel estranged from your religion?"

"I don't know. I said, I don't know. I'm willing to risk it."

He stood up and walked to the dresser. There he began putting back on his shirt. He looked at her, still and lovely, lying quietly in just her slip.

"Paulo don't go. I . . . I . . . love you so much."

"Goodnight."

"Paulo, please! Please, don't leave me!"

Then he shouted at her for the first time. "Stop it! My hell, Shielah, don't you see what you are doing. You love me but you won't marry me! You want me, but you won't be my wife! You are torturing me. I adore you and you just want me tonight . . . or forever. There is no middle ground for you. But I won't love you tonight—share the most intimate part of my soul with you—and then dry your tears when it's over and know you regret my love. What kind of love would that be? I have more pride than that!"

And he left her, alone and sobbing inconsolably on the bed.

He left the next day, by ferry, across the Straits of Gibralter. She left by plane and flew to Kennedy. Then she called the crew desk. She explained about the crash in Algiers. She needed time off, she couldn't function. She was given a week's vacation. She deserved it after Algiers. Then she flew home, home to Utah, to Clarksville, to her roots and a life she understood.

At Will's place she changed into her jeans and sweater. It was still a little chilly, even in May. She saddled Sheba and took with her only a light jacket. She never called Stephen. She couldn't. She said she'd be back in a few hours. But she wasn't.

She rode Sheba across the hills that were just beginning to blossom with the kiss of spring. They stopped beside a stream once and rested. Then she rode on, not really noticing where they were going. Sheba knew those hills like a friend. It was her back yard. Shielah wasn't thinking about direction. She could think of nothing but Paulo and Stephen and the pain in her heart. She didn't see the beauty of the mountains she so much loved. She didn't see the beauty of the little streams that cut their ways between the mounds of hills. She didn't see the blue of the sky growing white with clouds, then gray as they filled with a spring rain. She was enwrapped in her own dilemma, loving and hurting and knowing she was choosing a life. Today she would choose and not look back. There was no place for both men in one lifetime, although she loved them both. Instinctively she felt that Paulo needed her more, though his quiet strength belied that need. But Stephen shared her every dream; her very thoughts he knew almost before she knew them herself. How could she say goodbye to either of them?. Either way half of her heart would die, half of her life would be cut away.

She rode and agonized and cried out to her Heavenly Father. And the storm took her completely by surprise. She was riding Sheba down hill, letting the mare pick her way between the rocks and oak brush. The wind stiffened and forced her to put on her jacket. But still she was oblivious to her surroundings. It was late now. The sky grew dark as the mare headed home. She knew the way and she had her head. When the lightning cracked, Sheba bolted. Shielah was almost thrown then, but she clutched the golden mane and clung on, trying to rein the mare in. Across the hillside, they plunged headlong until Shielah was frantic, afraid the horse would break a leg. The lightning flashed again, a huge crooked serpent striking the ground not six feet away. And Shielah lost the mare. Sheba reared straight up. Shielah leaned forward in the saddle, trying to keep her seat, but the horse went down. She was pinned beneath the squirming ton of horseflesh and saddle for just a few seconds while Sheba struggled to regain her feet. When the animal succeeded she was off, streaking across the darkened hills. Home was seven miles away.

Shielah was too numb to cry, too disconsolate to pray or to fear. And she hurt all over. Her ribs were bruised, her elbow bleeding, her shoulder bleeding, and she couldn't make her leg move. She gave up the effort and lay back against the sharp, bumpy dirt, her face to the wild heavens above.

It's really lovely, she thought with inane serenity. Even when it is black, and wild and deadly, it's lovely. The rain came in driven sheets, and still she lay there, open to the storm and the night. What use were defenses and strugglings now? Her puny strugglings would not amount to anything in this storm. It swept down upon her and possessed her as she lay there, given up to the lashing of the wind and rain. Lightning struck all around her and still she didn't move. The effort was too great. She was tired, too tired of the struggle. She would simply go to sleep here and let death take her if it wanted her. Hadn't Stephen said that there were two friends that walked the earth. The one friend hadn't been terribly kind to her. It was cantankerous and whimsical and painful to understand. Shielah had hurt for as long as she could remember for this friend called Life. Now, perhaps the other friend waited just beyond the door, and maybe he would be more kind.

Her thoughts went back to that night with Paulo. She had been ready to give up everything she had valued in her life just to be his. Was God offended? Did He understand that love or condemn her? Sobs tore her again as she mourned the futility of a love so precious. Could she endure this life, if she should be so unlucky as to live, without ever having loved him, without ever truly being his, even once. Then came the vision of Stephen's face, clear as a summer day. It was as dear to her as the sparkling lights on Temple Square. They shared a lifetime. He knew her grief and had loved her always. He was as much a part of her life as the mountains and the church they both loved. Either way, a part of her would mourn forever. She cried aloud into the storm many times and begged her friend to take her.

But death had no power that night. Over the suffering girl, through the blackest night she would endure, stood another friend. A woman, streaming white light from the center of her being, stood above Shielah and held back the ravages of the storm. She looked down with pity and understanding, for she had been here once when life was merciless. Shielah slipped into a deep, unconscious sleep. As the storm raged, Charlotte guarded her from the powers of darkness.

Morning came and Shielah woke. She was stiff and sore, her leg was swollen. Delicately she touched it and winced. It ached miserably. It was probably broken. The sky had cleared but the wind was still brisk. In the cold, clear light she could see where she was. On the side of a mountain, with the river meandering through the valley below, she had wandered far from the main road. She searched the landscape for several minutes and then recognized that just beyond the scrub oak was the little cabin she and Stephen discovered last winter. She painstakingly dragged herself a few feet. Her knee hurt and she could only move by inches. She scanned the sky. It would rain again, and she was already soaked and shivering. It was strange she was not frozen stiff after the storm last night.

She didn't think at all that day about Paulo or Stephen. Inching along toward the cabin, she deliberately drew on all the lovely memories she had. She thought of Will and Maddie and pieces came back to her of the year she had lived with them, pieces she had long ago lost in her mind. She dwelt with pleasure and tenderness on the memory of her grandmother, and numbered all the childhood games that she and Buck had played. No tears, no anger, no hard times please, she commanded her memory. There have been good times in my life, and there has been joy. I just want that now. I've lived in the pain too long.

Stephen scoured the hills for her, along with Will and Drew, Wayne and Howard. At two o'clock, Wayne rode back home to call out the other volunteers. She mustn't stay out in the chill mountain air another night.

But it was a needless gesture. Stephen found her, lying in front of the cabin door, too weak to push it open, the rain puddling around her.

"Shielah!" he called to her as he jumped out of the saddle. "Shielah, where are you hurt?"

She looked up at him, her blue eyes rimmed with dark circles and suffering clearly etched in them.

"In the heart."

"I can see that. Anywhere else?"

"My knee and leg. I couldn't get in," she said, nodding toward the cabin. "The door is stuck tight."

"You need to get warm." Stephen shoved his shoulder against the door and thrust it open. She might have been a child again, he gathered her up so quickly and easily in his arms. In moments he laid her on the rough mattress of the cot and knelt beside her. Through the pant leg of her jeans his fingers searched for broken bones.

"I can't tell if anything is broken, but as soon as I get you warm and dry and rested, I'll take you home."

"I don't have a home. I was just thinking about that."

"I told you before, I'll make you a home."

He was kneeling on one knee, his hat pushed back from his forehead. Blue eyes were smiling in relief at having found her, and his jaw line was working strangely. He seemed to know what she had been sorting through and he didn't want to intrude unless she wanted him.

"Are you ready now for that home?" he asked.

"Will it be a happy one?"

"I guarantee it. Maybe not rich. Maybe not always easy, but happy yes."

"Stephen, I thought I wanted to die out here last night."

He wasn't surprised. He just listened thoughtfully.

"I could have, I know. I thought about your two friends, Life and Death, and decided for Death. It seemed so much friendlier. I offered myself, but he didn't want me. I guess I'm supposed to go on."

"You have a purpose, and there are lots of people who still need you."

"I'm not sure I have anything to give."

"You're a deeper well than you know. You're a stronger spirit than you know. The best have been saved for the last days, and you are here to prepare your own corner of the world for the coming of the Lord. You have been tried. You have been tested; and you have been refined. Now, love, come out of the fire and give your gold to others. It's time to throw off the past and the questioning and the struggles. It's time to go forward with no more looking back." He paused slightly and grinned engagingly. "We could go together."

Her eyes softened at that smile so dear to her. Then she turned her eyes away. "You wouldn't say that if you knew why I'm here. I almost gave myself to Paulo. I love him and I thought he had died in that airplane crash in Algiers. He was the one who walked away or I would be his now. Not because I don't love you, but because I couldn't stand the struggle any longer."

His blue eyes never left hers while she told him. They narrowed, they blinked, they lost the perennial twinkle, but they never left her face. After a few moments Stephen said, "He walked away. But will you ever be able to forget him enough to love me with all your heart?"

She was limp on the cot. Her strength was totally gone. Her spirit cried out for the right answer, the right decision. The moment had come. She felt as though her whole life had been building for this moment, and she knew her future for eternity hung in the balance. It was too much! She was torn apart with the agony of choice. Small, tight cries of pain broke from her while tears streamed down her face. She closed her eyes. Paulo's eyes looked into hers and she thought her spirit would leave her body, the pain was so intense. Then she opened her eyes and Stephen knelt beside her, looking into her soul. In that moment, as she hung in the balance of eternity, she saw, for the first time that she was not choosing either *man*, for she saw in Stephen's eyes the compassion of the Savior. Love unfeigned, unconditional, eternal—the pure love of Christ reached out to her and she decided for *that* love.

Shielah reached up for Stephen, touched his face, his soft hair. "Oh Stephen, I do love you with all my heart, because . . . because I see my Savior in your eyes. He makes us one. Why it has taken me so long to realize it I don't know. But I see it now. If you'll have me I'll build that little cottage with you, and we'll grow flowers and vegetables and little children there."

He held her in his arms securely, gently. She was glad she couldn't move.

His eyes filled with tears of relief. Still he smiled. "I have you right where I want you now," he wiggled his eyebrows.

She smiled weakly and shook her head at his antics. "Haven't you any sympathy for my hurt?"

"Respect yes, pity no. I'm a very good doctor. I put my own self back together. It's a little trick I learned. It's called light and love." He bent to delicately touch her lips. "I give you my light. You give me your love." He kissed her again, more possessively this time. "See how nice. Then you give me *your* light and I give you *my* love. See how simple. And there is no end to the cycle, no end at all."

The struggle was all dissipated. Enclosed as she was in his arms, in his love, there was nothing to struggle against. They were a match, an easy, perfect fit that needed no surgery. There was peace in this love, and joy! Loving Stephen was as natural as breathing. It was right! He was right! The struggle had disappeared with the storm. She had a home.

At seven a.m. on June fifteenth, Shielah and Stephen crossed the street at the light, hand in hand, and entered the Salt Lake Temple of the Church of Jesus Christ of Latter-day Saints. With them walked Aunt Maddie and Uncle Will and Drew—her oldest cousin, just ready to leave on a mission—Mary and Cam Gailbraith, holding hands for the first time in ten years. Waiting in the lobby for his sister was Buck, newly ordained an elder, and soon to be married in the Hawaiian temple to Bridget.

Buck put his arms around his sister and hugged her close. "We made it, didn't we? We both made it! Mom and Dad will be so proud. And maybe Grandma can rest, at last."

In another part of the temple grounds Brandy spent the morning with Tami and Michael Gailbraith, looking through the visitor's center, watching the informative movies there and contemplating the Mormon concept of eternal marriage. Shielah had written from Utah and asked her to come to her wedding as the maid of honor. Brandy was indeed honored by the eloquent expression of true love by her friend. She had never stayed in the home of a white person, never been treated as truly an equal before, and she loved her friend intensely. Prejudice could all be wiped away if people could only know and love as she and Shielah did.

Maddie went with Shielah to the bridal room for the short instructions on the temple clothes given all the new brides. She squeezed her niece's hand before the instruction started and whispered, "I wish Ginny could be here with you in my place. She would have loved that."

Tears started quickly today. Shielah kissed her aunt's cheek, and wiped tears from both their eyes. "I think she is. I'm no mystic, but I think she is—and Grandma too."

Maddie's mouth trembled with persistent tears. "This is a place of healing and peace, my dear. Be healed. That is what Heavenly Father wants for you, what your mother and grandmother want. Come back here often and you will be healed, I promise!"

All through the temple ceremony, instructing her in eternal principles, and leading her through covenants with the Lord, Shielah felt the deep cleansing of her lifelong pain. Peace seemed to envelope her being, erasing the scars, the questions that had tormented her. Old bitternesses evaporated and the freed spaces of her soul filled with serenity and joy. There was Stephen, across the aisle from her, dressed in the pure white clothing of the temple. His eye caught hers and twinkled as only Stephen's could. She smiled back at him and wiped her eyes again. Then it was time to cross from the Terrestial Room into the Celestial Room of the temple, signifying that she was coming into the presence of the Lord. The voice behind the curtain was the beloved voice that had consoled the tears of her youth and proposed eternal marriage to her. He took her hand, and she stepped into the Celestial Room at Stephen's side.

The small wedding party gathered into the simply elegant sealing room. Stephen still held her hand, even through the greetings of old friends and missionary companions who came to witness the wedding. When the temple president took his place at the head of the altar and invited Stephen to escort his bride to the altar, Shielah knelt on a velvet bench and joined her hand in marriage with Stephen. Across his shoulder she saw herself and him reflected endlessly in the mirrors that illustrated the endless union of two lovers. Deep within her welled an overflowing fountain of joy, of laughter, of tears.

"Do you, Stephen Gailbraith, take this woman, Shielah Sorensen, to be your lawfully wedded wife before God, Angels and these witnesses?"

He did! She saw the same fountain rising up in him, and before the rest of the vows could be spoken, both of them were laughing and crying at the same time, their eyes irresistibly locked together in joy and wonder.

279

"Do you, Shielah Sorensen, take this man, Stephen Gailbraith, to be your lawfully wedded husband, for time and for all eternity?"

In that magic moment everything beautiful was contained in his face, everything joyous in their union. And she did! Oh yes, she did!

When they finished the temple ceremony, they went out onto the temple grounds for picture taking. They stood on the steps of the temple, Stephen's arm around her protectively, and smiled the promise of tomorrow for all the cameras to capture.

Across the street stood a dark-haired man, watching. Shielah had written the longest letter of her life to Paulo, recounting her night on the hillside and explaining, as best she could, the spiritual confirmation she received that her life belonged to Stephen. Paulo read the letter in front of the fireplace where they had often lain and talked. He was not surprised. He knew when he left her in Algiers that it was over, that he would never have her. The gulf between them was too wide. Love cannot bridge all seas after all. He took the picture of her off his bookcase, a picture he had taken in front of his mother's home, and he stared at it for a long time. Who was she? Why had they loved so profoundly if it was never meant to be? Probably he'd never know those answers or why the visions and the dreams had seemed so real. Life was more of a mystery to him now than it had ever been.

June fifteenth approached. He watched the calendar with dread. On the fourteenth he bought an airline ticket to Utah. He couldn't bear the thought of knowing that somewhere, far away, she would marry another man. He had to go, to be there, to see for himself, as loved ones go to funerals. And now he stood on the sidewalk by the Hotel Utah. Across the street the high, black, wrought-iron gates enclosed the temple. Paulo read the words inscribed in granite, "Holiness to the Lord." He saw them climb the stairs together. He saw her smile at the tall, blonde-haired young man by her side, and then he saw them kiss as man and wife. He could stand no more.

Paulo drove back to the airport and took his seat on a flight to New York. Tomorrow was lost for him and he didn't know that he would ever be able to deal with the loss. Two young men in dark suits sat beside him. After an hour, one of them turned and spoke timidly to him, asking, "What do you know about the Mormon Church?" Then Paulo wept.

THE END

280

To all my readers who now hate me: Look for the third and final book of the Trilogy. Encompassing The Second Coming of Christ, it will blend Paulo's life with Charlotte's and with Shielah's. Watch through Paulo's eyes the events at Adam-ondi-Ahman. Walk with Stephen through Spirit Prison to re-claim the spirit of his best friend Buck. Thrill with Shielah as she witnesses the coming of Christ in Glory.